**FOR EDWARD ARMSTEAD,
BEING FIRST WITH THE NEWS
WAS NO LONGER ENOUGH.
HE WANTED THE POWER TO MAKE IT.**

Beautiful young Victoria Weston and seasoned Nick Ramsey were both ace reporters. They'd never missed a scoop and weren't about to start now—not when it centered on the kidnapping of a king, the assassination of a prime minister. Not when it had happened right before their eyes.

They'd been sent to cover trivial stories in Spain, in Switzerland, in Israel, and in France—stories that had turned, suddenly and unpredictably, into front-page headlines. Yet each time they phoned in the news, Edward Armstead, billionaire publisher of the New York *Record,* already had it. Until they had to wonder if something wasn't strangely askew . . . if their assignments might not be part of some huge and infinitely terrifying plan . . . if Edward Armstead was not only playing the role of the all-knowing, but of . . .

THE ALMIGHTY

BY IRVING WALLACE

FICTION

The Almighty
The Second Lady
The Pigeon Project
The R Document
The Fan Club
The Word
The Seven Minutes
The Plot
The Man
The Three Sirens
The Prize
The Chapman Report
The Sins of Philip Fleming

NONFICTION

The Intimate Sex Lives of Famous People (Coauthor)
The Book of Lists 1 and 2 (Coauthor)
The Two (Coauthor)
The People's Almanac 1 and 2 and 3 (Coauthor)
The Nympho and Other Maniacs
The Writing of One Novel
The Sunday Gentleman
The Twenty-seventh Wife
The Fabulous Showman
The Square Pegs
The Fabulous Originals

THE
ALMIGHTY

Irving Wallace

A DELL BOOK

Published by
Dell Publishing Co., Inc.
1 Dag Hammarskjold Plaza
New York, New York 10017

Dell ® TM 681510, Dell Publishing Co., Inc.

ISBN: 0-440-10189-1

Reprinted by arrangement with Doubleday & Company, Inc.

Printed in the United States of America
First Dell printing—January 1984
Second Dell printing—February 1984

*For Sylvia
with Love
and
Gratitude*

George Washington was a terrorist.
To describe a man as a terrorist is
a term of honor.

—A member of the Baader-Meinhof gang

He stared down into the open coffin. What surprised him most was that his father looked so small. The old man had always been a giant to Edward. Now, stiffly cushioned in satin, he seemed small. It was because the air of life had gone out of him, Edward realized. Ezra J. Armstead, the greatest and most autocratic press lord of modern times, had always been full of life, a force of energy, overwhelming. Now he was small and still. Otherwise, everything was in order. Maybe not the cheeks. E. J.'s cheeks were unnaturally red. The undertaker had applied too much rouge, as they always did.

Turning from the coffin, another surprise. Edward Armstead felt no loss.

And yet another. He felt rather good. Almost buoyant.

He scanned the cascades of flowers that formed a colorful semicircle behind the coffin. There was one discordant note. On an easel sat a gaudy American flag made up of red, white, and blue carnations. It had come from the staff of the New York *Record*, Edward Armstead was sure. One of the employees had heard or read that such a floral flag had decorated William

Randolph Hearst's coffin in 1951, and decided that E. J. deserved as much. Terrible taste, in keeping with his father's newspapers, Edward Armstead told himself.

He heard his wife, Hannah, just ahead, utter a muffled sob, and felt a stab of guilt. Quickly he stepped forward to join her, supportively linking his arm in hers. Her arm felt as thin as a matchstick. He had almost forgotten how frail and ill she was.

She turned her moist eyes up at Armstead. "Roger," she murmured. "Where's Roger?"

For a moment Armstead blinked uncomprehendingly, and then he remembered something else he had briefly forgotten. Roger was his son. He looked behind him and saw that Roger had just reached the coffin from the family room, and was standing over it, his long face set in bewildered grief. As always, Armstead was annoyed with his son. Or displeased. Perhaps as his own father had been with him. But no, his own displeasure was different. The boy—grown man, actually thirty-six-year-old man—was too tall, too tan, too outdoors-healthy and uncreative to be his son or his father's grandson. He worked for some strident environmental group in Wisconsin, always off in the woods or on a lake or river. Armstead was sure Roger had not read a book in years. He couldn't write at all, not even a letter. He came to New York once a year, at Christmas, and kept in touch by sending pamphlets. Where in the hell had his genes come from? Probably some pioneer on Hannah's side.

Armstead summoned his son. "Roger, take care of your mother." Although Hannah was ambulatory, standing any length of time was painful for her. Armstead added, "Help her into the wheelchair."

Armstead released Hannah to her offspring and started for the open chapel door, outside of which the pallbearers had been gathering. He reminded himself not to walk too briskly, and to keep his handshake limp. Gravely he shook hands with the six famous pallbearers—with the Vice-President of the United States, two governors, the mayor, the Army Chief of Staff, a senior astronaut—accepting their condolences, giving his thanks. Through his head flitted a picture of the editorial cartoon that had graced the front page of the black-bordered New York *Record* that morning: a gauzy drawing of E. J. climbing the clouds toward an Olympus where the filmy images of Dwight D. Eisenhower, Winston Churchill, Charles de Gaulle, Anwar Sadat, Francisco Franco, John Wayne waited to welcome him. It gave Armstead a start to recall that his father had known those dim and distant figures, had lived to eighty-one and known all the greats of his time, had indeed been considered one of them.

Armstead abandoned the pantheon of immortals and took in the crowd of personages and faithful nearby. He moved heavily toward them, hoping his Roman visage bore some semblance of contained bereavement. He nodded at his own loyal aides, Harry Dietz and Bruce Harmston, clasped the hand of his father's managing editor, Ollie McAllister. He was briefly surprised to find himself confronted by his father's arch rival, Paul Eldridge, publisher of the New York *Times*. But then not surprised, because Eldridge was Ivy League and Eastern Establishment and this was the gentlemanly thing to do (although, Armstead suspected, Eldridge probably held some admiration for the less couth E. J., for his father's self-made success, brashness, drive). Eldridge squeezed his hand comfortingly and Armstead squeezed back, reminding himself that they were brothers in the publishing fraternity.

Armstead wandered toward a cluster of conservatively dressed, mostly tailored, women, recognizing some as belonging to the newspaper, some as other men's wives. He nodded, and nodded, and found himself searching for Kim Nesbit. He tried to find her, the willowy youngish woman with corn-silk hair and limpid green eyes. But then he knew that she would not be there. He knew also that she had always been one of the reasons he had resented his father. He tried to believe the resentment grew out of the fact that his father had kept this woman for so many years when his mother had been alive and the fact that Kim had been

so young, much younger than he himself was. But the resentment
had come from none of these reasons. It had come from the fact
that he had envied and been jealous of his father. He was glad
Kim had not come to the funeral. It showed she had class. And
perhaps it showed that she had not cared for his father very much
after all.

His fruitless search for Kim Nesbit ended, Armstead became
aware that Horace Liddington was approaching him. Liddington
was over six feet tall, with a grayish crew cut, trim, impeccably
attired in a dark mourning suit with a vest.

"I'm sorry, Edward," he said crisply, taking Armstead's hand
with one hand and gripping his shoulder with the other.

"Well, he lived a good life," said Armstead. "He had a good
time."

"Yes, he did."

"I guess we'd all settle for that," Armstead added.

"We certainly would," Liddington agreed. He cleared his
throat, as if uncomfortable with the small talk and eager to get
onto something else. "Uh, Edward, whenever you have the
time—when this is over—I'd like to see you. I'm not rushing
you. It can be a day or two. There is some business to clear up."

"Business? What business?"

"Your father's will. It shouldn't take too much of your time.
It's a short document. Much of it concerns you. He was a very
wealthy man, as you know. It is important to maintain a continu-
ity in his affairs. Anyway, as soon as you are up to it, let's get
together. Possibly tomorrow, if you can."

"What about today?"

Liddington was startled. "Today? Of course. Why not, if you
think you can get away."

"I can get away. I think I should know what's in my father's
will."

"Absolutely. You should. Well, I'll be driving directly to my
office after the interment." He plucked a gold watch from his
vest pocket. "I should be there by two o'clock."

"I'll be there right after," said Armstead.

As Liddington turned from him to greet family friends, the full impact of his new situation hit Armstead. The lawyer's remark had made it clear: *Much of it concerns you.* Positive reassurance that his father's will concerned principally Edward himself. He was not merely a grieving son. He was an heir, an heir to empire. The king was dead. He was the king, the new monarch of all E. J.'s possessions. The millions and millions of dollars, the newspapers and television stations, the power. This had to be. There was really no one else who counted. Edward's mother had died senile three years ago. There was Roger, the grandson, and a few secondary relatives, but the old man had given very little time to any of them. Edward was E. J.'s only child, only heir.

The thought of such power gave him a momentary feeling of headiness.

Before he could enjoy it, he heard his name being called. "Edward." He heard the cackle a second time and knew it had to be his wife. He looked off and saw Hannah in the portable wheelchair, being steered toward him by Roger. God, he thought as he waited, how awful she looks. She was hunched in the wheelchair, shriveled and withered as an Egyptian mummy, her overpainted face prematurely wrinkled. How had she let it happen to her? She was only fifty-six, his own age, and yet she looked twice as old. Giving in to all those ailments, spending all that time in bed, that had done it.

She was beside him. "Edward," she said, "they're driving the casket to the burial site right now. We should be there."

"We'll be there. Let me get the driver out here." He nodded at his muscular son. "Roger, get your mother to the curb."

He started to leave, but Hannah's voice caught him. "Edward, as soon as the service is over, we had better return home. You heard the announcement. There may be a hundred guests dropping by to pay their respects. We should both be there to receive them."

"We'll be there," he said with impatience. "After the burial,

you and Roger go on ahead. I'll be there a little later. I have to
attend to some urgent business first.''

"Business? On a day like this?''

He wanted to tell the old woman: The king is dead. On a day
like this, a new king must be crowned.

Instead, he told her, "It's important, very important. I'll catch
up with you . . .'' His voice drifted off. ''. . . sooner or later.''

Hannah and Roger had left in the Cadillac limousine, and
shortly afterward Edward Armstead's standby Silver Cloud Rolls-
Royce and chauffeur had taken him from the cemetery into
Manhattan and dropped him off at the aluminum-encased Citicorp
Building. He had ridden the express elevator to the twenty-sixth
floor and headed for the office suite whose entry door bore the
gold lettering: LIDDINGTON AND KRAUS, COUNSELLORS-AT-LAW.

Ushered into Horace Liddington's familiar office, he enjoyed a
quick high of anticipation at the prospect of coronation. The
business of the dead was done for the day. The business of the
living was all that mattered.

At the far end of the room, Horace Liddington was engrossed
in some kind of document—probably *the* document—and with
Armstead's entrance he raised his head and removed his spectacles.

"Ah, Edward, glad you could come right over,'' Liddington
said, getting to his feet.

"Wouldn't miss it.''

Armstead had started across the Aubusson rug that stretched
before the lawyer's antique walnut desk, when he saw a silver
tray holding brandy and cognac bottles and glasses on the secretaire that stood beneath a baroque mirror with a gilt frame.
Abruptly he detoured to the secretaire. "Mind if I have a drink,
Horace?''

"Please do, please do,'' Liddington said hastily.

Armstead uncorked a half-empty bottle of Rémy Martin cognac and hoisted the bottle. "Can I pour you one?''

"Thank you, Edward, but I'll pass for now. But you—by all means you have one. I'm sure you can use it."

"I can use it," Armstead agreed, pouring more than an inch of cognac into the snifter. He inhaled the aroma, then slowly drank as he walked toward the elaborately carved French armchair resting next to the Louis XV fruitwood game table.

As he settled into the armchair, he saw Liddington watching him with concern.

"If you're worrying about me, Horace—don't," said Armstead. "I'm all right."

Liddington bobbed his head jerkily and lowered himself into his walnut desk chair. "It would be understandable if you didn't feel all right. Losing a father—it doesn't happen every day." He shrugged. "But as it must to all men, his time had come."

"I thought it would never come," said Armstead.

Liddington seemed taken aback.

Armstead smiled. "Have I shocked you? I've been in the wings a long time, Horace. I'm fifty-six. I never thought I'd get a chance to go on. But now it's my turn. At least, I think it is." He took another sip of cognac and placed his glass on the table. "Is it my turn, Horace?"

"Oh, yes—yes, of course. You were his only real heir. He had no meaningful charities."

"Well, let's get on with it. Make it official, Horace."

Liddington was unsettled. He made an effort to pull himself together. He drew the document across his desk closer to him. He took a moment to compose himself. "Would you like me to read you the will, Edward?" He hurried on. "It's a short testament. Hearst's will was 125 pages long, I've heard. E. J.'s is only 37 pages. Relatively short for so complex an estate. I could read it to you."

Armstead grinned. "You mean formally, like in those movies where relatives get together in a room to hear the old man's will?"

"Well . . . ." said Liddington lamely.

Armstead sat up. "Just give me the essence. I'll read the whole will when I have more time. You can send a copy over. Right now the essence. Did I get all of it? Or most of it?"

"He left you the bulk of the estate. He provided a trust for his grandson—your son, Roger—and he gave the title to one of his seven homes, the château near St-Paul-de-Vence, to Hannah—to Mrs. Armstead. Of his public holdings, he owned half the stock, which he passed on to you. Hannah, of course, always owned the other half—"

Armstead dismissed her with a gesture. "Hannah's no problem."

"Very well. The other six homes went to you. There are some token bequests—mainly minor shares in the magazines and syndicate—to some of the old-timers who have been in his employ for years. Perhaps a dozen bequests to various distant relatives."

"But the rest to me? The ranches—"

"Just about everything will be yours, Edward. The mines in Utah and Nevada. Oil wells in Oklahoma and Texas. The chain of markets. The New York real estate. The merchant ships. The art works, except for a few he left to the Metropolitan Museum."

A sudden curiosity prickled Armstead. "What about Kim?" he inquired. "Kim Nesbit."

Liddington appeared hesitant. "What about her?"

"Is she in the will?"

The attorney was still hesitant. "No—not exactly."

"What does that mean?"

"Well, the will is a public document, you know. It can be read by anyone after probate. I—I don't think Ezra wanted to invite speculation about his relationship with Miss Nesbit."

"Speculation," Armstead snorted. "The old hypocrite. Everyone knows he kept her from day one. He must have left her something."

"I did not say he left her nothing," said Liddington. "I was merely saying she was not in the will. Miss Nesbit was provided for a year before his death, at the beginning of his last illness."

"What did he give her?" Armstead wanted to know.

Liddington was reticent about replying. "I'm not sure it would be right for me to go into that, Edward. There is a confidentiality in a relationship between—"

"I know, I know," Armstead interrupted. He finished his cognac, and raised himself to his feet to take a cigar from the humidor on the walnut desk. He bit off the end of the cigar. "I just wondered how he felt about Kim at the end. Did he leave her flat?"

"Oh, no, no—"

"Did he let her keep her condo?"

"He gave it to her years ago. And he made her a cash settlement. A generous arrangement. She will always live in comfort."

"I see." Armstead put a lighter to his cigar, and puffed. "Now back to me, Horace. How much of the estate did he leave me?"

"As I said, the bulk of it. About three quarters of it."

"I only understand numbers, Horace. How much?"

"I should estimate—a worth of over a billion dollars."

Armstead sat down. After a brief silence, he spoke. "Horace, where's the zinger?" he inquired placidly.

"The zinger?"

"The needle, the shiv. You can't tell me the old man went to the grave and just left me everything without trying to needle me some way, exert some influence on me after he was gone, make something difficult?"

"Well . . ." Liddington hesitated momentarily. "I repeat, he left you the bulk of his estate."

"Clean?" persisted Armstead. "No ifs, ands, or buts?" He had a sudden intuition. "The newspaper," he said. "Does the estate include the newspaper?"

"The newspapers," Liddington corrected him. "He had liquidated most of them, as you know. But there are still five left."

"I'm interested in only one," said Armstead sharply. "The

New York *Record*, his flagship paper. The others are rags. But the *Record*, that could be important." He held on the attorney's face, and detected a certain evasiveness. "He left me the *Record*, didn't he?"

"Ah, yes," said Liddington. He fumbled with the pages of the document. "Yes, I was about to get to that."

"What's there to get to?" said Armstead impatiently. "It's his one possession that matters to me. That paper made him famous, until he became inattentive. I grew up on that paper. I know what to do with it. It is mine now, isn't it?"

Liddington was turning the pages of the will. "Well, yes and no," he said. He found what he wanted and reread it to himself. "Concerning the New York *Record*, there is a restrictive clause—"

"What kind of clause?"

"He bequeathed the newspaper to you but there is a restrictive condition."

"What condition?"

"It's—it's an odd clause. I remember when he inserted it. I didn't understand his reasoning, but I did as I was told, I included it."

"Will you tell me what the damn thing says?"

"You are to have the New York *Record*, of course. But conditionally, for a trial year. During that year you must at some point exceed the daily circulation of the New York *Times*. If you can do that just once, the paper is yours, permanently. If you fail, the newspaper must perforce be sold to Paul Eldridge of the New York *Times*. Eldridge had made your father an offer some months before his death. But, of course, that clause is inoperative if—"

"The bastard!" Armstead burst out. He was livid. "I knew it was too good to be true. There had to be a zinger. I knew E. J. had to shiv me somewhere. He knew what that paper means to me. He knew it hasn't topped the *Times* once since 1954. He set a condition that he knew couldn't be met. He didn't want to appear the bastard that he was. He wanted to show the world he was the good parent, leaving me what I wanted most, but then to be sure I lost it. He wanted to show the world what he always believed—that I am incompetent, not worthy—''

''Wait a minute. Hold on, Edward,'' Liddington broke in, trying to placate him. ''Even if you lost the paper, you'd get the money from its sale. You could start another newspaper in New York.''

''You don't understand,'' said Armstead angrily. ''You didn't know him the way I did. After a point, he never cared about money, and neither do I. He cared about his newspaper. It had made him—made him internationally famous. I was raised on it. I wanted the *Record* above everything else. Having it would give me my chance to prove myself, prove I was worthy. But he didn't want me to have the paper. He didn't want me to have my chance.''

''Edward, perhaps you are being somewhat unreasonable. I repeat, you could start your own newspaper—''

''You can't start a newspaper, not these days. A newspaper has to *be* there. It is like a person. It has a heart and soul. It's a friend, a part of every reader's family and life. The *Record* is part of the daily lives of hundreds of thousands of people here, and I could have carried it on, made it more, returned it to its highest glory—but no, he wouldn't let me.''

''You can still do so, Edward,'' Liddington said. ''The paper is entirely yours for a year.''

''A year,'' repeated Armstead bitterly. ''He's given me a year to do what he was unable to do in decades. He knew it couldn't be done. The bastard.''

The lawyer made one more effort at reason. ''Edward, he must have thought highly of you. He left you almost everything. He left you the television stations, the big one here in New York. Everyone watches television.''

''Fuck television,'' said Armstead. ''A picture book for illiterates and morons. Two or three minutes on any one subject. No time for in-depth, for understanding, for absorbing and reflecting.

The only things treated with care are the commercials. He left me television?''

''And a billion dollars.''

Armstead ground his cigar into a pewter tray. He stood up. ''He left me shit,'' he said bitterly. He shook his head. ''You'll never understand.'' He cast about him. ''Is there a telephone where I can make a call privately?''

Liddington came to his feet. ''Let me take you to the conference room next door. It's not in use. Can I put through the call for you?''

''It's personal. It's something I want to do myself.'' He had brought a small address book out of his jacket pocket. ''There's someone I have to see.''

''I wasn't sure you'd keep your appointment today,'' said Dr. Carl Scharf, closing the office door and directing Edward Armstead to the cracked and faded brown leather chair directly across from his own sand-colored armchair.

Usually when he sat down for one of his three-times-a-week sessions Armstead made some derogatory comment about the leather chair—that it looked as if it had come secondhand from a garage sale. Always he made some critical comment about Dr. Scharf's cramped and untidy office. Once he had even offered to lease and pay for a more commodious and modern suite in a better neighborhood for his psychoanalyst, but Dr. Scharf had politely declined. Armstead had then suspected that the analyst retained his Black Hole of Calcutta because it was contrary chic. To headquarter in a rotting and dangerous ancient building on Thirty-sixth Street off Broadway and there receive famous and wealthy patients showed a certain individuality, eccentricity, and disregard for façades that would finally impress overindulged neurotics.

Armstead had given up on Dr. Scharf's shameful apparel long ago. True, the analyst was not built to be a Beau Brummel, and apparently from early on had decided to go with what he had. Dr.

Scharf was a short, round man—round bald pate circled by a fringe of thinning hair, and fat round physique. A disgrace to the New York Psychoanalytic Institute, Armstead was sure, a psychiatrist who did not like to listen. But he was insightful, he was warm, he was brilliant. He had tried for years to get Armstead to break away from his father, to swim on his own, but that had been asking too much. This afternoon, as ever, he was attired in a rumpled and worn tweed sports jacket, turtleneck sweater, and unpressed slacks.

Dropping into his armchair, Armstead hardly noticed. Nor was he aware of the shabby office and its disreputable furniture. Armstead was blind, blind with rage.

While Armstead sat fuming, the analyst rearranged some back copies of the *Journal of the American Psychoanalytic Association* on top of the ottoman before his own chair. Then he wriggled more comfortably into his shallow seat, propped his feet up on the magazines, put a match to his smelly briar pipe and said again, "I didn't think you'd come by today."

"I didn't intend to. But I just heard his will, and I got so pissed off I had to see someone—even you."

Dr. Scharf puffed placidly on his pipe. "You did go to the funeral, Edward, didn't you?"

"Just to make sure he was dead."

Dr. Scharf nodded gently. "Reminds me of the old Harry Cohn story. You know, Harry Cohn, who was head of Columbia Pictures—"

"For chrissakes, Carl, I know who he was."

"When he died, a great crowd turned up for the funeral. Observing the crowd, someone said, 'Just give people what they want, and they'll show up.' I guess that's it."

"That's it," said Armstead.

"So you saw that he was dead."

"He was dead as a doornail. I'm sure of that."

"And still you don't feel free?"

"How can I? He won't let go. You should have heard what he put in his will, the bastard."

"Okay, Edward, what did he put in his will that's upset you so much?"

"He left me everything, except what I wanted."

"Tell me."

Armstead launched into a recital of his visit to Horace Liddington, the contents of the will and the conditional clause about the New York *Record*. When he finished he was almost asthmatic with anger. He stared at Dr. Scharf, waiting for his reaction.

"You're a rich man," said Dr. Scharf. "He made you a rich man. It could have been worse. He could have left it all to the Salvation Army."

"Come on, Carl, you know what this is all about."

"Of course I know," said Dr. Scharf mildly. "I'm just trying to give you some objectivity about your situation."

"He always looked down on me, he never respected me," said Armstead. "Never once did he show confidence in me."

"It's hard for big men, self-made men who have everything, to consider their puny sons as their equals, and to trust them."

"I don't want to keep repeating myself," said Armstead, "but this last will of his caps it off. He couldn't resist, even after he was in the ground, letting me know how he felt. I wanted to be a journalist, a publisher, right from the start, just like he was. He could never find a place for me. When I was a kid, he gave me a menial job on the *Record* when it was the leading paper, and I was proud and happy and loved it. But instead of moving me up, he moved me away. Shipped me off to his San Francisco tabloid. Then to that rag he had in Denver. Then to Chicago, which was better. Just when I thought I'd got going, he brought me back here to New York. Did he give me a position of responsibility? No. He trusted others. Me he made Special Projects officer. What was that? I never did find out. Whenever I came up with a new idea—and in recent years the *Record* needed new ideas—he would ignore it. When I protested to him—you know, I did stand up and protest to him—''

Dr. Scharf nodded. "Yes, you did."

"It got me nowhere. He always exiled me to secondary jobs. He forever had me learning the business—that's what he'd tell me when I protested: You've got to learn the business, Edward, he'd say—but Jesus, here I am fifty-six years old and he still had me learning the business. When he died, I was never more excited or happy. At last I'd have the paper. At last I could show the world. Then, an hour ago, I heard his will, and the provision that unless I could do the impossible—I couldn't keep the paper. It would be sold off. It would be gone. That was his good-bye message to me."

Dr. Scharf tried to speak, but Armstead would not let him. The venom in him was running over. He could not stop spilling out his poisoned past. He remembered how well he had started doing on the Chicago paper, and just when he was getting his identity, his father had recalled him to New York. He had been certain that this was a promotion and a reward, that his father had finally recognized his worth, but instead his father had refused him advancement, had relegated him to a back room with a couple of assistants, and had made believe he didn't exist.

"That's when I came to you, Carl. I was desperate. I needed help."

"Yes."

"He had real contempt for me, you know."

"Well—"

"He did. Everybody saw how he treated me, and they treated me with the same contempt. On every one of his papers, his editors treated me like a fool, a relative they had to endure. Only in Chicago, there were one or two people—well, mainly one, the managing editor, Hugh Weston, the old-timer who became the President's press secretary last year—who gave me some respect, knew I was intelligent and creative, tried to give me a chance.

But then E. J. yanked me back to New York and degraded me, and his editors here, they too treated me like a retarded son."

Dr. Scharf noisily emptied his pipe bowl of ash, filled it with fresh tobacco and lighted it. He peered through the smoke at Armstead.

"Edward," he said, "you own the newspaper now."

"For a year," said Armstead angrily.

"Even for a year. Those editors, they are your editors now. You can show them who's in charge."

"You mean, get rid of them?"

"Build your own team of loyalists from scratch. Are there any experienced newsmen you'd trust?"

"Harry Dietz, of course. You've heard me speak about him. And Bruce—Bruce Harmston. They were with me in Chicago. They were on Special Projects with me here in New York. They believe in me. They'd do anything for me."

"Then take them to the top with you, and do something about the paper. Yes, you always said the paper was the most important thing you wanted from your father."

"In fact, I used to tell you my father had only two things I ever wanted—the paper . . . and Kim—Kim Nesbit."

"Well, now you've got the paper."

"And Kim—well, of course, she's my father's—"

"Your father is dead, Edward."

Armstead blinked at Dr. Scharf through the smoke. He was silent a long time. "I guess you're right," he said finally. "He is dead. It takes time to get used to." He paused. "What about Kim? Does she ever come to see you anymore?"

What Armstead had remembered was that five years earlier, during one of the rare times he had seen her, Kim Nesbit had noticed and been aware of his own depressed state. She had spoken kindly to him, almost as a momentary ally against his father, and she had admitted that his father had driven her to see an analyst. She had found a good man, a wonderful man named Dr. Carl Scharf, and if Edward ever needed someone to talk to,

he might do well to see Dr. Scharf. So Armstead had come to
Dr. Scharf.

"Do I see Kim Nesbit anymore?" Dr. Scharf was saying.
"No. She drifted away. She felt I couldn't really help her.
Actually, she did come here one last time, about a year ago."
Dr. Scharf thought about it. "She wasn't in good shape. Loneli-
ness can be devastating. She was drinking too much. I hoped to
see her again, but she never came back."

"How did she look?"

Dr. Scharf rubbed the pipe bowl against his nose. "Why ask
me?" he said. "Why don't you see for yourself?"

She herself had opened the door.

Armstead stood stock still. All that he had imagined and
fantasized for so long was there before him.

And she was beautiful, absolutely beautiful.

She gave a little shout. "Edward! This is so unexpected. I'm
so glad you came by." She offered up her arms, and he stepped
into her embrace and kissed her on each cheek. The sweet smell
of her flesh mingled with the smell of whisky. "Come in, do
come in," she insisted, gripping his arm and pulling him through
the entry hall into the vast living room.

Momentarily, the lightness and brightness of the room made
him feel giddy. His eyes passed over the multicolored pillows on
the lime green sofas—three sofas that surrounded a coffee table—
across the patchwork carpet to the cream-colored grand piano.
Near it stood an elaborate television set airing a soap opera, and
near that a portable bar.

Kim Nesbit had come into view again. She was trying to draw
together her white lace negligee, and apologizing. "Sorry the
room's such a mess, but the maid's off today." Starting across
the room to the television set, she staggered slightly, then walked
with deliberate care to the set and shut it off.

She moved to the portable bar. "Can I make you a drink,
Edward?"

"If you'll join me," he said politely.

"Oh, I'll join you," she said, holding up an almost empty glass. "I've had a head start." She touched a half-filled bottle of J & B scotch. "I'm having scotch. I don't remember—what do you drink?"

"The same."

As she poured, she said, "It's been a long time, Edward."

"Eleven months," he said.

It had happened by chance. His father had planned to take her to a play and supper for her birthday, but at the last minute had been forced to fly to Los Angeles. Rather than let Kim spend the evening alone, E. J. had telephoned his son and asked him to escort her. Nervously, Armstead had agreed.

Her presence that evening, he remembered, had made him feel like an unsure adolescent. After the play, at supper at La Caravelle, he had been mostly mute, unable to take his eyes off her, yet forcing himself not to stare at her. Vividly now, he remembered his mingled discomfort with her and attraction to her . . . and he remembered how he had envied and hated his father that evening and wondered what she could see in the old man.

She could not have loved him, Armstead had decided. E. J. had been nearly three times her age, and not particularly good-looking. But he had been a power, a legend, and wealthy.

Armstead crossed to a sofa and sat down, once again not able to take his eyes off her. Her negligee was flimsy, transparent, and he could make out the outline of one of her naked inner thighs. She was probably wearing nothing underneath, being alone. Armstead studied her at the portable bar. There was something marvelously wanton about her, the way her long flaxen hair fell over an eye, the way one almost bare shoulder moved, the outline of that fleshy thigh.

It reaffirmed what he had felt when he saw her last. She had retained her beauty, no question—hardly faded, more mature and provocative. She was fairly tall, her lissomely curved body firm yet full at the bosom and hips, her legs long and slim. His father was a lucky bastard—*had been* a lucky bastard. Had been.

He tried to calculate Kim's age. She had been singing and dancing in a mediocre Broadway musical, one that would close in weeks, when his father first set eyes on her and went backstage. When her show closed, his father began seeing her more frequently, and eventually installed her in a small luxury apartment near Carnegie Hall. That had been eighteen years ago. Kim had been twenty-one, his father sixty-three, and he himself thirty-eight. Now she was thirty-nine, and he was fifty-six, and his father was—gone. She was young, much younger than he, but he was much younger than his father.

She was standing over him, handing him his scotch and water. "There you are."

He took the drink and absently took a swallow, looking up at her. "Were you at the funeral?" he asked. "I couldn't find you."

"I didn't think he would have wanted me to go." She downed a portion of her drink. "How was it, Edward?"

"Let me put it this way—" He recalled Dr. Scharf's irreverent story about Harry Cohn's funeral, and he retold it to Kim, ending with the visitor's comment, "Just give people what they want, and they'll show up." He did not smile and neither did she. He drank some more. "He was a bastard, my father," Armstead said. "Does that offend you?"

She gave a toss of a bare shoulder. "Not at all. He was never very nice to you."

She sat down on the sofa a few feet from Armstead, inched back against the corner pillows, and swung her legs onto the sofa, lifting her knees, hastily making sure the bottom part of her negligee was closed.

Armstead kept his gaze upon her. "Was he nice to you?"

She was silent a spell, taking a long pull on her drink, contemplating the glass in her hand. "Was he nice to me? I don't know. Yes, I suppose he was, in the beginning. I was just a gangly kid, and he was kind. After that, for some years, he was—well, attentive.''

Armstead tried to recall those earlier years. His mother, Sadie, had suffered her first stroke and was partially paralyzed. His father had spent more and more time at work, actually with Kim, determined to make Kim a Broadway star. His father had financed five musical comedies to star her. Four had closed within a week. One ran a limping *Variety* season. Kim did not become a star. But she did become an object of curiosity and gossip.

It was after his mother's second stroke, Armstead remembered, a more debilitating one, that his father had bought Kim this new condominium on Sutton Place. He had bought her the entire floor, remodeling two large apartments into one huge one. He had also bought her endless clothes, furs, diamonds, cars. His father had been very possessive of her, concerned about his age and her youth, and he had rarely let her venture out in public. Apparently this had been fine as long as he saw her regularly. Only after Sadie Armstead died had E. J. allowed Kim to accompany him in public. But gradually, as his father became older, tired more easily, and devoted himself increasingly to chasing honors, he had neglected not only his flagship newspaper but he had neglected Kim as well. Eventually, as far as Armstead could learn, his father had begun seeing her only occasionally. As for Kim, afraid to go out on her own, long cut off from friends her own age, Armstead guessed that she had become more and more of a recluse. A recluse and, he supposed, a heavy drinker, maybe an alcoholic.

He watched her finish her scotch. "Kim," he said, "when was the last time you saw my father?"

She tried to think. "Maybe six, seven, eight months ago. Although he didn't come around much at any time in the last few years.''

"You hadn't seen him for that long?"

"Not at all. He'd phone once a week. That was about it.'' She swallowed the last of her drink. "Any more questions?" she said a little thickly.

Armstead hesitated. "Yes. When was the last time he slept with you?"

She tried to focus her eyes on Armstead. "You mean fucked me, Edward? I don't know—it was that long ago. Maybe six, seven years ago. And not very good. In fact, it was never very good. Ezra was just not much interested." She frowned. "I shouldn't be saying these things about your father."

"What have you done for sex?"

"Oh, you don't need to do much when you're drinking. Sometimes I masturbated."

"That can't be much fun."

She stirred, reached around to put down her glass, and started to get up. "I never heard you suggest anything better," she said. Her negligee had come apart above the waist. He could see the milky mound of one breast.

Then she was standing. He could feel the throbbing and hardening between his legs. He fixed on her swaying form above him. "What are you going to do with yourself now? You're young. You're beautiful."

"I'm going to have another drink," she said. But she did not move. "You think I'm beautiful? Are you just being nice because it's today?"

He came quickly to his feet. "I'm telling you I want you, Kim. I want you. I always have."

Her face was expressionless. She wavered, but remained where she was standing. He had her in his arms, embracing her roughly. He kissed her on her open mouth, pressing until he found her tongue, then shoving his body against hers until she could feel his erection.

With difficulty, she drew her head back. "Edward," she said with a gasp, "do you know what you're doing?"

"Just what I've always wanted to do since I've known you."

She sighed. "Yes." Slowly her arms snaked around him. Her mouth found his lips and his tongue.

As their embrace tightened, their kissing more heated, he lowered one hand and opened her negligee. His fingers touched her naked flesh, groped downward from her belly until they reached the fluffy soft pubic hair, massaging the distended clitoris, gliding over the moistening vulva.

She began to moan in his ear, her hand fumbling below until it found his erection.

"I—I always wanted you," she whispered.

He scooped her up, carried her down a hallway to the master bedroom illuminated by a single floor lamp. He lowered her to the downy rose-and-white comforter that covered the bed. Yanking off jacket, tie, shirt, he undressed completely. He could see himself in a full-length mirror, his flat pale-blue eyes holding on himself at this moment of fifty-six. Just under six feet, thickset but not fat, sturdy and strong, no blotches and few wrinkles. In the mirror, he could see Kim behind him, on the edge of the bed, wriggling out of her white negligee. He could see how young she was, the flawless peach-colored skin, straight full breasts with large hardened nipples, the rise and fall of her abdomen, the long triangle of soft pubic hair.

His eyes returned to his reflection, to his penis standing straight out.

He turned around. She was lying back on the bed now, watching fascinated as he walked toward her. "You feel that way about me?" she said in an undertone.

"More than ever." He was on the bed. "Move over."

She worked herself sideways and he was beside her. He caressed her breasts, and pushed himself to his knees. She covered her eyes with an arm, licked her dry lips, lifted her knees, and spread them apart.

He was over her, and between her fleshy thighs, and into the vaginal opening, slowly and slowly, and deeper and deeper between the clinging lips of the vulva. It was delicious, this entry, and as he slid back and forth he was aroused to a bursting point. He thought that he might come right away, and slowed, fighting it, until the wave passed, and then he settled down to a steady, relentless rhythm, fucking her straight and hard.

After a few minutes her hips began to rise and fall with him, and make undulating circular movements that quickened and heaved, and she began to emit throaty orgasmic sounds. He was ready, and suddenly her fingers dug into his shoulders and she was ready. She opened her eyes and began to come, and with that he pumped mindlessly, felt the perspiration in his eyes, and then he came big.

She was slack beneath him, gulping air, and he rolled off her.

"Did you?" he asked her.

"Oh, yes."

Her hand went down to her clitoris, and he pushed her hand away and massaged her clitoris briefly until she lifted her hips and came again. After that, she had three more orgasms and wanted no more. He lay with his head between her breasts and her fingers played with his mussed hair.

After a while, he lay back and thought of what a fantastic fuck she was, so ready, so warm, so giving. He relived their coupling in his head, and suddenly he felt an involuntary movement between his legs. This had not happened so soon since he had been a young man. But then, he told himself, he was a young man.

His hand found her breasts and he fondled them, rubbing the large nipples of each, feeling them grow under his fingertips. She came around on her side, felt his growing erection, held it until her hand was full and able to contain only part of its hardness.

She pulled him to her, and raised her knees, and opened herself to him. He rose above her and comfortably entered her once more, resuming as if he had done it with her all his life and this was a dance they had always done so well together.

This time it was even better, the best. His body was slick with sweat and her skin slippery from his when she came in one long-drawn-out eruption, and seconds later he came too.

He managed to push off her, and they both lay there side by side as if dead.

Once she whispered sleepily, "You're never going to let me be alone again, are you?"

He touched her cheek. "Never."

He lay there a long time, resting, letting his mind wander. He had told his analyst today that he had been denied only two things in his life he had always wanted. One had been the newspaper. The other had been Kim. Now he had possessed Kim. She belonged to him. That left the newspaper. It was his for the moment. Tomorrow morning he would go into the publisher's office, remove the pictures from the wall, sweep the massive oak desk clear of its artifacts. It would be his alone. And now, for the first time, revitalized by his conquest of Kim, he felt confident that anything was possible and it could be his for all time. He had told Scharf that he would kill to keep the paper. And now he knew he could.

Satisfied, he got out of bed and walked to his clothes, which were heaped on a chair. He sought and found his watch. It was early evening. If he stayed away a little longer, he would miss the wake, and the mourners, and Hannah. He would phone Harry Dietz and Bruce Harmston and have them bring in some food, bring it up to the publisher's office of the *Record*. They could dine together, celebrating, and plan his new stewardship and his ultimate victory over the king who was dead.

Dressing, he looked over at the bed. Kim was breathing shallowly, sound asleep.

Going to the bed to cover her, one thought came to him as he stared at that wonderful naked body.

He and Kim, they had fucked each other. But one of them had also fucked his father.

2

Immediately after landing at National Airport in Washington, D.C., from Chicago, on this sunny late morning, Victoria Weston took a taxi to her father's two-story townhouse located on Prospect Street in Georgetown. Her father, Hugh, had come home for his lunch break and was waiting for her.

After the black housekeeper, Selma, had greeted her with a kiss, picked up her overnighter and garment bag and shouted for her father, Hugh Weston appeared almost immediately. Victoria flung herself into her father's arms. She loved him and had not seen him in months.

At last he held her off and scrutinized her. "Far as I can tell, you look great, fit and trim," he said. "Maybe you could stand a few more pounds—"

"I'm 118, and I'm staying that way until I find me a man."

"What's with this man stuff? Ever since I can remember you've had dozens of men at your heels."

"I mean the right man."

"How old are you? Twenty-four."

"Twenty-five, going on twenty-six, almost thirty."

"Twenty-five. Correct. Forgive me. At sixty, one tends to get hazy about birthdays, other people's as well as one's own." He looked her over again. She was a tall, willowy girl with loose blond hair, luminous eyes, a pert nose and wide grin; she was vivacious and cheerful, and particularly attractive in her pale apricot sweater, slim rust-colored skirt, hand-woven leather sandals. "Sorry, Victoria," he said, "I'm not worried about you. There'll be many right men." He took her hand and led her into the living room. "I can't tell you how tickled I was with your winning the Chicago Hildy Johnson Award, a great coup in journalism. Congratulations again."

"Thanks, Dad."

"I read those clippings at least three times. That was a helluva series, that exposé. Imagine all those so-called respectable married women working part-time for that madam on Lakeview Avenue. What got them to do it? Surely they didn't need money."

"They needed excitement. They were bored."

"Well, you deserved the Hildy Award. Was your mother pleased?"

"I think she was embarrassed that her darling daughter could write publicly about such things."

Hugh Weston was not surprised. "Yes, that figures." He eyed his offspring. "How is your mother?"

Hugh Weston's wife of thirty years had been unhappy as a newspaper widow. Their only child, Victoria, had been the product of many efforts to hold together their marriage. In the end, it had not worked. Six years ago they had enjoyed an unacrimonious divorce, and less than two years later his wife had married a wealthy businessman and now dwelt luxuriously in Evanston, Illinois.

"Mother?" she said. "She's a meat-packer's widow, but he keeps better hours than you ever did. He comes home long before dawn. Mother is Mother, which is why I moved to Chicago and got my own apartment as soon as I could. We still talk. I see her maybe once every two weeks. Sa-ay, what about you, Dad? How's the new job holding up?''

A year ago Hugh Weston had been appointed press secretary for President of the United States Thomas Callaway. He had given up his job as managing editor of the Chicago *Journal* and moved to the White House and this Georgetown house.

"It is not exactly *The Front Page*," Hugh Weston said ruefully, "but I like being on television and meeting rich socialites. Now I've got to leave you for an hour."

Victoria pointed at him. "I've just figured it out. Those are tennis shorts you're wearing. You mean you find time to play tennis? I know you did when I was a kid, but—"

Hugh Weston held up a hand to stop her. "Victoria, this President likes to play tennis on Sundays. And he likes to play me because he can beat me." He went to the french windows, where a tennis racket was propped up against the wall. "I have a confession to make. I liked it so much, I joined two neighbors in the block in buying a court. I own a third of it and use it when I can. I don't have to be back at the White House until three, so I'm using it now. Want to watch me?"

"Thanks, Dad. I think I'll shower and freshen up. Then I'll make us lunch. What do you want?"

"The special Victoria Cheese Omelet. Maybe a small salad first."

"You've got it."

He started to leave, then turned around. "Hey, what are you doing here on a weekday? I thought you were a working girl?"

"I was. I quit the paper last Friday, Dad. I came here because I want to talk to you about it."

He nodded. "Okay. Make me that omelet and we'll talk. See you in an hour."

After her father had left, Victoria Weston went upstairs to the spare bedroom where her overnighter and garment bag were waiting and unpacked. After that she undressed, took a quick shower, and put on a red-and-white-checked blouse and faded jeans. She went downstairs to the kitchen, told Selma to go back to her favorite soap opera, and started to make lunch.

An hour and a half later Victoria and Hugh Weston were enjoying their lunch in the sun-filled dinette. During the salad he had discussed the tennis game, and his partners. Now, pushing the salad plate aside, waiting as his daughter served him a generous portion of the cheese omelet, he said, "Okay, Vicky, you quit the *Citizen*. You came here to talk. Tell me what you want to talk about. I'm listening."

"My future," said Victoria, taking her seat across from her father. She sampled the eggs, approved, and looked up. "I want to talk about my future, my immediate future, like tomorrow."

"Go ahead."

"Dad, I was on that Chicago weekly for a full year, after getting out of Northwestern. Then I put in two years at that suburban daily, but I wasn't going anywhere. I was the best feature writer on the paper. In fact, too good for it. There was a monotony, a sameness to the kind of stories that could be dredged up. I needed more. I needed a challenge. So I quit. That way I knew I had to find something better." She paused for her father to say something, and when he remained silent she said, "Well, maybe there's more to it than that."

"Want to tell me?"

"One part's professional, the other personal. The professional part first. There I was on the women's page; I wanted out of that rut. I always wanted to be on the news side. You know that. I thought all my extra work on that exposé would do it. Especially after I won the award. But no, my managing editor wouldn't promote me. He was probably raised on Godey's Lady's Book. Woman's place? In the recipe and lovelorn section. I was really furious."

"I see. What about the personal part?"

Victoria hesitated. "A brief involvement. He was married, and promised to get unmarried. He didn't."

"Were you hurt?"

"Only momentarily." She considered the episode. "Not really. I'm sure it was just as well. As I told you, I'm still looking for Mr. Right."

"And as I told you, you'll find him."

"Anyway, I wanted a change. Above all, I wanted to get away from that crummy suburban paper." She added with certainty, "Dad, I know I'm ready for something big-time."

"I'm sure you are. Maybe you've made the sensible move." He paused. "I was going to suggest that you let me make a pitch for you with my old sheet in Chicago. But you say you want a change."

"Thanks, Dad, but no. It's more than just a change. There's been one Weston there, and he can never be surpassed. My feet aren't big enough to fill your shoes."

"I think you're overdoing it a bit."

"I'd really like to leave Chicago. I'd like to try at the summit."

"New York?"

Victoria nodded. "Yes, New York."

Weston ate his omelet and thought about it. He wiped his mouth with his napkin. "It's pretty crowded there, Vicky. Would you consider a slight detour, maybe upward, editorial staff of a magazine or book publishing house or even television? I have some contacts—"

Victoria leaned against the table. "Dad, I want what you had, newspapering. I've always envied your life, the excitement, the craziness, the day-to-day aliveness."

"The short money," said Weston with a wry smile.

"To hell with the money. I'll live in one room in a ghetto, eat an apple a day, mend my own panty hose—as long as I can wake up unable to wait for my job to begin, and go to sleep knowing I want more hours of the same. I want to be Nellie Bly. I want to be Annie Laurie. I want to be Dorothy Kilgallen."

Hugh Weston sat back in his chair. "Well . . ." he said.

"Well what?" Victoria asked intently.

"New York," he said. "Tough town. Let me think."

He rose, wandered about looking for his tennis jacket, found it, extracted a caked pipe, tobacco, pouch, and lighter, and moments later was seated across from his daughter once more, smoking. She eyed him intently, waiting.

"I was just reviewing my contacts in New York," he said, "and I just had a notion. My mind went to Ezra J. Armstead. Remember him?"

"E. J. Armstead. 'The Giant,' they called him. You worked for him on his Chicago paper. He died this week, didn't he?"

"Yes, he died. That means the New York *Record* will probably go to his son, Edward Armstead—Edward was his only heir, far as I know—and Edward and I were very close in Chicago."

"I remember him well, Dad. You used to bring him home for dinner sometimes. You practically treated him like a son."

"A good man, not that much younger than I, but in a sense he didn't have a father, and he would often turn to me. We had a close relationship. I haven't seen him in a while, but I think he still feels kindly toward me. Perhaps I should give him a buzz. We might luck out—"

Victoria clasped her hands. "Oh, Dad, that would be perfect. The New York *Record*—"

"Whoa, there." Weston pushed himself to his feet. "There are a few ifs along the road—if Edward Armstead inherited the sheet, if he is looking for new personnel, if he'll consider you . . . well, let's find out."

Weston went into the living room, where a telephone sat upon the rolltop desk that he had brought from his office in Chicago. While Victoria nervously removed the lunch dishes, Weston called long-distance information and got the number of the New York *Record*. He dialed the number and waited.

"*Record?* I'd like to speak to Mr. Edward Armstead. Tell him Hugh Weston is calling from Washington, D.C. . . . Okay, I'll hold on."

Weston saw that Victoria had materialized in the living room, untying her apron, also holding on.

The telephone crackled. Weston was instantly alert, receiver pressed to his ear. "Yes, this is Hugh Weston," he said and listened. "Harry, Harry Dietz! My God, it's good to hear your voice again . . . Oh, I'm fine, fine . . . Yes, it is a little drafty in the White House, but I'm enjoying it. I just wanted to give Edward a ring, to see how he's doing . . . What? He's right there? He wants to speak to me? Great. Put him on."

Hugh Weston saw his daughter's tense face and gave her a wink.

He was engaged on the phone again. "Hello, Edward. How are you? . . . I'm glad. Anyway, my condolences. The old man had a long run and a good one, and you had a long wait . . . Edward, I understand exactly how you feel." He paused. "I assume you're taking over the papers, and the *Record*." He listened. "Good, good, good. And just in time. The paper needs an infusion. You'll do a super job, Edward, nobody knows it better than I." He listened. "Well, thank you, Edward, that's kind of you, and I appreciate it. But I'm out of the newspaper business for good. I wanted to retire. Where's a better place than the White House?" He laughed. Then he sobered. "Actually, I'm calling not only to wish you well but to find out if you're going to be assembling your own team." He kept the receiver to his ear attentively. "Well, that fits in with something I want to speak to you about. You were kind enough to want an old Weston—but in fact, you can have a new Weston as good if not better than the old one."

"Oh, Dad," Victoria called out. "Don't do that."

Her father hushed her with his hand. "Here's what I mean, Edward," Weston said into the phone. "You remember my daughter, Vicky—well, she's a grown woman now, and a crack reporter. She's worked for three years in the Chicago area, two of them on an important suburban daily. She knows the ropes. She's decided to move on to a job that's more challenging. She quit her Chicago position last week, and came here to ask my advice this morning. I thought of you, and I wondered if you'd

have the time to see her, would want to—'' He stopped, listened,
and smiled broadly at the mouthpiece. ''That's wonderful, Edward,
wonderful. You won't be disappointed. What? . . . It's Victoria,
Victoria Weston . . . All right, perfect. Good luck to you, too,
Edward, the best of luck. You deserve it. Let me know the next
time you're coming to D.C. We'll hoist a beer together. . . .
Good. I'll tell Victoria.''

He hung up and turned to Victoria, beaming.

''Armstead's looking for people. He's ready to look at you.
Your appointment at the New York *Record* is for two o'clock
tomorrow.''

At the corner of Park Avenue and Forty-sixth Street, the light
gray Armstead Building stood sixteen stories high, dwarfed by
the taller new buildings leading uptown. The heart of the structure,
the one that pumped activity into all the other stories, was the
sixth floor. Most of it was given over to the New York *Record*'s
newsroom, with one portion of it reserved for the publisher's
suite, which included the publisher's main office, the office for
his personal secretary and receptionist, a conference and electronic media room, two offices for the advertising director and
his assistant, and smaller, glassed-in cubicles for the managing
editor and the assistant managing editor.

By the third day following E. J. Armstead's funeral, the temporary heir to this suite and to the building had made few personnel
changes. Edward Armstead had retired his father's elderly female
secretary on a generous pension and replaced her with his own
secretary, Estelle Rivkin, a smart, brisk, thirtyish woman with
short-cropped dark hair and horn-rimmed glasses who had served
him with devotion for five years in Special Projects. He had
moved the advertising director and his assistant down to his old
Special Projects offices and brought Harry Dietz and Bruce
Harmston up from the fourth floor and installed them in the
nearby advertising offices. For the time being, he had allowed

managing editor Ollie McAllister and assistant managing editor
Jim Crutchfield to remain in their glassed-in cubicles.

Now, this early third afternoon following the funeral, Edward
Armstead, having finished his box lunch (tomato and lettuce on
wheat bread, a dill pickle, a spinach salad, a diet drink—he had
decided to diet to make himself even more attractive for Kim
Nesbit), summoned his personal secretary and asked her to remove the cardboard box.

As Estelle placed the empty paper plates and cup into the box,
Armstead retrieved a toothpick and began to use it as he surveyed
the forty-foot office.

From the door Estelle said, "It's beginning to look right, Mr.
Armstead." She indicated the stretch of office.

Armstead gave a nod of assent. "Yes, I think we've got it in
shape."

After his secretary had gone, Armstead glanced about the
spacious office once more. In his shirt sleeves, behind the formidable oak desk, he was pleased with what he saw. It *was*
beginning to look right, his own office, no longer E. J.'s. Most of
the reminders of his father had been eradicated. For one thing,
the wall decorations. During the preceding two days he and
Estelle and a newspaper handyman had taken down all of his
father's favorite framed photographs, laminated honor scrolls,
and French paintings. Gone from the Irish linen matte wallpaper
were E. J.'s pictures of himself, self-styled "the Giant," with
five United States Presidents, with foreign royalty, with baseball
superstars, with movie and television luminaries. Only one photograph had been allowed to remain hanging, a portrait of Edward
Armstead's mother taken with Edward himself at the age of
fourteen.

Since Edward's own pictures with celebrities and his framed
awards had been pitifully few, he had filled the empty spaces
with artistic photographs by Julia Cameron, Stieglitz, and Steichen,
and substituted for his father's Matisses, Picassos, Cézannes his
own favorite Yugoslavian primitives, Generalić, Rabuzin, Lackovic,

a gaudy collection of naïfs acquired on several visits to Hlebine, Zagreb, and Belgrade.

Armstead cast his gaze further about the room. The fern planters on either side of the sliding doors that led to a balcony overlooking Park Avenue were new. The ultramodern seventy-two-inch television screen before the fireplace was also new. The pull-up rattan chairs before the oak desk had taken the place of his father's pompous leather ones. The desk top itself, always kept clean by his father, Armstead had defiantly cluttered with mementos—ivory miniatures from Tokyo, tiny military figures from Paris, several small bronze golf trophies from St. Andrews, an ancient coin in a velvet-lined case from Masada.

Of the larger pieces, only his father's custom-made oak desk retained its place. There had been magic here once. Armstead had not wished to tamper with magic.

His housekeeping inspection done, Armstead directed his sight toward his desk calendar and was suddenly eager to get going. His father's will had made him extremely sensitive to the passage of time. He reached for his ivory-colored computer telephone, pressed the ICM button and then the intercom code for Harry Dietz's private telephone.

"Harry, I'm ready for the meeting. Bring Bruce with you."

"Be right in, Chief. We have everything set."

A few minutes later Harry Dietz and Bruce Harmston appeared, Dietz carrying a handful of folders, and Armstead motioned his lieutenants to the rattan chairs across from his desk. Armstead felt comfortable with them, the only persons, besides his secretary, he depended upon. Certainly his reliance on Dietz was without equivocation.

Dietz was the taller of the two, with sandy hair, a chalky complexion, an adenoidal smile, and a smooth, suave manner. Harmston had a rounder face, receding hairline, bulbous nose, and lots of chin. Neither was as creative as Armstead, but they were perfect when it came to reading his mind, even to finishing his sentences. They were aggressive, daring, filled with energy, and both had hated E. J. These were Armstead's confidants and his loyalists, since Chicago, and from now on they would be properly rewarded.

"First things first," Armstead said to Dietz. "Did you check out the daily circulation of the New York *Times*?"

Dietz found a clear area on the desk, set his folders down, picked up the top one and opened it. "According to the Audit Bureau of Circulations, the latest daily circulation figure on the *Times*—four months old—is 873,255. That's subscription and newsstand."

"And the *Record*, what's our latest daily circulation figure?"

"Approximately 533,000."

Armstead frowned. "So we'd have to pick up around 350,000 readers to pass the New York *Times*."

"I'm afraid that's it, Chief," said Dietz.

"The bastard."

Both Dietz and Harmston knew that he meant his father, and they bobbed their heads in agreement.

Armstead sat up in his swivel chair and loosened his tie. "Well, if we want to keep this paper we'd better get to work. You've got the records of the editorial staffers and the reorganizational charts?"

Dietz patted the folders on the desk. "Right here."

"Okay, I'll get at them later. Let's start with the two of you. I've been giving it some thought. You will both be answerable only to me. Outside of general orders, everything I tell you will be kept in strictest confidence. Harry, this is a bigger job, much bigger, than Special Projects, and so your work will be greatly expanded. As always, you'll be the one to develop and carry out my ideas. You, Bruce, will have a double work load. Not only do I want you to serve as my liaison with the two hundred editorial people out there, but I also want you to act as my personal public-relations man."

"For yourself, not just the paper," said Harmston.

"For me. I come into this position as the Giant's son, an heir who got lucky, an obscure relative, a faded copy of the legendary press lord. I want to climb out from under that image. I want to be my own man, a known individual.''

"I'd love that,'' said Harmston enthusiastically.

"You did public relations in Chicago,'' added Armstead. "You have the background to do the job. See that I get a fair shake for everything I do. And work up a program that will get me both attention and prestige.''

"I can do it,'' Harmston promised.

"To do anything, we've got to hold on to the paper,'' said Armstead. "To hold on to the paper, we've got to revitalize it. To become Number One, we've got to give people what they can't get in any other newspaper. How do we do it? By finding exclusives. By digging for exposés. By having what no one else has. Harry, you and I will revamp the staff, get rid of the weaklings, hire some bright young pros. Bruce, I want you to revive Special Projects. Find out what the staff can offer. Meet with McAllister and Crutchfield. And that fellow, that investigative reporter who came up with that last Special Project for us, the groundwork for that series on the inside of world terrorism that my old man turned down. Who was that reporter?''

"Nick Ramsey,'' said Harmston.

"Sharp fellow. Milk him for some thoughts for Special Projects. Then—''

The ICM on Armstead's telephone sounded. Estelle's voice came through the speaker. "Mr. Armstead, there's a young lady here who claims to have a two o'clock appointment with you. Miss Victoria Weston. I don't have her in my book—''

"Miss—who?''

"Miss Victoria Weston. Apparently you were to interview her for a job as a reporter.''

For a moment Armstead's face was a blank, and then recognition came. "Yes, I remember—Hugh Weston's daughter. I promised to see her. Tell her to wait a minute.''

As Armstead turned away from the phone Dietz said, "Want me to interview her?"

"No, no, I think I should handle this myself. You remember how Hugh treated me in Chicago. I owe him this." He stood up. "Why don't you two get together with McAllister and Crutchfield in the conference room. Do some brainstorming. I'll join you when I finish with the girl."

Armstead sat on the sofa in his office, fingering the resumé and considering Hugh Weston's daughter seated at the opposite end of the sofa.

What was surprising was that he had expected Hugh Weston's daughter to be a child and instead found her to be a woman, very much so. She was a pretty, leggy young lady in a Chanel-style tweed suit and tan sling-back pumps. She had arresting, large hazel eyes and an attractive, tentative smile. She looked disarmingly innocent, deceptively so, he hoped.

"You know, your father and I had a close relationship," Armstead said. "I admired him."

"He always thought highly of you," replied Victoria. "He still does. He was sorry to see your father go—" She hesitated. "—but he felt it might be good for you."

Armstead acknowledged her frankness with a fleeting smile. "Yes, Hugh understands. Wasn't it Freud who said a son can't be a man until his father dies?"

"I recall reading that."

"How is your father these days? Does he like his new career?"

She wrinkled her nose. "I'm not sure. He's a die-hard journalist at heart. He doesn't like being put in an adversary position with the Washington press. He's on the side of the White House correspondents when he has to spoon-feed them the daily dose of hokum."

Armstead laughed. "Poor Hugh. But it's exciting for him, isn't it?"

"Oh, yes. Very much so."

"And now you want to follow in his footsteps?"

"Well, he had pretty big feet."

"But you're sure you want to be a newspaperwoman?"

"I *am* a newspaperwoman, Mr. Armstead. I've been one day and night for over three years. As you'll see in my resumé—"

"Ah, the resumé, yes. Let me have a look at it." He unfolded the sheet and read it carefully. He folded it again. "Impressive. Solid experience. You seem to lean toward investigative reporting. That can be a mean field."

"I can be a mean reporter. I'm persistent, resilient, acceptably devious."

Deceptively innocent, Armstead decided, and was pleased.

"My role model has always been Nellie Bly," Victoria continued.

"The little lady who went around the world in eighty days in—whenever it was?"

"In 1889. And she did it in 72 days for Pulitzer's New York *World*. She started on a ship named *Augusta Victoria*—well, Victoria—I always thought that was a good omen for me."

"It is," said Armstead with another smile. He was enchanted by her enthusiasm and seeming lack of guile. "As of now, you've got a job on the New York *Record*."

"You mean it?" She almost jumped off the sofa with joy, wanting to kiss him, but she restrained herself. "That's wonderful, Mr. Armstead. I promise you won't be sorry."

"I don't expect to be. I expect great things from you." He stood up, and she was quickly on her feet beside him. "We can use another investigative reporter," Armstead said, "especially a female one. The two or three we have are men. The best of them is Nick Ramsey."

"I've read his stuff. He's marvelous."

"When he's not drunk," said Armstead. "A little real competition from you might be a sobering experience for him." He started her across the room. "You'll begin tomorrow, nine o'clock sharp. Check in with Mrs. Crowe, our personnel director. She'll discuss your salary, which I'm sure you'll find satisfactory, and then she'll turn you over to Ollie McAllister and he'll assign you a desk. Right now I'm taking you next door to meet Ollie and his assistant and two of my other executives. I want them to meet the first person I've hired as publisher of the *Record*. So you see, I have a very personal interest in you. But tomorrow, no assignments. I want you to spend the day with Nick Ramsey. He'll show you around and break you in.''

At the entrance to the conference room, Armstead stopped her.

"I'm curious about something," Armstead said. "Did Nellie Bly carry a gun?''

Victoria was startled. "I—I don't know."

"Considering the business she was in, she should have. Ask Nick Ramsey when you meet him tomorrow. He'll know. He probably carries one, and if you're going to be an investigative reporter, you'll probably carry one, too.''

For Victoria Weston, her excitement the following morning was dampened only by the initiation formalities of a new job. She had sat a long time with Mrs. Crowe going through everything from salary to health insurance forms to social security. It was twenty minutes before noon when she reached the office of Ollie McAllister, the managing editor. He was a dour, lanky Scot in his middle fifties. When she had met him the day before, she had worried that he did not like her, until she realized that his frown was a permanent one and carried no judgment.

He was concentrating on some teleprinter strips when she entered, and he waved her to a chair.

In a minute or two he was through. "All squared away, Miss Weston?" he inquired.

"I think so," she said. "I'm told I'm to be turned over to Nick Ramsey. He's going to show me around and he's supposed to break me in, whatever that means.''

"It means he's going to show you where the toilets are and tell

you why you shouldn't waste your time working on a newspaper.''
He reached for his phone. ''Let me get him.''

McAllister spent a vain minute trying to locate Ramsey. Failing to do so, he glanced at the clock on his wall and shook his head.

''Almost a quarter to twelve. I should have known he'd be out. He's always off for P. J. Clarke's early, to be sure he beats the lunch crowd to the bar. Then he usually goes on to several other watering holes. That means you won't see him until three o'clock.''

''Isn't he on assignment?'' Victoria asked with wonder.

''Not at the moment. When he works, he works hard. When he doesn't work, he does nothing at all.''

''Is there anything special you'd like me to do until then, Mr. McAllister?''

''Have lunch. It's lunchtime, so have lunch. After that, if you have free time—you're new to New York, aren't you, Victoria? If that's true, you'll have plenty to do.''

''As a matter of fact,'' said Victoria, ''I talked to some friends last night, and one of them knew of an apartment that's just become available. I should go see it.''

''See it,'' said McAllister. ''You don't have to be back until three o'clock.''

Victoria came to her feet. ''I'm supposed to be assigned a desk.''

''Yes, of course,'' said the managing editor. He joined her at his door, opened it, and surveyed the vast hangar of the newsroom. There were endless desks, half of them occupied.

''I've never seen so many desks,'' Victoria said, excitement returned and mounting.

''Two hundred of them,'' said McAllister, ''and the newsroom is over an acre.'' He scanned the room. He pointed. ''Look down this row to the left. About the tenth one down. You can't miss it—it's the only clean desk on the floor. That's the metropolitan section, where we'll probably start you, where you can drop anchor. Now go to lunch, Victoria.''

Feeling that she belonged, she clutched the strap of her shoulder bag and strolled along the nearest row of desks, boldly meeting the stares and smiles of young male reporters along the way, until she arrived at her desk. It was a brown metal desk bearing a telephone, some phone directories, an "In" and "Out" paper tray, and a word processor on a stand beside it.

Satisfied that she had found her place, she was ready for lunch, for an apartment, and for the elusive Nick Ramsey.

Victoria was back at her desk at the *Record* by two-thirty, hoping Nick Ramsey had returned early. But he had not appeared.

She had rushed through her lunch break. She had gulped down a hamburger, found a taxi, and hurried up to West Seventy-third Street, where a female college friend was waiting to show her the vacant apartment. It consisted of a small living room with a sofa bed and small kitchen, was furnished in contempo modern and had just been cleaned. Victoria quickly signed a rental agreement and gave the landlady a deposit.

Now, breathless at her desk, she sought Nick Ramsey in the vast newsroom, not having the faintest idea of what he looked like, and at last knowing that he would eventually find her. Settled down, she filled out a requisition for supplies. Then she dug her compact out of her purse and freshened her makeup. Finally, she began to read this morning's edition of the New York *Record,* which she had taken from a pile at the foyer entrance to the newsroom.

She skipped the Mideast news and other foreign dispatches, skimmed the national news from Washington, D.C. (noting the mention of her father's name in one story, and reminding herself to call him after work), and concentrated on the metropolitan news. The major attraction playing in New York, it appeared, was crime, mainly murder. The monotony of this mayhem was relieved only by a few pieces about graft in the city government.

She had become engrossed in this seemingly endless parade of the sordid when she felt a hand on her shoulder.

She heard him before she saw him.

"Ms. Nellie Bly, I presume?" His voice carried a lilt of mockery.

Victoria's head came back, and she looked up as he added, "I'm Nick Ramsey, at your service."

She scrambled to her feet, somewhat surprised and disconcerted by his good looks. She had expected Armstead's best investigative reporter to resemble an aggressive ferret or a mole. Instead, he resembled an aging collegian who still did well with the young girls. He was certainly six feet tall, with poor posture, rounded shoulders. His face was somewhat narrow, sunken, craggy, and it wore a faint air of amused cynicism. His dark hair was combed sideways—a recalcitrant strand in back stood up— and he had gray eyes, absolutely marvelous gray eyes meant to make women weak-kneed. He wore a maroon pullover and cord slacks. Middle to maybe late thirties, Victoria guessed.

And he smelled of breath spray.

"I'm Vicky—Vicky Weston," she said, trying to regain her poise.

"Oh, not Nellie," he said. "Incidentally, she never carried one."

"What?" she asked, truly bewildered.

"A gun. Nellie Bly never carried a gun. And you won't either, unless you like to shoot stray cats. I'm told you've been hired on as an investigative reporter, junior grade. Well, you won't have to confront anything more ferocious than Ma Bell. The telephone's the weapon we use. My orders are to break you in this afternoon."

"I have a good telephone voice. Will that help, Mr. Ramsey?"

"It'll get you a lot of dates. First step in breaking you in: my name's Nick."

"Okay, Nick."

"Now you're broken in." He looked at his watch. "We've got two hours. I guess we can best use it by me showing you around—where the ladies' room is, where the Coke machine can be found, and how to get to your desk without being seen when you've come in late with a hangover.''

"Sounds great."

"You don't have to walk close to me," he said. "I can see you can't stand the breath spray. Let's have an open relationship. I've been drinking, and I had too much."

"Are you all right?"

"Too much breath spray," he said. "But under your cool and upright gaze, I'm sobering quickly." He took her arm. "Let's start our fateful odyssey here in the newsroom—where the life of a big city paper throbs, as the documentaries say. Ready, Vicky?"

She adored him. "I'm ready, Nick."

He walked her about the endless newsroom, introducing her to a blur of receptive editors and reporters, mostly male, as he tried to explain the organization of the newsroom. Very little of what he said was new to Victoria. It was similar to the organization of her suburban Chicago paper, only there was more of it, much more.

Ramsey pointed out the location of the desks of the metropolitan editors, national editors, foreign editors, and the partitioned offices holding the sports desks, financial desks, culture desks. Victoria lingered with him beside the copydesks, formed in the shape of a horseshoe. They watched editors sorting publicity releases and going through folders containing leads to future news events. Victoria followed Ramsey into the wire room, where thirty-five teleprinters pounded out news from around the world— most of this from the *Record*'s own special correspondents, the rest of it from Associated Press, Reuters, Dow Jones, and other agency sources.

The flood of words pouring in dazed Victoria. "How many words come in here every day?" she wondered.

"You mean just on the wires? Or from their local reporters, police headquarters, city hall, and in general?"

"From everywhere."

"About a million and three-quarters words every twenty-four hours. We print about 125,000 of those words."

Victoria groaned. "How'll I ever get a word in edgewise?"

"It's not how much you get in, but what you get in," Ramsey told her. "If you make it as an investigative reporter, your words will get in, plenty of them. Don't worry."

After that, Victoria trailed Ramsey through one department and office after another—advertising with its staff of 250, the morgue with its rows and rows of clipping files, the reference library with its thousands of books, the picture editor's office and finally the composing room, where each story came out in computerized strips that were cut up, pasted onto boards, converted into plates that were photographed electronically.

Leaving the composing room, Ramsey gave Victoria a long look. "You must be wiped out," he said. He studied his watch. "Almost six. I have to leave you now anyway. I have a business date—got to be at the Oak Bar of the Plaza in fifteen minutes."

"Thank you for the Grand Tour, Nick."

Lighting a cigarette before leaving her, he hesitated. "What are you going to do now?"

"I guess I'll do some grocery shopping and lug it back to my new apartment and make myself something to eat."

"I think you can do better than that your first night as a gainfully employed person in Manhattan."

"Like what?"

"Like having dinner with your mentor. I'll be free if you are."

Her face brightened. "I'd like that, if it can be Dutch treat."

"Since I intend to have some drinks, let's make it Armstead's treat. See you at eight-thirty. Oak Room, the Plaza. Don't bring a notebook. This'll be strictly holding hands."

They had not held hands at all.

It would have been impossible, Victoria knew, because each of his hands had been otherwise occupied during the hour in which they had been sitting at a secluded rear table in the Oak Room.

Ramsey's right hand had not once been without a glass of gin and tonic, and his left hand had been permanently busy holding a cigarette, one lit off another.

She had nursed her drink while he finished three. She felt faint with famine, and was about to tell him so when he opened the menu and ordered dinner for both of them without consulting her. But she was grateful, and then concerned when she heard him order a fourth drink.

She had been nervous but stimulated in the presence of this attractive stranger. He was definitely dissolute and definitely cynical, the real-life embodiment of Sydney Carton, a fictional hero of her youth. Her tension was heightened by the belief that he would make a pass at her, and she was not certain how she would react. But Ramsey had made no pass at her, had not even sat close to her, and she knew that she was disappointed.

Her edginess had made her talk more than she normally did. The moment they took their seats she started to tell him about paying the rent and the security deposit for her new apartment before getting the key from the landlady. There hadn't been much time to do anything else, yet she recited to him the details of unpacking her single suitcase and garment bag; the jubilant call to her father in Washington, D.C., to tell him that she had got the job on the *Record;* a more contained call to her mother in Evanston to repeat the news of the job (an irritating exchange in which her mother had said, "Well, I suppose I am happy you're pleased, but I really had hoped you'd get out of that miserable newspaper business") and to ask her mother to arrange with a shipper to pack her clothes and books and other effects and send them on to New York; a quick bath and change of clothes before finding a taxi to the Plaza.

Ramsey's only reaction to her inane, compulsive recital had been to say, "You don't sound as if you like your mother very much."

"Oh, I like her, of course. You've got to like your mother.

But not 'very much.' She resents me because she thinks I take after my father.''

"Do you?"

"I hope so," she said sincerely.

"Well, your mother's right about one thing."

"What?"

"That the newspaper business is miserable, no place for a decent young lady. It makes you devious, hypocritical, immoral. It makes you forget people are human beings with feelings. It makes you warp truth for stories. How in the hell did you get into this jungle?''

Taken aback by the anger underlying his easygoing manner, she began to cover her upset by compulsively going into the highlights of her autobiography. Her father, his exploits, his cronies had, of course, been major influences. But even beyond that, she had always been fascinated by newspapermen, by their memorable scoops, by the romance of reporting. She had spent five years at Northwestern University, had served on the college newspaper where she was the best on the staff, and upon receiving her master of science from the Medill School of Journalism had landed a job on a weekly paper. She had worked in newsrooms ever since.

"Did you have time for a love life?" he had asked.

"It's none of your business, but I certainly did."

"With newspapermen?"

"No, but—"

"But don't," he had said.

"Why not?"

"Like actors, reporters are too self-involved. As Wilson Mizner once put it, 'Some of the greatest love affairs I've known involved one actor, unassisted.' ''

She wondered what it would be like to have a love affair with a newspaperman, someone with her own kind of mentality, maybe someone like Nick Ramsey. She'd had four affairs—what might have been called affairs at the time, although each was of short duration—in her life. The first, in high school, had been to get it over with, to lose her virginity. The second and third had been in college, to find out if it could be fun (in one case it had been, a little, while they were in bed, but he hadn't been much fun otherwise). The last affair, the one she'd mentioned to her father, was with a married lawyer she had interviewed for her paper. He had offered her his total love and promised that he would leave his wife, but he was impossibly selfish and had never intended to get a divorce.

No matter what Nick Ramsey said, could a newspaperman be worse?

At that point the waiter had come with Ramsey's fresh drink. Ramsey took it and lifted it as if in a toast to Victoria. "Again, as Wilson Mizner put it, 'I am a stylist, and the most beautiful sentence I have every heard is, "Have one on the house." ' "

He ignored the Caesar salads being placed before them, and devoted himself to an almost nonstop swallow of his drink. Victoria, who had been prepared to ravage her salad, now had less stomach for it.

Fork in hand, she asked weakly. "Who was Wilson Mizner?"

"Who was Wilson Mizner?" Ramsey repeated, a bit dimly, slightly drunkenly. "Now there's a question that—that's hard to answer. He was a writer and gambler and lots of other things. He was mostly a wit. He was mostly cynical, which is why I like him. He never lived up to his potential, which is another reason I like him. He once said to a small, no-goodnik guy, 'You're a mouse studying to be a rat.' "

Victoria couldn't help but laugh.

Recovering, she considered her plate once more. "You asked something," she said, "so I guess I can ask it, too. What about your love life?"

"No comment."

"Not fair."

"I have no love life," he said, "only a sex life. In my

lexicon, love is a four-lettered word. Don't ask me to explain my troubled past. If you ever regard me as a love object, forget it.''

"Don't grow old worrying about that.''

"Love and news, two four-lettered words.''

Picking at her salad, she observed him out of the corner of her eye. He was drinking steadily, bemused.

"If you dislike journalism so much," she said, "how come you're in it?''

"How come a whore's a whore?'' he retorted.

"That's no answer.''

"And that's no question you asked.''

"I mean, something got you into journalism. What got you into it?''

"That's a question," he decided. He set down his glass and began to eat his salad reflectively. "I was born in Oakland," he said. "Ever know anybody in Oakland?''

"No," admitted Victoria. "All I know about Oakland is what Gertrude Stein said about it. 'When you get there, there's no there there.' ''

Ramsey eyed her with bleary respect. "Exactly," he said. He concentrated on his salad, then seemed to recall what he had been speaking about. "I was no good at sports, but good at writing. Not from my parents—they had a clothing store. Writing was a natural gift. I intended to write books. Those writers seemed to live well and independently. But after two years at a junior college I was given a scholarship to the School of Journalism at the University of Wisconsin. That was my downfall.''

The salad plates had been removed, and they were being served rack of lamb, with new potatoes and fresh peas. Ramsey considered the food, and finished his drink.

He became aware of his partner. "Where was I?'' he asked.

"In Madison, Wisconsin.''

"Yes. I was a feature writer on the *Daily Cardinal*. I was very gifted, too gifted. A magazine in New York—forget its name—

gave me a free-lance assignment. An exposé about Big Ten football. Recruitment. Did I tell you it was an exposé?''

"You were starting to.''

"It was very good. Result, the New York *Times* hired me. Features. Some by-lines. Result, the Giant—E. J. Armstead—he offered me more money. Almost ten years ago. Been on the *Record* ever since.''

"So what's so bad about that?'' Victoria wanted to know.

"Books,'' Ramsey mumbled. "Always wanted to do books.''

"Why didn't you?''

"I did. Wrote one.''

"You did?'' She was surprised. "You wrote a book that was published? What about?''

"Novel about Rousseau. Not Jean Jacques. Henri, Henri Rousseau. French primitive painter, died 1910. A real primitive, toll inspector, sometimes postman, turned painter.''

"I'd like to read it. What was it called?''

"*The Postman Always Rings Twice*. Naw, I'm kidding. Never mind what it was called.''

"I would like to read it, Nick.''

"Unavailable, even in rare-book stores. Sold 344 copies.''

"Why don't you write another one?''

"Would you, with that kind of encouragement?''

Victoria nodded her head vigorously. "I would, if that's what I wanted to do most in the world.''

He snorted. "You would. You're a romantic. You even think newspapers are romantic. You think there are big beats around every corner, derring-do, clandestine meetings, earthshaking news. That's what you believe in, isn't it?''

"Yes, that's what I believe. I think being on a newspaper is one of the last romantic things in the world.''

"Honey, this is big-time, big commercial time, and you're going to lose your girlish laughter fast. Maybe newspapers were romantic once. When your father was a young newsman, battered felt hat, ancient Underwood typewriter, stubby pencils, underworld connections, making deadlines, Extras in the street. Honey, that world is as dead as the one-hoss shay. You know what a newspaper is now? Something you read if you happened to miss last night's television. Something that shovels in words between the ads. No more regular typewriters, no more stubby pencils, no more Extra-read-all-about-it. Just one big electronic rig-up, filled with computers and tapes. It's one big bore, with no future. Take my word for it and spare yourself a lot of grief.''

"I hope you're wrong," she said.

"For your sake, I hope I am." He signaled a passing waiter and held up his empty glass. "One more for the road," he called out.

When he turned back, he found her eyes hard on him.

"Nick," she said, "why do you drink so much?"

He gave her a wicked smile. "I don't know," he said. "You're the investigative reporter. You find out."

The next morning, at her desk early, Victoria Weston was still thinking about Nick Ramsey when she heard her name on the loudspeaker. It was a summons from the managing editor. Taking up a notepad and ballpoint pen, she hurried to Ollie McAllister's office.

Studying the contents of a manila folder, he told Victoria to draw up a chair.

"Your first assignment," he said.

"I'm ready," she said, indicating her pad and pen and wondering what the assignment would be.

"Since Edward Armstead has just taken over, we haven't as yet had time to determine what investigative stories we want to get into. However, to keep you busy we have some news features that need doing. Especially one we want to get into the works right now."

Victoria waited tensely.

McAllister looked up. "Ever heard of Sam Yinger?"

"Who hasn't? He murdered all those kids.''

"He's going to die in the electric chair at Green Haven prison two days from now. Since his crime—horrendous as any I've heard—has imprinted itself on the public consciousness, we figure there's wide interest in how Yinger spends his last hours or last day. Especially now that the state has restored capital punishment. He'll be one of the first big names to burn under the new law. What we want is a color story, really. There you are in a cell on Death Row. Soon you are going to be extinguished as a human being. How do you spend your final hours? What are you doing? What are you thinking? Do you get the picture?"

"I get it."

"Is it scary, or isn't it for a subhuman like Yinger? We don't know. We hope to find out. Unfortunately we—and all of the press—have been refused visits or interviews. We can't get to Yinger directly. But as it turns out, we can get to him indirectly—that is, at second hand."

"I'm not sure I understand."

"You will in a moment," said McAllister. "Here at the *Record* we have on the payroll a large number of tipsters in every field. We have some in city hall, some in the D.A.'s office, some in the state capital." He paused for effect. "And we have some in the underworld."

Victoria was not surprised. But because McAllister obviously was playing it for effect, she said, "Really? Isn't it terribly dangerous for them, informing on their friends?"

"Yes, it is, although they rarely give us anything important. But they are people always short of money. They tip us off to small things, when they think they can do it safely. Well, one of our more productive underworld tipsters is a man named Gus Pagano. Does the name mean anything to you?"

"I don't think so."

"Probably not, because Gus Pagano was a local story and you were in Chicago at the time. Three years ago Pagano was a minor crime figure. Not a killer, but a thief. One night the cashier of a hotel on the Park, on Fifth Avenue, was held up. She set off a

silent alarm. Just as the robber was making his escape, a squad
car arrived and two of the city's finest got out of it. The robber
gunned them down, killed them, and got away. The police, as
you know, don't take murder of a policeman lightly. A wide net
was thrown out. Suspects were pulled in, and among them was
Gus Pagano. Immediately three witnesses pointed him out as the
police killer. He denied it, protested his innocence, but then what
else would one expect from a hardened criminal? Anyway, Pagano
was tried, found guilty, sentenced to the chair. He was incarcer-
ated at the Green Haven Correctional Facility. He continued to
insist upon his innocence. Although unlettered, he liked to read,
and he began to read up on the law. Then Pagano began to file
appeals, as well as write letters to all the New York newspapers.
A few of us on the *Record* were impressed by his letters, and we
decided to have our legal staff monitor one of his appeals. As a
result, there was a long delaying action and his execution was put
off time and again. Finally Pagano lost his last appeal, and a firm
date was set for his execution. He was on Death Row, getting
ready to meet his Maker, when another man was picked up for
murder in Atlanta and confessed to the killings of which Pagano
had been accused. In fact, the real murderer very much resembled Pagano, so the mistake by all the witnesses was understandable. Anyway, Pagano was released from Death Row and released from prison and was a free man.''

"And now he's working for you?"

"Yes. It came about quite simply. Some time after he'd gotten
out of prison he came up here one day to see us, ostensibly to
thank us for our help in appealing his case. Actually he was
looking for money. He admitted to being back in the mob, back
into petty crime, but the pickings were poor. He wondered if
we'd pay him to be an informant. We were wary. He could
hardly be regarded as the most trustworthy of parties. But Dietz
said he was street-smart and ordered me to give him a chance.
So we put him on a modest retainer. Most of his leads were too
vague and cautious to be of any value, but gradually he began to

phone in tips—three, four, five—that led to fairly big stories. We've kept him on the payroll ever since."

"What's he got to do with Sam Yinger?" asked Victoria.

"Pagano knew Yinger slightly before either of them was in Green Haven. I don't know if that amounts to much. More important, Yinger now occupies the cell on Death Row that Gus Pagano occupied before he was found innocent and released."

McAllister waited for Victoria's reaction, and she reacted almost at once. "I get it. Since we can't get to Yinger, we find out what he's going through in that cell before his execution from Pagano, who went through the same experience."

"You've got it. Get the material from Pagano—and write it about Yinger."

"When do I see Gus Pagano?"

"Any minute. He's on his way here. He has an idea what we want from him. You can talk to him in our conference room next door. Here's a file of clips about the Yinger crime. Brief yourself on it. When you're finished with Pagano, go write the story. No more than eight hundred words. Turn it in to me this afternoon." He directed her to a side door. "Good luck, young lady."

Gus Pagano proved to be a dapper, slender, youngish man, perhaps thirty-five, who looked like a fugitive from an Edward G. Robinson gangster movie. His five-foot-eleven-inch frame was encased in a tight pinstriped double-breasted blue serge suit. He wore blue suede shoes. He had a full head of curly black hair, close-set eyes, a long hawklike nose, thick lips, and pocked cheeks. He was indeed street-smart, and book-smart, as well as a fast and glib talker.

Setting eyes on Victoria, he removed his snap-brim felt hat, carefully placed it on the round conference table and offered her a small bow. "I'm Gus Pagano," he said. "You're the first looker I've seen on this paper."

"Thank you, Mr. Pagano." She settled into a wooden chair.

Although there were eight chairs around the table, Pagano took the one next to Victoria.

"So you're writing about Sam Yinger," he said, "and what it's like to get ready to die."

"What it feels like, waiting for the electric chair, and what a cell on Death Row is like."

"They can't get to Yinger, so they want to know what I know."

"That's right."

"They told you I was on Death Row right up to the wire, before I was sprung? You know about that?"

"Mr. McAllister told me."

"And Yinger's in the cell I used to have. Okay, I can't tell you from my feelings what Yinger feels like today. I was a special case. I was in there on a bum rap, and all I could think was that I was going to roast for something I didn't do. I was bitter, just plain bitter. Yinger's another case. He finally admitted he did it. You know what he did, don't you?"

Victoria tapped the folder on the table. "I read the coverage of the trial by the *Record*."

Pagano shook his head. "A real crazy, and sick as hell. He goes out with this woman—what was her name—?"

"Caroline."

"Yeah, Caroline, a schoolteacher. Yinger goes out with her twice, and she finds him too weird to go out with him anymore. She doesn't answer his calls. One night he spots her with another guy on a date, and he goes berserk. Next day he goes to her school, into the classroom where she's teaching English to six young ethnics—six young kids eight to ten years old, one little boy and five girls—and he shoots Caroline dead, and then he goes around the classroom and murders all six kids."

"I know all that," Victoria said.

Ignoring her, Pagano went on. "He almost gets away, until someone spots him a few days later." Pagano shook his head again. "He went into Green Haven after I got out. It's loons like him who give all of us a bad name. I can't help you about Yinger."

"What about his living conditions? How does he live? How does he spend his time?"

Pagano waited for Victoria to find her notepad and take out her pen, and then he began talking. "Death Row is on the third floor of the Hospital-Segregation Building. It's actually the wing called K gallery. The cell I was in, the one Yinger is in—well, what's to say about it? A cell's a cell. You've seen plenty of them in prison movies."

"Yes, but I'd like you to describe it."

"It's a small, gloomy room. There's a cot. There's a toilet with no seat. There's a sink on one wall. Also a water fountain. There's a peephole in the ceiling so the guard on the walkway above can check you out from time to time. You don't get what the other cons get."

"Meaning what?"

"Meaning you don't get to eat in the mess hall with the rest. You get your rations in your room. You can have cigarettes, but no matches. You want a light, a guard lights you up. Your pants better fit, because you can't have a belt. Same with your shoes. No shoelaces. You can borrow a safety-lock razor, but you've got to give it back after shaving."

"Do the guards ever let you out of the cell?"

"One hour a day, for supervised exercise. And when you have visitors."

"You can have visitors?" Victoria asked.

"My old lady used to visit me, and my older sister. Also my lawyer. Also a doctor, and my old lady's priest. Anybody else has to have a court order."

"How did you spend your time, Mr. Pagano? I mean in the days before your proposed execution date."

"Me, I was different. I read books, mostly legal books. I kept writing up briefs, appeals, letters to the press. I had no time for nothing else. But Sam Yinger—naw, no chance he'd ever crack a book or write a single thing.''

"Would he read the newspapers?"

"No newspapers allowed. My guess is he's probably watching television most of the time."

"Television?" said Victoria. "You mean they let you have a television set?"

"Yeah, sure. Didn't I tell you? Green Haven's a so-called civilized slammer. But Yinger's never going to know how the characters in his favorite soaps make out."

He grinned at Victoria, and she tried to smile back. Gus Pagano appraised her awhile as she wrote.

After she had finished writing, he said slyly, "Of course, I didn't tell you how I spent *all* of my spare time."

She knit her brow. "I'm not sure I understand you. I thought you had no spare time?"

"I had some," he said mysteriously. "Hey, mind if I smoke?"

She pushed an ashtray toward him as he put the flame of his lighter to a cigarette.

He inhaled deeply once, seemed to consider saying something, and finally said it. "Tell you a funny thing," he said. His demeanor and tone were serious. "The funny thing is, I could have got him out."

"Got whom out?"

"Yinger, Sam Yinger. I could have got him out of prison, saved him at the last minute from getting fried, but I didn't do it because he doesn't deserve to live. Anybody that kills six poor little children—anybody like that deserves to die. But I could have got him out if I wanted."

"You could? How?"

Pagano reconsidered briefly. He drew on his cigarette in silence, then gave Victoria a wink. "Just between us, for the hell of it," he said quietly. "Off the record. Do I have your word?"

"You have my word," she said wonderingly.

"Just to show you what goes on that people don't know about, not even Yinger. I can trust you?"

"I promise."

"Okay, I'll tell you." He waited for Victoria to put down her pad and pen.

Rapidly, in an undertone, he began to talk again.

Two hours later, just before lunch, Victoria sat tautly in front of Ollie McAllister's desk and strained to catch a flicker of reaction on his face as he read her feature story on Sam Yinger's Death Row cell.

The managing editor was a veteran nonreactor. There was no expression on his face as he continued reading Victoria's story to the end and put it down.

"It's well written, of course," said McAllister, "but—"

The "but" hung ominously in the air.

"—I don't know," McAllister concluded. "Basically, the piece is weak. No human information."

"I used everything Pagano gave me," said Victoria defensively, "only he wasn't able to give me enough. He hardly knew Sam Yinger at all, let alone knowing anything about Yinger's feelings and emotions. Their cell, well, what's to say—there was nothing personalized about it. Pagano's smart all right, but he simply didn't have anything more to give. The best information he had was something we can't use."

"We can't use? Why not?"

"Pagano said it was not for publication. He made me promise not to use it."

"Promise not to use what?" McAllister asked mildly.

"The story about the escape tunnel that's been dug below Yinger's maximum security cell across the prison yard and under the concrete prison wall."

"A tunnel, did you say?"

"A tunnel that goes from Death Row to the outside."

"A real tunnel?"

"According to Gus Pagano, it's there and it's real. After Green Haven was built and became operative, one of the first Death Rowers discovered a vent cover that could be detached in this particular cell, and there was room enough for a man to squeeze into the vent shaft and lower himself down a pipe to an abandoned subbasement. He calculated that a tunnel could be dug from this room to a place just beyond the prison wall, but it would take a number of years. Using some old tools that he found in the room, he started the tunnel. He deposited all the dirt in that little-used storage room. He was executed before he got very far. But he was able to pass on word of it to the next occupant of his cell. So each occupant dug further, hoping to be the one to use it. When Gus Pagano was thrown into the cell, he soon learned about the tunnel. There wasn't too far to go to complete it. With all the delays and postponements that Pagano got, he was able to finish the job. He planned to use the escape route if he didn't receive a reprieve. But he did get the reprieve and he had no reason to escape. When he heard that Sam Yinger was to replace him in that cell, he decided not to tell Yinger about the tunnel. Because he hated Yinger and didn't think he should be free." Victoria caught her breath. "Yinger has the means to escape, but doesn't know about it. What a great story! What a pity we can't use it."

McAllister's eyes held on her. "It is a shame," he agreed. "And you promised Pagano we wouldn't use it?"

"Yes. I gave a solemn promise, I swore to it."

He sighed. "Then that's that." He came to his feet. He held up Victoria's story. "I want to go in and show this to Harry Dietz, our publisher's assistant," he said. "See if we can do something with your story, salvage it in some way. Thanks for a good first effort. We'll have something else for you tomorrow."

After Victoria had gone, McAllister pressed the intercom button on his telephone and stood by until he heard Harry Dietz respond.

"Ollie here," McAllister said. "Could I come over and see you for a moment?"

"Can it wait?" Dietz asked. "I'm really busy." He paused. "Is it urgent?"

"It's urgent."

"Okay. I'll see you now."

When McAllister entered Dietz's office, he found Dietz standing before a wall mirror combing his sandy hair. Once he was satisfied, Dietz pocketed his comb and returned to his desk.

"What is it, Ollie?"

The managing editor handed him Victoria's story. "It's from Victoria Weston. Her first piece for us. She got the material from Gus Pagano. I'd like you to have a look at it."

Dietz gestured McAllister to a chair, sat comfortably in his tall suede-covered swivel chair, and skimmed the story. When he finished, he handed the typed pages back to McAllister with a show of disgust. "It's a piece of shit," Dietz said. "She can write, but Pagano gave her nothing to write about. You didn't come here to bother me with this story, did you?"

"No, I didn't," said McAllister calmly. "I came to tell you something she didn't put in the story."

Dietz was instantly attentive. "Go on."

"Pagano told her he was one of many who had been digging a secret escape tunnel from beneath Sam Yinger's Death Row cell to the outside. Yinger doesn't know about the tunnel. Of course, Pagano told her about it off the record."

Only Dietz's small eyes reacted, narrowing. "Tell me more, Ollie."

In an effective, contained monotone, McAllister related the details of the Green Haven prison tunnel. When he had finished, he shrugged his shoulders. "I thought this was something you should know," he said casually.

Dietz sat up. "You've told me everything?"

"Everything I know."

"Very interesting," said Dietz. He tendered the managing

editor a tight-lipped wisp of a smile. "That was smart of you, coming right in here with that."

"I thought it was something you and Mr. Armstead would want to know."

"Yes, I'm sure he'll be interested. He'll appreciate your—your sharpness—and your loyalty."

"I know you can't do anything with it," said McAllister, "but I thought you should be informed of every tidbit."

Dietz considered him briefly. "As no doubt you, and everyone else suspects, with a new management taking over the *Record* there will be a reappraisal of the staff. Inevitably, some major changes will be made. Mr. Armstead intends to clean house, sweep out some of the incompetents that his father kept on. When your name comes up, I'll be sure to remember this. It may be only a tidbit, as you say, but passing it on shows a certain alertness that we're looking for and appreciate. It is also evidence you are on our side. Continue to keep your eyes and ears open for us. Of course, I'll see that Mr. Armstead is informed."

"Thank you, Harry."

Edward Armstead had been sitting squarely behind his massive oak desk, staring up at the row of Yugoslavian primitive paintings on the office wall as he listened to Harry Dietz.

After ten minutes there was no more that Dietz could add. "There it is, Chief," he said.

Armstead continued to stare at his paintings, absorbing what he had heard. Slowly a smile opened on his face. He swung his attention to Dietz. "Beautiful," he said. "Just beautiful, Harry."

"We must keep in mind that Pagano told her this was off the record."

Armstead's smile disappeared, and he seemed to examine his assistant's face to see if he was serious or not. "Pagano said off the record? You're not serious, are you? Who in the fuck is Pagano? A tinhorn crook whose neck we saved. Screw Pagano.

Whatever is off the record—that's what we're going to publish from now on.''

Dietz indicated his assent. "You're going to run the story, then?''

"I'm not going to run it," said Armstead. "I'm going to do better than that.'' He savored the information he had just heard. "An unused and unknown escape tunnel running from Sam Yinger's cell to freedom. What if Sam Yinger knew about that tomorrow?'' Armstead was all action now. "Let's not waste any time, Harry. Find out the name of Yinger's attorney. Call him and tell him to meet me for a drink at Perigord Park at seven tonight. If he gives you a hassle about being tied up—tell him to get untied. Tell him this is really important.''

Yinger's defense attorney, George Tatum, was waiting for Edward Armstead when the publisher arrived at Perigord Park. He was seated alone in a booth to the left of the entrance in the otherwise empty room. He was a pale, middle-aged man wearing thick glasses and an unfashionable brown suit. He had probably not received as much attention in his entire life, Armstead surmised, as he had received in the Sam Yinger case. He certainly had never been in this fancy restaurant before.

George Tatum was nursing a drink when Armstead approached him.

Armstead stuck out his hand, introducing himself, then called over his shoulder for a double scotch and water as he pushed himself into the seat across from the lawyer.

Tatum seemed embarrassed about his drink. "I thought I'd get started,'' he said. "It's been a long day.''

"By all means,'' said Armstead, unpeeling a cigar. He guessed that Tatum was impressed to be with him. Impressed, and curious.

"Do you know why I wanted to see you?'' Armstead asked.

"Only that it is about my client, Mr. Yinger, and—and that it is important.''

"Correct on both counts,'' Armstead acknowledged, accepting

his drink from the waiter. He tasted his drink, assessing his tactic
with the lawyer, and swallowed slowly. Armstead put his glass
down, lit his cigar, then exhaled a puff of smoke. "I'll tell you
why I wanted to see you," said Armstead. "You know I'm the
publisher of the New York *Record*."

"Yes, of course."

"What would you say if I told you I'd like one of our reporters
to have an exclusive interview with your client before his
execution?"

Tatum's disappointment was immediate. "I'm afraid," he said
with reluctance, "I'd have to say that's impossible."

"Absolutely impossible?"

Tatum pushed the thick glasses higher on his nose. "Mr.
Armstead, believe me, it would be impossible."

Having expected this reply, Armstead remained nonchalant.
He sucked at his cigar until it was aglow again. "All right, let's
try it another way. How much would you like to see your client
go free?"

"Go free?" Tatum was plainly bewildered. "He can't go free.
He's condemned to death. He's going to the chair the morning
after next. I spent the entire day trying to get the governor to
modify Mr. Yinger's sentence from death to life. The governor
turned us down. It's the chair for sure."

Armstead measured his words. "Mr. Tatum, I'm not asking
you if your client can go free. I am asking you how much *you*
want to see him go free."

Tatum's bewilderment remained. "I'm not sure what you mean,
Mr. Armstead. I am Mr. Yinger's defense attorney. I defended
him. I tried to get him free. I appealed the verdict. I went to the
governor. I've done my job."

"Your job aside," said Armstead, "do you want him to die in
the electric chair?"

"Of course not. He doesn't deserve the chair. I'm not saying
he's a good guy or that he's innocent by any means. If the
witnesses were right, and he did what he did, then he's a

maniac, totally insane, and was insane when he did it. We don't send the insane to the electric chair. I'm against that. It's not humane."

"So you would like to see him go free?"

Tatum hedged his answer. "I don't want to see him executed."

"You'd do anything to prevent that?"

"As a matter of principle—yes." Puzzlement had crept over Tatum's face. "I don't understand you, Mr. Armstead. What are you leading up to?"

Armstead laid down his cigar. "Simply this. You want to prevent Yinger's execution? I can help you prevent it. I can get him out of it."

"Out of the electric chair?"

"Out of prison," Armstead said flatly.

Tatum's expression was one of total disbelief. "Are you serious?"

"Very serious."

"I repeat—the governor turned down the stay of execution. It's the chair, morning after next. There's no way out."

"And I repeat—there *is* a way out." Armstead was beginning to savor the game.

"What are you talking about?"

"I'll be happy to tell you in a minute." He retrieved his cigar and relit it. "Presuming I can get your client out of prison, would you let my reporter see him before that?"

Tatum nodded. "Under those circumstances, yes. It could be arranged. No problem with the warden. And I could persuade Yinger to cooperate."

"You guarantee you could arrange it?"

"I could arrange it. But the deal you're offering is impossible. It simply makes no sense."

Armstead became businesslike and brisk. "It simply makes no sense *if* you don't know all the facts." Armstead dropped his voice. "All right, Mr. Tatum, come closer and listen. The facts. You can convey everything to Sam Yinger—only to Yinger—

otherwise it is confidential and could get us into trouble. All
right, I want my reporter in—and you want your client out—and
here is how we do it. There is a tunnel way down beneath Sam
Yinger's cell.''

Lowering his voice even more, Armstead went on without
interruption.

3

Victoria Weston had been thrilled by the unexpected assignment given her by Harry Dietz personally.

She had rented a new Chevrolet sedan, charged it to the *Record*, and obtained an intricate set of directions. She had been told that the eighty-mile drive from Manhattan to Green Haven prison would take her about two hours. Since her appointment to interview Sam Yinger had been arranged for three o'clock in the afternoon, she had left at noon to be certain that she would arrive on schedule.

Once she had attained the East River Drive, after passing the United Nations Plaza, she had believed that she would have time to formulate her questions for Yinger. It had been a marvelous surprise, getting the interview, although it was a natural follow-up piece to her backgrounder—how could it possibly have been arranged?—and a chilling assignment to talk to a real live person of flesh and blood who little more than a dozen hours later would be laid out on a slab, an unmourned corpse.

But the drive proved to be too complicated for Victoria to be able to work out many questions. Around the entrance to the

Triborough Bridge there was a confusing interchange, she had
missed the turn onto the Major Deegan Expressway and had
gotten badly lost in the Bronx, but eventually found herself on
the New York Thruway. Finally she had taken the Taconic State
Parkway that brought her to Interstate Highway 84 and the
turnoff for the small hamlet of Stormville, located on State
Highway 216. The countryside, with its undulating hills, had
been beautiful. Suddenly the two-lane road had dipped, and the
thick concrete wall of the prison had loomed before her. Off to
one side there appeared to be a farm, with green-garbed men,
obviously prisoners, toiling in the fields. Straight ahead, beside
the entrance, a metallic sign read: GREEN HAVEN CORRECTIONAL
FACILITY.

Leaving her car in the parking area outside the thirty-foot-high
wall, Victoria had climbed the stairs near the main gate to the
glass-enclosed reception room. There she had cooperated in the
routine procedure of establishing her identity, having her shoulder bag searched, going through the metal detector, and allowing
her left hand to be stamped with invisible ink. After that she had
descended a staircase that brought her to the grounds inside the
prison wall.

Now, five minutes before her interview, she was ascending
another flight of steps to the lobby of the Administration Building.
There, escorted by a surly, hefty blue-shirted guard, she was led
to one more security check, where a new guard took her left
hand, examined the back of it under an ultraviolet light beam.
Signaled on, she caught up with her personal guard, followed
him through a dimly lit corridor, up one more stairway to the
red-brick Hospital-Segregation Building. Striding beside her guard,
she found herself led through a gate into what seemed to be one
of the visiting rooms. She was directed to sit at a table bisected
by an eye-level screen built to prevent a caller from passing
anything to a prisoner on the opposite side. As Victoria extracted
her notepad and pen from her shoulder bag, she observed beyond
the table the ominous presence of one more unsmiling guard, a

sergeant, on a raised platform at a desk. Near him she detected a closed-circuit TV surveillance camera.

Victoria's escort guard was addressing her. "Instructions are to sit you here instead of the Death Row visiting rooms. Guess it's because the bulletproof glass and hole make it too hard to talk through. The new visiting room is better." He pointed to the sergeant up on the platform. "He'll be keeping an eye on you and your pal, to see that you don't pass him anything or—" he made an evil grin"—try to make love. The inmate's on his way."

Five minutes later Sam Yinger was brought in and led to a chair across the table. Yinger, hands cuffed and shackled to a special belt at his waist, was flanked by two huge, grim guards. Yinger was smaller and blander in appearance than she had anticipated. His thinning blond hair, watery eyes, undershot chin gave him the look of just another figure in a crowd. Outwardly he resembled an unsuccessful door-to-door salesman, not the callous murderer of seven human beings, six of them mere children.

Yet from his first words spoken after his uniformed chaperons stepped back, Victoria knew that she was dealing with a savagely angry man.

"You the broad I'm supposed to talk to?" he said, once seated.

"I'm Victoria Weston of the New York *Record*, and I was told you would be willing to give me an interview."

"I'm not willing, just doing it as a favor to my lawyer," Yinger snarled. "I don't know why I'm here. What in the fuck's in it for me? What good's doing an interview you'll never be able to read?"

"Maybe something will turn up before morning."

"Shit, you know nothing'll turn up. The governor was the only chance and he turned us down. I'm a dead man, good and dead."

Victoria squirmed, uncertain as to how to proceed. She wanted

in some way to justify her interview. "Well, Mr. Yinger, to
begin with, everyone has to die sometime—at least you'll have a
chance to justify yourself, speak your mind by speaking through
me. You can let the world know how you feel—and your friends
and relatives. Surely you have some friends and relatives out
there?"

"Sister, I got nobody out there I give a damn about."

"Not a soul?"

"There's nobody I give a damn about except Caroline, and
she's dead."

"Are you—are you sorry you shot her?"

Yinger did not reply.

Victoria swallowed. "The children—what about the children . . . ?"

"I had to," he said, his voice suddenly reasonable.

"Had to? Why?"

"It was logical, that's why. They were eyewitnesses against
me. What's the difference? They won't miss much." He reflected.
"They didn't know what hit them."

"I suppose not," she muttered weakly, busily writing her
notes.

He watched her write awhile, and finally caught her eye.
"You know what, lady, let me tell you something. You can print
it. You can tell them Sam Yinger said it. I don't mind dying. I'm
just as glad I wasn't commuted to life. Imagine having to spend
your whole goddamn life, years and years of it, in this two-by-
four concrete sewer. Dying is like going to sleep, sort of. Before or
after, you don't know what happens. Blink and you're out of it.
Darkness. Big long sleep. No dreams. No thinking. Nothing. Just
rest. I'm not scared of that. You tell them Sam Yinger isn't
scared one bit. How's that, lady?"

"It's a philosophy," Victoria said, writing furiously.

"Yeah," said Yinger. He thought for a moment. "There are
worse things than dying. There's living." He paused. "My life
was lousy."

"Do you want to tell me about it?"

"I don't know." He picked his way through remembrances. No parents that he knew. Bleak orphanage years. In and out of several gangs. Handyman jobs. Night school to make something respectable of himself. Still no decent work. Scrounging, more handyman jobs. Something better with the city—truck driver for the garbage department. Only relaxation, cheap midnight movies. And women. Whores who gave you syph and clap. First grownup love was the schoolteacher, Caroline, and she doublecrossed him, a whore like the rest with all her men. The bitch. He stopped. "What the hell," he said.

"That's the past," said Victoria. "What about the present? What do you do with yourself in your cell?"

"Only two things to do. Watch TV and jerk off. The first's not as bad as they say, and the second doesn't give you pimples." He appeared pleased that he had embarrassed her. "Anything more, miss?" he wanted to know.

"There's one more question—well, maybe a few more."

"Go on."

"I was wondering about this: how you look at life on the outside today. Is there anything you wish you could do out there?"

"Not a fucking thing, nothing. Not even screwing." A grin. "Not even screwing you."

She tried to avoid reacting.

"Not a put-down," he added quickly. "You got nice tits. It's just, I got bigger things—like maybe the chair—on my mind."

"So there's not a thing you want on the outside."

Yinger was lost in thought. Victoria did not prod him. "Yeah, there's . . . there's something."

He fell silent again.

Her pen paused, she inquired, "Do you want to speak about it?"

"One thing," he said quietly. "I'd like to get out to have

revenge on the people who treated me unfair in the trial. Especially one. I'm talking about the D.A.—what's his name?''

"You mean District Attorney Clark Van Dusen?''

"Yeah, him. Cheap-shot bastard. I never liked the way he talked about me to the jury—to the reporters after—even to the governor yesterday, when he put in his two bits against commuting." Yinger gnawed at his lip. "Van Dusen, yeah. He said I deserved to be removed from society. He called me an animal, did you know that? An animal. I'd like to show him you can't treat another human being like that. It's the only thing I'd like to be free for—to kill that prick Van Dusen."

Victoria concentrated on her writing, but her mind was boggled. Here was a man who had cold-bloodedly taken the lives of six children, put bullets into the heads and bodies of six innocent youngsters, yet his only grievance was that the district attorney had characterized him as an animal.

"Anything else?" Yinger was asking.

Victoria finished her writing, and busied herself thumbing through her notes. "Let me see—"

At that instant a deep, booming voice intruded upon them, and Victoria jerked her head up, startled. It was from the sergeant behind the raised desk at the end of the table. He was addressing Yinger. "Hey, Sam, hate to butt in on your tête-à-tête," the sergeant called down, "but you got another visitor waiting."

"Bet it's the governor," Yinger called back with a grin.

"You know who it is," the sergeant said. "Your attorney, George Tatum, he's waiting. Guess he's come to kiss you good-bye." The guard pointed at Victoria. "None of that's for your paper, ma'am."

"Don't worry," said Victoria, tucking her notes and pen into her purse.

"Old Tatum," Yinger murmured. "I was expecting him."

The sergeant at the raised desk interrupted once more. "And you and your mouthpiece, you speak English, I'm telling you."

"Fuck off," Yinger said to the guard good-naturedly. Yinger saw the inquiry on Victoria's face. "What he means is that Tatum and me, he doesn't understand the way we talk. When Tatum took on my defense, he taught me a little Esperanto, like he does with all his clients like me. We put in some Esperanto words so what we're saying is confidential. Don't like that asshole to hear everything. No rule against it."

"No," said Victoria, coming to her feet. She was uncertain what to say. She said, "Hope you get your reprieve or whatever."

"Don't bet a penny on it."

"Well, I'd better let you see your attorney. Thanks, Mr. Yinger."

He didn't bother to stand. "If you got any more questions tomorrow, send them care of Somebody Up There." He pointed the forefinger of his shackled hand upward.

"Okay," she said. "Thanks again."

For Victoria Weston, getting into Green Haven prison had been hard enough. Getting away from it proved harder.

The main obstacle was her car. The rental service had given her a lemon. Try as she would, the car refused to start. A dead battery, a deputy superintendent surmised. There was no one available in the facility to assist her. She'd have to get help from the garage in Stormville.

Victoria tried. The sole repair truck in Stormville was out on another call. No telling when it would be back. She was advised to telephone a garage in Beekman. The only repair truck there was also out on an emergency call, but it would be back soon. It would be sent along. Just be patient, she was advised.

The wait was almost two hours, and it was dark when the repair truck came coughing to the floodlighted parking area in front of the prison. During that time Victoria had reviewed her jottings, reflected on her encounter with Sam Yinger, tried to determine a lead for her news feature. She had observed the comings and goings outside the prison, including the early departure of the man she presumed to be Yinger's attorney. All the while she had been supremely impatient.

Now she watched the youngster from the white repair truck trying to jump-start her car. It seemed endless. When he finally succeeded, and was putting away the jumper cables, she said, "Can I leave now?"

"You'd better follow me back to the station," the youngster said. "If you try to get straight back to New York, I ain't guaranteeing you'll make it. If you stall—"

"What do you have to do to get me to New York?"

"Give the battery a quick charge. Just follow me."

A losing battle, she knew. Her car was temporarily functioning and she slowly followed the crawling truck away from the prison wall and to the station in Beekman. When Victoria learned that it would take at least three quarters of an hour for a quick battery charge, she tried to buy a new battery. The station was sold out. Frustrated, she decided to call Ollie McAllister at the *Record*.

She had some difficulty getting through to the newspaper, but when she did she was connected with the managing editor immediately.

Agitated, she explained what had happened to the car and why there was a continuing delay.

"Now I'm stuck in this nothing town," she went on. "I may not get out for an hour. After that I have to drive back. It took me most of three hours coming to the prison. It may take me as long returning. Would you prefer that I call the story in?"

McAllister remained calm. "What kind of story is it? Did Yinger give you anything?"

She peeled through her notebook, stopped here and there to read McAllister the quotes.

"Not bad," the managing editor conceded, "but no hard news."

"I think it's pretty interesting."

"A sidebar, a human interest feature."

"From an animal," Victoria said.

"What?"

"Never mind. Yinger resents being called an animal. Do you want me to write it here and call it in to the news desk? Or just come back and write it at the paper?"

McAllister sounded strangely detached. "Would you prefer to write it here?"

"Well, naturally. I'm in a gas station, in the middle of a bunch of oilcans. But I can do it if—"

"No rush, Vicky. I'll see that the bullpen editors have a summary. We'll make a place for you in the dummy. Even if you're as late as ten o'clock—"

Victoria peered at her wristwatch. "Oh, I won't be."

"Even if you're that late, you can make the Late City Edition that rolls at midnight. If you miss that, there's a two A.M. deadline for the cleanup edition."

"I'll be there way before."

"We're running a little behind tonight, anyway," he said vaguely. "So don't worry. You don't have to phone anything in. Just come home."

"I'll be on my way soon. Be sure to alert Photo for some pictures of Sam Yinger—close-ups, I think—"

"They're already on my desk."

"Repeat—I'll be back soon."

But it was not soon at all. Victoria's original relief that she did not have to phone the story in from the gas station was soon replaced by growing distress at her constantly delayed return to the city. The recharging of the battery would have thrown Job into a fit. Then, using a map, she tried to reverse the route she had taken from Manhattan. Reading the map was like reading the Rosetta stone.

The early part of her journey through the Hudson Valley went hummingly. Nearing the city, at night, she had to slow down. Before she crossed the Harlem River, she became confused by the maze of interchanges and constantly took a wrong turning and constantly was lost.

The third time she got badly lost, she left the Expressway and found an all-night Gulf station, determined to get the rest of the way right. As she walked toward the station, located at a busy intersection, she saw that there was a newsstand on the corner, and a number of pedestrians were crowding about the elderly proprietor who was kneeling over a bundle of papers, distributing copies left and right. He was shouting something indistinctly, but she thought that she heard him use Yinger's name.

Curious, Victoria detoured toward the newsstand and the old man. It was the New York *Record* that he was selling and the front-page headline was bold:

YINGER ESCAPES PRISON ON EVE OF EXECUTION.

The headline shocked her, and she moved quickly into the newly formed line for a copy of the paper. Biding her time, she could see piles of the New York *Times,* its front page without mention of the Yinger escape. There were copies of the New York *Daily News* and New York *Post,* and they were also Yingerless, but then they were earlier editions.

The New York *Record* alone had the sensational beat, and she had a copy in hand now, while paying the man.

She unfolded the front page and swiftly scanned the exclusive story. There it was. Yinger's incredible last-minute escape. His cell had been found empty at dinnertime. There had been some laxity in not spotting his flight earlier, the guards lulled by the fact that his cell was on Death Row. Yinger had apparently wriggled down a vent pipe to a subbasement, found a tunnel beneath Green Haven prison, inched his way through the narrow tunnel and under the prison wall and, many yards beyond, had broken through the thin layer of turf and got away in the darkness. He might be armed and dangerous. There was evidence, an imprint in the soil, that suggested some excavating inmate had stashed a gun at the escape hatch. There was also evidence, footprints and other signs farther on, that Yinger had been headed south toward New York City. There was an all-points bulletin out for his capture and arrest. To Victoria, that meant that Sam Yinger would be shot on sight.

Going toward the filling station, Victoria's mind reeled at the turn of events. How could Yinger have known of that secret tunnel? Only two of them at the newspaper knew about it—she herself, and McAllister. And McAllister had known it was off the record. Nor would he have had reason—or the means—to convey the information to Yinger. Then she realized that she and McAllister had known because Gus Pagano had informed her about the tunnel. Pagano, of course. He was hardly what one would call a sterling character. He was a criminal. He would have sold the information for a payoff, and the information had gone to another convict on Death Row who had passed it along to Yinger. And Yinger had acted fast and daringly. And successfully. Somehow the *Record* had it as an exclusive.

She caught another glimpse of the corner newsstand. More people gathering. More papers selling steadily. But only one paper was selling because it had the big story. The New York *Record* was a runaway tonight.

Somehow, she felt a pride in belonging.

Continuing to the station, she wondered if her interview with Sam Yinger meant anything anymore. His pre-execution story had been fully supplanted by his freedom story. Her own interview would no longer be as newsworthy, Victoria realized, but it still might make a colorful sidebar. She must keep going and write that story.

Once inside the filling station, she had a ten-minute wait before a gas pump attendant was free to help her. Again, an open map. Again, a Rosetta stone. But now the directions were clearer because her destination was nearer.

Eager to get to her story, eager to satisfy her curiosity and her paper's scoop, Victoria was on the run to her Chevrolet. She pulled away from the curb fast, but was soon enmeshed in heavy traffic and slowed to a crawl.

It was slightly after nine o'clock in the evening when she turned into Park Avenue and headed for the Armstead Building. She had rewritten the lead of her interview with Yinger a half-dozen times in her head, and even in light of the new development it worked. Nor was she worried about her tardiness. She recalled that McAllister had said the deadline for the Late City Edition was ten o'clock. Her dashboard clock promised her that there would be time to make it if she got straight to her desk and banged the story out.

By the time she was idling at the next stoplight, she was mentally writing her story one last time, editing out Yinger's foul language. Her mind reached the final paragraph:

"When asked whether there was anything he was interested in doing if he could get out of prison, Sam Yinger made it clear that there was only one reason he would like to be free. 'I'd like revenge. There were people who treated me unfair in the trial.' " Victoria visualized the closing quote: " 'I'm talking about the D.A. . . . I never liked the way he talked about me to the jury . . . He called me an animal . . . I'd like to show him you can't treat another human being like that. It's the only thing I'd like to be free for—to kill that Van Dusen.' "

In those last seconds, a cold chill began to creep over Victoria's flesh.

Yinger *was* free right now, tonight.

He had a gun, and he was thought to be heading for New York.

If he was to be believed, he had only one animal motive to take him there. To kill. To kill for revenge. To kill District Attorney Van Dusen.

Victoria knew it, but no one else in the city knew it—least of all District Attorney Van Dusen.

In those seconds of realization, Victoria was immobilized by fright.

The horns of the cars behind her startled her into action.

Aware that the stoplight had turned green, she stepped on the gas, moving her vehicle slowly until she could cut into the right-hand lane. At the first opportunity she spun off Park into a one-way street and searched for a telephone. Past Madison Avenue there were restaurants open, but no place to park. When she reached Fifth Avenue, she recalled there were two public telephones on a corner a block away. She swung into Fifth, followed the traffic, gratefully spotted the telephones outside the Doubleday Book Shop. Desperately seeking a place to leave the car, she saw a cab draw away from the curb, and quickly slipped into the empty parking space.

Shutting off the engine, she jumped out of the car and ran to the telephones. One was unoccupied. She knew that she had plenty of small change.

Now she must keep her wits about her. Yinger was after District Attorney Van Dusen. She must locate Van Dusen. Not easy at this hour, but she must find him and warn him before it was too late.

She started dialing. It was as if a Great Wall of Operators blocked her. Casual, unhurried operators, not interested in her frantic haste.

At last she had an operator at the Criminal Courts Building.

"Give me the district attorney's office," Victoria begged. "I've got to speak to Mr. Van Dusen. It's urgent."

Another gum-chewing voice. "He's not in. No one is. Hey, don't you know what time it is? Try tomorrow."

"Tomorrow may be too late. Someone's life is involved."

"Well, maybe I can find somebody to talk to you. Let me connect you with the supervisor in the complaint room. He's sure to be there. Hold on."

There was a series of clicks. Some static.

A man's voice. Tired voice. "Berger. Complaints."

Victoria tried to keep her tone steady. "I'm Victoria Weston. I'm a reporter on the New York *Record*. I must speak to the district attorney on an urgent matter—"

"I'm sorry, miss, you have the wrong department."

"I've got to get hold of Mr. Van Dusen. It's important, I tell you."

"I'd suggest you try his office in the morning."

"He may be dead in the morning."

"We all may be," said the supervisor cheerfully. "Now if you have a legitimate complaint—"

"My complaint is that no one will help me contact the district attorney."

"Forget about doing it tonight. He's at the testimonial dinner for the mayor at the Plaza."

"Where?"

"The Grand Ballroom of the Plaza Hotel."

Victoria thanked him, slammed the receiver down on the hook. The Plaza wasn't too far to make it on foot, but she reconsidered. Too far to walk in an emergency. She made for her car, and tried to find the quickest route to the Plaza.

Twelve minutes later she pulled up in front of the Fifty-ninth Street entrance to the Plaza. She gave her car (and a generous tip) to the uniformed doorman to park and hurried up the steps into the busy lobby of the Plaza. She lurched into an open and crowded elevator, calling out to be let off at the Grand Ballroom.

Emerging into the jammed marble foyer, she noted the time, ten-thirty, and noted dressy people leaving the ballroom. The mayor's dinner was just beginning to break up. She looked for a familiar face, an official face, and her eyes came to rest on a blue-uniformed policeman.

She clutched at the policeman's sleeve. "Officer, can you help me?"

He seemed surprised by her anxiety-ridden countenance. "Something the matter, miss?"

"I've got to speak to District Attorney Van Dusen."

"Forget it, young lady. He's on the stage with the mayor, with orders not to be disturbed. There's no way they'll let you in there."

"But listen—"

"Sorry, miss."

Victoria slumped in frustration, backed off, and became aware of an anemic-appearing, bespectacled young man staring at her. He took a few tentative steps toward her.

"Pardon me, you're Vicky Weston, the new girl on the *Record*, aren't you?"

"Yes," she admitted.

"I met you yesterday when Nick—Nick Ramsey—was taking you around. We were introduced. I'm Jim Purdy, metropolitan desk. What are you doing here?"

She grabbed hold of him as if he were a life belt. "Jim, listen, you can help me. I've got to see Van Dusen—"

"Not much chance of that right now. Can't it wait?"

"No, it can't. Will you listen to what's happened?" She spilled out the details of her interview at Green Haven with Sam Yinger, the killer's statement that if he were free he'd go after Van Dusen, and now the knowledge that Yinger was free.

Purdy was cautiously impressed. "He actually stated he'd try to get the D.A.? Did you believe him? Maybe he was just crowing for you, for your story."

"You'd have believed him if you'd been there and heard him say it. Anyway, I think Van Dusen should hear about it. Do you know anyone who can get to him?"

"I can get him," said Purdy. "My beat is Van Dusen and criminal courts. Let me see what I can do."

Victoria followed Purdy to the ballroom doors, heard him whisper to two police guards, saw a door open, and was able to peer around the reporter's head as he looked inside. Victoria could see, beneath the two magnificent chandeliers, tables and tables of formally attired men and women. Dignitaries on the distant stage were standing.

Purdy called back to her, "Van Dusen's just said good-bye to the mayor. He's coming down the stage steps toward the aisle. Let me see if I can get to him. Wait here."

With assent from the guards, Purdy entered the room, hurried down to the carpeted aisle where a tall, thin man in a tuxedo, obviously District Attorney Van Dusen, was making his way between the tables, acknowledging greetings from guests. Halfway along, Purdy intercepted him and began addressing him. Van Dusen leaned over to listen, glanced up, and started toward the doorway where Victoria was waiting.

The district attorney reached Victoria, towering over her. "You Miss Weston? Purdy tells me that you have important information—something about Sam Yinger wanting to kill me—it's not clear—"

"You know of Yinger's escape?"

"I know from Green Haven—and from your newspaper," he said wryly.

"I interviewed Yinger at the prison this afternoon. I asked him what he'd like to do if he were free. He told me that the one reason he'd like to be free is to kill you."

Van Dusen frowned. "He really said that?"

"I have my notes. He actually said it."

"You think he meant it?"

"I think he did. After all, he had no compunction about killing six children." Victoria wanted to emphasize her belief. "I'm sure he meant it. He hates you for calling him an animal in court."

"He is an animal," Van Dusen said.

"And now he's on the loose," said Victoria.

The district attorney beckoned to a man who had just come out of the ballroom. As Victoria wondered who the man was, she found Van Dusen taking her hand. "I want to thank you, Miss—"

"Victoria Weston. The New York *Record*."

"—yes, Miss Weston. The chief of police, here, will take immediate precautions. He'll double my protection. Can you spare a few moments more? I want you to tell the chief what you told me. Again, my thanks. I may owe you my life."

*   *   *

It was several minutes before midnight when Victoria, on the verge of exhaustion, stumbled through the thinly populated newsroom of the *Record* on the way to her desk. She pulled her notebook out of her purse, praying she had enough strength left to write up her Yinger interview before it was too late.

When she arrived at her desk, she found her swivel chair amply occupied. A lazy, and perhaps partially intoxicated, Nick Ramsey lolled in her chair, one long leg hooked over the armrest.

"Just keeping the seat warm for Lois Lane," he said.

"I appreciate that," said Victoria. "Now if you don't mind moving, I have a story to write."

"Don't bother."

Victoria's brow furrowed. "What do you mean?"

"Your story's just been canceled."

"Why?"

"Hotter news. What you have is old news by now." Ramsey removed his leg from the chair arm and straightened up. "Sam Yinger is dead."

"What?" Victoria said with disbelief.

"Yup." Ramsey stood up. "Purdy phoned it in from the D.A.'s Gracie Square residence five minutes ago. Van Dusen was returning home from the mayor's testimonial. Sam Yinger was lying in wait with a gun, ready to assassinate the D.A. Before he could take aim, the D.A.'s guards gunned him down. Maybe a dozen shots to Yinger's chest and head. He was killed instantly. The D.A. survived unscathed." Ramsey smiled. "Thanks to you."

Victoria moved her head dumbly, trying to comprehend the sudden turn of events.

"It's right there in Purdy's lead. Girl reporter from the *Record* saves D.A.'s life. Van Dusen gave you credit by name."

"But my story? There's still a story."

"Old news, Vicky dear. After that Yinger escaped. Yinger stalked the D.A. Weston alerted the D.A. Yinger was executed hours earlier than planned. Good-bye, Yinger. Old news."

"Old news," said Victoria dully. "Maybe I should have got my story in earlier. What will Mr. Armstead think?"

"Can't say. Van Dusen thinks you're a heroine. Edward Armstead—he'll either fire you or give you a raise." Ramsey hooked his arm through hers. "Right now, I'll tell you what *I* think. I think you need a drink."

Harry Dietz could not remember, in all their years together, ever before having seen Edward Armstead as cheerful as he was this morning.

The publisher's handsome office was bathed in sunshine, which streamed in through the sliding glass doors that opened onto the balcony. It was as if Mother Nature had directed a special yellow spotlight on Edward Armstead. He leaned back, deep in his leather swivel chair, letting the sun warm his beaming face as he called across his massive oak desk to his assistant, "Tell me again, Harry."

Dutifully, Harry Dietz once more reviewed the sheet of paper on his lap. "Unofficial figures, mind you, but even if they are off, they won't be that much off. Yesterday, the daily New York *Times* sold, in round numbers, 860,000 copies." He cleared his throat. "The New York *Record* sold 940,000 copies—all our new presses could turn out. You crushed them. You did it."

"Fantastic," crowed Armstead. "A runaway. The Yinger escape did it. Wow."

Armstead heard the intercom, and then his secretary's voice. "Mr. Armstead, I have Horace Liddington for you."

"Thanks, Estelle," said Armstead. "I'll take it." He winked at Dietz. "This'll knock our old legal-beagle on his ass." Armstead punched the button on his phone marked CO #1.

"Horace?"

"Hello, Edward," Liddington said. "How are you?"

"Have you heard the news about what the *Record* did in sales yesterday?"

"I had an idea—"

"You what?"

"I guessed what was happening. When I heard them break your story on the late television news, I went out to buy the paper for more details. I had to visit three newsstands before I could find a copy. People were buying it everywhere. You have my congratulations—my heartiest congratulations—"

Armstead cupped his hand over the mouthpiece and said to Dietz, "Liddington says he guessed it. We were a sellout in his neighborhood. He's congratulating us now."

Armstead gave his attention to the telephone once more.

"—I couldn't be happier for you," Liddington was saying.

"Well, thank you, Horace, thank you."

"How on earth did you ever get a scoop like that?"

"Never mind how we got the scoop. The zinger in my father's will was obliterated by Yinger." He savored the poetic justice. Zinger, Yinger. He resumed. "Let me give you the figures on sales yesterday." He reached out, took the sheet of paper from Dietz, and said into the phone, "We exceeded the sale of the *Times* by 80,000. Listen to the numbers." He read them to Liddington. "How does that sound?"

"It certainly sounds as if you're in."

"You bet I'm in."

"I'll only require some official confirmation to fulfill the condition in your father's will. You'll take care of that?"

"Yes, I'll send you the official figures as soon as I receive them from the Audit Bureau of Circulations in Chicago. But there's no question—"

"I'm merely speaking of a formality, Edward. To all intents and purposes, you have done what was required."

"Good, good, I'm glad to hear you say that," said Armstead. "I have fulfilled the condition in the will. The *Record*, from this day on, is *my* newspaper."

"Let me repeat, I couldn't be happier."

"Thank you, thanks again. Believe me, Horace, this is only the beginning. From now on, it's straight onward and upward."

"Myra and I want to share your achievement, to celebrate by taking you and Hannah to dinner next week. I'll promise you a bottle of Moët and Chandon Brut Imperial at the table to toast your triumph."

Armstead could not resist a chuckle, aware that his father's attorney was a Yankee and knowing his reputation as a tight man with a buck. "Thanks, Horace," he said. "I will accept that generous dinner offer—and the champagne. See you shortly."

No sooner had Armstead laid down the receiver than Estelle was on the intercom again. "The phone is ringing off the hook, Mr. Armstead. I'm not bothering you with most of the calls. I'll leave you messages. But maybe you want to take this call. It's the mayor, the mayor himself."

Armstead grinned at the telephone. "I'll take it," he said. He punched the lighted red button. "Hello, this is Edward Armstead . . . How are you, your honor? . . . Why, thank you, that's very kind of you. But after all, we are a public service newspaper. We are only too pleased to be of use . . . Yes, I'll be delighted to have lunch with you next week."

Armstead slammed the receiver down with a grimace and looked at Dietz. "His honor congratulating me. You know what for? No, not the Yinger beat. He's congratulating me for having a reporter enterprising enough to have alerted the district attorney to the danger he was in and for helping save Van Dusen's life. Which brings us to Victoria Weston. What do you think?"

"I don't know," said Dietz frankly.

"I think I know how to handle her. Be a good guy, Harry, and send her in."

Edward Armstead watched Victoria as she crossed the office from the door to his desk.

She was a fairly tall girl, he saw again, with long blond hair, a bright, alive, pretty face, firm breasts that moved with her motion beneath a clinging gray sweater, long legs. Not as mature as Kim Nesbit, not as sensuous, less a full woman.

But he could see that she carried herself with ease, great poise, and there was a smartness about her that he found enticing. He had to remind himself not to be seduced and softened. He had a hunch that she would make a first-rate reporter. She would seduce and soften other men. She would be an asset for the newspaper. Nevertheless, he would have to be tough with her. The molding of a real reporter had to begin today.

As she sat down across from him, he heard her say, "Congratulations, Mr. Armstead. The word's out all over the plant—that the *Record* topped the other New York newspapers yesterday. That's wonderful."

"Yes, it is. Thank you, Victoria. We're ahead, and we mean to stay there."

"How did you ever pull it off, the exclusive on Yinger's escape? You had it all alone."

This was dangerous territory, but Armstead moved through it smoothly. "You're referring to the Green Haven tunnel, of course?"

"I can't imagine how Yinger found out about it."

"Well, you found out about it from Gus Pagano. You kept your word not to use it. But I doubt if others were as trustworthy. At any rate, someone in the prison told Yinger, and at the same time someone tipped us that Yinger was using the tunnel. I think we had the story on the presses just as he broke out. I'm not at liberty to give any details."

"Oh, I'm not prying, Mr. Armstead."

"Nothing wrong with prying, Victoria—as long as it's into someone else's affairs. We simply want no one to pry into the paper's affairs. I know you can be depended upon."

"Absolutely, Mr. Armstead," she said.

With deliberation, he extracted a cigar from its case and fiddled with it. "I'm aware, of course, that you had an excellent interview at the prison with Yinger."

She became wary. "It was—interesting."

"During that interview, you learned that Yinger wanted to kill our district attorney, and after you learned Yinger had escaped, you went to great lengths to contact Van Dusen and alert him to the danger." Armstead put a light to his cigar. "In fact, by so doing you may have saved the district attorney's life."

She was still wary. "Yes, I suppose so."

"I gather everyone has been congratulating you on your humanity and good citizenship. In fact, the mayor called here to congratulate us on your act. And others have as well. But there is one person who is not going to congratulate you. That person is me. I can't congratulate you for something you should not have done."

Armstead knew that she knew what he meant. Nevertheless she asked, "What do you mean?"

The publisher exhaled a balloon of smoke. He followed its rise, disintegration, evaporation. "I'll tell you what I mean by telling you a story I heard or read somewhere, a story about another woman reporter. I forget her name, but I believe she worked for the New York *Daily News*. This was back in the days before the young Prince of Wales became King Edward VIII and finally Duke of Windsor. It was a time when the young prince was frivolous news, but news all the same, a glamorous playboy. The prince, the real Prince of Wales, was an enigma, and the public wanted to know more about him personally. Well, he was visiting Quebec under an assumed name, although everyone knew he was the Prince of Wales, and the New York *Daily News* decided to attempt a ruse to find out more intimate facts about him. The paper assigned one of its youngest and most beautiful female reporters to go to Quebec, pose as a debutante, meet the prince, gain his confidence, and learn his most private thoughts. Well, it worked—but it didn't work. Are you following me, Victoria? Are you wondering what went wrong?''

Squirming, Victoria stammered, "I—I'm wondering, Mr. Armstead."

"Yes, the stunt worked," said Armstead. "The girl reporter posing as a debutante attracted the Prince of Wales, danced with him endlessly, entranced him, gained his confidence, got her story. But then she couldn't write it. She felt that the prince had become her friend, that she couldn't betray him, make his confidences public, write the personal story she was supposed to write. She wrote something, but not the real story she'd been assigned. In the end, her loyalty was to the prince and not to her newspaper. As a reporter, she failed her publisher. Do you see?''

"I do see," said Victoria in a small voice.

"In the same way, you failed me. You had a story to write for us. Instead of writing it, you devoted yourself to worrying about the district attorney."

"But I couldn't let him be killed!" Victoria exclaimed.

Armstead poked the stub of his cigar at her. "Don't be childish. There was little chance Yinger would have been able to kill Van Dusen under any circumstances. The district attorney is always well protected."

"But Van Dusen himself thanked me."

"Nonsense, nonsense, Victoria. A political ploy to play up to the press. Also to create more human interest for himself. You were dealing with a consummate politician, Victoria. No, you had your priorities wrong. You must learn, once and for all, that you are not in the public service business. You are in the dog-eat-dog newspaper business. Your first duty—your only duty—is to me, to me and this newspaper. You had an exclusive story for us, one we had considerable difficulty arranging. You got a good story. Your instinct should have made you come directly here and write it. We might have had a second beat—and you would have had a by-line. Yes, a second beat. A natural. I can see the headline: 'Escaped Murderer Vows to Kill D.A. Van Dusen.' That would have hiked our circulation even higher. Once Yinger was dead, your story was pointless, and Yinger's death was everyone's story, not ours, and it became routine news. You had your priorities wrong. Do you understand what I am saying, Victoria?''

"I—I think I do, Mr. Armstead. I'm sorry.''

"You may get a medal from the district attorney. But you won't get one from Edward Armstead—until you realize that the paper always comes first. Next time you have a big story, see that you deliver it to the *Record*. Then you'll get the right kind of medal.'' He saw that she was unstrung, and he did not want to unravel her completely. "Okay, you've learned your lesson. You'll do better from now on.''

As she left, he wondered if he had been unduly harsh. He decided that he had not. He had, indeed, taught her a lesson. From now on she would be a perfect reporter, and a good member of a winning team.

Armstead was determined to have a winning team, a newspaper that was the constant leader.

In pursuit of this goal, he had spent the next hour going through the latest editions of all the New York papers, and the Washington and Chicago papers as well. He had riffled through the future folder, the file folder of potential news stories that might develop in the days ahead.

He wanted another Yinger. More of the same.

A thought had materialized, and he had asked McAllister to locate Nick Ramsey.

He had Nick Ramsey on his phone now. "Nick, this is Armstead.''

"Yes, sir.''

"Do you remember that last Special Project we conceived, the one I had you research abroad—the one my father turned down?"

"Certainly. It was the terrorist thing, the series we were going to call 'The Time of the Terrorist.' "

"That's the one, the series. As I recall, you did quite a bit of background work on it. Do you still have your notes?"

"Every note in mint condition."

"Good. Leave them with my secretary. I want to read them again. We just may want to reactivate the series."

"Great idea. It could be a scorcher."

"We'll see. Let me have a look. I'll let you know."

As he put the receiver down, Armstead heard Estelle's voice and had to pick it up again.

"Gus Pagano is here for his appointment."

Armstead had quite forgotten. "Send him in," he said.

Seconds later Gus Pagano came into the room, twirling his hat in his hand.

Inside the office, he halted and surveyed the space. "Quite a layout," said Pagano, impressed. "Lots of elbowroom."

Armstead presumed that his visitor meant the office was more habitable than a cell in Green Haven prison. He motioned Pagano to a chair across from him. Armstead had never met the informant before. What surprised him was that Pagano looked like what he was supposed to be, as if type-cast for a small-time racketeer or gangster. The jet-black curly hair, hooked nose, swarthy complexion, pinstriped suit—perfect, except there were no bulges that might indicate a weapon.

Pagano had made himself comfortable and was shaking a cigarette loose from his pack. "Do you mind?" He lit the cigarette without waiting for an answer.

"I've been looking forward to meeting you, Mr. Pagano," Armstead said.

"Likewise," said Pagano.

Armstead wasted no time. "Your tip about the prison tunnel—that was pretty good."

"You used it."

"You bet I did."

"You weren't supposed to," said Pagano. He wasn't angry at all. Just a flat statement. "It was secret."

"Mr. Pagano, once a secret is revealed to another, it is no longer a secret. That should be evident."

"I told her it was not for publication."

"It wasn't published," said Armstead simply. "It wasn't published until Yinger's escape revealed its existence."

"Okay, if you want to be technical."

"Mr. Pagano, hear me out. I have a business proposition for you. But before presenting it, let me state my policy unequivocally—I believe that there is nothing in the world not for publication once it has been given to the *Record*. Everything on earth is for publication. If I know it, it is for publication. What did you get paid for talking to our reporter about Yinger and the cell?"

"Two hundred and fifty bucks."

"Not enough," said Armstead. "For services rendered, you deserve better. I'm making that payment a thousand dollars for the tip. And I'm offering you a proposition. How'd you like to be on my payroll at a thousand a week?"

Pagano sat up, his beady eyes brightening. But he was hesitant. "For doing what?"

"For doing what comes naturally. I don't want a thousand dollars a week to make you go straight. I want you to stay where you are—underground. Give me more leads like the Yinger one."

"They don't happen often."

"You need come through only once in a while. Look, I know a little about you. You like to live well. You're always short of money. This would give you enough to live on, and to live well. At the same time, I don't want you to lose your contacts. I just don't want you involved in armed robbery anymore. Hang around with your regular friends, but take no risks. Keep your ears open."

"And let you know what I hear."

"If it might be a lead to a news story, yes. Just give us a little more."

"I wouldn't want to get my friends in trouble."

"You don't have to. What you report doesn't have to involve them exactly."

Pagano stubbed out his cigarette thoughtfully. "It's still a dangerous scam," he said. "My friends wouldn't like it if they learned they had a stool pigeon around."

"You won't be a stool pigeon. You'll listen a lot. You won't hurt anybody. You'll be selective, tell us what you can tell us."

"Yeah."

"A grand a week, Gus. Maybe some bonuses down the line for special services."

"Yeah."

Armstead stood up. "What do you say, Gus?"

Gus Pagano came to his feet. He stuck out his hand. "You got a deal, Mr. Armstead."

Armstead shook his hand heartily. Releasing it, Armstead came around the desk. He was beaming again. This was a good day. Things were falling into place. He joined Pagano and took his arm. "Come one. You need to talk to Harry Dietz. He is now my assistant, and he'll be the one you keep in touch with. I want you two to work out a *modus operandi*. Okay?"

"Okay."

Armstead was about to leave his office when the telephone call had come from his wife Hannah.

She had wanted to know if he would be coming back for dinner, because she had something she wanted to discuss with him.

"I can't be home for dinner," he had told her, "but as a matter of fact I will be coming by right now, just for a few minutes. I've got several appointments lined up, and I want to change clothes before going out again. I'll be by in a little bit. We can talk then.''

Now, in his bedroom of their penthouse apartment overlooking Central Park, Armstead had finished his dressing. He had three appointments ahead of him, and it was for his second appointment—date, really, a date with Kim Nesbit—that he had come back to change from a staid business suit into a younger and sportier outfit, lively cashmere sports jacket and Savile Row slacks. Inspecting himself in the full-length mirror, he was pleased. He hadn't looked better in years.

He realized that time was closing in, he would have to be on his way shortly. He had better leave five minutes for Hannah, who was still waiting for him in the living room. He wondered what she wanted to talk about when he was so busy. He had already told her about the Yinger beat at breakfast this morning. What more was there to discuss? If it was something Hannah had on her mind, it couldn't be good. He hoped it would be nothing to mar his perfect day.

He went through the corridor into the living room. Hannah, he was pleased to note, was not in her usual wheelchair, the constant invalid. She was seated, instead, in the armchair near the television set. She even had color in her face. Going toward her, he wondered if he should sit briefly, but decided against it. Relaxing might invite a prolonged conversation. He decided to remain on his feet.

''Meant to tell you,'' he said, ''we passed the New York *Times* today, beat them out all the way. How's that?''

''Congratulations, Ed. I'm pleased for you.''

''I knew I could do it, and I've done it,'' he said, extracting a cigar from his sports jacket and unpeeling it. Snipping off one end, he brought out his pocket lighter and lit up. ''Okay, Hannah, now what can I do for you? You wanted to talk about something.''

''About our son Roger,'' she said.

''What about Roger?''

"I had a call from him a little while ago, from a hospital in Green Bay, Wisconsin."

"A hospital? What do you mean? What's wrong? Is it anything serious—no, it couldn't be or he wouldn't have been able to call you, and you'd have told me on the phone."

"It's not serious," said Hannah, "but it is still the hospital. Roger was climbing a mountain, and slipped and fell—"

"Climbing a mountain? There are no mountains around Green Bay."

"A hill, then," she said. "Maybe I heard it wrong. Anyway, he took a fall and injured himself. Roger sustained two leg fractures. Not serious, but incapacitating. It'll keep him laid up a little while."

For some reason, hearing about this outdoors nonsense irritated Armstead. "What in the hell was he doing climbing?"

"It had something to do with his job."

"Idiotic," Armstead muttered. "Serves him right." He couldn't think of another Armstead in the family who had ever climbed anything, except into bed. The thought amused him, and he said more cheerfully, "Well, as long as he's all right. Let me know how he's coming along. Is this it—what you wanted to talk to me about?"

"Not completely," said Hannah. "Ed, I wanted to ask you to come to Green Bay with me for the weekend."

Armstead scowled. "To do what? Hold his hand? God, Hannah, he's not a child anymore. Besides, he's got a doctor, plenty of friends there."

"It's not the same as family, Ed. He's flat on his back. You know how he hates to be confined. I'm sure he'd like more company, be happy to see his parents. It would be comforting."

Armstead waved his cigar in disgust. "Hannah, you know better than that. I've just taken over. I've just made my mark. I'm up to my ass in business, in the very middle of everything, with a million plans in progress—"

"Can't you put it aside for just one weekend?"

"Hannah, for chrissakes, I can't spare the time. Look, if you feel Roger needs company, then go to Wisconsin yourself and see him for the weekend. I'll arrange for a nurse to accompany you. How's that?"

With effort, Hannah said, "I think he wanted so very much to see you, Ed. He told me on the phone he'd read about your Yinger exclusive in the local newspaper up there. He said to tell you it was fantastic. He was very proud of what you'd done."

Armstead was both surprised and pleased. "Well, now, the boy has at least some sense." He searched for the time. "Tell you what, I've got to rush out now or I'll be late. But leave Roger's telephone number out for me. I should be back not too much after dinner. A short victory celebration with Dietz and Harmston. When I get back I'll give Roger a call myself. You go up and see him for the weekend. I'll miss you, but he needs you more. Now I'd better hurry."

Once Armstead had left the apartment and stood waiting for the elevator, an odd thought occurred to him.

It occurred to him that he himself had been a son so long, he'd never had time to be a father.

Well, he told himself, maybe his own sonhood was coming to an end. Life would belong to him alone (and Roger—of course Roger). He'd have to get into it in today's session with the shrink.

Edward Armstead had sunk into the worn brown leather chair in Dr. Carl Scharf's office, and he had been talking for forty minutes, forcing the psychiatrist to listen. It had been a test of strength, and Armstead had enjoyed it.

Now he ceased talking and shifted his weight in the leather chair. Then he said, "Carl, when are you going to get a new chair or have this one fixed? Christ, the springs are practically coming out. I have a sore ass every time I leave you."

"It's to remind the idle rich of the Spartan life. To remind you life is real, life is earnest, and it is also a pain in the ass."

"If I have to, I'll buy you a new chair for Christmas."

Armstead knew that Dr. Scharf would use the last ten or fifteen minutes to do a sum-up of their session. It was his pattern. It was all right. It always allowed Armstead—and other patients, too, he supposed—to leave with a clear picture of where he stood and where he should be going. Emotionally, that is.

Waiting for the sum-up, he kept his eyes on the psychiatrist. Momentarily Dr. Scharf had taken on a resemblance to a beach ball. He was very globular this afternoon. His protruding curved belly hung over a narrow belt. He was as untidy as ever in the turtleneck sweater and wrinkled slacks. Dr. Scharf was busily adjusting his feet on the footstool.

Armstead waited for wisdom. Or at least support for his own good cheer.

"Well, I must say, that was quite a scoop you pulled off, Edward," said Dr. Carl Scharf.

"We don't call them scoops anymore," said Armstead. "We call them beats."

"Your scoop was on the television news," Dr. Scharf said. "That's where I heard about Yinger's escaping."

"You didn't read it in my paper? You know that paper is my life."

"I bought three copies, just to keep you affluent," said Dr. Scharf. "I wondered, how did you get that story so fast, and exclusive yet?"

"Professional secret."

"Hey, I'm your analyst, Edward. You're not supposed to have secrets. If I'm to be of help—"

"I don't need help today," said Armstead complacently.

"Well, I'm proud of your—of your achievement," said Dr. Scharf. He clasped his hands over his belly. "You must be pleased with yourself. You officially won the right to keep the paper. You overcame your father's mistrust, *and* you accomplished what your father had not been able to accomplish in a decade. You're a *mensch*."

"That's the way I feel."

"You're free, free to do what you want to do, go as high as you want on your own."

"I'm only beginning," said Armstead. "The Yinger beat was no flash in the pan. I'll see to that. I have a million plans. Once I get ready, I'm really going to shake up the media world. Everyone will know who I am."

"That's still so important?"

"To be me, yes."

"Is that it?"

"Well, you know what's in my head. I've got to eclipse my old man completely. Anything wrong with that?"

"I didn't say so."

"When people speak of Armstead, they're going to mean Edward Armstead, not Ezra."

"Anything else you want to say about your father?"

Armstead considered it. "No, I think that's it. Well—I guess there's something else I should mention. After I saw you the other day, I dropped in on Kim, Kim Nesbit."

The psychiatrist nodded. "How was she?"

"Drunk. Also, beautiful."

"Was she pleased to see you?"

"I think so." He held back a moment, then added, "I fucked her." He paused. "It was good, very good. I—I intend to see more of her."

Dr. Scharf took his feet off the ottoman. "Why?" he asked.

"I don't know. Do you object?"

"You know I'm not here to judge you. I'm just curious about why you were intimate with her."

"I don't know. Why not?"

Dr. Scharf pushed himself to his feet and said pleasantly, "Was it to show your father you were a man—or to show yourself?" He waited for his patient to rise, and then accompanied him to the door. "Let's talk about that next time."

* * *

It was to show no one anything, Armstead decided as he rested on the lime green sofa in Kim Nesbit's apartment. His eyes followed her graceful movement as she walked to the portable bar. He needed a woman, a passionate woman, because he needed the feeling of youth and strength and purpose. His wife had dried up on him years ago. Except for occasional worry about their son Roger such as she had displayed earlier in the day, Hannah's main concern had become herself and her ever more sickly body. Kim was vibrant and pleasure-giving and a discovery that he had dreamt of and only now was able to explore. He did not have to prove anything to his father or to himself. It was far less complicated. He wanted this woman, and he had her, and would have her again and again, and it was delicious. He would have to convince Dr. Scharf of his true feelings at their next session.

"Scotch and water?" Kim called from the bar, pouring.

"Exact."

"I'm learning," she said, bringing him the glass. "I want to please you in every way, Ed."

"You do, you do." He saw that she was empty-handed. "What about you? Aren't you drinking?"

"I'll have a Perrier."

"That's not drinking."

"I don't need it anymore," she said, sinking into the sofa beside him. "I have you, darling." She took his head in her hands and drew him closer. He found her moist lips, felt her tongue, felt the softness of her breasts against him.

Ending the kiss, he could see her bare breasts beneath the opening of her diaphanous negligee, and he was fully aroused.

"Are you still as happy as you were when you called me this morning?" she asked.

"I know what could make me happier," he said, getting to his feet and pulling her in front of him.

"Darling—" she said, about to turn to the bedroom.

"One second, Kim." He fumbled in his pocket and brought

out the small velvet Tiffany box. He pressed it into her hand. "For you. To celebrate."

She fussed over it, lifting the lid. "Oh, Ed," she murmured, near tears. "It's beautiful."

"Like you."

She took out the shining pink sapphire ring and slipped it on her finger. "Are you buying me?" she said, trying to smile. "You don't need to, you know."

"I'm adorning you." He smiled. "You don't need it, you know."

She held up her hand with its pink sapphire. "I love it," she said. Her arms went around him. "I love you."

"Show me," he said as they parted.

She clasped his hand tightly and walked into the bedroom. He undressed quickly, and when he was naked he saw that she was naked lying on her back on the bed, arms outstretched.

"Let's not play," she said. "Let's love."

She lifted her legs and spread them apart, and he was atop her immediately. She clutched him tightly as he pressed between her legs and entered her.

She gave a throaty outcry, and he groaned.

He quickened the pace, thrusting hard, pushing her against the headboard. He rose and fell as she held on, gradually rolling her hips, until he was in a frenzy.

They went on and on, for long minutes, until their mutual eruptions.

He came off her, on his back, wet and panting. She dropped her legs, brushing her corn-silk hair from her eyes, trying to catch her breath and even it out.

Side by side, they lay in silence.

"Never stop loving me," she said.

"It's all I want to do," he promised.

Later, when she was breathing regularly again and sound asleep, and he had raised himself on an elbow, ready to get out of bed and leave her, he knew that his last words to her had been a lie.

Loving her was fantastic, a small fulfillment, but it was not all that he wanted to do, or intended to do.

Sex was not first-best but second-best.

Power was first-best.

Power to manipulate, control, dominate—everything, everyone, the world.

It had come to him with clarity after he came, what to do, how to do it. It was dangerous, very dangerous, this bigger seduction, this rape of life. But he would attempt it. He would enjoy the ultimate orgasm.

5

Tempting as it had been to bask in another morning of sunshine, Edward Armstead had firmly adjusted the blinds to minimize the brightness. He wanted no relaxing atmosphere in his office. He wanted the tone to be somber and businesslike.

When Nick Ramsey and Victoria Weston answered his summons to see them, Armstead greeted them curtly. After gesturing them to places before his desk, he went behind it, sat down, and picked up the sheaf of typewritten notes that Ramsey had left for him yesterday.

Although he had read the notes twice, Armstead reviewed them once more.

"You can smoke," he said without looking up. Ramsey immediately extracted a bent pack of cigarettes and lit one. Victoria remained with her hands folded in her lap.

Presently Armstead put down the sheaf of notes. He was ready to tread the path—a trailblazer's path—toward which the Yinger affair had directed him. He would have to ascend it cautiously, a step at a time, conscious always of the possibility of fatal pitfalls.

First step.

"Nick, I've been reading the notes you originally made for our Special Project, the one we called, 'The Time of the Terrorist,' " said Armstead. "It's still good stuff."

"I really enjoyed digging it up," said Ramsey. "I wish it had worked out."

"It may yet," said Armstead. "I have something in mind. Something that would require cooperation from both of you. First, I want to find out more about these notes from you, Nick. For the time, Victoria need do no more than listen. Then we'll see. You ready to discuss your terrorist researches, Nick?"

Ramsey came out of his slouch, more alert. "I'll be glad to tell you anything that's not in my notes, Mr. Armstead, anything I can remember or help you with."

"I want an evaluation from you, Nick," said Armstead. "There are so many of these terrorist groups running around, I was wondering—well, simply put, which ones are most important?"

"The most important in what sense?" inquired Ramsey.

"Relatively, a lot of these groups must be fly-by-nighters or Mickey Mousers. Ignore them. Which are the most powerful and effective?"

"Of those currently in existence?"

"Right now," said Armstead.

"The most powerful, the most effective . . . ." repeated Ramsey. "Easily the biggest, the best trained, the best financed is the Popular Front for the Liberation of Palestine, known as the PFLP. They're a Marxist organization directed out of Damascus. Saudi Arabia gives them $25 million a year. Colonel Qaddafi of Libya gives them at least $50 million a year. One of their cadres pulled off the Munich Olympics massacre in 1972."

"Name some others."

"Others who are powerful?" mused Ramsey, giving it some thought. "Without ranking them exactly, I'd say the best disciplined and the most active after the PFLP are the Red Brigades of Italy, the Baader-Meinhof gang in West Germany, the Japanese Red Army, the Irish Republican Army or IRA, the Turkish

Popular Liberation Front, the ETA Basque separatists in Spain and—down in South American—the Tupamaros in Uruguay.''

"Any common bond?" wondered Armstead.

"Revolution in our time, down with capitalism," said Ramsey. "Most of them are supported with money, weapons, training, by the Kremlin, the Soviet Union. I suppose the one person who's had something to do with a majority of the groups is the leading terrorist hitman, the man known as Carlos."

"Ah, Carlos," said Armstead, touching the research folder. "The Venezuelan playboy turned killer. I saw several of the photographs you had of him. A fat, soft, moon-faced young man. He looks harmless."

"Don't let his looks fool you," said Ramsey. "Carlos is ruthless. Human life means nothing to him. Before Carlos was well known, he was living in a third-floor apartment in the Rue Toullier in the Latin Quarter of Paris. A friend of his, a Lebanese named Moukarbel, was forced to turn informer, and he led three French intelligence detectives to Carlos. During his interrogation, Carlos got permission to go to the bathroom. He came out with a 7.65mm Russian automatic blazing, killed two of the detectives, seriously wounded the third, shot the informer in the head, and escaped. All in ten seconds. His other credits are in my notes."

"I don't recall the details," said Armstead. "There's so much."

"Carlos helped organize the Japanese Red Army massacre at Israel's Lod Airport," said Ramsey. "He tossed a grenade into Le Drugstore in Paris, killing two, injuring twelve, burning the store down. He drove a Peugeot to a runway at Orly Airport and unleashed a hand rocket launcher against a Boeing 707 El Al plane with 136 passengers. That was a miss. He set up the hijacking of an Air France plane in Athens that led to the Entebbe rescue by the Israelis. I personally think his most successful caper was the one in Vienna in 1975, when he and five comrades took a streetcar to OPEC headquarters in the Texaco Building. Carlos and his group walked in and murdered three security guards, took eleven oil ministers hostage, flew them to Algiers

where they were released once he had his payoff. That took
planning and guts. He's a tough one."

"You speak as if he's still around. Is he?"

"I don't know," said Ramsey. "He was when I researched the
story for you in Paris. That's the last I heard."

"You don't know if he's alive?"

"I really don't know. But I'd guess so. There's been no word
of his death. He was alive in 1982 when he sent a threat, with his
thumbprints, to the French Interior Ministry from somewhere in
Holland."

"Where would he be now?"

Ramsey shrugged. "Could be in London, in Bonn, in Damascus.
But he's probably in Paris."

The publisher stared past Victoria reflectively, then engaged
Ramsey again. "Nick, tell me what this is all about. This Carlos,
is he a Commie?"

Ramsey shook his head. "Oddly, I don't think he is. From his
background in my notes, you might believe so. His father was a
Colombian who moved to Venezuela and made millions in real
estate. The father had three sons and he named them after Lenin.
The father was a rich Marxist. He gave his son Carlos the name
Ilich after Lenin's middle name. Carlos was Ilich Ramirez Sanchez,
born in 1949. He got Communist training at Camp Matanzas,
outside Havana, under a KGB colonel. Later, Carlos attended
Patrice Lumumba Friendship University in Moscow. He was
thrown out for drinking and womanizing—probably a KGB ploy
to get him underground. But I don't think he was a Communist.
You know, when he did that OPEC caper in Vienna, one of his
hostages was Sheikh Yamani, the oil minister from Saudi Arabia.
Yamani talked to Carlos a great deal, and had no sense that
Carlos believed in either the Communist or Palestinian cause."

Armstead remained puzzled. "Why has he been going around
kidnapping and shooting people?"

Ramsey lifted his shoulders. "Not certain. He is supposed to
believe in international revolution, Maoist variety. Don't bet on

it. Maybe he likes the adventure. Maybe he likes the money. Maybe he likes the power. He's supposed to have his own group, hand-picked German and Arab assassins. All the other groups are purely political. Carlos's group may or may not be.''

The publisher busied himself unwrapping a fresh cigar. After a few moments he inquired, almost casually, ''How'd you get all this material on Carlos and his gang?''

''Many sources,'' said Ramsey. ''The best one was an informant in the Carlos group. A minor member who mostly did errands, but a member. I was in Paris, spreading money around, and met this Middle Eastern type who had a girl friend in the Carlos group and did errands for her. I asked Mr. Dietz for a thousand dollars, and I paid off the informant for the information you've just read. It was all I could get.''

''I want more,'' said Armstead, standing up and lighting his cigar.

Ramsey showed his surprise. ''On Carlos?''

''On Carlos and his group.''

''I'm not sure that's possible,'' said Ramsey.

''Anything is possible,'' said Armstead. He made a meandering tour of his office, talking as he walked. ''I want to reactivate the terrorist series, now that I'm in charge. I want Carlos to be the focal point, at least to start with. I want you to go back to Europe, Nick, to Paris—you and Victoria Weston together; you'll need all the assistance you can get.''

Ramsey met Victoria's eyes, and frowned. ''I'm not sure this is woman's work—'' he started to say to the publisher.

''Nick, stop it,'' Victoria interrupted. ''Male chauvinism went out with bloomers, or should have. I can speak French. I've been to Paris, to every part of France, three times. I can be of real help, and you know it. I'm not afraid.''

''I am,'' said Ramsey.

Armstead intervened. ''I agree with Victoria,'' he said. ''I want her on this series. For two main reasons. One is, I want you to continue to break her in. Another is, I want the female touch, stories that can appeal to women as well as men.''

The other main reason, the one he had mentioned to Dietz, he now left unspoken. He wanted to do something for Hugh Weston's daughter, because he wanted to please Hugh even more. After all, he had told Dietz, Hugh Weston was now press secretary to the President of the United States. It would help to have him grateful to them. Someday a favor could be needed. Besides, Victoria might do well on the assignment. She was capable, even if relatively inexperienced. Armstead felt that this was a smart move.

''Also there's a lesser reason I want Victoria along on this assignment,'' he went on smoothly. ''I want a good façade in Paris. With both of you there, you can pose as married tourists, at least while working on the outside. In the hotel, I'll register you as separate individuals. I want the *Record* left out of this investigation. You're not journalists. You want to see the Eiffel Tower, have duck at the Tour d'Argent.'' Armstead returned to his desk. ''I think, Nick, you might start off by reviving your Carlos contact. What's his name?''

''Ahmet.''

''Okay, Ahmet. Learn if he's still in Paris. Can you do that?''

''I had a bartender who used to be able to reach him.''

''Try to reach him,'' said Armstead. ''Mainly, I want to know if Carlos has some action coming up.''

''That's asking a lot,'' said Ramsey, doubtfully.

''I'm paying a lot,'' said Armstead. ''You can pay that informant of yours, Ahmet, ten thousand dollars to find out. I'll pay others more to find out even more. What do you say?''

There was concern in Ramsey's expression. ''I can't say what we'll learn from Ahmet about Carlos. I can say you'll find money won't buy you anything from the other terrorist gangs. They can use money, but they are not after it. Their interests are purely ideological.''

''Money is ideology,'' said Armstead flatly. ''Money is

everything, as you'll find out when you start passing it around. Right now let's start with Ahmet. You and Victoria get ready to take off for Paris.''

Ramsey rose to his feet, followed by Victoria.

"When do we leave?'' Ramsey wanted to know.

"Tomorrow. Concorde. There'll be a Mercedes and driver to meet you both at De Gaulle, and a two-bedroom suite waiting for you at the Plaza Athénée. You are going as first-class tourists. When you have news, call my private number. After that, Harry Dietz or I will have your next assignment ready.''

"Also first-class?'' asked Ramsey.

"If your work is first-class,'' said Armstead. "Bon voyage.''

The following gray day Air France Concorde had taken off from New York's John F. Kennedy Airport at 1:00 in the afternoon and landed at the almost deserted Charles de Gaulle Airport 3 hours and 32 minutes later, at 10:32 in the evening, Paris time. Once they had cleared passport control and picked up their luggage, Ramsey and Victoria found their young French chauffeur, who led them in the cool late evening to the Mercedes sedan.

By midnight, they had settled into suite 505 of the Plaza Athénée Hotel. Although neither was hungry—they had just had a full lunch on the plane—they telephoned room service for sandwiches Gruyère. Ramsey located the small refrigerator behind a cabinet door in the entry hall, mixed himself two scotches before the sandwiches arrived and a double scotch after, and Victoria had a soft drink labeled Frampoise-Raisin de Fruité with her meal. Even though it was six hours earlier in their heads, Victoria found herself exhausted by the movement and change and she retired to the larger bedroom after her snack. Ramsey, a more seasoned traveler, was less tired and stayed awake two hours longer, going over his old notes on terrorism and nursing his drink. When he had finished both notes and drink, he yawned twice and knew that he was ready for sleep. He also knew what he must undertake the next day.

After an early breakfast in the suite, and accompanied by a rested and eager Victoria, Ramsey strolled along the Avenue Montaigne, chose the longer way up the Champs-Élysées toward the Étoile to give the bar time to open. Paris was not new to Victoria, but she hadn't visited it for five years and she was stimulated and wanted to talk. Ramsey did not want to talk. The tension of his first act preoccupied him.

They turned into the Avenue George V, then into the Rue Pierre Charron. Ramsey led Victoria to a modest bistro where four outdoor tables were being set up by a waiter.

Ramsey touched Victoria's elbow. "We're going inside. Let me do the talking. You just be quiet and have a drink."

"What should I drink?"

"Anything."

Victoria felt a flare of resentment at the way Nick was taking over, treating her as an unwanted appendage. She had felt constrained by this foreign assignment anyway. When Armstead gave it to her, despite his apparent reasonableness she had felt a twinge of suspicion that there might be nepotism involved. It was a possibility, the publisher currying favor with her father for some payoff down the road. She couldn't prove this was true, but the thought of nepotism niggled at her.

Instinctively she jutted her jaw, resolving to prove herself on her own on this trip. She quickly followed Nick into the bistro, going between the empty tables and the pinball machines being played by two tieless older men. With Nick, she went to the abbreviated zinc bar.

Ramsey perched on a stool, and Victoria sat next to him. A hunchbacked bartender sorting bottles left his work to request their order. Ramsey lit a cigarette and said, "Scotch and Evian."

Victoria had determined to order whatever Nick ordered, to show that she was tough and experienced, too, but the very idea of hard liquor at this hour in the morning nauseated her. She decided to be her independent self. Fearlessly she said, "I'll have a Coke."

The bartender fixed their drinks, and when he served them Ramsey said to him, "Monsieur, last time when I was here, a year ago, there was a bartender named Henri. I wondered—"

"Henri is here, *oui*. He has arrived. He is in the back changing."

"Would you tell him a friend would like to see him?"

The hunchbacked bartender disappeared through a doorway at one side of the bar, and seconds later a handsome, gray-haired, broad-shouldered man emerged, pulling on a white jacket. He squinted at the only occupants of the bar, coming toward Ramsey.

"Hello, Henri," said Ramsey. "Remember me?"

Henri's face broadened into a smile of recognition. "Monsieur Nick. How are you?"

"Better than ever. As you can see. I'm a newlywed. Meet my wife, Victoria."

Henri greeted her with a gallant kiss of her outstretched hand. "My best to you. Why do you marry such an old man?"

"For money," said Victoria, falling into it.

"And you, Henri, how are you?" inquired Ramsey.

"I now have a grandson." He fished inside his jacket for his wallet, withdrew a snapshot and handed it over. Ramsey and Victoria dutifully clucked over the picture.

Handing it back, Ramsey said, "Congratulations, Grandpa."

"You must not waste time," said Henri. "You are here on a honeymoon?"

"On business," said Ramsey.

The bartender's expression sobered. "The same business?" he asked softly.

"The same," said Ramsey, lowering his voice. "Is he still in Paris?"

"Yes."

"Can I speak to him?"

"When?"

"Soon."

"Where do you stay?" asked Henri.

"Plaza Athénée. Suite 505."

"He will call you there in an hour."

"Thanks." Ramsey swung off the stool, paid for the drinks, left 500 francs for the bartender, and departed from the bistro with Victoria at his heels.

They took a shortcut back to the hotel and waited nervously in their suite for the telephone to ring.

They had waited fifty minutes when the telephone rang.

Ramsey, sitting on the sofa, grabbed for it. "Hello."

"Mr. Ramsey?"

"Yes, this is Nick Ramsey."

"I am Ahmet."

"Hello, Ahmet, I'm glad you called. Can you speak?"

"No. Not now. I will be fishing in the Seine, near the Quai de Montebello stairs. Three o'clock this afternoon. We can speak then."

"All right, that's fine. See you there at three o'clock."

Ramsey hung up. "That was quick," said Victoria. "Any luck?"

"He was jittery. Didn't want to talk from wherever he was. He indicated the best way to talk would be to see him at three o'clock. He will be fishing in the Seine. He told me where on the river."

"You mean literally fishing—trying to catch fish in the Seine?"

"As good a place as any. Better. Hard to be picked up by electronic devices or bugged there. Carlos may keep a close eye on his crew." Ramsey glanced at his wristwatch. "Well, we have a few hours to waste. I think I'll look up Sid Lukas, head man at the *Record* bureau. We broke into this business at the same time. Anything you want to do?"

"Nap," said Victoria. "Wake me when the countdown begins."

By midafternoon she was refreshed, her face shining and apprehensive as she strode beside Ramsey on the Quai de Montebello above the river and across from the towering Gothic cathedral of Notre-Dame.

"Down here," said Ramsey, pointing to stone steps leading

from the street to the banks of the Seine. Victoria followed him
down the steps to the cobblestone walk that ran along the river.
Orienting himself, Ramsey looked about, then searched off to his
right. Victoria could see what he saw—four or five fishermen
scattered at intervals along the riverbank.

"He's the nearest one, the one with the cowboy hat," said
Ramsey. He started along the bank, and she chased after him.
They went on for thirty yards, and as they neared the fisherman
with the broad-brimmed cowboy hat, Victoria could make out the
concave face of a brown-skinned youngish man, thin, seated
holding a bamboo pole and line, with a closed wicker basket next
to him.

Ramsey halted to light a cigarette and said to Victoria in an
undertone, "You can come along, but stay in the background.
Don't talk. I'll tell him you're my wife. Okay, let's go."

Ambling nonchalantly, dragging on his cigarette, Ramsey approached the fisherman, with Victoria lagging to the rear.

Reaching the fisherman, Ramsey stopped at the basket. He looked
off. The rest of the fishermen were farther up the river, well out
of earshot. Ramsey pointed to the basket. "How's the catch
today, Ahmet?"

The swarthy young man in the cowboy hat and sweater shrugged.
"See for yourself."

Ramsey kneeled close to him and opened the basket. It was
empty.

Ahmet said quickly, "Who's the woman?"

"My wife."

"All right. Make it fast."

"Like last time," said Ramsey. "I need some information. Is
Carlos in Paris?"

"He could be."

"I'd like to know if he's planning anything soon."

"Impossible. Go away."

Ramsey did not move. "It would be worth ten thousand
dollars to know *something*."

For the first time Ahmet glanced up at Ramsey, as if to be sure he had heard right.

"Ten thousand dollars," Ramsey repeated.

Ahmet went back to his fishing. After an interlude of seconds, he spoke out of the corner of his mouth. "Tonight. Midnight. I phone you. Good-bye."

Ramsey straightened up, went back to Victoria, took her by the arm and started away.

"Get anything?" she whispered.

"A nibble," he said.

Early that evening, in a cheerful mood once more, Ramsey announced to Victoria that he had made reservations for them at Tong Yen, his favorite restaurant in Paris. It was a confined, yet airy place in the Rue Jean-Mermoz, a busy short thoroughfare off the Rond-Point. They were warmly received by the young Chinese proprietress, who kissed Ramsey on each cheek and seated them in a large booth downstairs. Ramsey refused scotch but had a Chinese beer, letting Victoria taste it from his glass. He ordered for both of them—won ton soup, spareribs, deep-fried chopped beef and onions, and jasmine tea.

They were in their hotel suite before eleven o'clock, pretending to be interested in this morning's *International Herald Tribune* and the London *Telegraph*, listening for the sound of the telephone.

At eight minutes before midnight the telephone rang sharply, several times, until Ramsey lifted the receiver.

"Ramsey here."

"It is Ahmet."

"Hello, Ahmet."

"I could find out nothing from my main source."

"Too bad, but—"

"There is something else."

"Yes, go on, go on," Ramsey urged him.

"I have heard something interesting from another source that I will tell in person."

"Good, very good."

"California Hotel," said Ahmet. "Five o'clock tomorrow afternoon. Room 110. Door will be unlocked."

"Five o'clock, I'll be there."

"Not you. Send your wife. She will bring the money in cash, American dollars."

"Okay, she'll be there."

"Room 110. Do not forget."

"No, no, don't worry, I won't forget. Thanks, Ahmet."

Ramsey bent down to replace the receiver on the hook, and pivoted to meet Victoria's inquiring gaze.

"We may have something," he said.

"Tell me what, Nick. Don't be exasperating."

Ramsey was lighting a cigarette. "Ahmet said, 'I could find out nothing from my main source.' Meaning his girl in the Carlos group. Then he said, 'I have heard something interesting from another source that I will tell in person.' He said he will be waiting in Room 110 of the California Hotel—"

"Where's that?"

"A block and a half off the Champs-Élysées in the Rue de Berri. It's a nice old commercial hotel. He wants you to make the contact—'Send your wife,' he said—Room 110, first floor European style, second floor our style, and he said the door would be unlocked. He also said, 'She will bring the money in cash, American dollars.' We'll pick up the money in the morning. I have Armstead's authorization for this. Then you'll deliver it at five o'clock *after* Ahmet tells you what he's found out."

"What do you think he's found out?"

"Some hint of Carlos's next move, I hope."

"God, I'm nervous."

"Let me treat you to a drink." He started for the refrigerator.

"Maybe this could be our big break, Nick."

"Sure. The Pulitzer, at least."

*   *   *

The time was six minutes to five o'clock in the afternoon when they arrived at the entrance to the California Hotel.

They paused briefly under the glass canopy of the hotel while Victoria took the compact out of her leather purse, snapped it open, examined herself in the mirror. She licked her upper lip, put away her compact, pushed back a strand of her long blond hair.

She became aware that Ramsey was eyeing her critically. "What's the matter?" she wanted to know.

"Next time, do your hair up in a bun or something before we go out," he said.

"Why? Is it unattractive to you?"

"The opposite. The long hair attracts too much attention. You don't look like a wife—or an undercover agent."

"I'm neither," she snapped, but he had her arm and was leading her inside.

The stretch of lobby, caught between day and night, was dusky. They went past the nearest desk, where a uniformed concierge was marking directions on a map of Paris for a tourist, on past the reception desk largely obscured by a registering company of Japanese, to the metal grille of the elevator.

Ramsey pressed the button. "Remember, this is the ground or first floor. You'll find Room 110 on the next floor."

"Nick, I've been to Paris as many times as you have. I know how they count floors here."

"Sorry. Now, when you get to his room the door will be unlocked. Go straight in. You have the money?"

She patted her swollen purse. "Right here. Nick, what if he's not there? Do I hang around?"

"No, come back." He watched the elevator descending. "Don't worry, Ahmet will be there."

"I'm to write down what he has to say first, and then I'll pay him."

"You've got it."

"What if—if his information isn't anything much?"

"Pay him anyway. He'll mean well. We want to keep the contact."

The elevator had ground into place. Ramsey opened the grilled outer gate to let her inside. About to enter, she said, "Nick, where will I meet you?"

His head indicated an archway behind him. "The dining room and bar are back there. I'll be in the bar." He closed the grille. "Push the button for the first floor. Good luck."

She saw his comforting figure disappear as the elevator rose and seconds later jarred to a halt at the first floor. She left it, read the sequence of room numbers, and walked down the dim corridor to Room 110.

The door was closed. She wondered whether she should rap. She gripped the doorknob and turned it. The door opened. She stepped inside the bedroom and closed the door.

The old-fashioned room was obscured in shadow, no windows except the drape-covered french doors undoubtedly overlooking a court below. She could hear the monotonous splashing of a fountain in the court. Some sparse illumination was coming from a low-wattage bulb in the lamp standing between the door and a large brass double bed. She could make out a mirrored green-painted armoire and a stiff settee covered in maroon velour. The room seemed unoccupied, and then her gaze lighted on him. He was on the other side of the bed, in an armchair, bent forward, apparently changing his shoes.

"Ahmet," she called out, "it's Mrs. Ramsey—"

She went around the brass bed, unclasping her purse to bring out her notebook and pen, and was halfway there when she became aware of the silence. He had not acknowledged her.

"Ahmet," she said again, and stopped midway, waiting for his response.

Silence.

He had not moved, not straightened up to greet her. He was immobile.

She edged several steps closer to him. She could see him clearly now, the top of his head, his shoulders.

The hilt of the knife stuck in his back.

She strangled her scream. Her body went numb. She froze. The one sound in the room seemed to be her thumping heartbeat.

"Oh, God," she gasped.

At once, cold fear. Was there someone else in the room? The assassin? She animated herself to find him. There was no one, just herself and the corpse.

She forced herself unsteadily nearer until she could make out the darkish drying blotches around the knife, everywhere around his torn sweater, numerous stab wounds.

She backed off, willed herself to kneel so that she could see his face, to make out if he was still alive. His eyes were white sunken ovals in his brown flesh, the pupils almost gone, the eyes sightless. The mouth hung gaping, a thick trickle of blood from it clotted on his chin.

Horror-stricken, she recoiled to an upright position, spun about on rubbery legs, her foot hitting the cowboy hat on the carpet, and rushed to the door. At the last moment, conditioned by years of murder-mystery movies and novels, she held back, hunting in her purse for a handkerchief. With shaking hand she wiped her fingerprints from the doorknob, pulled the door open, searching to left and right in the corridor. There was no one in sight. She stepped into the hall, shut the door after her, and wiped the knob on the outside of the door.

Trying to regain her poise, she fled.

A half hour later, still trembling, she was in the secure haven of the Plaza Athénée suite with Ramsey. Pouring herself a straight gin at the refrigerator, drinking it, she could hear Ramsey on the telephone with New York. He had awakened Edward Armstead at his private home number, and had been telling him of the informant contacted and the informant found dead.

Victoria continued drinking as she walked into the sitting room of the suite.

Ramsey was saying into the telephone, "Okay, Mr. Armstead, we'll stay in place until we hear from you. Good-bye." He hung up.

"I—I've never seen a dead person before," Victoria said.

Ramsey sat on the sofa, staring at the carpet. "I guess Carlos has given us his answer," he said. "Armstead says stay away, research other terrorist groups, until we hear from him with a definite assignment." Ramsey looked up at Victoria. "You've never seen anyone dead before? You'll see more." He placed his flattened hands on his knees, pushed himself up and off the sofa. He reached for Victoria's glass and took a swallow, and handed it back. "I'd better have a couple on my own. And your hair— yes, do it up next time."

The reality of the murder in faraway Paris had not penetrated Edward Armstead's mind until that evening at dinner in New York.

He had invited Harry Dietz to join him at Nanni Al Valletto after work. It was a cozy, quiet Italian restaurant on Sixty-first Street, not far off Park Avenue and a short walk from the office. It was a nice place to talk, and Armstead wanted to talk tonight to the one person in the world he could fully trust. He guessed that it might be the most important talk he had ever had with anyone in his life.

Watching Dietz being served, Armstead regarded his confidant with affection. He knew full well now that Dietz's dedication to him was the meaning of Dietz's life. Before embarking on this crucial conversation, Armstead once more assessed his associate's loyalty and their relationship to each other. Dietz's selfish, disinterested mother, a spare hatchet of a woman, had raised her son through correspondence with a series of boarding school headmasters. Dietz had grown loveless and friendless to maturity, and not until Armstead (who understood such deprivation) had seen valuable qualities in him, and given him a job in Chicago that provided faith and respect, had Deitz been so close to another

human being. From the start, Armstead had perceived, Dietz had
loved him, even worshipped him, and would have done anything
to please him, even kill his own mother (whom he hated, anyway) or himself for the authority figure who had given him
identity and purpose. In turn, welcoming a subordinate who
could be an ally, a sounding board, an errand boy, Armstead had
been unfailingly considerate of his assistant. Both men understood that their relationship gave each of them *someone,* and it
worked. Now that Armstead had at last come to a position of
power, inherited a great enterprise, he felt that he had the confidential companion and alter ego he would require readily at hand
and groomed for a great role.

Yes, Armstead reassured himself, his plan was safe with Harry
Dietz.

Not until he was consuming his spaghetti—Armstead had ordered spaghetti and meat sauce for his entire entrée—did he
begin to relate to Dietz what had happened to Ramsey and
Victoria in Paris.

"The informant had something about Carlos that he was ready
to pass on to Ramsey for the money," Armstead was saying.
"The informant wanted Victoria to be the go-between. So she
went up to this hotel room and found the informant all right, only
he couldn't tell her anything. He was sitting there dead, murdered."

Harry Dietz's eyebrows shot up. "No kidding? Murdered?"

"Stabbed between the shoulder blades. Stone cold dead. There
was nothing Victoria could do but get out of there fast. Empty-
handed." Armstead brought a napkin to his lips, replaced it
neatly across his lap. "That's the big leagues we wandered into,
Harry. They play for keeps."

"They sure do."

"I knew it was for real from the beginning," said Armstead,
eating once more, "yet I didn't. It was an assignment. Even the
murder sounded like a paper murder. But it's finally got to me.
That was a human being they killed."

"It was, Chief."

"It also made me realize that they were sending me a message. Stay away. Don't poke around in Carlos's affairs. Unless you want to get killed, too."

"I guess that's the message."

"With no uncertainty," said Armstead. "And I'm sure every other active terrorist group will have the same message for us."

"No question," agreed Dietz.

"That's what gave me my great idea," said the publisher. "That's why I wanted to have this talk with you tonight."

"What do you have in mind, Chief?"

"A tremendous idea. Actually I got the idea, the glimmerings of it, after our Yinger beat. The Yinger success made me realize that exclusive stories don't just happen. You have to make them happen, the way we did, and that way we trounced the *Times* and every paper in town." He rested his fork and tablespoon on the plate and leaned closer to his assistant. "You see, Harry, even before sending Ramsey and the Weston girl to Paris, I anticipated that nothing positive would come of their investigation. I sensed right away that no terrorist group anywhere would give us anything. But I wanted to be certain. That's why I sent our reporters over there. To find out. So they found out all right."

"They sure as hell did."

"Terrorist groups do their own thing for whatever reasons. They're not interested in us or our problems. To them, we're only obstructionists. They prefer to be on their own. Once they do what they plan to do, it is news of course, big news, but it is news that every paper in the world publishes at the same time. Those terrorists are not handing out exclusives to anyone."

"They're useless," said Dietz.

"Exactly," said Armstead. "Just the way most of the upcoming news is useless for our purposes. I was going through our future file the other day to see what's coming up. There's a lot coming up, certainly. The king of Spain is scheduled for a visit to the Basque country. There's going to be a nuclear disarmament conference in Switzerland. The prime minister of Israel

is arranging for another meeting in Cairo. There's talk of the
Pope going to Lourdes. All of it news. None of it exclusive.
We'll report it, the New York *Times* will report it, everyone will
report it. Some papers will exaggerate or distort their stories to
make them seem newsier, exclusive, but none of them will be.
They'll all be exactly the same stuff in print and on TV."
Armstead unpeeled a cigar, and pointed it toward Dietz. "Harry,
there's no real news—unless you make it yourself."

"I'm trying to follow you, Chief."

"Follow me closely. The whole impact of it, of what should
be done, hit me last night after I finished screwing Kim. How did
we get the big beat on Yinger? By making it happen, by making
it become our exclusive news. You saw the results. We zoomed
to the top. I saw at once that I had to pick up where I left off with
that one. I thought of trying to work with some well-known
terrorist group. I had a gut feeling that this was the wrong way to
go. Now my feeling has been confirmed. It is the wrong way to go.
But there's a right way. It is this: When there is no exclusive
news—you invent it. When a story happens, it's your own. Do
you get the idea, Harry?"

"Vaguely. How—how do you make it happen, Chief?"

"By having your own terrorist group to make news for you,"
said Armstead quietly. "The existing groups won't cooperate. So
we buy our own. Our own does what we tell it to do. The news it
creates is exclusively our own. That could keep us Number One
in New York and make us the top-selling paper in the world.
What do you think, Harry? Is it harebrained? Yinger wasn't. Is
this?"

Dietz was shaking his head vigorously. "Absolutely not, Chief.
It *is* a big idea, the biggest. A perfect concept. I think you're on
the right track, but—" He hesitated.

"But what?" Armstead wanted to know.

"Can it be done?"

"It *has* been done—with Yinger."

"I mean, getting a terrorist group. Where do we start?"

"With Gus Pagano," Armstead said instantly. "That's where we start. Presuming we still have the goods on him."

"We have."

Armstead smiled complacently and held a flame to his cigar. "Then that's where we start."

All through the night, Edward Armstead slept and awakened with the notion that he was onto something earth-shattering, a big idea that Gus Pagano could make possible. The immediate question was: Did Pagano have any important criminal connections or would he be acquainted with only the underworld small-fry? Given the important criminal connections, the more vital question was: Could he be trusted?

Then Armstead remembered the file folder on Pagano that Dietz had left for him. Having read it, Armstead *knew* that Pagano could be trusted. Reassured, he had fallen into a sound sleep.

Early the next morning, Armstead received Pagano in his office. Armstead knew that he would have to be frank with Pagano, but at the outset he was satisfied to nurse the informer along. They were drinking the coffee that had been placed on the desk between them. They had little in common with each other except for the fact that Pagano was on the payroll of the *Record*, so they talked about that.

Armstead was becoming increasingly impatient with the point-less chatter, and made up his mind to be direct and candid. He drained his coffee cup and put it down.

"Gus," he said, "I want to discuss something important with you. But I must be assured from the start of your loyalty to me."

Pagano's beaky countenance was bland. "You pay good. That's my loyalty."

"I can pay better," said Armstead, "much better."

"You have my *complete* loyalty. You mean, can you say something to me that's strictly between us? You can."

"Not enough," said Armstead. "I need more. I have to be absolutely positive that you are one hundred percent trustworthy."

Pagano sat up, curious. "Meaning what?"

"Meaning this." Armstead reached for the folder on his desk and opened it. "Whenever we hire anyone, we set up a dossier on him. And we keep it up to date. When we hired you as an informant, we set up such a dossier." He glanced up at Pagano. "And we've kept it up to date." He dropped his gaze to the contents of the folder once more. "The Acme Jewelers on Lexington. There was a stickup there two years ago. There was some shooting. Ring a bell?"

Pagano made no reply. He sat sullenly staring at the publisher.

"During the shooting, in the cross fire, a customer was killed—the widow of a well-known millionaire—and a guard was wounded, but the guard managed to kill the stickup man."

"What are you saying?" said Pagano. "I've never killed anyone in my life."

"I never implied you had," said Armstead with feigned innocence. "I'm merely saying a stickup man named Restell shot a woman to death during a holdup, and in turn he was shot to death. I'm also saying Restell had an accomplice. The accomplice got away. He was never caught. Because this was a big-name killing, one of my father's better crime reporters followed through. The reporter spent a lot of time with the jewelry shop guard showing him photographs of criminals on parole or with records. The guard identified one positively as the accomplice. The picture was of a man named Gus Pagano."

Pagano did not stir, did not even blink. He remained silent.

"We could have turned this over to the police," said Armstead, "got a minor story out of it, and the accomplice would have wound up back in jail. For a long time, I'm sure. But my father did not want to have the paper's good name tarnished by having one of its employees mixed up with a tawdry bit of violence. My father chose to confine the information to this private dossier. I hope to keep it there."

Armstead waited.

Pagano wriggled to reach the cigarette package in his pocket. He shook a cigarette loose, and calmly lighted it. He blew out some smoke, squinted through the smoke, and offered a half smile. "Mr. Armstead, you want to know if I'm one hundred percent trustworthy." He skipped a beat. "Mr. Armstead, I'm two hundred percent trustworthy."

Armstead's face was wreathed in a smile. "Good. Very good." He cast aside the folder. "We will never refer to this matter again," Satisfied, Armstead was prepared to plunge ahead with no further hesitation. "Let's begin with this," he said. "Do you know any gangs?"

"Gangs?" Pagano showed his surprise and relief at what he evidently regarded as an unexpected and childish question. "Mr. Armstead, I grew up with gangs—in the Bronx, Brooklyn, New Jersey—"

"No, no," Armstead interrupted, "not street gangs. I am speaking of international gangs."

"I—I'm afraid I don't get you."

Armstead tried again. "Terrorist-type gangs who work abroad."

"Oh, those," said Pagano, "like those Red Brigade kooks in Italy? Naw, I don't know any of them."

Armstead's heart fell.

Pagano was going on. "But international, like you said—yeah, I do have some connections to one outfit. It's not in Italy, though."

"I don't give a damn where it is. All right, where is it?"

"In London. They're not exactly what you'd call terrorists."

"What are they?"

Pagano was momentarily confused by semantics. "Maybe you could call them top-level crooks. When they need money, they get together and pull off a job."

"A job?"

"Like a robbery."

This offered a tantalizing possibility. "Little or big robberies?"

Pagano was positive now. "Oh, fat stuff, juicy ones."

Better. "And you have some connection with that gang?"

"Sure thing. It's through another Green Haven graduate—guy named Krupinski. For good behavior, he was assigned to the farm outside the wall. Not being a rural type, he got bored. So one day he skipped out. Krupinski made it all the way to London. He needed money. He had some introductions. He contacted the Cooper gang. Being a good man with dynamite, bombs, Krupinski was a natural for them. They took him on. I had a postcard from him not long ago. He's still in London. Even invited me over."

"Did you consider going?"

"Naw. I got a legal passport, you understand, but I don't want to live with foreigners. Besides, I have this steady job with you. Why go with them?"

Armstead lifted himself from behind the desk and went thoughtfully to the coffee table. He found a cigar in the humidor and readied it as he returned to his desk. "Gus, who's in it?"

"What?"

"This London gang. Who is in it?"

"It's a loose outfit that gets together every once in a while to plan and pull off a big job in England or in France. They're not amateurs. They've got savvy, and what you call credits. One of them goes way back to the Brink's robbery in Boston. There were seven of them wearing Halloween masks. They hit the Brink's building, the vault, for almost three million. A couple of them had a part in the Glasgow-to-London night mail train robbery. That took nineteen members of two gangs to pull off. That's the one that involved Ronnie Biggs—the guy who was caught, and escaped, and used a French plastic surgeon to fix him—he got away to Brazil, where he was abducted by British security people and taken out of the country, then returned to South America. That was a seven-million-dollar job."

"Not bad," said Armstead, impressed.

"There was better," said Pagano, warming to his subject. "There was the—I don't know if I can pronounce it right—the

Société Générale bank heist in Nice, in France, where they used the city sewer system to get into the bank, spent the weekend inside, emptied 317 safe-deposit boxes, made off with twelve million dollars.''

Armstead was definitely impressed. ''And you say some members of the Cooper gang in London were in on those—uh, jobs.''

''Absolutely. A real big-time crowd.''

''How many are there in this Cooper gang?''

''About a dozen, Krupinski told me last year. He was over here for a week to see his old lady who was sick. Headman is this Cooper, an American now British. Krupinski says he's a wizard brain. Then there's another dozen of them either on the lam in other countries or still serving time in jail. They're all pros at forging, safecracking, bombing, robberies. They're not interested in politics. Only in money. Lots of it.''

Armstead smiled. ''I have lots of it.''

Pagano also smiled. ''Yeah, I heard.''

''And I'm not interested in politics, either,'' said Armstead.

Pagano's eyes held on the publisher shrewdly. ''What are you interested in?''

''News.''

Pagano tried to make sense of it. ''News,'' he echoed. ''You've got me kind of lost. I don't know what you mean.''

''I mean I'm interested in making news—creating it—for my newspapers and television stations. I need exclusive news for my papers and TV news network.'' He paused. ''A gang could create that kind of news for me.''

Pagano tried to absorb it, and wagged his head slightly. ''That's kind of—'' He did not want to sound disrespectful. ''—far out.''

''You mean crazy?''

''I don't know. I suppose there is a business side to it. But it's far out.''

They were down to bare bones, Armstead decided. Now he would go all the way. ''You gave me the original idea,'' he said to Pagano, ''with the lead about Yinger's tunnel. That led to

Yinger's escape. It was a set-up happening, an invented one. And I had it all to myself. Yes, it was good business, the best. It doubled the circulation of my newspaper here in New York, and it upped the circulation of my other newspapers around the country, and it hyped the attention given the story on television stations everywhere. That gave me the idea of setting up and creating more news. Do I make myself a little clearer, Gus?''

''Yeah,'' said Pagano, with slight uncertainty. ''I'm catching on.''

''You see,'' Armstead tried to explain, ''there's not enough hard news around, exclusive news. Usually my competitors have the same thing to sell that I have. But we here want our news alone. Since it's not around, we might have to invent some of it. That's my big idea.''

''For that, you need a gang?''

''Who can pull off big jobs for only the New York *Record* to write about. To put it bluntly, I need an outfit of experienced, organized thugs to do what they do best. I want them to work for me full time. I want them to make news for me. No killing, no murdering. But a hijacking, a sensational robbery, most of all a name kidnapping. High-class stuff. Front-page caliber.''

This was closer to Pagano's area, and he understood completely. ''This could be dangerous.''

''So is deep-sea diving and riding a space capsule.''

''People'll be putting up their lives for—for news.''

''For money.'' Armstead enunciated each word. ''The Cooper gang wants money, you said. I've got money.''

''What kind of money would you be talking about?''

''Maybe three million dollars a job.''

Pagano emitted a low whistle.

''Think they'd be interested?'' Armstead wanted to know.

''Depends what you want them to do. But three mill. Yeah, they'd be interested.''

''Of course, I don't want them to know who I am. They must not know whom they are working for—or why. I want to assign them jobs—through you. No questions to be asked. I want the jobs done professionally, cleanly. For each job they'll get paid. You believe they'll be interested?"

"I'm guessing. I think so."

"Can you find out for sure?"

"You mean make contact with Cooper?"

"Yes."

"I can make contact," said Pagano.

"Then make it," said Armstead. It was an order. "There'll be plenty in it for you, Gus. Go to London and find out if they'll cooperate."

"You sound like you mean right away."

"I mean tonight. I'll make arrangements for you. I expect to hear from you in forty-eight hours."

At eleven o'clock in the evening, two days later, Armstead received his call.

He had just walked through the door of his Fifth Avenue penthouse overlooking Central Park when Hannah, from her wheelchair, a telephone receiver in her hand, raised her voice. "Is that you, Edward?"

"It's me."

"There's a long-distance call for you. From London."

Armstead's heart quickened. "Tell them to call me back on my private line. I'll take it in my study."

He yanked off his raincoat, threw it aside, hurried to his study, let himself in, and carefully relocked his door from the inside. He strode to the white telephone, his very private telephone that had an unlisted number different from the one for the other rooms of the penthouse. He waited a few moments for the phone to ring. Finally it rang.

Hastily he lifted the receiver. "Hello."

A female operator's voice. "Is this Mr. Armstead?"

"Yes, this is Edward Armstead."

"Mr. Pagano calling from London, person-to-person."

"Okay, put Mr. Pagano on."

The line from London crackled, but Pagano's voice came on distinctly. "You there, boss?"

"Hi, Gus. Okay, what's the word?"

"All signals Go."

"All signals Go. What does that mean?"

"Cooper is definitely interested," said Pagano. "But there's just one thing—"

"They *are* interested, you say—but what?"

"They want to meet with you in person, over here. I think they want to know exactly what you have in mind for them. We can fix it so's you won't be recognized. If it's not too much trouble, I think it would be worth—"

"It's not too much trouble," Armstead cut in. "If they want to see me first, I'll see them. I'll be there."

"Can you make it by tomorrow?"

"Yes, tomorrow's okay. I'll take the Concorde. I'll get on the first flight."

"If you'll let me know your arrival time, I'll meet you at Heathrow. Set you up for a suite in the Ritz."

"I'll let you know the time. You'll meet me at Heathrow? Fine. The suite at the Ritz is also fine."

"You won't be bringing anybody along?"

"Bringing anybody? No, don't worry. I'll be alone. See you tomorrow."

He hung up slowly.

He felt exultant.

He was almost—almost—in the terrorist business for himself.

6

The chauffeured black Rolls-Royce turned off Piccadilly, moved around the block to draw up before the Arlington Street side entrance of the Ritz Hotel in London.

Gus Pagano quickly stepped out of the car, with Edward Armstead right behind him. The doorman tried to take Armstead's Mark Cross bag and wardrobe, but Pagano insisted on carrying them himself. The evening was chilly, and they ascended the steps and hastened into the warmth of the hotel lobby.

Pagano guided Armstead away from the registration alcove to their left. "I've already registered you under my name, Mr. Armstead. We better go straight to your suite."

They proceeded through the long lobby, turned right to the waiting elevator, and rode up to the fifth floor. Rounding a corner, they arrived at 518, Armstead's suite. After getting rid of his hat and light topcoat, Armstead was eager to learn more about what lay ahead. At Heathrow Airport they had hardly been able to talk, since the hired chauffeur had joined them almost immediately. After that, during the drive to London, even though the chauffeur's window partition was closed Pagano had cautioned his employer against conversation.

Now, in the Ritz suite parlor, at 9:35, Armstead was at last able to ask Pagano, "How interested are they?"

"I'd say Cooper was very interested. Enough to tell me to bring you over to London right away. The three-million-dollar paycheck hooked him."

"You did tell him I'd pay that much for *each* job?"

"Yeah, I sure did. That's what got him. But he's not sewed up yet, boss. He wants to meet you, hear it from you exactly what you got in mind."

"I'm ready if he is," said Armstead. "When do we meet?"

"Now."

"Where?" Armstead wanted to know.

"Here," said Pagano. "Next door. I reserved a two-bedroom-and-living-room suite for you. They're in the other bedroom, waiting for you."

For the first time since his arrival Armstead felt a surge of anticipation, the kind a leading man must feel when the curtain goes up on a Broadway first night, or a football player feels before a crucial kickoff. There was also something else inside him, a pulsating curiosity to meet live terrorists in person, not actually terrorists yet but widely feared, successful criminals, men who inhabited a secretly populated world outside the law.

"How many of them are there?" Armstead asked.

"Should be Cooper and two of his aides. I showed Cooper to the room, and he said he expected two more of his crowd to join him. That was when I went to meet you at Heathrow. By now they should all be there." Pagano studied his employer. "Maybe you want to rest a few minutes first? I mean, you just got off the plane."

"It was no more tiring than taking a car across midtown Manhattan."

"So you're ready to see Cooper and his men?"

"I'm ready."

Pagano held up a hand. "Not quite," he said. He reached inside his sports jacket. There had been some object bulking it up behind the breast pocket. Pagano removed the object and handed it to Armstead.

"What's this?" said Armstead, flattening it out. "Looks like a ski mask."

"A *passe-montagne*," said Pagano. "A mountain climber's mask. Also, a ski mask. Better put it on if you don't want no one to recognize you. It's a little warm, but it'll hide your face."

Armstead gave Pagano an appreciative nod. "You're on the ball, Gus." He pulled the woolen mask over his head. Armstead stepped to the entry hall mirror and viewed his reflection. "Grotesque but efficient."

"Okay, let's get in there," said Pagano.

He unlocked the door to the second bedroom and pushed it aside. Armstead entered awkwardly and tried to get his bearings. The large room had been darkened except for a few lamps. There were two isolated folding chairs past the bed at one end of the room. Facing them were an armchair and a sofa bearing male occupants, each man in tie and jacket. None wore masks.

A rangy man with matted hair, hooded brown eyes, a drooping brown mustache, and a gaunt, seamed, expressionless face uncurled from the sofa, straightened his tweed jacket and came forward, hand extended. "I'm Cooper."

Pagano quickly introduced Armstead. "My boss."

"Walter Zimberg," announced Armstead, "for purposes of identification." He shook hands. "Glad to meet you." Cooper pointed to the other two in the bedroom, giving their names almost indistinctly. "Krupinski . . . Quiggs." He added, "If necessary, you'll meet the rest of our board of directors later—De Salvo, Overly, Shields, Lafair. Now we might as well get down to business." He headed back to the sofa and took a seat.

Armstead sat gingerly, well to the front of his folding chair, while Pagano occupied the chair beside him.

Armstead cleared his throat. "You all know the reason for this meeting?"

"Let's be certain that we have it right," said Cooper. "You want to hire an experienced organization in order to instigate a series of actions. You are ready to pay three million dollars for each individual action."

"Correct," said Armstead.

"We won't ask you why you want these jobs done," said Cooper. "That's your business."

"It's not political," said Armstead hastily.

"No matter," replied Cooper. "Before we can determine if we will work for you, we must know exactly what you want done. Does this involve murder?"

Armstead was horrified. "Absolutely not," he answered quickly. His woolen mask was beginning to itch. He clasped a hand more tightly against one thigh. The bland use of the word "murder" had unnerved him. He tried to recover his poise, his voice, his prepared speech. "I'm mainly interested in kidnapping," he announced. "Maybe robbery later. But the first job is a kidnapping. I want you to abduct a well-known person, keep him in hiding two days, demand a ransom—not too large a sum, a reasonable amount that can be raised and paid easily—you can keep the sum, the payoff. I told you this is not political, but I think it would be smart to make it look political, maybe instead of money ask for the release of a political prisoner, some minor radical figure. You'd free the kidnap victim after two days, because I want to lessen the risk of your getting caught. An important consideration is that Gus Pagano must be added to your organization as my representative. He will help you when he can; mainly he is to act as my liaison man, be accountable strictly to me. If this can be done, I'll be satisfied."

"Where does our first action happen?" inquired Cooper.

"San Sebastián, Spain," said Armstead.

"When?"

"Two weeks from tomorrow."

There was a pause. "Who do we kidnap?" Cooper asked.

Armstead held his breath, then blew it out of the mouth slit in his mask. He kept his voice even. "You kidnap the king of Spain," he said.

There followed what seemed an interminable silence.

Cooper broke it. "We'll have to talk about that," he said. "You go back next door. We'll call you when we are ready."

For Armstead, it was a restless hour's wait. Removing his mask, he wanted to call for room service. Pagano thought that it would be unwise to have a waiter around. Armstead undressed, busied himself taking a shower, dressed again. He unlocked his suitcase and extracted a manila folder, reviewing a number of alternate possibilities should the offer to the Cooper gang fall through. None was as promising as the Cooper connection, and Armstead prayed that it would work out. He was absently leafing through a London magazine when he heard the loud knock on the door to the second bedroom.

"It's Cooper," called a muffled voice. "You can come back in."

Pagano caught Armstead's shoulder. "Don't forget your mask. Put it on."

Armstead did so.

They were in the darkened second bedroom once more, and Cooper was confronting them with a stocky, short, pimply young Englishman in tow. "This is Quiggs, you remember," said Cooper. "He's the one with the most experience of Spain. In fact, he has a summer residence there. He'll take over. He has a few more questions."

Cooper returned to the sofa. Quiggs waited for Armstead and Pagano to reach their places. Once they were seated, he pulled a free folding chair closer to them and sat in it.

Quiggs spoke in a high-pitched nasal voice. "This is no simple assignment," he began.

"That's why I want experts," said Armstead mildly.

"Oh, the kidnapping itself might not be too difficult," said Quiggs with the confident air of a professional. "Ordinarily the snatch itself is a matter of preparation—deployment of members to create a diversion, to block traffic, to transfer the victim to an escape vehicle, to reach a predesignated hideout, to have shifts of guards, to negotiate. But the assignment you've requested is a more dangerous one."

"Aren't they all dangerous?" challenged Armstead. "Isn't that the risk entailed in any effort?"

Quiggs would not be baited. "This assignment is more dangerous than most because it will take place in Basque country. The king of Spain will mount heavy security against any attack by the Basque separatists, the ETA."

"I should think that would be in your favor," said Armstead. "The Spanish police will be watching out for the ETA. They'll give less attention to a sprinkling of curious foreign tourists. Any attack from ordinary British tourists is likely to be unexpected."

Quiggs agreed. "Yes, we've discussed all that." He hesitated. "Have you heard of the Blanco affair?"

Armstead knitted his brow beneath the warm wool mask. "The Blanco affair?"

"An ETA operation," said Quiggs. "We might be wise to imitate it, and let the Basques take the heat. We suggest this as an alternative plan that in some respects, might be easier to implement."

"Blanco affair," repeated Armstead. "I'm not sure I remember."

"Admiral Luis Carrero Blanco. He was prime minister of Spain. The Basque separatists wanted to get him. They observed that Blanco was a creature of habit. He drove his Dodge Dart through central Madrid on the same route daily. The Basques rented a basement along the route, patiently dug a tunnel under the street—"

Tunnel. Armstead listened more intently. There had been a tunnel involving Yinger. It sounded lucky. "Go on," said Armstead.

"The Basques imported over one hundred pounds of dynamite from the IRA, who had acquired it from the terrorist Carlos," Quiggs went on. "They planted it in the tunnel under the street. When Prime Minister Blanco drove over the spot, the Basques detonated the dynamite. The explosion blew the prime minister and his Dodge Dart up over a five-story building, a church I think. It was an extremely successful operation, and in some ways easier than a kidnapping."

Armstead peered through the slits of his mask at the stocky speaker. For the first time he fully realized that he was not dealing with mild and gentlemanly romantic robbers. He was dealing with cold-blooded killers. He was shaken. "Wait a minute," he forced himself to say. "Are you suggesting we try to blow up the king of Spain?"

"Just a thought," said Quiggs ingenuously.

"Christ, no," blurted Armstead. "I told you right off—no murder. I just want a—a harmless kidnapping."

"As you say," said Quiggs good-naturedly. "A kidnapping it is. But again, more complicated, more dangerous. We think it's too dangerous for three million dollars."

"I see. All right, exactly what sum would make it worthwile for you?"

Quiggs glanced over his shoulder at Cooper, and directed himself at Armstead again. "We could do it for five million," said Quiggs.

"You want five million dollars for one job," said Armstead, to be sure he had heard it right.

"We can guarantee a helluva job," said Quiggs. "The payment from you, that's not all. There are other conditions and costs."

"Name them," said Armstead nervously.

Quiggs looked behind him. "You better take over, Coop." Cooper rose and exchanged places with his confederate. "We have a force of exactly twelve men in London," said Cooper. "For this kind of operation we might need closer to twenty. We know where we can recruit eight more—some are in hiding, in exile, in retirement—all veterans. To get them in line quickly might take another half million American dollars. Of course, this is a one-time-only expense. Once the personnel are with us, we'll have them available for any future assignments.''

"Anything else?"

"Weapons," said Cooper. "We have a fair supply of small arms, but for what you have in mind we'd have to be able to do better, depend on more firepower. We wouldn't need anything heavy. We'd require light, portable weapons. You'd have to supply them, preferably buy them from an individual dealer, not from a national source. Another one-time expense. Once we had the arsenal, we could use it over and over.''

For some unaccountable reason, Armstead was beginning to feel stimulated. "You tell me what you want. They shouldn't be hard to find.''

"We'll give Mr. Pagano a detailed list of what we need, as well as information on how and where we'll take delivery.''

Armstead tried to think of where to turn for weapons, and Nick Ramsey over in Paris came into his mind. Surely Ramsey would know where to turn, or be able to find out.

"Is that all?" asked Armstead.

"Not quite," said Cooper. "Normally we could handle what comes next ourselves. But the shortage of time involved makes it clear we will require some help. I refer to two items. One is reconnaissance. We must know the king's schedule in San Sebastián, so that we can study it and assess his vulnerability. We must also know the degree of his security during the visit. Every detail will be useful. Can you give us a hand on this?''

"I can," promised Armstead.

"One final matter. The five-million-dollar payment to us. We must have half of it in advance.''

"It will be done. Pagano will deliver the information on the king of Spain's schedule, his protection, and he will deliver half your payment. Be sure to tell him where to contact you. I will tell him where to contact me. Is that it? Are you ready to go?''

Cooper gave a tic of a smile. "We're ready to go."

Armstead stood up. "Let's consider ourselves in business."

When Victoria let herself into the Plaza Athénée suite, after a full afternoon of rummaging through the reference files of the *International Herald Tribune* at their offices in Neuilly, she realized that Ramsey was already there speaking to someone.

In the sitting room she found him on the telephone. He cupped his palm over the mouthpiece and handed her a written message.

"He's in London," Ramsey said.

"Who?" Then she saw that the phone message was from Edward Armstead, who had called and missed them earlier this afternoon. "Armstead at the Ritz," she said. "What's he doing in London?"

"I've a call in to him," said Ramsey. "We should know any second."

In a few seconds Armstead's gruff voice came on. "Hello."

"Mr. Armstead? This is Nick Ramsey in Paris. We just came in—"

"I was wondering when you'd return my call."

"We were both out doing some research on other groups."

"Never mind," said Armstead. "I had to fly over here to London on some business. Getting away from the office gave me a little time to think. I've been giving some thought to your terrorist series. One thought has come to mind particularly. I keep wondering where they get their arms."

"From nations, big and small, through go-betweens," said Ramsey.

"You mean, the United States sells weapons to terrorists?"

"Not exactly. But as a matter of fact, the United States is the biggest arms dealer in the world, followed by the Soviet Union, France, Great Britain, Italy, and West Germany. Of course, there is government arms control in those countries, and most of their export is in heavy weapons—airplanes, tanks, so forth. Terrorists are usually interested in smaller weapons.''

"How do terrorists get weapons from us or the Soviet Union?''

"Not directly, of course,'' said Ramsey. ''A big nation will sell weapons to Libya, Ethiopia, Belgium, Liechtenstein. They, in turn, may resell the arms to terrorist groups. I'd say most weapons arrive in the hands of terrorists that way.''

"Hold on there, Nick. You say *most* weapons get to terrorists that way, through countries. How do other weapons get to terrorists?''

"Through individuals or private arms dealers. The legendary merchants of death.''

"Individuals are in this business?'' asked Armstead.

"Yes, there are any number around.''

"I'd like to meet one, interview him,'' said Armstead. ''For our series.''

"Oh, you don't have to bother, Mr. Armstead. Vicky and I can find one of them to interview.''

"No,'' said Armstead firmly. ''I'd like to do it myself. Talk to one of those merchants, as one businessman to another. I find the idea fascinating. Also gives me a chance to keep my hand in, keep my journalist skills from getting rusty.''

Ramsey glanced at Victoria as he spoke into the telephone. "Very well. You want to interview a private arms dealer. When and where?''

"Wherever he is. When? Soon as possible. In two or three days, if you can arrange it.''

"We'll have to make some inquiries, learn who the best and most available dealer is.''

"Good,'' said Armstead. ''As soon as possible. Don't tell him who I am or that this is for a newspaper. Say you're setting up an appointment for a buyer, an anonymous buyer—no, better if I have a name. Say you're representing Walter Zimberg, an American businessman.''

"Walter Zimberg. Okay, Mr. Armstead. Vicky and I will get

on the ball tomorrow morning. Soon as we have someone you can see, I'll call you back.''

"No more calls," said Armstead, "not about this. When you've set it up, come straight over to London with the information. In the next two days. I'll wait for you at the Ritz."

"Okay, Mr. Armstead. See you in a day or two.''

Hanging up, Ramsey related to Victoria everything that Armstead had discussed.

"Well, I guess our next assignment is clear," said Ramsey.

"Where do we find a private arms dealer for him?" asked Victoria.

"That's not what bothers me. We'll get a lead from some of the correspondents in town or from old clips. What bothers me is—why the hustle for an interview on weapons when we haven't even got the terrorist series started yet? What's the big hurry all about?''

The big hurry did produce results. Despite his complaint, Nick Ramsey had to admit that.

By late the following evening Ramsey and Victoria Weston were in London, were in the Ritz with Edward Armstead, who was pleased with their speed.

"I've reserved two single bedrooms for you for overnight, and you can check in downstairs when we're through here," said Armstead, propping himself on the sofa with his martini in one hand. "Pour yourselves drinks."

Ramsey went to the tray atop the television set and poured himself a straight scotch. Victoria refused a drink.

Now, gathered around the coffee table, Armstead seemed almost benign. "I received the Telex that you were on your way here. I assume you found someone reliable, and you've arranged an interview for me."

"We found several big-time arms dealers," said Ramsey. "But I think Vicky has the man you really want to meet."

Victoria spoke. "Everyone agreed he's the best," she said.

"He's the most important in the trade since Zaharoff. He's Helmut Middendorf in Frankfurt. I spoke to him on the phone. He'll see you, Mr. Armstead. He said he'll see you if you're serious."

"How do I prove I am serious?" asked Armstead.

Ramsey intervened. "By proving you have a Swiss bank account. All those arms merchants insist on that. You must have a Swiss bank account."

"I have one," said Armstead.

"In your name?" asked Ramsey.

"In the name of Walter Zimberg."

"The name Victoria used for you," said Ramsey. "Perfect."

"When do I go to Frankfurt?" asked Armstead.

"You don't," said Victoria. "Mr. Middendorf went to Antibes today for his vacation. He's at the Hôtel du Cap d'Antibes. He'll see you there."

"What day? What time?"

"The day after tomorrow at eleven in the morning. You go to the Hôtel du Cap."

"I've been there before."

"If it's a sunny day, he'll be down by the pool. He'll be poolside, in a lounge chair to the left of the clubhouse entrance, with a bare-breasted girl on a pad beside him."

Armstead smirked. "Rich old men with young girls, breasts unsheathed, that's routine for the Hôtel du Cap. A number of scenes like that on the Riviera."

Victoria looked down at the protrusion of her breasts against her blouse, and shook her head. "Anyway—" She determined to return to the business on hand. "You spot them. Mr. Middendorf described himself as a hairless—meaning bald—fat, middle-aged man wearing tinted glasses, blue jock trunks, and smoking a pipe. He'll probably be reading a Swiss magazine. You go directly to him. The bare-breasted girl will leave and make way for you on her pad. You settle down next to him and show him the deposit book for your Swiss bank account. After that you're on your own. Don't forget, he thinks you're a buyer.''

"Good work, Victoria," said Armstead, pleased.

"One last thing. If it isn't a sunny day, if it's not poolside weather, buzz Mr. Middendorf in his suite. He'll be waiting one place or the other."

"Fine, Victoria."

"Mr. Armstead," said Ramsey, "maybe you'd like us to come to the Riviera with you. We might be of some help."

"No, thanks," said Armstead emphatically. "As a matter of fact, I have something else in mind for you and Victoria. I have a new assignment for you. I want you to go to San Sebastián, Spain, tomorrow. That's the coastal city in the Basque area."

"I lived there one summer," said Ramsey.

"All the better. In less than two weeks the king of Spain is going to be visiting San Sebastián for a day. I have a file of clippings on the table here. There's talk that the ETA—the Basque separatist movement—may go after him."

"I doubt it," said Ramsey flatly.

"Well, there could be some trouble from them," persisted Armstead.

"Never," said Ramsey. "The odds are that local security will be covering every Basque who looks suspicious. I don't think anything newsy will happen."

Armstead's reaction was one of fleeting annoyance. "I still say the event is worthy of coverage. At least we should give it an advance buildup indicating that the king is going into a hornet's nest of potential danger. I want you and Victoria down there not so much to see if anything happens or does not happen, but to get the *Record* advance material on two aspects of the visit."

"Whatever you say, Mr. Armstead," conceded Ramsey reluctantly.

"You, Nick, I want you to find out exactly what the security setup is in San Sebastián for the king's visit. Also, what the

Basque separatists are up to. I don't expect them to tell you. But you can poke around, discover what the talk is.''

"I'll do my best, Mr. Armstead.''

"As for you, Victoria, I want you to find out details of the king's schedule in San Sebastián. When he will be arriving and where. Is it a ceremonial visit? Will he tour the city? Where will he stop? Will there be any meeting with local political and religious leaders? Someone in San Sebastián should have all that for you. If you have any difficulty, get in touch with the government offices in Madrid.''

Victoria nodded. "I'll dredge up his itinerary somehow.''

"After I've had my weapons interview, I'll come back to London. I'll be here the rest of the week. You two file your reports with me Friday afternoon by phone. I'll be here in my suite with a stenographer. I want the royal visit treated as a news story. Nick, whatever else you come up with on the Basque separatists we can incorporate in the terrorist series. I'll take that back to New York along with my notes on my weapons interview. Is everything clear?''

Victoria stirred. "What do we do after Friday?''

"Oh, I want you to stay on in San Sebastián until the king has come and gone. Just in case something *does* happen. After that, either Harry Dietz or I will call from New York and give you your next assignment.''

Once Armstead had accompanied the pair to the hall, wished them well and seen them off, he returned to the living room and picked up the telephone. He dialed Pagano's room. Pagano answered immediately. "Gus, it's all set. Get down to the hall porter and arrange for two first-class tickets on Air France tomorrow for Nice. Also, have him phone the Hôtel du Cap in Antibes and make a reservation for two bedrooms or a suite.'' Armstead repeated the name of the hotel and spelled it. "Reserve in the name of Walter Zimberg. There should be no problem with space. It's almost off season now. If there is, promise the reservations clerk a generous tip. Let's say two hundred francs. After all, anybody who's buying an arsenal can afford to grease a few palms along the way.''

At the corner of Cap d'Antibes, the Hôtel du Cap, like the rest of the ancient Riviera town, lay under the yellow glare of the late morning sun.

The hour was ten minutes to eleven when the elevator came to rest on the lobby floor and Edward Armstead emerged with Gus Pagano. Armstead was wearing a striped flannel beach robe over his red trunks, his bare feet encased in thonged beach shoes, and he was puffing on a cigar. Pagano was dressed in an open-necked white polo shirt and white slacks. Without conversing they crossed the lobby to the rear exit, emerged into the hot sunlight, and descended the stairs to the wide, long footpath.

As they walked in step along the path to the pool, Armstead pointed off toward the picturesque green forest to his left, indicating a bench in the foreground. "Wait for me there, Gus. I won't be more than ten or fifteen minutes."

They parted company. Armstead strolled on to the Eden Roc club, stepped inside the cool interior, went on between the locker room and the steward's desk. He swung left and entered the swimming pool area that stood on the cliff jutting out over the blue Mediterranean.

After surveying the scene a moment—at least a dozen bronzed bodies stretched out sunbathing around one side and the two ends of the large pool—Armstead looked over his shoulder at the nearest couple.

They were there all right. No mistaking the gleaming, reddening pate of the bald German arms dealer with the fat belly hanging over his blue jock shorts, resting on a poolside lounge, cold pipe in his mouth, Swiss magazine in his lap. Beside him, on a pad, lying on her back, which spread and flattened her bare breasts, her ample nakedness covered by no more than oversized pink sunglasses and a strip of pink bikini at her crotch, was his mistress.

Armstead pivoted decisively and strolled toward them. The second he reached the foot of the German arms dealer's lounge, the German's mistress snatched up her wisp of bikini bra and sprang to her feet. As she left, the rotund German dealer called after her, "See you at lunch, Gretchen."

Armstead addressed the German. "Helmut Middendorf?"

The German removed his tinted glasses and squinted up at Armstead. "You are Walter Zimberg, yes?" The accent was slight, the voice guttural. Middendorf nodded at the ribbed beach pad beside him.

Armstead removed his terry-cloth robe, folded it neatly, and lowered himself to the pad. He tried to make himself comfortable, and lighted his cigar once more. "Hot today, isn't it?"

"We are fortunate for this time in September," said Middendorf.

Armstead remembered his instructions. He reached deep into the pocket of his nearby robe, brought out his Swiss bankbook, and doubled over to lay it atop the German's magazine. Middendorf hardly gave it a glance, handed it back.

"Fine, fine," he rumbled. "What can I do for you?"

"I require a consignment of arms. Mainly light arms for guerrillas. I'm afraid there is a rush."

"There is always a rush," said the German complacently. "Of how much time do we speak?"

"One week," said Armstead. "One week from today."

"The delivery point?"

"Two destinations," said Armstead. "One to France, outside Lyon. One to England, outside London—actually, in Wales."

"It is possible. It will depend on the complexity of your order. You have your order, the exact order?"

"Everything spelled out," said Armstead. His hand had dipped into his robe pocket again and withdrawn two paper-clipped sheets of folded paper. Unfolding them, his eyes held on the

German's reddened bald head. "Aren't you afraid of a sunburn, Herr Middendorf?"

"When you come to the Riviera with a beautiful young woman, you do not like to be pale white like a businessman. You like to have a tan, and appear to be outdoors healthy and vigorous. I have only five days here. I cannot waste time." Nevertheless, his hand groped below his chair to retrieve his canvas hat. He covered his bald head with it. "You are right. I must not overdo." He reached out. "Your order, *bitte.*"

Armstead gave him the two sheets of paper.

Middendorf raised his knees and placed the papers against his bare thighs. He scanned the first page, then the second, in silence. "Very efficient," he murmured. "Let me read more carefully."

He set his tinted glasses on the bridge of his nose once more. They were obviously prescription sunglasses.

He reexamined the list conscientiously. He spoke as he read, almost to himself. "The Spanish Astra—we call it the .357 Magnum handgun—the very best, great penetrating power. You request fifty with ammunition. . . . The Skorpion VZ-61 from Czechoslovakia. Very light, serviceable. With silencers, I see. Also ammunition. . . . The AK-47 Soviet assault rifle, the Kalashnikov. Good, very good, we are amply stocked. . . . More Soviet goods. RGD-5 antipersonnel hand grenades . . . The SAM-7 Strela heat missiles, surface to air, portable, useful, *jawohl.*"

Armstead wanted to explain that he was having his people employ foreign-made weapons as much as possible, especially Soviet ones, to make any future raids resemble the act of a real terrorist group. He was tempted to explain the cleverness of this, but resisted because he instinctively knew that Middendorf would not give a damn.

The German continued to mutter over the list like a connoisseur. Lovingly he read aloud, "The German Heckler and Koch MP5 submachine gun. *Ja,* I can vouch for it . . . RPG-7 bazookas . . . Radio-fused bombs." He flipped over the page. "Mmm. What's this?'' His head came up. "Two helicopters. Heavier equipment. Might be more time-consuming. You must have them?''

Armstead remembered that Cooper had some ingenious scheme of collecting the ransom money in Spain, one that required armed helicopters. "I must have them," Armstead said.

"These to be delivered to the private airstrip near Lyon." Middendorf removed his tinted glasses, wiped his forehead with the back of his hand. He was calculating the possibility. "It could be done, through the port of Venice, at Mestre. I can deliver the helicopters, everything."

"In one week?''

"One week from today." He studied Armstead. "You care to know what this will cost?''

"Naturally. I know you will be reasonable for such an order."

Middendorf grunted. "My friend, to me it is a small order. There are no discounts on any order." He located a pen in the pocket of the robe lying under his lounge. "Let me add this up for you."

For five minutes he devoted himself to pondering and jotting down various prices. Then he spent several minutes adding up the figures. At last he showed the total to Armstead. "This is the full price, delivery included."

Jolted by the figure, Armstead had to remind himself that this was a one-time expense only, and that he himself was now a billionaire. "Acceptable," he heard himself croak.

"Very well." Middendorf neatly folded the sheets and deposited them, along with his pen, in the pocket of his robe. "Now as to the destinations."

"I have a colleague outside who will give you the exact details, if you'll meet with him."

"Fine, fine. He will tell me where to find the warehouse outside Lyon?''

"He has a map for you. Also, one for the location in Britain. Your shipment will go to Hay-on-Wye, a small village in Wales, perhaps a three- or four-hour drive outside London. The warehouse there, a book warehouse, is on the fringe of the village.''

"Then the light arms can be shipped as books. The rest can go as farm machinery.''

"You will have no trouble with customs?'' Armstead asked worriedly.

The German grunted. "There will be no customs,'' he said, rising with an effort. He picked up his robe and allowed Armstead to help him into it. "You leave it to me. Now, your associate, he is outside here?''

"On a bench in the woods near the terrace. His name is Gus Pagano.''

Middendorf waddled to the door. "Introduce me. We can finish our business.''

They descended to the wide path and started toward the hotel. Pagano was standing before the terrace steps, waving.

Armstead summoned him.

The German said, "We will take a stroll in the woods. It is refreshing.'' Then he added, "It is quieter.'' As they moved up the path, he promised, "We will discuss everything. To begin with, the mode of payment.''

Walking, Armstead marveled at one thing: It had all been as easy and innocent as ordering a shipment of Christmas toys. It was difficult to imagine that he had crossed the line.

He was now a terrorist.

7

They had arrived in San Sebastián in the early night, wearied by the British Airways takeoff delay in London and the changeover at Madrid's Barajas Airport to a Spanish Aviaco carrier, harried by the search for their temporarily lost luggage at the Spanish airport of Fuenterrabia, and exhausted by the fourteen-mile taxi drive into the Basque resort. It had been raining, the dark streets were windswept and desolate, and throughout the passage Victoria had derived no sense of city.

But this first morning was different. After a cozy breakfast with Ramsey in the gay dining room of the otherwise staid Londres y de Inglaterra hotel—fresh flowers everywhere—Victoria stepped outside into the cold clarity of the new day and found the view glorious. "Winning setting," her Fielding guidebook had promised her, "with its semicircular bay flanked by twin mountains and backed by green hills." It was all there.

Slipping her purse strap onto her shoulder, Victoria displayed her pleasure. "I'm going to love Spain!" she exclaimed.

Ramsey wrinkled his nose. "Maybe," he said. His eyes traveled over the curve of expansive beach below, La Concha, now almost lifeless in the low temperature of the early morning. "Don't forget, Vicky, you're in Basque country. Not as placid as it appears on the surface. There's a boiling cauldron of revolution underneath. These people don't want to be Spain. They want to be Euzkadi, their own country. They don't want outside dictators and they don't want monarchs."

"The king's showing a lot of courage, coming here."

"Either courage or foolhardiness," Ramsey said. "Although I still doubt if anything will happen. Armstead's way off. We're going to have a very routine and dull ten days here."

"Spoilsport," Victoria said cheerfully. "Where do we start?"

"Well, I know the city, and you don't," said Ramsey. "Since your assignment is to find out the king's schedule in his day here, you'd better become familiar with the sites he might visit. So to start with I'm going to show you around. This morning I'm going to be your guide, give you the Ramsey special—the highlights with colorful captions. It should take up the entire morning."

"Sounds great," she said. "Let's go."

They took a leisurely walk on the Playa de la Concha, then reached the Alameda de Calvo Sotelo, crowded with shoppers by midmorning, taking in the endless number of men's stores, fish restaurants, outdoor cafés. When they tired, Ramsey hailed a taxi, which drove them up a winding road to the lookout on Monte Igueldo, where the breathtaking panorama of the Bay of Biscay stretched beneath them. Then Ramsey directed their driver to take them back to the Old Town huddled at the foot of Monte Urgull, where they covered the Plaza de la Constitución on foot. Making their way past the old fishing harbor, they hiked to the Palacio del Mar and examined the exhibits at the Navy Museum inside.

Ramsey proved an indefatigable guide, leading Victoria through a procession of museums, municipal buildings, churches. Finally, to Victoria's relief, they wound up in a colorful upstairs restaurant, the Casa Nicolasa, in the last of its three jammed noisy dining rooms, where Victoria was able to get off her feet and kick off

her shoes. She consumed two glasses of cider, a crayfish and
spinach appetizer, *pollo asado* or roast chicken, and a custard
with caramel sauce.

When they came out of the restaurant Victoria asked Ramsey,
"What next?"

"You're on your own for the rest of the day. Me, I'm going to
go back to the Londres. I'm going to take a nap. Then I'm going
to get on the phone and try to make some appointments. It's not
going to be easy for either of us. Obviously, no official will want
to tell me very much about the king's security setup."

"You think it might be easier for me to get his schedule in San
Sebastián than from Madrid?"

"No. You won't get it in either place."

"It's just a state visit he's making."

"Vicky, in Basque country any Spanish leader is a target for
the dissidents. Why tell them where their target is going to be
every hour? Nobody's going to give you the king's full program
here. They'll either tell you it can't be done or they don't know,
or it hasn't been fixed yet. They'll tell you to contact them
mañana. The mañana after the king has come and gone, they'll
tell you where he's been."

"I'll say I'm a reporter here."

"All the worse."

"A pretty reporter."

"You may get laid, but you won't get the king's schedule."

She grimaced. "You can be so discouraging. Well, I'm going
to ignore your comments. I'm going to get that schedule, the
whole itinerary." She dug into her purse for a local guidebook
she had acquired. "I'm going to start with the city hall. I'm
going to see the mayor."

"Good luck," he said sarcastically.

"Even if you invited me to dinner, I might not go."

"I'm inviting you to dinner tonight."

"I accept."

"In the lobby at nine o'clock." And he strode off.

* * *

Awakening from his short nap, Ramsey doused his face with cold water, wiped it dry, and went to the telephone on the stand beside his bed.

Security was the word for the day, and he knew calling the San Sebastián police department would be a waste of time. Instead, he decided to call his favorite *farmacia* and arrange to see his favorite Basque friend, the pharmacist Josu, a secret member of the Euzkadi Ta Askatasuna, the underground ETA. If anyone would know about the state's security preparations for the king, it would be Josu.

A half hour later Ramsey stood before the cheerful window of the modern pharmacy in the Avenida de España. Amused by the gaudy color posters on display—from vitamins for infants to skin creams for women—Ramsey pushed the glass door and stepped inside. A young woman in a green smock was pouring some powder from a large jar into smaller jars, and next to her, his back to the door, opening and closing little mahogany drawers, was a gnome of a man wearing a rakish beret and thick spectacles, with a bristly gray mustache under a mottled bulge of nose.

Ramsey crossed the shop to the counter, greeted the woman assistant with a nod and said quietly, "Josu."

The gnome of a pharmacist spun around, squinting through his thick lens, and suddenly his mouth came out from under his mustache, spreading in a broad grin. "Nick!" he shouted. He sprinted around the counter, and fell on Ramsey with a bear hug. "Nick, Nick, it is so long. You are feast for eyes." He grabbed Ramsey by the sleeve. "Come, I have some wine for us in the back room."

Ramsey resisted, with a tilt of his head indicating the female assistant. "Maybe we should go somewhere—I mean where we can talk privately."

Josu tugged at Ramsey. "Not necessary." His head, too, indicated the assistant. "She does not understand one word of English. You can speak freely." He winked. "So can I."

He yanked Ramsey past the counter, and they went into the confined room behind the pharmacy. Unlike the modernized shop area, the room had never been finished. Actually a storage and accounting room, it contained a roughhewn wooden table that served as a desk, and two wooden chairs. The adding machine had been pushed to one side of the table, and a carafe of red wine and two plain glasses rested in the middle.

Josu shoved Ramsey into one chair and he squatted on the other, filling the wineglasses. "Chacoli wine," Josu announced. "Clears the cobwebs from the brain."

"Exactly what I need," said Ramsey, toasting and drinking.

Josu smacked his lips, licked at his wet mustache and set down his glass. "Why you here this week, Nick?"

"Why is the king of Spain here next week?"

"He, to mend fences."

"Me, to watch him mend fences."

"You are writing another book?"

"I'm gainfully employed this time. I'm on the newspaper again. The New York *Record*. I'm paid to be curious."

The gnome of a pharmacist sucked at his wine, poured himself a refill. "You are curious about our so-called king?"

"A Spanish king in Basque country? It could become a story."

Josu shook his head sadly. "No story this time. He is safe as if he wears armor. Because he comes here, he will be made safe. Normally, in Madrid, he is lax about protection. In San Sebastián he will have heavy protection."

"How much?"

"Who can say exactly?"

"You must have an idea, Josu. Make a good guess. I will not speak of my source, you know that."

"A good guess," mused Josu.

"An *educated* guess, based on knowledge."

About to pick up his wineglass once more, Josu left it untouched. He scratched his mustache. It was, Ramsey could see, as if he were trying to determine how far to go.

"I am your friend," Ramsey prodded him.

Josu appeared not to have heard him. He began speaking in a quiet monotone. "It is our practice to keep all major government officials in Madrid under constant surveillance. The king among them, of course. He is accompanied everywhere by six personal bodyguards in plainclothes. They are armed with handguns. If the king is flying up from Madrid, he will bring with him these bodyguards. The mayor of San Sebastián will meet him with three cars and military chauffeurs. The middle car, the limousine, will carry the king. The limousine will be preceded and followed by the other cars carrying the personal bodyguards."

"No additional personal guards?"

"No evidence of more," said Josu. "The king does not have a budget for a large security force. But even if he did, he might not use it. Spain tries to show it is a democracy, with the king a mere figurehead. As such, the officials do not wish to display too much protection. They do not want to look like a police state again. Of course, once he arrives in San Sebastián, you can certainly expect the *Guardia civil* will be on hand, stationed at every stop."

Ramsey conjured up a picture of the *Guardia civil*, the well-trained elite guardsmen with their unique tricornered hats, gray uniforms, rifles and revolvers.

"How many?" Ramsey wondered.

"I would not know. But for a special state occasion such as this, there might be fifty or sixty strategically placed, no more. Also, the province will furnish a military unit scattered in the streets, on rooftops and elsewhere."

"That's it?"

"As far as we can tell. There will also be the usual San Sebastián police in the streets for crowd control."

"The king's protection does not seem too heavy to me."

"It will not be heavy. But it is formidable."

"Still, if I were a leader of the ETA, I would think him vulnerable."

"No, Nick," said the diminutive Basque. "It is all too obvious a situation for the National Liberation. The king's security will be alert. We cannot sustain such losses or a failure."

"So the ETA will not move."

The gnome offered a wisp of a smile. "My *educated* guess is that they will not move." He pushed back his chair and rose. "Now I had better be seen in the shop. If you are still here when the king has left, call me. We will drink to his continued safety."

Ramsey escorted Victoria to a late dinner at an old two-story rustic restaurant called Salduba. They sat at a small table covered by a spotless red-checked tablecloth, under a wagon-wheel chandelier.

Ramsey had suggested *sopa de pescado*, a delicious fish soup, and *changurro al horno*, the local specialty of baked crab, and they had ordered both dishes, Victoria eating hungrily and Ramsey eating lightly as he devoted himself to his straight scotches.

Peering past the candles on their table, Ramsey could see that despite her appetite his partner was unhappy. Victoria's unlined pretty face remained uncharacteristically morose. It bothered him to see her so troubled, and he considered how he might cheer her up.

"Vicky, you didn't really expect to have anyone in the mayor's office hand you the king's schedule, did you?" he asked.

She shrugged. "Maybe not. Yet I expected something, a morsel or two. But they were totally uncommunicative, and a few of them were actually rude."

"Well, try to see their point of view," Ramsey said. "Handing you the the royal itinerary would be like handing out an invitation to assassination."

"I know," said Victoria, "but I wasn't expecting everything. Just a tidbit or two. They could even have lied to me, just to give me a couple of paragraphs to write about."

Ramsey smiled. "The Basques do not lie much, at least as far as I know. What did you do after Town Hall? Did you try anywhere else?''

"Of course. The police department. They thought I was crazy. They almost threw me out.''

"Did you try the local newspapers?''

"Yes,'' said Victoria. "The editors were friendlier. One even made a pass at me. But they insisted that they knew nothing. They'd know the king's schedule when he was here, when he kept it. What good will that do? Armstead is expecting something from us the day after tomorrow. What can I tell him?'' She pushed her plate aside and had a sip of white wine. "What about you, Nick? I haven't asked about you. Forgive me—I'm usually not this self-centered. How did you do on the security thing? I'm sure the city officials wouldn't cooperate with you, either.''

"I didn't bother with the officials, Vicky.''

"Oh.'' She looked at him harder, but posed no more questions. "But you got something, evidently.''

"Very little, very little,'' he told her, lighting a cigarette. "Vicky, as I knew from the beginning, this is a bust assignment. There's going to be no incident. Nothing's going to happen to the king.''

"You're sure of that?''

"Fairly certain. I won't have much more to tell Armstead than you do. Look, sweetie, you lose some, you win some. This is no win. Have a dessert.''

"I don't want a dessert. I want a story.''

"You've still got tomorrow,'' he said encouragingly. He signaled the waiter for another scotch. "We won't be talking to Armstead until the morning after. There's time.''

Victoria's eyes were fixed on Ramsey. "You did not go to official sources,'' she said. "Then you went to unofficial sources.''

He sized up the other diners at nearby tables. "If that's what you want to call them,'' he said.

Her expression was alive for the first time this evening. "That's what I'm going to do tomorrow, Nick. I think I know what to do.

I'm going to dig up something for Armstead after all. Thank you, Nick. Thank you very much. And yes, I will have a dessert.''

It was late Friday morning, and they were both in Ramsey's spacious single room in the Londres. Victoria sat on the side of the bed, listening as Ramsey dictated to the stenographer in Armstead's suite in London with Armstead on a second line. The ceiling lights were on. It was an overcast day outside, with a steady rain tapping at the window. Victoria watched the rain dance against the panes, nervously fingered her notes, and listened with more concentration.

Ramsey had no notes. He spoke fluently from memory. He said, ''The end,'' to the stenographer. ''There is no more.''

Victoria could hear the stenographer say, ''Thank you.'' Next, she could hear Edward Armstead's voice resound from the receiver.

''Nick,'' Armstead said.

''Yes?''

''You're sure of what you have?''

''Fairly sure.''

''Pretty light security for the head of state in a guerrilla center.''

''I can only repeat what I heard,'' said Ramsey evenly. ''Looks like a great big zero. No hit planned.''

''By the locals.''

''Right. No action, far as I can learn.''

''Thanks,'' said Armstead abruptly. ''Put Victoria on.''

''Here she is,'' said Ramsey. He got out of the chair, handing the receiver to Victoria, who sat down, sorting her notes in her lap.

''Hello, Victoria,'' Armstead said. ''Did you get an official schedule for the king?''

''There is no official schedule, Mr. Armstead. I tried every source. They were uncooperative. But I *do* have an unofficial schedule.''

''Unofficial,'' said Armstead. ''What exactly does that mean?''

"No one handed me a certified itinerary," Victoria said. "But I figured that if the king was going to be here for a full morning and afternoon, he'd have to go somewhere, visit something. So I sat down and made a summary of the most likely sites he would look in on. Then I beat the pavements all morning and afternoon yesterday calling on the minor individuals who are in charge of these logical places. They were easier to get to, easier to talk to—like a museum curator, the supervisor of the street cleaners in the main plaza, an assistant to the bishop at the biggest church—people like that. Some did not expect a visit from the king. Others had been instructed to expect him and to have everything in readiness. It worked out. I got together a list of where he'll be—"

Hearing her, Ramsey made a circle with his forefinger and thumb. "Smart girl," he whispered.

Pleased, she pressed closer to the mouthpiece of the telephone. "I can read it off to you right now, Mr. Armstead."

"You're sure of your sources?" said Armstead.

"Pretty much. There could always be some last-minute changes. But it's a tight itinerary and I believe the king will stick to it. Let me read it to you."

"Hold it, Victoria. The stenographer is on the line. You can dictate it to her. Here she is."

Armstead's voice faded. "Are you there?" inquired Victoria.

"I'm ready," said a woman with a British accent.

"Let's go," said Victoria. She organized the notes in her lap. "What follows is my dictation." She paused and read aloud from her notes: "9:00 A.M.—King arrives at Fuenterrabia Airport. 9:30 A.M.—King takes military helicopter to San Sebastián. 10:00 A.M.—King arrives at Palacio de Ayete, Generalissimo Franco's one-time summer residence. 10:30 A.M.—His Majesty takes motorcade to Casas Consistoriales, the Town Hall, where greeted by the mayor. 11:30 A.M.—King arrives by motorcade at Catedral del Buen Pastor for confession with bishop. 12:00—Royal party departs for Palacio de Escoriaza-Esquibel for luncheon hosted by

governor general. 2:30 P.M.—King addresses crowd from platform in front of Palacio for ten minutes." Victoria paused. "Am
I speaking too fast?"

"Go on," said the stenographer. "I'll want to check some of
the spellings when you're through."

"Very good, so far," Armstead cut in.

Victoria cleared her throat and resumed her reading.

Nightfall had come to London, and in the living room of
Armstead's suite in the Ritz the publisher had pulled on his ski
mask and allowed Gus Pagano to help him adjust it.

"How many of them are here?" Armstead asked.

"Only two. Cooper and Quiggs. Cooper wants to give you a
final report before leaving."

Armstead nodded and followed Pagano to the door of the
adjoining bedroom. The two went inside. Except for a few dull
lamps, the room was lost in darkness. Near the center of the
sitting area a large circular walnut table had been set up with a
half-dozen folding chairs around it. One chair held the rangy
Cooper, the other the pimpled, stocky British youth named Quiggs.

Armstead greeted them briefly and took a place opposite them
at the table, with Pagano beside him.

Momentarily the publisher was concerned by Cooper's unsmiling face, and Quiggs's phlegmatic one. Did this mean that something had gone wrong, that there was bad news?

But in seconds Armstead's apprehension was put to rest.

"We're leaving in an hour," Cooper began. "Before leaving,
I thought we should report to you on the status of the operation.
Everything is going exactly as planned."

Armstead exhaled his relief.

"Most of our team is in place for the secondary stage,"
Cooper went on, "some in Lyon, some en route to St-Jean-de-
Luz with equipment."

"With weapons?" asked Armstead.

"All the lighter arms are in hand. The Lyon shipment arrived early, except for the helicopters, which we won't require until next week. The other goods are being transported from Wales into France and to the Spanish frontier.''

Armstead was incredulous. "You mean most of the arms have been delivered? That's fast.''

"It's what you paid for,'' said Cooper. "We'll be crossing into Spain in the next forty-eight hours. We'll then begin to familiarize ourselves with the various locales and sites on the king's schedule.''

"You found our reports satisfactory?''

"Mr. Pagano delivered them right after lunch. That was prompt, and we found them thorough,'' said Cooper.

Quiggs shifted in his chair. "We hope the king stays with that schedule.''

"Don't worry about that,'' Cooper assured Armstead. "We'll be double-checking in the field, up to the very last moment. If the royal party makes any change, we will be able to accommodate it with our alternative plans.''

"Was our security report also satisfactory?'' Armstead wanted to know.

"Most useful,'' said Cooper. "Because of the nature of the king's security, we were forced to alter our original plan.''

At once Armstead was consumed with curiosity. "How do you plan to take him?'' he asked bluntly.

"I'm afraid I cannot tell you,'' Cooper replied with equal bluntness.

"I'm sorry,'' said Armstead, contrite. "I don't want to interfere.''

For several seconds, Cooper was silent. When he spoke, his demeanor had softened. "You are paying for this, so I suppose you deserve to know something.''

"It doesn't matter,'' said Armstead.

Cooper appeared not to have heard him. "I don't mind telling you, since it is no longer operative, that our original plan was the one most often successful in previous operations. Perform the kidnapping while the subject is in a car. Use two vehicles to intercept and block the target—swerve one car in front of his car, one in back of it, grab him, throw him into the front getaway vehicle and follow it with the second car. This was our original plan, and the one we abandoned.''

"Why did you give it up?" Armstead wanted to know. "The subject will be in his car, in a continuous motorcade, in San Sebastián."

"Let me tell you why we abandoned that plan," said Cooper. "Have you ever heard of an outfit called Control Risks?''

"Control—? No, what's that?"

"The insurance company, Lloyd's of London, has an underwriter that sells kidnap insurance. If you are afraid of being kidnapped, you apply for this insurance. Lloyd's sends a team of surveyors and consultants to visit you, determine the potential of risk, and brief you on how to reduce the risk. Then they issue you a policy in secrecy. Your policy is with an underwriter called Control Risks. They try to help you prevent a kidnapping. But if you are kidnapped and pay a ransom, they reimburse you. It's a little-known but popular thing now."

"Most unusual," said Armstead. "What does it have to do with your change in plans?"

"We have a woman in Control Risks. She's having an affair with one of our men. She does him favors. She has access to the Control Risks confidential files. From these files we learned that ninety percent of all kidnapping today, nine out of every ten cases, occur when the victim is riding in a car. We realized that if Control Risks works with that statistic, they must have developed better protection for potential victims who are riding in cars. We realized that if we went for the king while he was in his limousine, Spanish security would be prepared for it. The chance of failure would be too great. So we decided against this mode of kidnapping. We changed our plans. Now you understand."

Armstead understood and was impressed. He was tempted to inquire further and try to learn Cooper's alternative plan. Yet, earlier, Cooper had been adamant against revealing it. He would probably still refuse to reveal his plan. And suddenly Armstead did not want to know the *modus operandi*. He wanted to keep the operation at arm's length. He had to remind himself that he was a publisher and not really a terrorist, after all. "Now you think you can succeed" was all he could bring himself to say.

Cooper stood up. "We hope to succeed. We cannot guarantee it. We can only try. We must leave at once. You want Mr. Pagano to accompany us?"

Armstead came to his feet. "Pagano is essential. He will be my liaison with your activities. I will be leaving London tomorrow. Pagano knows how to reach me. He will keep us in touch with one another." He faced Pagano. "Are you ready to go, Gus?"

"All set," said Pagano.

"I'll wait to hear from you." Armstead hesitated. "You're sure you'll be able to contact me?"

"Minutes after it happens," promised Pagano, "I'll be on my way across the frontier into France, by the same way we smuggled the weapons in—underground. I have a phone reserved. I'll report to you immediately."

"Okay," said Armstead, satisfied. "Good luck."

Armstead stood by until the three of them had left the room. Alone, he returned to his suite, tearing off his uncomfortable mask. He would dispose of it somewhere later.

He felt unnaturally excited, and knew that he had a partial erection. He wished that he were already in New York with Kim.

But he knew his real orgasm would be in San Sebastián.

It was a luminous, cold morning in San Sebastián, and the king of Spain and his entourage had arrived on schedule.

Despite countless hindrances due to the crowds of monarchist followers and neutral Basques and the police, Victoria and Ramsey had followed the monarch's progress in the new Renault that Ramsey had rented.

At 10 A.M. they had witnessed the king's arrival at the modest

Palacio de Ayete, after they had parked the car and mingled with
the curious crowd of spectators waiting outside the building.
Ramsey had become restless at the inactivity, chain-smoking and
complaining until the king emerged, resplendent in his visored
cap and bemedaled sashed tunic jacket and dark trousers.

The people all around them had cheered, and Victoria had
been ecstatic, pointing at her watch, saying, "It's ten-thirty,
Nick. Right on schedule. Now he'll be heading for Town Hall.
Let's stay with the motorcade. Which way is our car?"

"If you insist," Ramsey had grumbled, elbowing ahead of her
through the mob of onlookers.

Back in the car, they tracked the royal motorcade to the San
Sebastián Town Hall, left the Renault illegally parked in a side
street, and made their way through more spectators in time to see
the king and his aides enter the Municipal Building with the
mayor.

They had lingered outside for twenty minutes, with Ramsey
becoming more and more restless and inattentive.

Now he was pulling at Victoria's coat sleeve. "What's
happening?" he asked.

"Nothing yet," she said.

"Nothing yet, and nothing now, and nothing later. Vicky, it's
a washout. I warned you this would be a non-news event, and by
now you should know that I'm right."

"Be a little more patient, Nick."

"For what? I've had it, Vicky. I'm cutting out."

"You're leaving?" she said incredulously.

"You bet. This is a drag, as predicted. You can handle any big
beat by yourself. If king bites dog, you've got it. As for me, I'm
going to walk back to the hotel, have a few drinks, and take a
nap. When you're ready to file your hot story with New York—
well, just wake me up and I'll give you moral support." He
handed the car keys to Victoria. "Stay alert, old girl, and sober."

He disappeared into the crowd.

Disheartened by his cynicism, feeling a little foolish about her romantic expectations, feeling sophomoric and inexperienced, Victoria planted herself firmly on the pavement and prepared to wait. Dammit, she told herself, this could be a story and I'm a reporter and Nick is a jaded old drunk.

By 11:15 the king had not yet reappeared, which meant that from this point on he would be running late. Victoria kept searching the spectators, hoping for some demonstrators or protestors, but there were none.

Ten minutes more passed, and then Victoria was brought to attention by an outburst of cheers and applause. Rising on her toes, she could see the impressive figure of the king. He was shaking hands with the San Sebastián mayor before departing for his limousine, while members of his entourage and the plain-clothesmen quickly surrounded him.

She whirled about, fought through the mass of people, burst into the open, and raced for the side street where the Renault was parked.

She breathed a sigh of relief that there was no parking ticket.

Once inside the sedan, she found her street map of San Sebastián, located the X's she had marked on the sites of the royal stops, pinpointed Town Hall and her present location, pinpointed the king's next scheduled stop, the Catedral del Buen Pastor. She traced the route, started her car, and was on the move through the less traveled back streets.

Finally, when she had the dominant 75-meter main spire of the church in view, she sought a parking place, and after many misses, she took the Puente Cristina across the Rio Urumea and found an empty slot near the Norte railroad station. Purse suspended from her shoulder, map in hand, she began striding briskly over the bridge. Shortly she was in the Plaza de Bilbao and approaching the massive neo-Gothic cathedral.

Once more there were thickets of onlookers. They ringed the church entrance and were being held back by a cordon of local police. She tried to edge her way closer for a better view, but was unable to get nearer than fifty yards from the entrance.

Her view was partially obscured by the applauding townsfolk, but she could make out that the royal motorcade had already arrived and that the king, caught up in his entourage, was making his way to the cathedral entrance. There, the members of the entourage appeared to melt to one side, and hold still as the king, followed by two personal bodyguards, left them to join a single clergyman. Together, the four men went inside the church.

This was unexpected, the king going into the cathedral with only two of his party, but at once Victoria realized what was happening. She recalled the itinerary that she had prepared. The cathedral was a brief interruption in the ceremonial day, during which the monarch would go to confession.

This was respect. Victoria sighed. It wasn't news.

Dumbly, and more weary now, she settled down for one more wait.

The interior of the cathedral had been tactfully cleared of tourists and worshippers, and except for the few clergymen who discreetly lost themselves in various shadowed recesses, the king of Spain was left alone with his cleric guide and pair of guards. Gesturing for the cleric and his guards to remain where they were, the king moved ahead.

Far below the majestic vaulted ceilings of his house of God, the king of Spain passed the rows of empty pews and made his way to the nearest confessional box. Arriving at the curtained entrance, far from the hue and cry of the multitude, isolated from the grave matters of state, the monarch paused to gather his thoughts, and then he stepped into the booth to cleanse his soul.

Inside the confessional, an openwork lattice was set into the wall that separated him from the priest who would hear his confession and give him absolution. The king knew that it would be the bishop himself beyond the lattice.

The king brought himself to his knees on the padded step, bowed his head before the lattice, and began in a low but distinct voice.

"Father, I have sinned."

"Yes, my son."

"I wish to confess—"

That instant, the lattice was pulled aside. To the king's astonishment, the bishop's face was not revealed. Instead, a gloved hand pointed a heavy Parabellum 9-caliber pistol through the opening and pushed the gun's metallic nozzle against the king's forehead.

"Silence," a harsh voice commanded. "Do as directed or die."

The king remained on his knees, petrified.

The curtain to the confessional was jerked open, and he could barely make out a person in clerical garb, holding a gun and some sort of garments, standing behind him. He felt the bishop's white miter being shoved down on his head, felt a clerical robe—plainly the bishop's own purple cassock—being forced on his arms and around his body.

"On your feet," a voice in his ear ordered in Spanish.

Incapable of rising, the king allowed himself to be yanked to his feet. Another armed clergyman, a gunman dressed in surplice and cassock, had now materialized.

The pair pulled the king out of the confessional into the cavernous hollow of the church.

Prodding with their guns, prodding, pushing hard, the pair were swiftly joined by two more men in the garb of clerics, who helped surround the monarch.

The four hustled him between the pews and altar.

The king had only a glimpse of his bodyguards and several other clergymen—the real ones, he assumed—being tied up and gagged while fake clergymen held submachine guns on them.

Close to the king's ear a breathless voice, the harsh one, said, "We take you outside to a car in the rear. Behave, and you are safe. One word from you, and you are dead."

The king nodded, remained mute, and allowed himself to be hurried away.

*   *   *

Outside, continuing to keep her gaze on the cathedral entrance,
Victoria was becoming increasingly tired.

Fifteen more numbing minutes had gone by, a wind chilled the
air, and still the king had not emerged, as members of his
entourage patiently stood by in front of the cathedral. Victoria
was almost ready to concede that Nick Ramsey had been right.
This was a day for no news, a cosmetic ceremonial day, disap-
pointing not only her but a disappointment for Armstead in New
York.

She weighed backtracking her car, walking to it as fast as
possible for warmth, and returning to Ramsey to have him assist
her in calling in her newsless story.

That instant she heard a shrill outcry ahead.

Startled, instantly curious, Victoria barged forward between
the peasant couple in front of her and fought closer to the cordon
of police to hear and see what was happening better. After a
minute she came to a full view of the church entrance, and what
she saw surprised her even further. In the entrance, a disheveled,
bareheaded elderly man, apparently the bishop himself, attired in
a cassock, was shouting frantically to members of the uniformed
Guardia civil and the royal entourage. A *Guardia civil* officer
now had the bishop by the shoulders, trying to calm him, and the
bishop ceased his shouting and was speaking hysterically to the
officer.

Abruptly the cordon of police heaved backward, and Victoria
would have toppled over except for the press of spectators around
her. Ahead of her there was an eruption of persons at the
cathedral entrance—*Guardia civil* officers, policemen, plainclothesmen rushing toward waiting cars—and breaching this avalanche,
other officials and clergymen were leading the hysterical bishop
back into the church.

All about Victoria, the babble of rising voices mingled with
the whine of automobile engines. Obviously something had gone
terribly wrong, but Victoria did not know what was happening

because she had not understood a word of Spanish. She raised
her voice, calling out to the spectators around her, "What's
happening? What's going on? Can anyone speak English?" Her
neighbors ignored her until one bespectacled young man, who
looked like a student, reached between the people separating
them and touched her shoulder to gain her attention. "I speak
English," he said. "The king has been kidnapped from inside the
church, abducted by terrorists at gunpoint. They tied up the
bishop, took his place. The rest dressed up as priests." Rattled,
disbelieving, Victoria held on to the young man's arm to keep
him from getting away. "The king kidnapped?" she shouted.
"You're sure?" The young man was nodding vigorously. "It is
true. He's been kidnapped." Victoria tugged at the young man's
arm. "Who did it? Do they know?" The young man was shaking
his head. "They did not tell—but for certain it must be ETA."
The young man was pulling away from her and she called after
him, "Thank you, thank you."

There was no time to think, only to act. She was clawing
through the crowd, battling to get out of the noisy mob, and after
minutes the crowd was thinning. Victoria scrambled free, fully
into the open, halting only to catch her breath.

Her mind reeled. She'd been right to stay with the royal tour.
Nick had been wrong to leave, to believe nothing would happen.
An incredible event had happened, and she was half-witness to it.
She had a—a scoop. The *Record* would have it. Armstead would
be out of his mind.

She was running away from the cathedral in the direction of
her car. The first thought that entered her mind was to find a
telephone somewhere, anywhere, and call New York. But reality
dampened the thought. The obstacles would be insurmountable:
she did not know the method of making a call outside the hotel,
she would be unable to deal with a Spanish operator, she would
have to make the long-distance call collect—impossible. She was
winded, now only half-running as she approached her parking
place. Her immediate destination had become clearer. She must

get back to the Londres hotel, to her room, use the hotel's English-speaking operator to get the first flash across to Armstead.

The king of Spain kidnapped!

She threw herself into the front seat of the Renault, started the car, gunned the engine, and was off as if flung from a catapult.

Safely inside her hotel room, Victoria had dialed the hotel operator, said that she wanted to call New York City, a station-to-station call prepaid, and she carefully enunciated the telephone number of the New York *Record*. "Hang up, please," the operator had told her. "I will call you back." Victoria had pleaded, "Make it as fast as possible." The operator, unperturbed, had replied, "I will call you back when I have the connection."

Now Victoria was waiting, trying to put the story together in her head, and silently beseeching the telephone to ring.

In less than a minute it rang, and Victoria grabbed it up.

"Yes?"

The operator's tone was maddeningly cool. "Miss Weston, on the call you have placed to New York—it cannot go through at this time."

"What?"

"Maybe later, in a few hours, by this evening."

"Why can't I make my call?"

"There is a police emergency. All calls going out of San Sebastián have been temporarily stopped. Your call cannot be placed. I will let you know when long-distance service is resumed."

Victoria knew that any further pleading with a minor functionary, a minor cog, would get her nowhere.

"I'll be waiting to hear from you," she said helplessly and hung up.

Only one bit of light alleviated her dark frustration. If no outgoing calls were being permitted during this emergency, it meant that other press people, rivals, were being similarly frustrated. No Spanish newspaper or foreign wire service would be allowed to send the news out of San Sebastián. Nor, she was sure, would any Spanish radio or television station be permitted to broadcast the news. This was an immediate clamp-down on word that the king of Spain had been kidnapped. Whatever the reason the police had for the censorship, she had no doubt that it was in full effect.

What to do?

Nick Ramsey, of course, Nick right next door napping, unaware of what had taken place and of the great scoop she alone had. She must enlist him, with his experience, ask him what they should do to get the story to New York.

Quickly she left her room, entered the corridor, and hurried to the next room. She rapped hard on Ramsey's door, to be sure to awaken him.

No sooner had her knuckles left the door than it was thrown open.

"Nick—" she started to say, stepping into his room, and immediately she stopped in her tracks.

Confused, she tried to take in the unexpected scene. Looming over her at the door was a uniformed soldier holding a rifle. He had opened the door. On the bed straight ahead of her sat Ramsey, barefoot, bare-chested, wearing just trousers, with two gray-uniformed *Guardia civil* men, holding guns, flanking him. At the far side of the room at a desk, using the hotel telephone, was another member of the *Guardia civil*, probably an officer.

Victoria stared at Ramsey. He looked terrible, as if in the throes of a hangover. The bedcover behind him was in disarray.

He lifted a hand in good-humored greeting. "Hi, Vicky."

"Whatever's going on here?" Victoria demanded, moving toward Ramsey. One of his two guards said something to her in Spanish. She didn't understand him, but she stopped. "Nick, the king's been kidnapped!"

"I just heard," said Ramsey, "and they think I'm the one who did it."

"But you've been here all the time! Anyway, that's idiocy. Why you?"

"I was followed last week—seen going into a pharmacy owned by an ETA sympathizer, and seen leaving a half hour later without making a purchase. They figured I must have been plotting with him."

"That's absolutely ridiculous!" Victoria exclaimed.

"Tell them, not me," said Ramsey cheerfully.

"Nick, I need your help—"

At once, he was serious. "I need *your* help first," he said. "Soon as you leave, get hold of Armstead and have him notify the United States ambassador in Madrid to get the police off my back, to spring me."

"That's just it," said Victoria frantically. "I can't reach Armstead with my story—or to help you. All outgoing calls have been shut down. How do I reach New York from here?"

"Quiet!" a voice bellowed from the far side of the room. The *Guardia civil* officer had set down the phone and was putting on his tricornered hat as he marched to the bed. He addressed himself to Ramsey. "Please, dress. I have spoken to my superiors. You are to be detained until everything has been cleared up. I must take you in for questioning."

"Here we go," said Ramsey, wobbling to his feet and reaching for his shirt. He made a gesture of distress to Victoria. "I guess we're both cooked."

The officer signaled for the guards to get rid of Victoria and then strode into the hall ahead of her.

Briefly, she stood fast. "Nick, we're not cooked. Listen to me."

"Better make it quick."

"I'm heading for St-Jean-de-Luz on the French side," Victoria called out. "It's about twenty miles from here, across the frontier. I've been there before, so I know the area. I'll take a train, or whatever."

"They won't let you through."

"When I show my American passport, I think they will. Nick, I'll be at the Chantaco Hotel—it's France, so the phones will be open to New York. I'll call Armstead for both of us—file my story and get you out of here.''

The bedside guards had finally converged to block Victoria, and to ease her toward the doorway and into the corridor. She stood there, immobilized, watching the guardsmen roughly push Ramsey out of his room. In the corridor, they surrounded him and marched him toward the stairway.

As he was led away, Ramsey caught a glimpse of her, tried to maintain his grin, and failed.

"Nick," she shouted after him, "I'll be waiting for you there!"

Then he was gone.

Animated once more, Victoria ran back to her room and the telephone to find a means of reaching St-Jean—that is, if they would let her, let anyone, leave San Sebastián or Spain itself on this violent day.

Although St-Jean-de-Luz was only a short distance away, it had taken Victoria a long time to get there.

For Victoria it had been a harrowing afternoon, because of the threats that had befallen her, and maddening in some respects because of numerous delays. Eager to get to a telephone to help Ramsey, bursting with her still exclusive story on the kidnapping of the king, she was taunted by the parade of hours.

She had sought assistance from the hotel's main concierge, buttering her request for transportation with a sizable tip. He had assured her that it would be time-consuming to go by train. At last the concierge had located a private car-rental service in San Sebastián that would have a BMW sedan and an English-speaking driver available in two hours to take her to France.

Not thinking, she had tried to put through a call to the Chantaco Hotel in St-Jean, but had once more been reminded that no outgoing calls or communications of any kind were permitted from San Sebastián. However, a local travel agent had assured her that as the resort season for St-Jean was almost over and the hotel would be closing down in a few weeks, it was probably no longer fully occupied. The agent was sure that she would find a room once she presented herself at the Chantaco.

Impatiently watching the wall clock for the time her driver and car would arrive, she had busied herself making notes on the kidnapping of the king. She had wanted to be prepared to pour her story out to Armstead once she had him on the phone. Then, in the lobby, having found and purchased a travel guide on the area that gave several pages to St-Jean-de-Luz, she had returned to her room to read the book and have a snack.

She had been packing her single bag, on the verge of leaving, when the police came.

There had been two of them, both in plainclothes and both speaking English. The more aristocratic of the pair had flashed his identification and verified that she was Victoria Weston and recited what was in her American passport. He had proceeded to interrogate her closely. There had been this day, he had said, an act of terrorism in the city. Did she know that? Yes, she had replied forthrightly, she had been a witness to part of it. Why had she been at the cathedral? As a tourist to see the king? No, she had replied, as a newspaperwoman to write about the king's visit. Could she prove that she was a bona fide member of the American press? She had shown him her press pass from the New York *Record*. He had returned her pass, remarking that it could be counterfeit. She had suggested that he contact her newspaper for verification that she worked for them. He had then gone off on another round of questions. There had been evidence that she had been nosing about San Sebastián in advance of the king's visit, trying to find out his schedule. Why had she been so interested? Well, she had retorted, why not? She had been assigned to write a story about the king's activities in San Sebastián. She had looked into his itinerary openly.

The plainclothesman had described her own visits around the city accurately, and had wanted her to explain the purpose of each call. Then he had described her activities in the company of one Nick Ramsey, and inquired into their relationship.

This questioning had gone on for over an hour. In the end she had been absolved of complicity. Hard as she had tried, she had not been able to learn more about the fate of Nick Ramsey.

Her departure from San Sebastián had been aggravatingly late. Once in the BMW, she and her driver had been stopped three times. After getting on the A-1 autoroute heading toward St-Jean-de-Luz, they had been brought to a halt by a roadblock just outside of town. Here they were questioned. When they reached the border and Irún, they had been held up by customs. And when they turned off the autoroute for the French town of Ciboure, they had been delayed yet again, this time by road construction and a detour.

When they had crossed the bridge over the Nivelle River and entered St-Jean-de-Luz, Victoria had given an audible sigh of relief. It was midevening and there were lights and life in the gay port town, but Victoria had not been distracted from her main purpose. A mile from the downtown, they had arrived at the elegant Chantaco Hotel. The haven of the hotel with its two-story fireplace near the reception desk and its Moorish arches had no interest for Victoria. Only one thing: Did they have a bedroom and a bath for her, a room with a telephone, for at least two or three days? They did.

Now in the room, despite hunger pangs there was only one thing on her mind. She put through a call to New York, to the *Record*, and in five minutes she had the newspaper and then Edward Armstead's secretary, Estelle Rivkin, and Victoria's excitement mounted. She must speak to Mr. Armstead immediately. She learned that he was out and could not be reached, and Estelle had no idea when he would be back. Victoria felt a lurch of disappointment, then asked for Harry Dietz, who was second-best. But Dietz was also out. Another disappointment. Victoria realized that she had wanted congratulations and praise at the highest level, but that was unimportant and she was pleased to settle for third-best, her managing editor.

Ollie McAllister was on the phone.

"Ollie, this is Victoria Weston. I've been trying all afternoon—"

"Vicky, how are you?" He sounded surprisingly cheerful for a dour Scot. "Where in the devil are you?"

"I'm calling from the Chantaco Hotel in St-Jean-de-Luz—"

"Where?"

"The French resort town across the border from San Sebastián. I'm at the Chantaco Hotel."

"Yes, Mr. Armstead mentioned—"

"Ollie, I've got a tremendous scoop. No one has been able to phone it out of San Sebastián. That's why I came here. The king of Spain was kidnapped this morning! I think we've got it alone!"

"We sure have, Vicky," McAllister agreed. "We have it alone, a big exclusive. We hit the streets with it an hour ago. The king of Spain kidnapped in the Cathedral of the Good Shepherd in San Sebastián by a group of Basque terrorists. They were dressed as clergymen. They pulled off the abduction without a shot. We've headlined it, a clean beat. I'm told the *Record* is selling almost at the pace of the Yinger issue—"

"Ollie," she interrupted. "I can't believe I heard you right. You know about the kidnapping of the king?"

"I told you. It's on the front page."

She sank down into the couch, deflated and bewildered.

"But Ollie, I had it exclusively. No one's been able to get it out of Spain."

"Well, someone did. Good try, young lady, but—"

"Who?" she wanted to know. "How?"

"It's by-lined Mark Bradshaw. I'm told he's a British hotshot Mr. Armstead hired to cover the continent."

"How did he get it out?"

"I don't know precisely. It was filed through our London

bureau. He must have found some means of getting it out. Maybe just as you tried.''

''Mr. Armstead didn't tell me he had someone else there.''

''Publishers don't always confide in reporters, or editors either.''

She tried to protest once more. ''But Nick Ramsey and I—'' She remembered. ''Oh, my God, Ollie, I nearly forgot to tell you. Nick Ramsey was picked up by the Spanish police around noon today. They dragged him out of the hotel for questioning about the kidnapping. They had spotted him earlier, meeting with an ETA sympathizer—''

McAllister chuckled, unconcerned. ''Good old Nick. Here we go again.''

''He's been arrested, Ollie.''

''He always is. Okay, the police in San Sebastián have him. You want us to try to get him free.''

''He wanted Mr. Armstead to contact the United States ambassador in Madrid—''

''I know. Nick always travels first-class. Don't worry, I'll get right on it.''

''I'm supposed to wait here for him. Also, to stand by for our next assignment. You can get Nick out?''

''Don't worry, Vicky. Enjoy the sun while you can. You'll see Nick soon enough, and you'll hear from us.''

After the call, Victoria broke into tears out of exhaustion and frustration. As a team player, she should have been happy that the *Record* had the story. But she was miserable that she had failed to make it alone, that she had been scooped by her own side. A few minutes later she recovered and picked up the telephone again, this time to call room service.

The next day, except for one long walk on the busy Boulevard Thiers and the crowded shopping mall of Rue Gambetta in St-Jean-de-Luz and a stop at the waterfront to watch the blue-and-white tuna boats in the harbor and the sun-lovers before their cabañas on the broad beach, she confined herself to her room, awaiting a call from Ramsey.

When the telephone rang, it brought her not a call from Ramsey but a long-distance call from Edward Armstead in New York.

"I hear you phoned me yesterday with news of the kidnapping," Armstead said. "I appreciate your effort, and I wanted you to know it."

She bit her lip and forced herself to say, "Congratulations anyway for getting the story before I could get it to you. You must be very happy."

"I'm ecstatic," crowed Armstead. "We're outselling every other paper in town. We're running alone, way out in front, with this one. And this morning we've got another clean beat."

"What is it?" she asked politely.

"Bradshaw filed the kidnappers' demands. He got hold of a communiqué they've just issued. Want to hear it?"

"Yes, of course."

"Let me read it to you," said Armstead proudly. "Here it is. 'The Basque Socialist Revolutionary Organization for National Liberation, Euzkadi Ta Askatasuna, ETA, assume responsibility for taking into custody yesterday the king of Spain.' "

"So it was the ETA."

"Naturally it was," said Armstead. "Who else could it have been? The communiqué goes on, 'Our action against the king of Spain and the Spanish government constitutes a major step forward for socialism in Euzkadi in our struggle against national oppression, as well as for the liberation of the exploited and the oppressed in the Spanish state.' " Armstead's voice had drifted off. "Then they make their ransom demand. They want a half-dozen Basque political prisoners in Madrid released from jail. When they are assured that this has been done, they will return the king unharmed."

"No money?" said Victoria, surprised.

"This was purely a political kidnapping," said Armstead. "By the way, I really called to let you know I've got onto the Nick Ramsey matter. I just received word from our ambassador in Madrid. He's been promised that Ramsey will be freed in the morning. You should see him sometime tomorrow.''

"I'm certainly glad to hear that.''

"When you're together again, give me a ring. We'll move ahead from there.''

The next morning, rested and bathed and wearing a Harris tweed blazer, a ruffled fine linen blouse, and a wool flannel skirt, Victoria was having a late brunch in the dining patio of the Chantaco. She had almost finished her pot of coffee and had read the long story in the *International Herald Tribune* on the kidnapping of the king, which gave entire credit for the beat to the New York *Record*, when she heard her name called out.

She looked up and there was Nick Ramsey, coming out from under a wisteria-bedecked archway and removing his new black beret to bow to her.

He kissed her on the forehead and sat down. "How's the keeper of the scoops?'' he said. He beckoned a waiter. "Ham and eggs and black coffee,'' he ordered.

Victoria was staring at him. "Nick, are you all right?''

He lifted his arms and inspected them. "Everything's in place. No signs of police brutality. Just hours of the same questions over and over again, which is worse.''

"Were you in jail?''

"No such luck. Nothing picturesque. Just put back in my hotel room under armed guard. Thanks for getting me released. Well, did you scoop the world?''

She poked the *Herald Tribune* at him, pointing to the lead story. "See for yourself.''

He read the story in silence.

"It's not yours,'' he commented, when he had finished. "Who's Mark Bradshaw?''

"I thought you'd know.''

"Never heard of him in my life."

"Ollie says he's someone Armstead hired abroad."

"I wonder how on earth Bradshaw got it out ahead of you."

"That was sure a letdown."

"Well, anyway, Armstead had it all to himself. I do give him credit. Never thought him that smart or perceptive, anticipating that this might happen, sending us down there."

A loudspeaker crackled. Miss Victoria Weston was requested to come to the reception desk.

She leaped to her feet and hastened to the desk. She was told that New York City was on the line asking for her, and was directed to a lobby telephone.

It was Harry Dietz calling long-distance.

"Hello, Victoria," he said. "It must be morning there. I tried your room, then had you paged."

"Here I am."

"Mr. Armstead asked me to find out if Nick Ramsey had arrived yet."

"He walked in moments ago. He's safe and sound. We were just having brunch."

"Good," said Dietz.

"Your story on the kidnapping—you broke big. Front page in the Paris *Herald*, with full credit to the New York *Record*."

"Wonderful. I'll inform Mr. Armstead. Incidentally, you'll be interested to know we've come up with another exclusive on the ETA kidnapping. The Spanish government capitulated to the ransom demand. The king was released quite dramatically. Flown by helicopter to an isolated hill outside San Sebastián, and lowered to the barren summit blindfolded and tied. After the helicopter had disappeared, the Spanish authorities received a phone call telling them where to find him. They found him, quite intact. We have it, totally exclusive, in our last edition off the presses for morning distribution."

"Congratulations again," said Victoria.

"One more thing Mr. Armstead wanted me to tell you and

Nick. You are to proceed to Paris today. You will be at the
Plaza Athénée as before. Mr. Armstead will be in touch with you
there tomorrow afternoon with your next assignment.''

"Do you have any idea what?" Victoria asked eagerly.

"Go to Paris and wait."

After hanging up, she realized that she had forgotten to ask
Dietz the one piece of information she wanted to know. She had
wanted to ask him, Who is Mark Bradshaw? Maybe, she decided,
she would find out in Paris.

8

With one hand Dr. Carl Scharf brushed the bread crumbs off the front of his green turtleneck sweater into the cup formed by his other hand, and deposited the accumulated crumbs in the paper plate on his desk, which still held the crusts of a tomato and lettuce sandwich. "Edward," he said to Armstead, "do you realize you've gone through this entire session—it's almost over— and you never once mentioned your father?"

Armstead was not sure whether he was being praised or chastised. He decided that it was a compliment. "My father is dead," he said matter-of-factly. "He's no part of my life anymore." He reflected on this and added, "Actually, I will give him credit for one thing. He may not have had respect for his offspring, but he certainly had respect for power. He always knew that success was the name of the game. Now I can see that he was right. It is. All things considered, that's the real orgasm."

"There's room for both orgasms," said Scharf gently. "They're both real."

"In my book," said Armstead, "success is the big one. The other is the little one—most anyone can have it."

Dr. Scharf locked his pudgy hands over the protrusion of his belly and regarded his patient with benign pride. "Well, I'm pleased you're pleased with yourself."

"That's a rotten sentence," said Armstead. "You'd never make it on the *Record*." He sat back. "Yes, I'm damned pleased with myself. I always knew that I could do it if I had the chance, and now I'm doing it. You've got to admit, Carl, it's no mean accomplishment—first the Yinger beat, and now the king of Spain blitz, two hot exclusives in a row. We've knocked everybody out of the box."

"You've certainly demonstrated a genius for your job."

"Only the beginning, Carl, only the beginning. I'm going to go right on. I don't intend to stop."

"How do you explain your instinct for what's going to happen, and being there when it happens?"

Armstead smirked. "Luck and my crystal ball." He turned serious. "No, it's more. It's knowing where important people will be at the wrong time. It's sensing when they're vulnerable. It's an awareness of what their enemies are thinking. In a way, it's like being God. It's like looking down from a high cloud and being able to see what's ahead for mere mortals. And being able to act on it."

"I think you really mean it," said Scharf.

"What?"

"That you feel like God."

Armstead gave a shrug of embarrassment. "No, that's not what I meant exactly. Don't bait me. I just meant I am pretty good in the premonition department. I knew what was going to happen to the king of Spain, and it happened. I was there with it first. Circulation soared. I've been able to put the word 'news' back into 'newspaper.' Not bad. I'm enjoying the power." He looked down at his watch. "I'd better be going."

"No hurry," said Dr. Scharf, taking in the wall clock. "We still have some time. I'll let you know when it's time to go."

Armstead came to his feet. "I'm busy. I have to talk to someone in Paris.'' He hesitated. ''In fact, I've been meaning to tell you. I'm too busy to see you three times a week anymore. My life is pretty much under control, so once a week from now on should do it.''

''If you're sure you feel that way.''

''I feel that way.''

Dr. Scharf rose. ''Very well. Let's try it once a week, on this day and time.''

''Much better,'' said Armstead.

Dr. Scharf followed him to the door. ''Incidentally, about what I mentioned earlier, I meant it as a compliment,'' he said.

''Meant what?''

''That you were able to let go of your father today.''

''Fuck him,'' Armstead said, and he yanked open the door and went out.

In his office, Armstead had divested himself of his jacket and was about to start for his desk when the door opened and Harry Dietz put his head in. ''Estelle said you were back,'' said Dietz. ''I spoke to Ramsey and Weston. They're in Paris, at the Plaza Athénée. They're standing by for your call.''

''Get them for me,'' Armstead ordered. ''Let me speak to Nick first.''

''Done,'' said Dietz, and he closed the door.

Armstead dropped into his leather swivel chair and ran his eyes over the row of telephone messages on his desk blotter. Most of them were from newspaper and television executives and editors around the country—from his own chain as well as friendly rivals—congratulating him on his series of stunning beats the past few days during the unexpected kidnapping and safe release of the king of Spain. Pleased, Armstead plucked them off his desk, placed one on top of another, and set the small pile aside but in view.

The ICM on his computer telephone sounded, and he heard Dietz on the speaker. ''Edward, I've got Nick Ramsey on hold.''

"Fine. I'll take it." Armstead sat still a moment, reviewing the overall pattern of his grand design. Satisfied, he lifted the phone receiver. "Hello, Nick."

"Hi, Mr. Armstead. Thanks for getting me out of Spain."

"Whenever we put you in a spot where it gets too hot, it is our duty to get you out."

"And congratulations on those tremendous beats."

"We're going right on from there," Armstead promised. "There are two events taking place in the next two weeks that I want to give special coverage. I want you to handle óne, and Victoria to handle the other. I'm splitting you up for the time being."

"Whatever you say, sir."

"I want you to go to Tel Aviv and prepare for the meeting that's going to take place between the Israeli prime minister and the president of Egypt in Cairo."

"That's in two weeks," Ramsey said.

"I want you in Israel first, cranking up on it. Could be a crucial meeting. There may be some violence attending."

He listened for Ramsey to contradict him, but Ramsey only murmured, "Might be."

Armstead smiled to himself. Ramsey had been tamed. "Burrow in for a couple of weeks," Armstead said. "Our bureau's doing only straight stuff. I want some color. Give me several back-grounders for our next two weekend issues—the prime minister himself, those in his cabinet who disagree with him, public opinion in Israel, and a dramatized version of the issues to be laid on the table. Got it?"

"Got it," said Ramsey.

"Okay, when the prime minister leaves Tel Aviv for Cairo, you leave with him. You've been accredited for the press plane. Stay put in Cairo for a series of sidelights on the meetings. And keep your eyes open for new imput to be used in our terrorist series."

"Will do."

"After those Mideast meetings, I'll route you elsewhere. As

for Victoria, I'm assigning her to Geneva—I'd better tell her myself."

"She's right here, panting to get her turn."

"Put her on." Armstead took a cigar stub off his glass tray and lighted it. He heard Victoria say something inaudible to Ramsey and then take over the telephone.

"Mr. Armstead. Victoria here."

"Look, Victoria, I've got an immediate assignment for you. I don't know if Nick has told you."

"He hasn't had the chance."

"I'm going to let you fly by yourself for the next week or two. I'm sending Nick to Israel. I want you in Switzerland tomorrow. Geneva, to be specific."

"Sounds good."

"You mean parting is not such a sweet sorrow?"

"I'll miss him, Mr. Armstead. He's so helpful. But I'd really welcome a chance on my own."

"Okay, here it is. You know about the Non-Nuclear Nations Conference set for next week in Geneva?"

"I'm up on the basics."

"The specifics will be waiting for you in your room at the Hôtel Beau-Rivage. Your assignments will be spelled out for you. The Non-Nuclear Nations Conference starts four days from now at the Palais des Nations, officially the office of the United Nations at Geneva. The secretary-general, Herr Anton Bauer of Austria, the United Nations head man, will arrive in Geneva three days from now. The last of the delegates from the twenty-five countries most likely to have nuclear weapons in the next five to ten years will also be arriving. The agenda for the conference will be in your briefing folder. It should have all the information you require—"

"I appreciate that."

"Yes, our Zurich bureau and the United Nations protocol officer will be providing you with all you require. Now let me tell you what we need for the *Record*. I want two advance

features—the first on the Palais des Nations and the specific
council chamber where the delegates will be seated and the
conference will be held. File that by phone tomorrow night on
the regular dictating system. Just notes. We'll get up the story at
this end. The day after tomorrow, I want you to tour the Hôtel
Intercontinental, the hotel where Anton Bauer and his staff will
be staying, and write up the details on his accommodations, his
suite, and file directly with me or with Harry Dietz, whichever of
us is handy.''

"The complete story?" Victoria interrupted.

"Complete notes. Repeat, that's to be done day after tomorrow.
Late afternoon your time. The day after that is when Bauer
arrives. You don't have to cover that. Our bureau people will be
on hand.''

"Anyone from the bureau I should meet?"

"Not this time. You're strictly on your own. They've been
there a long time, and I don't want you prejudiced by what they
know or influenced by what they take for granted. I want the
advance stories fresh, as seen through your eyes. Your third day
in Geneva is a free day. Give you a chance to mingle with
delegates, look around the city. But on your fourth day, I want
you in the press gallery, covering the preliminaries. Straight
news, if any. After that, we'll play it by ear. We'll see how
much reader interest there is in the coverage. If anything I've
said is unclear to you, it will be defined in the package of
material in your room. Now get yourself to Geneva by noon
tomorrow. You've been preregistered at the Beau-Rivage. Good
luck.''

It was a short flight from Paris by Swissair to Geneva, and only a
three-mile drive from the Aéroport de Cointrin to the hotel, and
Victoria arrived at the Beau-Rivage in midmorning.

She and Ramsey had parted late last night before her room at
the Plaza Athénée and they had both been quiet and a trifle
glum—she, because of the sudden separation, and he, she

suspected, because of having to go to the Middle East. Neither Tel Aviv nor Cairo was his favorite place.

There had been an awkwardness, too, last night outside her room. She had desperately wanted to invite him inside, and into her bed and body. Dissolute and cynical though he was, so different from Victoria herself in so many ways, she had found him more and more attractive as they traveled together, was drawn by his handsomeness, his Sydney Carton demeanor, his masculine scent, his downbeat but amusing charm. She had wanted to possess him, own him, but she had not been able to get up the nerve to be the aggressor. She had hoped against hope that he would invite himself in for a nightcap, one for the road, but if he had considered it he had let the moment pass. As in Paris earlier, as in San Sebastián and St-Jean again, he had sent her to bed with a chaste kiss on the forehead and a squeeze of her arms. Except last night he had added, "We'll see each other soon."

Preparing for bed, undressing, she had wondered why, obsessively wondered why he was not with her. She had never known a man not to desire her. This was a first. It was also a first in another way—because she desired him. She knew that she would not rest until she found out why he resisted her. Only just before sleep arrived did her curiosity about Ramsey give way to the more immediate concern of going it alone.

But this morning, alighting from her taxi a few feet from the blue canopy of the Hôtel Beau-Rivage entrance on Rue Fabri, she had put aside thoughts of Ramsey and overcome the fear of being on her own, allowing herself to be stimulated by a new adventure and opportunity.

Having paid the driver, standing by while the doorman removed her suitcase, typewriter, and briefcase from the trunk of the taxi, she could see the rise of the six-story hotel with its rolled-out yellow awnings shading ornate wrought-iron balconies and, across from the hotel, a wide promenade area with flower beds and green benches and, beyond that under a dazzling golden sun, a smooth blue carpet of water stretching across the river.

She had never been in Geneva before. She had expected something more austere, but what she could see was soft and lovely.

She went inside.

She crossed the tasteful lobby past pink marble pillars to the
reception desk. Armstead had, indeed, taken care of everything.

Five minutes later she was in her deluxe single room, patterned
blue carpeting, light blue bedspread on the wide bed, blue window drapes drawn apart so that she could see a magnificent
mountain—probably Mont Blanc—in the distance. Fresh chrysan-
themums stood in a porcelain vase on a glass-topped table between two brown armchairs, and on the bureau rested a silver
bowl of ripe fruit with plates, a fruit knife and napkins beside it.
In front of the bowl an oversized manila envelope, bulging, and
written across it in red crayon: *For Ms. Victoria Weston, Personal,
Hold for Arrival.*

Ridding herself of her coat, Victoria carried the parcel to the
bed, untied it, and carefully extracted the contents. There were a
number of cardboard folders, each labeled, one containing material on the Palais des Nations, another with brochures on the
Hôtel Intercontinental, another with Xeroxed papers listing the
nations and delegates attending the conference, another holding a
biography of the secretary-general of the United Nations, Anton
Bauer, another offering maps of Geneva and environs, as well as
a typed telephone list of personnel in the city who might be
useful. Armstead had left nothing to chance.

Eager to announce her presence before her lunch break, Victoria moved along the side of the bed to a cabinet that held a
telephone on its top and a built-in radio below. She lifted the
receiver and asked for the protocol officer's secretary at the
Palais des Nations.

Efficiently, she was advised to appear promptly at two o'clock
if she wanted to take the first of several afternoon tours of the
Palais.

Satisfied, on schedule, Victoria began to undress. There would
be time for a bath and a leisurely lunch in the terrace restaurant

overlooking the blue water. There would be time enough during the meal to read the material in several of her background folders.

Stripped of all her clothing, she posed naked to catch herself fully in the mirror above the bureau. She inspected her long blond hair, pouting lips, bony broad shoulders, straight full breasts with nipples centered in pink areolas the size of half dollars, the indentation of her navel, the slender hips and fleshy thighs encasing the triangular mound of light pubic hair.

Surely Nick Ramsey could not think her a child.

Surely he had no idea of what he was missing.

Wrenching her mind back to the work that awaited her, she went into the tiled bathroom and ran the water in the short, square tub.

Where was the story here in this neutral clean enclave of plenty? A handful of nations, each with the technology to produce nuclear weapons, about to be admonished by the head of the United Nations that they must promise restraint in an era of disarmament. Yes, a story, but one that was old hat. What she wanted was a new explosive story, something that would make everyone in New York sit up.

Where was a king of Spain?

Where a terrorist group?

Did anything ever happen in Switzerland?

Before lunch, Victoria had arranged for the rental of an auto, and after lunch the Jaguar was ready along with explicit instructions from the concierge on how to reach the Palais des Nations.

Once she was on the curving Avenue de la Paix, she watched for the building set well above the street that would have two red crosses on the sign topping its sloping roof. The CICR or Comité International de la Croix Rouge, the headquarters of the International Red Cross. Immediately past it and across from it, she had been told, was the visitors' entrance to the Palais des Nations. The instructions were excellent. She identified the CICR building, and past it she spotted the booth that sold tickets for the Palais tours. She drove past the rambling modernistic Palais structure and then turned off the Avenue de la Paix.

Victoria had no trouble finding a parking place on a nearby side street. She hurried back to the ticket booth, where she showed the attendant her press pass. Immediately she fell in behind a stream of tourists walking toward the door of the reception room, where she had been advised to meet up with her press tour.

Several groups were already gathered inside, and in one, many of the persons seemed to be armed with notepaper and pens or pencils. Victoria approached it, certain it must be the assembled press tour, and she was right. After a five-minute wait, when two others joined the group, the guide in charge, a tall, young Frenchwoman, was satisfied that everyone expected was on hand. To make sure, she read the roll aloud from the clipboard she held. In English, she read the person's name, the newspaper or magazine or television station the person represented, and the country each came from. Victoria was surprised by the variety of nations that had sent special reporters—reporters from Israel, Japan, Italy, Sweden, Pakistan, Romania, Turkey, two from Austria and, nearly at the bottom of the roll call, "Victoria Weston, New York *Record,* United States."

The guide tucked her clipboard under an arm. "We are all here, so we can begin," she announced in French. "This is unusual, but I will give my descriptions in French, English, and German, so please be understanding. We wish to serve everyone reporting on the Non-Nuclear Nations Conference." She cleared her throat and continued. "We are now in the new wing of the old League of Nations Building, officially the Palais des Nations. This new wing, added in the year 1973, enlarged our façade length from 400 meters to 575 meters, and gave to this European headquarters of the United Nations an additional ten conference rooms and seven hundred offices. If you will come with me, we will proceed."

Victoria and the others followed their guide through a maze of corridors until they reached a long hallway, one wall lined with plastic-covered brown sofas set between the marble pillars. "Over five thousand international meetings take place here annually," the guide explained as they walked. "It is by far the busiest meeting place in the world."

Now they were led into the gallery of an attractive and stately council chamber. Looking down, they could see rows of black seats, similar to bucket seats, facing the speaker's table where the secretary-general would be addressing the conference. Victoria learned that the glassed-in section at the rear of the room, above the delegates' seats, would hold members of the simultaneous-translation staff. Above that was the balcony where they were sitting, the press and visitors' gallery, which was surrounded by powerful wall murals of gold leaf on sepia painted by Spanish artist José Maria Sert. The murals, Victoria realized, depicted the end of wars and the birth of peace.

The guide encouraged them to ask any questions that they might have about the Non-Nuclear Nations Conference that would start in three days. Victoria had one question: What is the purpose of the conference? The guide had a prepared answer: To persuade those countries most advanced in nuclear technology to limit its application to domestic energy needs. Anton Bauer was lending his personal prestige to the meeting to bring about a treaty to supplement the nuclear weapons freeze already agreed upon by the United States and the Soviet Union.

When the questions had ended, the group was led through more corridors and down various flights of steps until they reached the souvenir shop. After browsing for a while, most of the group emerged from the building and strolled across a path toward a flagpole flying the blue United Nations flag. Victoria was instantly entranced by the landscape—a rolling green lawn, in the center of the lawn what appeared to be a giant bronze or gold sphere set above a reflecting pond, and behind the monument an array of hoary cedar and cypress trees backed by the shining waters of Lake Geneva.

Victoria pointed. "That gold ball—I can't figure out what it stands for?"

"I was just reading about that," said the young woman next to her. "What you see in the center is the Woodrow Wilson armillary sphere—an ancient astronomical instrument; the rings represent the positions of the planets. This was a gift from the United States, dedicated to the memory of President Wilson and his efforts on behalf of permanent peace."

Victoria gazed at the globe in wonder. Fifteen minutes later, she was walking back to her car with her notes.

One contradiction was clear to Victoria and it bewildered her.

The assignment was dull, dull, dull.

Yet, Armstead was shrewd.

It didn't make sense at all.

Once in her car, starting back to the Beau-Rivage, she made up her mind not to resist or be difficult. It was a job to be done, and she would dutifully phone New York and report what she had seen. Tomorrow's assignment, she hoped, would be better.

As it turned out the following morning, tomorrow's assignment proved to be worse.

Victoria had always prided herself on her imaginative ability to turn anything, no matter how static, no matter how unpromising, into a readable story. But the notes for this second story that Armstead had ordered her to prepare—raw material for an advance feature on the luxurious Hôtel Intercontinental in Geneva, and the accommodations that Anton Bauer would have here— baffled her. Bauer himself, from what she had read, might be a good story. This dynamic, athletic blond Austrian, from a poor family and with a background in music, had worked his way up until he became a leading international diplomat and currently head of the United Nations. He could be written about. But his hotel in Geneva? His accommodations in that hotel? Impossible.

Yet, led by an assistant manager with buck teeth and swallow tails into the hotel's presidential suite, prepared for Bauer's

arrival the next day, Victoria doggedly determined to make the
story possible.

Her notebook was already filled with scribblings about her
drive on Route de Ferney to the Hôtel Intercontinental, the
doorman with black plug hat and emerald green coat and white
trousers, the large ground-floor lobby with twin escalators connect-
ing it to the mezzanine with its shops and reception desk (padded
counter) and elevators.

Now, from the elevator, she had come to Bauer's suite.

Slowly she wandered through the vast sitting room, the assistant manager beside her babbling away. An awesome room, a
majestic one. At the left was a great grouping of two four-
cushioned sofas and four deep velour armchairs. To the right, a
grand piano and bench, a bar, a table circled with straight-backed
chairs, another table bearing an oversized basket heaped with
fresh fruit.

When she had finished her inspection and was at the door
ready to leave, she looked back once more.

In her mind's eye, she tried to infuse the suite with life, tried
to animate it with Bauer and nuclear conference delegates in
private consultations.

But it didn't happen. The rich living room remained what it
was—a room.

Disgusted, Victoria left the suite and the hotel, embarrassed by
what she would have to report to Armstead.

When her Jaguar was returned to her, she tipped the doorman
for helping her in behind the wheel, snapped on her seatbelt, and
considered the time on the clock dashboard. It was still morning,
far too early to telephone Armstead in New York—he would not
be in the office yet—and she knew that she had three or four
hours of freedom ahead of her. She had planned tomorrow, her
day off before the conference, to take a tour of the city. She had
the choice of moving that up, doing that now, and then decided
against it. She was in the mood for the countryside. Her map of
Switzerland lay folded on the passenger seat. She opened it. As

she scanned it, her focus held on the Geneva-to-Lausanne high-way along the lake, labeled N1, and on instinct she felt that the drive gave promise of being colorful. She started the Jaguar and wheeled away from the Intercontinental to find the N1.

The leisurely drive outside Geneva did indeed prove to be colorful. Victoria drove at a slackened pace, inhaling the fresh air, taking in the villas built along the lake, the placid small farms, the fruit orchards. After half an hour on the road she had covered only twenty kilometers and found herself in the ancient town of Nyon, which she decided to explore.

She had slowed to a stop at the intersection of the avenues Viollier and Perdtemps, idly casting about for sight of an outdoor café where she might pause to have tea, when she thought she saw something—someone—that made her blink.

What she saw was a man sauntering toward, and turning into, a building that might be a hotel—that *was* a hotel, she could see, a five-story building with a sign reading: HÔTEL DES ALPES. She had blinked because she thought that she recognized the man, knew him from some other place, and because it was so surpris-ing to see him here in this little-known Swiss town.

She'd had only a glimpse of him at the corner, turning away and entering into the hotel, disappearing from sight. She tried to recall who he was. Her glimpse of him had been of a slender, youngish man, around six feet, a brimmed hat sitting on a head of dark curly hair, close-set eyes, hooked nose, thick lips, maybe a blemished complexion.

Like a fugitive from an Edward G. Robinson gangster movie.

She had characterized him like that the first time she had met him, and instantly she made the association and had full recognition.

Gus Pagano.

Of course. Gus Pagano, the onetime petty thief and informant whom she had interviewed in New York as her first assignment on the *Record.*

What was Pagano, of all people, doing in someplace called Nyon, Switzerland?

A horn was honking behind her, and immediately she wanted to park and have a reunion with Pagano. Out of curiosity. Out of a sudden need to talk to someone from faraway who was familiar. Out of a desire to have a companion for tea or lunch.

The honking behind her was persisting, and Victoria tried to get her bearings. Then she saw that a parking lot was right at hand, the Place Perdtemps, a huge free parking lot for tourists who had come to visit the château that housed a museum down below.

Victoria stepped on the gas pedal, wrenched her Jaguar off the street into the half-empty lot, and pulled into the nearest parking space.

Jumping out of the car, she traversed the lot and the street and entered the Hôtel des Alpes.

It was a confined lobby with only three lounge chairs, and a reception desk toward the back. There was no one in the lobby, not Gus Pagano or anyone else. Victoria strode quickly to the reception desk, but this was also empty, unattended. She saw a bell on the counter, obviously to be rung for service, and so she pushed it.

In seconds a swarthy young waiter, possibly Italian, popped out of the adjacent restaurant, sized Victoria up, determined that she was American, and spoke apologetically in English. "Forgive me," he said. "I am waiting on the restaurant tables but I am also the reception clerk today. You wish to register?"

"No," said Victoria. "You have a guest here who is a friend of mine. I'd like to see him. Can you tell me his room number?"

The waiter went behind the reception counter, and brought the guest register closer. "His name, please?"

"Mr. Pagano. Gus Pagano. From New York."

"I will see." The waiter-clerk went down the open page, turned to the previous page, then to the one before that. "Will you spell the name for me, please?"

"P-a-g-a-n-o. Pagano."

The young man ran his finger down each page again, shaking his head. "Sorry, there is no name Pagano."

"Let me see the register," Victoria said. He handed it to her. She scanned both pages. No Pagano. Puzzled, she said, "I saw him come in here a minute ago."

"Not registered."

"Maybe he was just going to the restaurant?"

"No, not there. No one has come there for a half hour. Miss, maybe he is just visiting a friend who stays in the hotel. Then, of course, we would not know his name."

This was a possibility that had not occurred to Victoria. More than a possibility, it was a likelihood. She thanked the young man, and walked out of the Hôtel des Alpes lobby. She felt vaguely disappointed. Which was ridiculous, she told herself, because she hardly knew Pagano and could not even remember if she had liked him.

Glancing at her watch as she left the hotel, she decided that it might be best to skip Lausanne and get back to Geneva. She would want a little while to review her notes before telephoning Armstead.

She still dreaded phoning her publisher—when the most exciting sight she had seen today was only another member of his staff, a part-time one at that, in Switzerland on a holiday.

By midafternoon Victoria had made her connection with New York City and was holding the receiver to her ear, waiting for Estelle to put Edward Armstead on the phone.

The loose pages torn from her notebook with their scribbled information on the Hôtel Intercontinental were assembled on her lap, and she reviewed them a fourth time, helplessly.

"This is Armstead. That you, Victoria?"

"Yes, Mr. Armstead. You wanted me to call you with my notes on the Intercontinental."

"You're right on time, I see. Did you confirm that Anton Bauer is still going to be staying there?"

"He's checking in tomorrow." She hesitated, and swallowed. "Mr. Armstead, I must tell you, I did my very best at the hotel. They gave me every cooperation, a bright assistant manager to show me around—"

"I'd expect that. I used to stay there."

"—so I'm not complaining about their part. But I must say, Mr. Armstead, despite seeing everything, there's very little to write about."

"Let me be the judge of that, Victoria."

"Yes, of course. I was simply trying to point out—true, it's a five-star hotel—but really nothing special—"

"No special preparations for the UN secretary-general?"

"Not that I could observe."

"Well, you go ahead and dictate what you saw and heard."

"Are you going to take down every word of it?"

"No, don't worry, young lady. I have Estelle on the line with me. She'll take what you dictate in shorthand. I'll stay on the line to listen in, in case I have some questions . . . Estelle, you ready?"

"Ready," Victoria could hear his secretary say.

"Okay," Armstead said to Victoria, "you can dictate—go ahead."

Victoria held up her notes and began to read them. She described the interior of the Hôtel Intercontinental from the shops in the lobby to Anton Bauer's presidential suite. Several times she faltered, as if to apologize for the blandness of the material that she was dictating. She went on for ten minutes, uninterrupted. At last she was finished.

"The end," she said. "You've heard all of it."

"Thank you," said Estelle, and got off the line.

"You still there, Mr. Armstead?"

"I'm here, Victoria."

"I told you," she said hastily, "I didn't think there was much. I don't know if there's a story."

"It'll do," said Armstead. "It's exactly what I expected.

We'll run a short feature—the secretary-general of the United Nations in the lap of luxury, while preparing to tackle recalcitrant non-nuclear nations—or we should say part-nuclear nations who threaten to go all the way. Yes, it'll do.''

Victoria wanted to say that she did not think the angle a very good one, but she held her tongue. She said, ''I'm glad.''

''Okay, you've done your job. Take tomorrow off, then get back to the opening of the conference for a few sidebars—''

''Oh, one silly thing I must tell you, Mr. Armstead,'' she interrupted. ''I had some time to spare before I could call you, so I took a spin into the Swiss countryside. Guess whom I saw—or thought I saw? One of your employees—''

''One of my what? Employees?''

''Gus Pagano,'' she blurted.

''Who?''

''Gus Pagano. Remember the first assignment I had the day after I started on the *Record*? I was told to talk to one of the informants who worked for the paper. A fellow who had occupied the same cell Yinger occupied later? His name was Pagano.''

''I remember. What about him?''

''I was out driving in the countryside a few hours ago. I came to a little town named Nyon. There I saw Pagano go into a hotel. I thought I'd say hello, so I went into the hotel. But he wasn't registered. I thought it was Pagano—anyway, that's all unimportant—''

''It wasn't Pagano,'' said Armstead. ''You're quite mistaken.'' He chuckled. ''He could hardly be in two places at the same time. He's right here in New York. Harry Dietz and I saw him just a half hour ago.''

''Oops, my goof. I was chasing the wrong man. That could have been pretty awkward. Sorry to bend your ear with such nonsense, Mr. Armstead.''

''Never mind. Enjoy yourself in Geneva. And stay with the conference. Good-bye.''

*   *   *

For more than a minute Armstead remained motionless in his swivel chair. Inside, he was steaming.

He pressed the button of his intercom. "Harry?"

"Yes, sir, Mr. Armstead."

"Come right in here," Armstead ordered. "I want to see you."

Harry Dietz materialized in Armstead's office almost at once, his chalky countenance perplexed.

"Anything wrong, Chief?"

"Anything wrong?" Armstead exploded. "That fucker, Pagano, almost blew the ball game."

Dietz came forward, more perplexed than ever. "What do you mean?"

"That idiot, Pagano, he was seen in the town where he's staying—"

"Nyon."

"Whatever. He wasn't supposed to be seen."

"But how—?"

"One of our staff, the Weston girl—she was out taking a drive, eating up time before calling here. She got to Nyon, and there she saw Pagano. He was going into his hotel. She parked and chased after him. Luckily, she couldn't find him. Luckily, too, he wasn't registered."

"He's registered as James Ferguson." Dietz seemed to be thinking. He wagged his head slowly. "I don't know, boss, I don't know if it's a good idea to have both of them out there—Weston and Ramsey—even if they're in different places. Something like this can always happen again—"

"I need them there," Armstead insisted. "They're useful. The material they've been digging up helps. This run-in was a wild coincidence. If Pagano had followed instructions—" He slapped his hand on the desk. "Harry, you get Pagano for me right away. I'm going to eat his ass out. Before you do, tell Estelle to type up those pages as fast as possible. I've got to pass the information on to Pagano. Now get me that fucker on the phone."

Dietz dashed out of the office.

Soon Armstead heard from Dietz on the intercom. The long-distance circuits were tied up. There would be a short delay.

For twenty minutes Armstead remained in place, constantly drumming his fingers on the desk, gradually building up a head of steam.

When word came through the intercom that Gus Pagano was on hold, Armstead was ready for him.

"Gus?" he shouted into the phone.

"What's going on, boss?"

"You goddamn idiot, you let yourself be seen!" Armstead bellowed.

Pagano sounded confused. "I don't get it."

"Somebody saw you," persisted Armstead, trying to simmer down. "Somebody on our staff, one of our reporters—remember the girl, Victoria Weston, who once interviewed you?"

"Don't remember." Then he did. "You mean the good-looking broad who talked to me about Yinger?"

"She's the girl on our staff who's in Switzerland researching the Intercontinental. She was taking a drive, and she got to wherever you are, and she saw you go into your hotel—"

"She was in this godforsaken town—?"

"Sight-seeing, dammit. The point is, what in hell were you doing out in the street in the daytime where you could be recognized? You had your instructions about that."

"Listen, boss, let me explain. Cooper—"

"Is this a safe line?"

"Nobody gives a damn about this line. I'm just another crummy tourist here to see the museums. Let me explain. I know my instructions. But Cooper buzzed me from the Hôtel Xenia in Geneva and wanted me to case an alternate site for the—the hideout—so I had to leave the hotel—"

"He should have known better. Don't you ever let it happen again."

"Well, sometimes I may have to move around—"

"Then grow a beard or mustache or some goddam thing. No, there won't be time. Buy one. Buy a disguise, anything."

"Okay, boss." He was disbelieving still. "You mean that girl really saw me?"

"She saw you all right and told me so. I was able to persuade her it hadn't been you. That you were in New York and I'd just been with you. She bought it. So no problem there."

Pagano sighed with relief. "I'll be more careful from now on."

"I've got the Intercontinental material for you."

"Good. Though I don't think Cooper will need much of it. He's already had one of his own men in and out of the place. Anyway, I'll pass it on to him. Want to give it to me?"

"One second. Let me get the notes."

Armstead left his chair and opened the door to his secretary's office, holding out his hand. She leaped to her feet with the typed pages and gave them to him. He shut his door and returned to the phone.

"You set with your pencil?" asked Armstead.

"All set."

"I'll try to read it to you slowly."

Lovingly, with care, Armstead read the three and a half pages of typescript aloud. Victoria had done an admirable job and Armstead was pleased.

When he was finished, he inquired, "Got it all?"

"Got it."

Armstead dropped his voice. "Is the event on schedule?"

"Day after tomorrow at the time planned. No change."

"I'll be in the office here. You'll get word straight to me."

"The second I hear, I'll let you know."

"It's an important one, Gus. Hope they get it right."

"They'll get it right, boss. They can't afford to get it wrong. Don't worry."

But hanging up, Armstead *was* worried. When news just happened spontaneously you were not involved, except to report it.

When you made the news happen, that was another matter, a strain. You had a stake in it, full responsibility.

You had to worry.

It wasn't all that easy, playing God.

The day after tomorrow in Geneva.

Nine twenty-five in the morning.

The press and visitors' gallery of the Spanish chamber in the Palais des Nations was jam-packed. Victoria had arrived early to be sure to claim a place at the best vantage point. She had a seat in the front row of the balcony. Bending forward, arms on the brass railing, she once more surveyed the scene in the chamber below. The chamber was crowded with delegates, most in their seats, a few moving about, many of them chattering in many tongues.

It was a colorful spectacle, this polyglot gathering, and Victoria was eager to see the proceedings get underway. As timepieces clicked closer to nine-thirty, more and more of the delegates became attentive to the speaker's table and the chair that at any moment would be filled by the arrival of Secretary-General Bauer from his headquarters at the Hôtel Intercontinental.

Nine-thirty.

Victoria sat alert, notebook and pen poised.

Nine-thirty-five.

The secretary-general's chair remained empty.

Nine-forty, nine forty-five.

Yet another fifteen minutes passed, and still Anton Bauer had not appeared.

Victoria could detect, for the first time, a degree of restlessness among the delegates below. Some of them were standing, stretching, wandering about. To Victoria, Bauer's tardiness did not seem unusual. Men of state were often engaged in many great enterprises, and had much to handle in limited time, and Bauer would be here shortly, she was convinced.

Five minutes later, in response to grumbling in the chamber

below, Victoria heard a voice call out, "I am informed that Herr Bauer has left his suite!"

This calmed the delegates for the moment.

Time continued to tick away, and still Bauer had not appeared. Victoria found herself fidgeting, and at last, on impulse, she came to her feet and left the gallery.

In the hallway she saw a cordon of Swiss federal policemen. She approached the nearest one. "Pardon me, but do you speak English?"

"Yes, madame."

"Has Anton Bauer shown up yet?"

"Not yet. We are expecting him for some time."

There would be some logical explanation for this delay shortly, Victoria told herself, and she should get back to the balcony and her press place to be on hand for the opening of the conference. But she did not return to the balcony. Instead she walked swiftly down the series of corridors that led to the exit, hurried outside, and made for her car. The automatic reporter's instinct that something might be amiss had surfaced in her. The nonappearance of Bauer was odd. It might even be news. It was worth looking into.

Victoria settled into her Jaguar, started it, and headed for the Hôtel Intercontinental, only a few blocks away. Driving, she tried to define what was in her mind. Illness was one possibility. Anton Bauer might have suffered a heart attack. This would explain the delay. She must find out what was going on.

At the entrance to the hotel she left her car with the doorman, asking him to keep it handy, and then she hurried into the entry, made for the escalator, and rode it up to the mezzanine. She surveyed the area between the reception desk and the elevators. There was a large party of men, some in uniform, some in plainclothes, gathered near the elevator, a few milling about impatiently. Bauer's security detail, Victoria surmised, still waiting for him, but she had to be sure.

Victoria's eyes went to the reception desk again, and this time she saw the buck-toothed assistant manager who had been her host during the tour of the hotel. She went directly to the counter.

"Hello," she said. "Remember me?"

The assistant manager looked blank for a moment, and then recognition came. "Yes, of course. Good day, Miss Weston."

She jerked her thumb over a shoulder. "Is that Anton Bauer's escort party?"

The assistant manager glanced off. "Yes, it is."

"What happened to Herr Bauer?"

The assistant manager shrugged. "We do not know."

"Is he in his room?"

"We have called. There is no answer."

"Maybe he's sick and can't answer."

"No, Miss Weston. We have been in his suite. There is no one there. Herr Bauer has left."

"But—"

That instant the assistant manager's head came up, his gaze fixing fast on something or someone behind Victoria. She immediately turned to see what had diverted his attention. There was a stocky gentleman, black hair pomaded flat, horn-rimmed spectacles, nattily dressed even to a vest, beckoning imperatively. The assistant manager came erect. "Excuse me, miss," he said nervously, "the manager must see me." He left the counter in a hurry and trotted toward the manager. Victoria saw the manager's arm go around his assistant's shoulders and forcefully lead him away toward one of the squarish white marble pillars that held display cases framed in teakwood.

The bulky manager was leaning close to his aide, beginning to whisper conspiratorially as they disappeared behind the pillar. Victoria's inquisitiveness was instantly piqued. She started toward the pillar. The pair might be discussing only hotel business, but nevertheless it might be worth eavesdropping. Casually, Victoria sidled up to the near side of the pillar, tilted her head closer to the corner behind which the pair had disappeared.

She was safely out of their sight, but she could hear the

manager's voice distinctly now. He was speaking rapidly in French but she could understand every word, and what she heard made her stand stock-still.

Listening intently, she heard the manager saying, "Yes, it is true, Pierre, it is confidential from the police headquarters where they are interrogating the bodyguard. What happened, as far as I can learn, is that Bauer went with his bodyguard into the elevator we set for express, to bring him straight down to his escort. But somehow it was stopped and opened before the mezzanine. Armed terrorists—we now know it is the Carlos gang—abducted both men, rushed them out of the hotel to a large car, blindfolded them both, and drove them out of the city."

"Impossible," Victoria heard the assistant croak. "The secretary-general of the United Nations kidnapped in Geneva—no."

The manager was going on in French. "But true, Pierre—alas, it is true. It is all from the bodyguard. Carlos took him not only to keep it quiet until they had a good start, but to use him to report the kidnapping to the police and to reveal the ransom terms. I do not know these terms yet. They not only blindfolded the bodyguard but bound his hands behind his back. After an estimated twenty or thirty minutes' driving, the vehicle stopped, and the bodyguard was pulled out of the back seat and left in a field and the vehicle sped away. He was loosely tied, deliberately so I am sure, and after a while he was able to free himself, remove his blindfold, and hike to the main road. He realized that he was outside Coppet. He caught a ride from a motorist, went to the village and reported to the police, who brought him back to the headquarters here. He remembered his captors' mentioning Carlos, how pleased Carlos would be. He was addressed directly only once, when they released him. He was given ransom terms to pass on. The police called me to cooperate."

"But how?"

"They want no word of this out yet. But they want me to inform the escort party that it need not wait any longer—but there must be some innocent explanation given—"

"That Monsieur Bauer is ill—ill for a day or two—must rest—"

"Perfect, Pierre. You will so inform the escort party. Meanwhile, I am requested to phone the Palais to have this morning's conference postponed because of Bauer's indisposition. The truth must not be revealed, Pierre—it will hurt the police effort— perhaps do damage to the hotel—"

For the first time, Victoria stirred.

She must not be caught eavesdropping. She must get the incredible news to New York as fast as possible.

Quietly she left her post at the pillar. Although her cheeks burned with excitement, she tried to appear calm as she approached the escalator to the lobby.

In seconds she was off the escalator, and on the run for her car and the biggest story of her career.

Once locked in her room at the Hôtel Beau-Rivage, Victoria tried to relate the time in Geneva to the time in New York City. It was slightly after the noon hour here, therefore only daybreak or early morning in Manhattan. No one important would be in command at the *Record*. What she had ready was too big to pass on to any underling. She must go straight to the top.

Eager to call Edward Armstead, she realized that he would be at home and she did not possess his apartment phone number. No use trying New York information for his number. It would be unlisted. Calming down, she remembered that Harry Dietz had told her that if ever there was an emergency she could call him at his apartment, and that was a suite he had recently purchased in the Sherry Netherland Hotel.

She snatched up the telephone and put through her call to the Sherry Netherland.

Apparently the circuits to New York were open at this time of day, because in a few minutes she had a woman operator in the Sherry Netherland. Victoria announced that she wanted to speak to Mr. Harry Dietz.

The hotel operator, like most lonely night operators, was a

chatty type. "I dunno," she said, "usually he has his phone shut off at two A.M., won't be disturbed until eight in the morning. Lemme see. No, it's not shut off this morning. Maybe he's not in. Let's find out."

There was a brief ringing, and a quick answer.

"Hello, there."

Victoria's heart leaped. The voice was unmistakably that of Harry Dietz.

Victoria wanted to shout out her news, explode it in his ear, but she also wanted to be a cool professional. She contained herself. "Mr. Dietz, this is Victoria Weston in Geneva," she said briskly. "I'm sorry to wake you at this hour but—"

"Don't worry about it, you haven't awakened me," Dietz interrupted. "Matter of fact, I haven't gone to sleep yet." He sounded a trifle slurry, like someone who had recently had two or three drinks. "Edward and I just now left the paper. What a night this has been, but we got a big one going, just got it off on the presses, should hit the streets very soon."

"Well, listen, I—"

Dietz ignored her, went right on speaking. "In fact, it's from your neck of the woods. A real big one, and we have it all by ourselves. Not a peep from the wires anywhere. What a beauty. The secretary-general of the United Nations—Anton Bauer—he's been kidnapped—grabbed while leaving his hotel room—"

"By the Carlos gang." Victoria's voice had gone flat. She sank down on the side of the bed. She felt pain, as if she had suffered a stomach blow.

Dietz seemed not to have heard her. "—Abducted by Carlos and his terrorist gang. Ed and I saw the ransom demand just as we were leaving to get some sleep. We've got a full crew back at work—this'll give us an exclusive follow-up for the next edition—"

"What was the ransom demand?" Victoria asked dully.

"Weird, real weird. But guess it makes sense if you know about someone like Carlos. The ransom is to break up the Non-Nuclear Nations Conference and send the delegates home.

Because the conference was a big nations power ploy to keep the smaller nations disarmed and weak. It was to discriminate against them. So if everyone is sent home, allowed to make their little bombs, it will be fair. Once everyone is sent home, sent home from Geneva, Anton Bauer will be set free.''

"Can't there be another conference soon?''

"Sure, but Carlos promises if there is he will terrorize it once more. Whole thing, just his way of making a political statement. Well, the *Record* and Mark Bradshaw score another beat. Read about it in the *Record*. Hey, I better hit the sack and get a few winks of sleep. Got a long day ahead tomorrow—mean today. Thanks for calling, Vicky.''

She heard him hang up, too spaced out even to have asked her why she had called.

She sat there, limp and dazed.

A scoop kicked out from her again. Mark Bradshaw, the whiz kid of the *Record* again.

How?

Her wristwatch told her the kidnapping had happened only three hours ago. She'd had it, owned it, herself alone. Yet she hadn't. Someone else had reported it before her, and in New York the thunderous story would momentarily be in the streets and on the airwaves. Yet, in Geneva and in the wide world out there, no public knew. They would know only when the infallible *Record* told them.

How?

Maybe an old master like Nick Ramsey would have an answer. She must find him and tell him, and hear what he had to say.

9

Relieved to be in an air-conditioned place again, Nick Ramsey sat sprawled in one of the chairs available in the Israeli press officer's temporary room on the second floor of the terminal at Ben Gurion International Airport and watched as the officer poured scotch from a quart bottle for the other foreign correspondents lounging along the walls. When the officer reached him, Ramsey was pleased to note that there was still plenty of liquor in the bottle. He held out his glass, empty except for two ice cubes.

"Say when, Nick," said the Israeli press officer, pouring slowly.

Ramsey said nothing until his glass was filled to the brim. Then, with a grin, he said, "When."

He brought the glass of scotch to his lips and enjoyed a long drink. His body's response seemed almost instantaneous. The throbbing ache of fatigue in his muscles, chest, arms, gradually his thighs, began to disappear.

Now the press officer was addressing the group of reporters. "Prime Minister Salmon will be boarding, taking off for Cairo to meet with Egyptian President Massouna, in one hour. Well, it

could maybe be an hour and a half. It depends." He squinted
down at his wristwatch. "The prime minister should just be
finishing his meeting with Egyptian Ambassador Nahas at the
Knesset about now. Salmon mentioned something about detour-
ing briefly to take the Egyptian ambassador to the Dead Sea
scrolls museum across the way. A quick fifteen- or twenty-
minute tour. As you know, Salmon is pretty proud of the role his
father played in acquiring the scrolls. After that they'll both head
straight for the airport here, to catch the official plane to Cairo."
The press officer picked up his own drink. "You'll board your El
Al 707 press plane in fifteen minutes. There'll be an open bar,
but I advise a minimum of insobriety. Egyptian President Massouna
is personally welcoming our prime minister. There will be a little
ceremony for you to cover."

"Meaning we'll have to hang around the Cairo airport for over
an hour before the ceremony," protested Ramsey.

"You'll be well taken care of at Cairo International Airport,"
said the Israeli press officer. "The Egyptians will be putting on a
fancy Faroukian feed for you in the press area. Food catered by
the Nile Hilton, and served by those *zaftig* waitresses. I promise,
you won't suffer. Well—" The officer held up his glass.
"Shalom."

Ramsey stifled a yawn, and drank again.

He did not like the idea of leaving. He felt comfortable in Tel
Aviv, and constantly interested in Jerusalem. He hated Cairo, the
crowdedness of it, the dirt and poorness of it, and no sum on
earth could induce him to go out to the pyramids once more, to
suffer those nagging and lying hawkers with their awful trinkets.
Staying on in Israel would have been preferable, except for the
fact that there was not much doing these days on the story side,
certainly no event that would make the first four pages of the
New York *Record*. The coming meetings in Cairo between the
heads of Israel and Egypt promised little more. There had been
endless similar meetings in the past few years, and not one had
produced a decent international news story.

Lazily, Ramsey finished his drink and wondered what was happening to Victoria Weston. He missed her brightness, her chatter. Almost every morning since their separation he had awakened picturing her, her body, and had an erection. He wished that she were here to accompany him to Cairo and make the visit more bearable.

The thought that he would see her one day soon, and perhaps stop acting as foolishly as he had, made him feel even more relaxed.

He held out his glass for another shot of scotch. Leaning forward, he picked a few more ice cubes out of the bowl on the desk, dropped them into his glass, and drank again, waiting for the last ache of exhaustion to drain away.

For Ramsey, the past ten days had been wearying. No sooner had he reached the Tel Aviv Hilton Hotel from Paris than he had heard from New York and from Ollie McAllister. There was a new priority assignment for Ramsey. Instead of merely researching background material for coverage of the Israeli prime minister's flight to Egypt and his meetings there with his Egyptian counterpart, Ramsey was to accompany Israel's defense minister on an inspection tour around the country. This would take five days. The sixth day he was to go to The Shrine of the Book—the Dead Sea scrolls museum in Jerusalem—and cover an anniversary of the museum, which was to feature a gathering of eminent international archaeologists.

The defense tour of Israel had quickly worn Ramsey to a frazzle not because he was in soft physical condition, or because of the unremitting heat, or because the military provided few comforts (no hotels on this tour, only barracks and tents), but because the young, vigorous defense minister was a dynamo. Ramsey had ridden with the minister or hiked at his heels from Haifa to Afula to Gaza to Beersheba, and throughout the Negev. The resultant story—Israel's preparedness for a possible war in the near future against any combination of Arab states—proved interesting enough until Israeli censors emasculated it.

The sixth day, in Jerusalem, Ramsey had gone to cover the ceremony at the Dead Sea scrolls museum. He had never before visited The Shrine of the Book, the Israelis' name for the sacred sanctuary that housed and preserved the seven priceless Dead Sea scrolls discovered in a Qumran cave in 1947. Walking between the white dome—fashioned after the cover of the scrolls' earthen jar—and a black basalt wall, descending to the subterranean main repository, Ramsey had found himself interested but doubtful that the inanimate story of a musuem could provide much excitement for the busy readers of a harum-scarum, hyped-up New York metropolitan newspaper.

Yet, once inside, Ramsey had been forced to suspend all doubts. He had been utterly intrigued by what he was shown beneath the double parabolic dome. As he followed an archaeologist guide during an inspection tour before the ceremony, Ramsey had been open-mouthed with fascination. An arched tunnel lined with showcases ascended to the central circular main hall, which was highlighted by an elevated main column displaying the Isaiah scroll, the entire book of Isaiah. It was as if the ancient Qumran community of two thousand years ago had come to life, resurrected by the numerous jagged leather sheets bearing in Aramaic their accounts of the persistent struggle of Good against Evil.

With reluctance Ramsey attended to his job, made notes for his story, noted everything from the fact that the museum's interior architecture was in the form of the cave in which the scrolls had been found to the fact that the scrolls were enshrined behind thick glass in ten display cases to the fact that the fragments of the main scroll, the Isaiah, were not the originals but clever photocopies, since the fragile real fragments might be destroyed by exposure to light in the building.

Ramsey, with an interpreter at his side, had joined other guests in the makeshift seating arrangements, had tried to be attentive to the ceremony, had half-listened to speeches by biblical scholars and archaeologists. For Ramsey, the speakers had been relatively lifeless. What had pumped life and blood into the day had been the scrolls themselves.

That evening, in the King David Hotel, Ramsey had tried to infuse some of that energy into his story. Calling New York to dictate the piece, he had been modestly pleased with his handiwork. But he had still suspected, despite knowledge that Armstead had personally suggested the assigment, that the story would be given little prominence in a normal New York day replete with murders and muggings, bribery and graft, and at least several sex scandals.

This morning, which was hot as ever, Ramsey had hired a taxi to take him the three quarters of an hour drive from Jerusalem to the Tel Aviv Hilton. There had hardly been time for a shower, a change of clothes, a sandwich on the run, and no time at all to reply to the phone messages from Victoria—who, to his surprise, was in Paris, not Geneva—before he had to catch the press bus to Ben Gurion International Airport.

He was still in the airport's temporary press room, finishing his second drink, when he realized that he was being paged on the public-address system.

Setting down his glass, he came to his feet. "They're paging me. I missed it—where do I pick up the call?"

The Israeli press officer beckoned him. "You can take it next door. Let me help. Come along."

They walked to the claustrophobic adjacent room. The officer picked up the phone, spoke twice in Hebrew, handed over the receiver. "Paris on the line for you. They're making the connection." He went to the door. "Don't forget, we're leaving any minute."

Once he was alone, Ramsey brought the receiver to his ear. "Hello. This is Nick Ramsey."

"At last," a distant voice sighed. The voice belonged to Victoria Weston. "Where have you been, Nick? I was so worried. I've been trying to get you for over a week—"

"Hello, Vicky. I got your messages when I stopped by the

Hilton, but there wasn't time to call you back. How'd you know I was at Ben Gurion?''

''The hotel told me you were on your way to the airport.''

''Boarding a plane to Cairo any minute. When I came to Tel Aviv, Armstead had an interim assignment for me.''

''Terrorist stuff?''

''I wish it had been,'' said Ramsey. ''A tour of defense installations. A day covering ceremonies at The Shrine of the Book.''

''The what?''

''The Dead Sea scrolls museum. Good story, but it's not going to help the *Record* soar. Sa-ay, these calls—is anything wrong?''

''Everything—or maybe nothing.''

''And what are you doing in Paris? I thought you were—''

''In Geneva, you thought. Well, that's part of it, and I wanted to talk to you after it happened. I mean the Bauer kidnapping. The secretary-general of the United Nations was grabbed by Carlos while I was there.''

''I read the stories in the Jerusalem *Post* and the *Herald Trib* along the way.''

''I had it alone, Nick,'' she said quickly. ''Did you read the by-line on the big scoop?''

''There was no by-line on the first story I read. The wire services credited the New York *Record*.''

''There was a by-line on the story in New York. Want to guess?''

''Mark Bradshaw? Not again?''

''Again. I phoned Dietz immediately, positive I was the only one to have it, and he told me they were already on the presses with it. What is Armstead doing—double-covering our stories with another staffer?''

''I suppose he wants to make sure. That Bradshaw's a lucky bastard. I wish I had some of his luck. And Armstead—I would never have predicted it, but he's turned into something of a genius.''

"How do you mean?"

"Sending us and Bradshaw to hot spots where things happen. He should rank high with the Central Premonition Registry. But this time he's going to miss out, with me in Israel and you in Paris. What are you doing in Paris anyway?"

"Armstead recalled me from Geneva until he had another assignment. Until something happens, I'm twiddling my thumbs."

"Well, not a thing is going to happen there, and as far as I can see, not a damn thing is going to happen here. This trip is zero, zilch. Good to know that our publisher is human—wins some, loses some, like everybody else. Anyway, maybe we'll see each other soon."

"I hope so, Nick."

"Ditto on this end. Hey, somebody out there is calling for me. I'm afraid it's bon voyage time."

"Nick, call me when you get to Cairo."

"Real soon, baby. We'll have plenty of time together yet."

At midafternoon the blue minibus, moving at moderate speed, turned off Herzl Boulevard in Jerusalem and entered onto Ruppin.

Inside the rented bus, Cooper, the model of a businessman tourist attired in a light summer suit, with conservative necktie and white Oxford-cloth shirt, leaned closer to the window until his nose almost touched the glass. To his right, he could see the buildings of Hebrew University passing by and the university stadium ahead. Pulling away from the window, he caught a glimpse of the stately pillared Knesset, Israel's parliament. Narrowing his eyes, gazing up the aisle through the bus windshield, he could make out the graceful arc of a white dome, the roof of the Dead Sea scrolls museum, not quite directly ahead, somewhat to the right in the near distance.

"We're almost there," Cooper proclaimed, straightening in his seat. He raised his voice so that the other seven men in the bus could hear him. "We'll be there in a few minutes, so on your toes. You've all been to the museum. You know your way around. You have your assignments. You know what to do.''

"Clear enough," called back Quiggs from the front seat.

Cooper sat in silence for a half minute as the bus rolled on and the white dome grew larger in the windshield.

Cooper resumed speaking once more, almost idly. "Krupinski will drive this bus into the parking lot beside the museum. He will leave the wheel, abandon the bus, and with Pagano go to the two empty Fords in the lot. They will stand around, have a smoke, watch the time, be ready to get into the driver seats. Meanwhile, the six of us will alight from this bus like tourists, a tour party from Liverpool, remember. Queue up at the ticket office—there's a sign in English and Hebrew that identifies it—and when we have our tickets, move on singly or in pairs to the glass entry booth. Once through the booth, there'll be the long black-pebbled concrete walk to the Israel Museum on the small hill ahead. Before that, second turn off to the right, there'll be a sign reading THE SHRINE OF THE BOOK. That's it. Make your way casually to it—no running. You're sightseeing—you're tourists, remember. Go up the rise in the turnoff, four steps, more walk, two steps, to the head of the steep staircase leading down into the courtyard. The second we start down, we go into action.''

Lafair waggled his hand. "What if we get mixed in with some other tourists, real tourists, going down the staircase?''

"Odds against it, but possible," Cooper replied. "If that happens, you stop them at that point and cover them, immobilize them there until the getaway." He addressed the others. "We all keep going. Fast. I'm allowing three minutes from entry of the museum to exit. Got it?''

"Got it," called back Quiggs.

"Any questions?" asked Cooper.

There were none.

"One caution," stated Cooper, "based on last-minute intelligence from Pagano.''

Everyone in the bus except the driver turned around to listen attentively to their leader.

"You recall, after the entrance hall and souvenir area in the museum, there's the tunnel with its lighted glass showcases," stated Cooper. "Ignore those. Don't bother with them. They display the Bar Kokhba manuscripts and Masada scrolls and coins, potsherds, and other artifacts. Those are not the great treasures. Go on past them into the main circular central hall. Avoid the elevated pedestal in the center of the room. It contains leaves of the Isaiah scroll, but these are photocopies, fakes, not the original. Go for the ten showcases around the room. They contain the originals of the Dead Sea scrolls from the Qumran cave. Don't try to break the glass in the display cases. We don't know how thick the glass is. We don't know if the glass is tied into an outside alarm. Instead, use the duplicate keys we have made. The keys may take seconds longer, but they are surer and safer. Each display case has a keyhole in the wooden frame at the bottom. Insert the key, lift the lid, remove the scrolls. And away we go."

The bus jolted into a turn.

Cooper looked out the window. "Here we are. We're passing the two Fords we'll use. To the rear, Krupinski—park there."

As the bus eased across the parking lot, they all sat tense with expectation, noting only three other unoccupied vehicles.

As they parked, Cooper spoke quickly once more. "About the getaway. If it goes well, we leave as casually as we went in. The four of you go nice and easy to your cruise ship in Haifa. Leave your bags of scrolls with me. Gus and I will head back into Jerusalem to do what we have to do before flying out of here. If anything goes wrong, if we're pressed, then we'll scram fast as we can, follow the alternate plan, take a different route, drop you off in pairs at your contact points where you'll have changes of clothes, and then you'll leave the country." He addressed himself to Krupinski and Pagano. "In either case, when we leave this lot, remember, no speeding, no jumping red lights. The

Israelis have camera boxes over their traffic signals to take pictures of offenders. Once we're on the wing, we'll meet up in Paris as agreed."

Cooper looked out the window. The bus had drawn to a stop. The engine died.

"All right, boys," Cooper said quietly, "we've got work to do. Let's move."

The bus door opened. Krupinski left the wheel, descended, followed by Pagano. Momentarily Cooper watched them saunter away toward the Fords. He stepped into the aisle of the bus and trailed after his colleagues and out onto the baking parking lot.

They broke into two groups, ad-libbing conversations with each other as they headed across the lot to the booth with the sign reading TICKET OFFICE. They fell raggedly into line, each finding Israeli change, each paying for his ticket, each moving on to the neighboring booth, a glass enclosure framed in blue, with a sign that said ENTRANCE.

Cooper led the way into the entrance. Inside, there was a disinterested young man with a Band-Aid on his chin and a museum badge on his sports jacket, chatting in Hebrew with a fat adolescent Jewish girl who was seated nearby munching on an apple. The young man automatically glanced at each ticket, hardly noticing them as he passed them through.

They were gathered in the open again, on a broad pebbled concrete walk. Cooper stepped ahead of the others, as if guiding a tour group. They trudged along slowly, several of them mopping their foreheads with handkerchiefs and complaining of the heat. They went past the first pathway to their right, the museum's exit from the rear bookshop and rest rooms, and straggled toward the walk that led to the museum. A posted sign read THE SHRINE OF THE BOOK.

At the sign they slowed, assembled behind Cooper and turned off to another walk, stepping up the pace, climbing three short sets of steps. They were dwarfed by a towering black slab of wall on one side and the white dome on the other.

Rounding a corner, they assembled once more at the top of a sharply angled stone staircase leading down to a courtyard. There were no real tourists in sight.

Cooper squinted at his watch, lifting his head to encompass the others, and dipped his head toward the staircase. "All right," he ordered.

As if on signal, the six of them whipped out their grotesque colored woolen ski masks and pulled them over their heads. Quiggs had already extracted his Koch submachine gun from one of the shopping bags he was carrying. Hurrying down the staircase, each of the others tugged free his loaded Spanish Magnum handgun. They hit the floor of the courtyard almost in concert. They spun left and dashed across the court to the actual entrance to the underground museum.

In the lead, Cooper could see the personnel he had expected—at the open metal doorway, inside the entrance, two museum employees, one a ticket taker wearing an ordinary suit, the other an elderly guard in some semblance of a uniform, wearing a drooping gun holster. Not far behind them, seated next to a souvenir stand of booklets and tapes, a beardless clerk sat reading a paperback.

Cooper's sudden appearance in the frightening slit-eyed mask, brandishing a gleaming handgun, startled all three members of the museum personnel into temporary paralysis. Cooper burst inside, and the other five masked figures streamed in after him. As Shields came abreast of him, Cooper reminded him, "The alarm you located yesterday—probably off, but make sure it's fully disengaged."

The ticket taker had his hands up, and so did the souvenir clerk. The only one who tried to resist, the elderly entrance guard, slid one trembling hand to his holster. Cooper took a rapid step forward, lashed him on the head with his gun. The old man groaned, began to crumple. Cooper caught him, jerked free the guard's gun, and let the limp body fall to the floor. Quiggs, having set aside the submachine gun and shopping bags, was in back of the ticket taker, bringing his arms down. Tying his wrists behind him with a thin hemp rope removed from the pocket of his suit coat, Quiggs shoved the man to the floor, then dipped into his own pocket again for a wadded-up handkerchief and stuffed it in the ticket taker's mouth. At the same time Cooper was binding the wrists of the unconscious guard and gagging him. Overly was doing the same with the souvenir clerk.

Swiftly Cooper leaped to his feet. Gesturing for Quiggs to remain at the entrance, he snatched up the shopping bags, passed one to Overly, passed the others out to Lafair, De Salvo, Shields as they ran into the museum tunnel. Overly followed them and Cooper brought up the rear.

On the run, they scurried through the crushed-basalt tunnel between the illuminated display cases holding the Bar Kokhba and Masada documents. As they approached the ascent to the main curcular museum room, a squat uniformed museum guard materialized. Cooper sprinted ahead, gun high, and saw that this guard was unarmed and already had his hands up. Cooper gestured for his cohorts to bind and gag the second guard.

As they did so, Cooper quickly circled inside the exhibit room to see if it was otherwise occupied. Hidden by the central pedestal, a short couple, apparently man and wife in their sixties and apparently both partially deaf from the hearing aids in evidence, were peering intently into a showcase bearing the brown Habakkuk Commentary scroll. Cooper was upon them with his gun before they knew it. They were too bewildered to resist, and Cooper hastily herded them, stumbling, to the others, where they were tied and gagged and ordered to lie down beside the prone guard.

Without the loss of a second, members of the gang fanned out around the room, each inserting his key into a preassigned display case. Five glass lids went up, the genuine fragile Dead Sea scrolls, sheets of ancient leather, some sewn with threads of flax, were drawn out and stuffed into the shopping bags, several

scrolls coming apart. Five more glass lids went up. More scrolls
were dropped into the shopping bags.

The heist was over.

At the entrance to the Israel Museum and The Shrine of the
Book, Prime Minister Salmon of Israel, with Egyptian Ambassador Nahas beside him, had quickly left the limousine and escort
at the curb, had ignored the public entrance and led his guest
through the open gate next to it.

Despite his seventy-two years, the prime minister was striding
across the pebbled concrete walk as rapidly as an athlete, fast
enough to force the Egyptian ambassador to gasp for air and the
three younger bodyguards, two mustached Israeli onces and the
ambassador's clean-shaven Egyptian one, to break into a trot to
keep up with him.

The prime minister was late, very late. A politician who
always took pride in his promptness, he considered tardiness an
unforgivable sin. But the last-minute meeting with Ambassador
Nahas had gone on longer than he had expected. Salmon had
been painfully aware that his entourage, the consultants, aides,
ministers accompanying him to the Cairo meeting, were already
on the plane awaiting his arrival.

Still, this further delay was necessary. Leaving the Knesset, he
had promised the Egyptian ambassador a brief glimpse of the
Dead Sea scrolls museum. For Salmon, it was a matter of pride.
His father, as much as any man, had been responsible for the
museum's holdings. The new ambassador had not yet seen them,
and Salmon was eager and proud to show them off.

The prime minister slowed down slightly. "You know the
story of the discovery of the scrolls?"

"Yes, I had read about it," Ambassador Nahas puffed.

"My father, Yitzhak, was one of the main people responsible
for their acquisition. On the eve of the United Nations vote to
partition Palestine, and the outbreak of fighting, my father accompanied Professor Eliezer Sukenik, the Hebrew University archae-

ologist, from Jerusalem to Bethlehem where a dealer had the
recently discovered scrolls. Very dangerous, very dangerous. But
the trip was made safely and the ancient parchments purchased,
and now they reside here for all the world to see. Nearly two
thousand years old, those scrolls!''

Salmon pointed to one aide.

"Let's take a shortcut, go into the museum by the back way.
It'll save time, give us a few minutes extra to view the treasures.
Then we'll be off, fast as we can, for the airport and Cairo.''

Inside the Dead Sea scrolls museum, Cooper had run to the
tunnel opening and whistled loudly three times. He waited,
heard Quiggs whistle back three times and was satisfied. The
signal for all to depart. He waited again, saw Quiggs and his
submachine gun coming toward him swiftly. When Quiggs joined
him, Cooper whirled, shouting to the others for the benefit of his
bound victims, "Carlos says let's get out of here!''

He and Quiggs and their colleagues, with their filled bags,
were rushing across the room to the doorway leading into the rear
corridor when suddenly, unexpectedly, the doorway was filled
with men, strangers—one, two, three, four, five of them entering
the museum, two in mufti, three in uniforms and armed. Cooper
saw the startled looks on their faces and realized that he, Quiggs,
and the others were still wearing their slit-eyed masks and were
obviously recognizable as terrorists.

One of the uniformed men already had his gun out and had
opened fire. As a member of the Cooper gang, Shields, took the
first shots and crumpled lifeless, Cooper heard Quiggs next to
him go into action. Quiggs's submachine gun raked the entering
party from one side to the other, and then back again, and then
over again. Like so many wooden dolls, each member of the
entering party toppled over. All five of them lay sprawled on the
floor, with blood beginning to ooze from their wounds.

The massacre had taken seconds, and Cooper prayed that the
chattering sounds of gunfire had not been heard outside.

Fiercely Cooper signaled for his survivors to get out. Leaping over the prone bodies, they rushed from the room into the rear corridor, hurrying to the right into the exit corridor as they yanked off their masks and hid their weapons in their pockets. Going past the bookshop and the puzzled female clerk behind a counter, they were immediately outdoors.

They were in the open air once more, racing for the nearby museum exit gate, abruptly following Cooper's lead in slowing to a brisk walk as they retraced their steps toward the unlocked final gate next to the glass ticket booth. As they strode to it, no one running, the young man inside and the escort personnel around the limousine at the curb never even looked up. Cooper exhaled his relief. The sounds of gunfire had been too distant to be clearly heard, or if heard at all had been misunderstood.

As a group, walking steadily, they were crossing the parking lot to the two Ford sedans where Krupinski and Pagano were standing by, posing as chauffeurs.

Advancing, Cooper gestured the drivers to their wheels.

Splitting up, members of the group ducked into their respective cars, closed the doors.

"There was a shoot-out," Cooper growled to Pagano, "so it's the alternate plan. Let's beat it."

As Pagano hurriedly started the car, Cooper called to those in the rear seat, "Who in the hell were those two with the guards?"

"One of them looked like the Israeli prime minister," answered Lafair.

"Shit," said Cooper. "And losing Shields besides. Shit. Okay, Gus, make it cool and easy—but fast."

They drove out of the parking lot, the bookless and bloody shrine receding quickly behind them, quiet in the sunny afternoon.

The deed was done.

In Cairo, darkness had fallen.

From a window of the Cairo International Airport, fifteen miles northeast of the teeming city, a foot-weary Nick Ramsey watched the lights come on below, illuminating the asphalt airstrips. Most of the jets that had been landing in daylight, and were landing now, belonged to Egyptair. There was still no sign of the Israeli prime minister's El Al 747. Ramsey looked down below where the president of Egypt, the vice-president, the minister of trade, and the sprucely uniformed Egyptian honor guard had been attentive for so long. Now Ramsey could see that the president and other officials had left their places, probably had gone indoors, and the soldiers of the honor guard, standing at ease, looked wilted and bedraggled.

The nonappearance of the Israeli prime minister was inexplicable.

Ramsey had been advised, much earlier, that the prime minister had been delayed, would be leaving Ben Gurion Airport two hours behind schedule. Ramsey had used up his time with more drinking, some eating, chatting with fellow journalists. During the waiting period word had come up that the prime minister would arrive at Cairo International Airport within the hour. But that hour had passed, too, and since then yet another hour, and the prime minister's plane was nowhere in sight.

The Israeli leader's plane had never before been this long overdue. Its nonappearance was mystifying. No further explanation had come to the restless and puzzled members of the press contingent.

Ramsey turned away from the window, wondering whether he should continue his vigil or dared leave his station and go into the city to the room reserved for him at the Nile Hilton Hotel, where he might get some deserved rest.

He was trying to make up his mind when he heard someone call out, "I say there, Nick!"

He turned further to see a sandy-haired, freckle-faced young man coming swiftly toward him. He recognized the person who had hailed him as an acquaintance he had made on his previous trip abroad, a British reporter, Brian Enders, of *The Times* of London.

Enders came up, face wreathed in a broad smile. He offered his hand. "Congratulations, your people in New York have done it again."

Ramsey dumbly took the handshake. "Congratulations for what?"

"For the tremendous exclusive by the New York *Record*. Moments ago I heard it on the wireless." He stared at Ramsey. "You mean you don't know?"

"Know what?" said Ramsey.

"Ah, you *don't* know. Let me be the first to tell you. In Jerusalem, the Dead Sea scrolls museum was invaded by Carlos and his terrorists earlier today. They ransacked it, made off with almost every damn scroll. Incredible. Most daring theft I've ever heard of in my entire life."

Ramsey stood astonished. "Carlos and his crowd made off with the Dead Sea scrolls? I can't believe it."

Enders laughed. "You better, old boy. It's emblazoned over the whole front page of your own newspaper, according to the wireless. The *Record* has the bloody story alone. An absolute whopper of a scooperoo."

Ramsey nodded toward the terminal window. "I guess that explains the prime minister's no-show. He heard the news and postponed his trip."

"I don't think so. The Egyptians told us he would be on his way at least an hour ago."

"Well, the news was probably radioed to his plane, and he made the plane turn back."

Enders seemed doubtful. "I don't know."

"I don't know either," said Ramsey thoughtfully. "I'm going to try to find out. Failing that, I'm going to my hotel and take a dip in a hot tub. Thanks for the flash, Brian." He threw the British reporter a mock salute and began to stroll away with him. "Looks like a crazy day. The Dead Sea scrolls missing. Now the prime minister disappearing. What's going on?"

But he had a hunch that Edward Armstead might somehow know.

*   *   *

Once he had checked into the Nile Hilton Hotel, Ramsey told the
Egyptian bellboy to wait while he made a few purchases at the
newsstand. He crossed the busy lobby to the stand, and in the
shop he bought two packs of American cigarettes and three
English-language newspapers. Riding the elevator to the fourth
floor, he scanned the front page of each paper for details about
the theft of the Dead Sea scrolls. Ramsey could find no mention
of the event, and finally realized that the papers were a day old.

Being let into his plush double room, Ramsey had something
else on his mind. The lingering mystery. The prime minister of
Israel had departed from Ben Gurion Airport for Cairo, and had
not arrived. Tipping the bellboy and watching him leave, Ramsey
tried to speculate on the mystery. Even if he could project no
logical solution, and tempted as he was to immerse himself in a
bath of hot water and try to arrive at some conclusion, he knew
for certain what he must do first. A non-event could also be
news, and his duty was to report that news or at least alert
Armstead in New York to what was happening—or hadn't happened at all.

He was about to go to the telephone on the table beside the
couch when it began ringing.

Surprised, Ramsey lifted the receiver, sure that it was a wrong
number. It was not a wrong number. It was a long-distance call
from Paris and the caller was Victoria Weston.

"Nick, is that you?" he heard her say.

"All me," he answered. "How'd you know I'd be here?"

"I knew you had a reservation at the Nile Hilton."

"But I was supposed to be at the Cairo Airport."

"I figured you wouldn't be hanging around there any longer—"

"Then you heard the prime minister never showed up?" he
said. "I was just going to report the mystery to Armstead."

There was silence, and for an instant Ramsey thought that they
had been disconnected. But Victoria came on again.

"You haven't heard yet? Nick, you haven't heard?"

"What?"

"The Israeli prime minister was gunned down by the Carlos gang during the theft of the Dead Sea scrolls. Then the Israeli government put the lid on that part of the happening, on the shooting. For security reasons."

Ramsey lowered himself to the couch, stunned. "The prime minister shot? You're kidding."

"Heard it with my own ears on French television, a French newscaster quoting a terse government announcement."

"What condition is Salmon in?" Ramsey wanted to know.

"No idea. Just the delayed government announcement that he'd been shot in the museum by the Carlos terrorists and was now in some Jerusalem hospital. No further details."

"I—I don't know what to say," Ramsey finally muttered. "What am I doing here?"

"Only knows God," said Victoria, quoting from an old profile of *Time* magazine's Henry R. Luce, and adding, "In translation that means, Only knows Armstead—maybe. Don't forget he had the heist part of it exclusive."

"Armstead," repeated Ramsey. "I better hang around until I hear from him. And the prime minister—" he said wonderingly. "What's happening with him?"

"They what?" said Edward Armstead, paling and rising out of his office chair, unable to believe his ears.

Nervously, Harry Dietz squirmed in the chair across from the massive desk. "They shot him, Chief," he repeated.

"They shot the prime minister of Israel? Is that what you're saying? They wounded him?"

"Apparently. Because the government announcement said he was taken to a hospital. The government release on that—it just came through—was curt, but according to my information, the prime minister is probably in critical condition."

"You heard that from Pagano?"

"From Gus Pagano, yes. When he reported the scrolls operation to us, he didn't want to tell us about the shoot-out. First, because it might have revealed that someone in the gang was reporting to us. Second, because he was uncertain whom they had cut down. But once he heard the government announcement, he phoned again with a few of the details."

"What details?" Armstead demanded. "How did it happen?"

Dietz cleared his throat. "I don't know exactly, but I do know this much. Cooper and his men had just grabbed the scrolls and were about to clear out when the prime minister and some guest, with three armed guards, walked in on them. Seeing our men in masks, one of the guards immediately understood what was going on and opened fire. He brought down one of Cooper's regulars, Shields, apparently killing him instantly."

Armstead stood unnerved. "They actually killed one of Cooper's men?"

"No question," said Dietz. "Pagano was certain of that."

"What happened next?"

"The terrorists retaliated—"

"I don't like your calling them terrorists," interrupted Armstead. He sat down behind his desk. "Then what happened?"

"One of Cooper's boys opened up with a submachine gun— just mowed them down, the five of them, one after another, the prime minister, his guest, the three guards. They were lying there on the floor like those bodies in the old St. Valentine's Day massacre in Chicago. Pagano said Cooper couldn't tell how many were dead and how many injured. It was all too fast."

"And Cooper and his gang got away safely?"

"Absolutely."

Armstead shook his head. "Thank God for that. But they had to leave Shields, they had to leave him behind."

"No choice. Every second counted."

"Shields—there wasn't any identification on his body, was there?"

"None whatsoever. None of them carried any identification."

Armstead shook his head again, unhappily. "I never wanted there to be bloodshed."

"There had to be sooner or later," said Dietz in a practical tone of voice. "Besides, our men had no choice. It *was* self-defense."

"I suppose you're right," mused Armstead. "Who will be blamed for this?"

"The Israeli government announcement has already blamed Carlos."

Armstead frowned. "Too bad we didn't have the shooting exclusive, too." He looked up. "But the details of the shooting—no one has the details except us."

"That's right, Chief."

"Well, when's it coming off the presses?"

"Chief, it hasn't even been written yet. I just got Pagano's second call. I—"

Armstead slammed his fist on the desk. "Goddammit, Harry, get on the ball. We don't want anyone else getting it into print before us. Let's roll with it fast—another Armstead beat—another exclusive. The full and inside account of the shooting of Prime Minister Salmon—the story of the year." He came off his chair and around the desk as Dietz stood up. Armstead took him by the arm. "Let's keep moving, Harry. We're on top of the world. Let's stay there."

"I'll hustle it into print, Chief. Do I by-line it Mark Bradshaw again? We credited him with the beat on the theft of the scrolls. It would be logical for him to report on the rest of the story, the shoot-out."

Armstead approved. "You've got it, Harry. Let's keep him our star."

"Okay. Oh, one more thing—"

"Yes?"

"—what about Ramsey?" asked Dietz.

"Better get Nick Ramsey out of Cairo. Bring him back to

Paris to join up with the Weston girl. I think I may have something new brewing.''

Dietz hesitated at the door. ''I was just thinking, Chief. Maybe it would be wise to have a breather between stories.''

''Since when have you become cautious, Harry?''

''I haven't really, but—''

''Leave the planning to me,'' said Armstead. ''When you're running the world, you don't get off.''

10

To Nick Ramsey, riding the unusual, undulating arrival escalators in Charles de Gaulle Airport was always an enjoyable sport, like taking a roller coaster standing up, no hands. But this day, returned to Paris from Cairo before one in the afternoon, he hardly noticed the escalators. He was bemused by the violent events that had swirled about him in Egypt and the Middle East.

He reached the ground-floor luggage conveyors and sought out the one that would be delivering his suitcase and typewriter. He watched the Cairo luggage sliding down the moving conveyor belt, spotted his own rubbed black leather bag, stepped forward to catch it as it came around and lifted the suitcase free. Shortly after that he had his portable typewriter.

He was surprised to see a young woman with an arm raised motioning to him. As he arrived at the customs exit, he could see that the young woman was Victoria. Finished with customs, he could not help smiling as he approached her—she was wearing her tweed jacket over a brown silk blouse and hip-hugging beige pants, and was a dream walking—but Victoria was not smiling at all. She was dead serious, even grim.

"Nick," she said. He wanted to kiss those full red lips, but gave her a smack on the cheek instead.

He studied her expression. "Anything wrong?"

"Nick, the prime minister of Israel—he's dead."

"Dead?"

"He died in surgery."

"Dammit," Ramsey said under his breath. "Where'd you hear that?"

"They broke in with a bulletin on French television. Salmon recovered consciousness only once before surgery. Someone told him the Dead Sea scrolls had been stolen, and told him the ransom demand. In return for the scrolls, release of the five PLO terrorists who attacked the kibbutz Kfar Hanassi last month. The prime minister whispered, 'Never, never in a million years. The scrolls are precious to all of us, but the safety of our people is more precious. Israel does not give in to terrorists, now or ever.' And then they rolled him into surgery. And then he died."

"That's the whole story?"

"Not quite. French television also had the details of what happened in the museum, details of what led to the killing. They had these by quoting an exclusive from an American newspaper."

"I assume they were quoting the *Record*," said Ramsey quietly.

"Yes."

"A by-lined story by Mark Bradshaw."

"Yes."

"I see," he said. But he did not see a thing.

"I think it's odd," Victoria said, as they walked out of the terminal to the street.

Ramsey said, "I think a lot of things that happen in this world are odd."

She put up her hand to get the attention of a chauffeur smoking nearby, and he acknowledged her signal and strode off. "I have a rented car at the hotel, but I was afraid if I used it on the autoroute I'd get lost and miss you. So I hired that driver with his Mercedes."

"Extravagant, aren't you?"

His tone had been light, but Victoria remained serious. "It's Armstead's money, and he's making more and more with all these scoops."

"Well, I guess he's earned it."

"Armstead, he's becoming famous, practically a legend."

"I guess he deserves that, too."

"He *and* Mark Bradshaw."

Noting her emphasis, Ramsey glanced at her.

She touched Ramsey's arm. "Nick, I want to talk to you about all this. Can we talk about it?"

He knew that he was supposed to ask her exactly what she wanted to talk about, but he was not ready for that yet.

The driver had drawn his Mercedes up to the curb. Ramsey opened the rear door for Victoria. "All right," he said, "we'll talk. But not yet and not now. Give me a chance to shake off the dust of Cairo, take a shower, get a change of clothes. Let's just neck on the way to Paris."

"Nick, I'm really serious."

"So am I," he said.

"I'll tell you what," she said. "When we get to the city, drop me off at the *Record* bureau. I have to do something there. You go to the hotel, check in—same suite—and when you've come down, let's meet at a café on the Champs-Élysées for a snack."

"You name it."

"Let's say the Maison d'Alsace at Rue Marbeuf on the Champs-Élysées an hour from now. It's only a short walk around the corner from the Avenue Montaigne."

"You've got a date."

"A serious talk," she said.

"A serious talk," he agreed, and wondered what it would be about.

Victoria was seated at a table under a red umbrella in the front row of Maison d'Alsace, sipping her sweet sherry, idly observing

pedestrians streaming past her in both directions along the Champs-
Élysées. Because speculation on the backgrounds of various
passers-by diverted her thoughts, Victoria shifted her gaze to the
red awning that served as a canopy over the umbrellas and tables
of the café. She tried to concentrate on what was uppermost in
her mind and to organize her discussion of it with Nick Ramsey.

She and Nick had agreed to meet here an hour after he had
dropped her off at the Paris bureau of the *Record* and she had
come to the café on time ten minutes ago. She had expected Nick
to be waiting for her, but he was nowhere in sight and the
black-and-white-striped chair opposite her remained unoccupied.

Eager to have the conversation with him and to have his
opinion, although she had foreseen that he would be skeptical,
she stretched her neck and looked off toward the Avenue
Montaigne. At once she saw Nick. Although he was a half block
away, he was taller than the French pedestrians ahead of him and
easy to identify. She could not help but smile. He appeared neat,
for him, in a gray suit, and refreshed, and was advancing
purposefully, impeded only now and then by window-shoppers.
She supposed he would invite her to dinner, but first she determined to have her talk with him here and now in the café.

For a moment her gaze had strayed, and she had lost him.
Then she had him in sight, and her brow furrowed.

Nick was no longer walking. He had stopped or been stopped.
He had been partially blocked out by a stout man in a dark suit
who was speaking to him. Another man—shorter, even heftier, a
person in a black leather jacket who resembled a Lebanese—had
come up behind Nick, seemed to bump into him.

Curious, Victoria tried to make out what was happening.

She saw the pair who had detained Nick jostle him, pushing
him off the sidewalk and nearer the street. The action was unclear,
but it looked as if the pair was forcing Nick toward a sedan at the
curb.

Alarmed, Victoria opened her purse, pulled out some loose
francs, threw them on the table and searched for Nick once more.

The threesome, the two strangers and Nick, had reached the low sedan. What was taking place was even clearer now. Nick was definitely being forced into the back of the vehicle.

Victoria jumped to her feet, wondering why Nick did not resist the bullying tactics. Instantly she realized that he couldn't. He was being forced into the car, probably at gunpoint. Nick was being abducted. He was being kidnapped.

And Victoria was running.

Obstructed by pedestrians, she dodged and wove and kept running toward the sedan.

Closing in on it, she could make out a driver at the wheel, the two abductors with Nick between them in the back. Before she could open her mouth to cry out, the sedan, a light blue Citroën, darted away from the curb, then tried to wedge into traffic, blocked by a parade of other cars, all honking horns.

Victoria cast about frantically for someone in a blue uniform, a gendarme, but saw at once there was none in sight, and then she saw something else. A taxi had drawn up along the edge of the Champs-Élysées and was disgorging a passenger. The passenger had paid his fare and was about to shut the rear door when Victoria stumbled up and grasped it.

As she flung herself into the taxi and fell back into the seat, the beetle-browed, unshaven Gallic taxi driver twisted around and released a torrent of French. "No, no, no!" he protested. "I am finished for today. No more fares. I go home for dinner."

Victoria leaned forward, gripping his arm in both hands and shaking it. "Listen to me, monsieur, this is an emergency!" she cried out. "I will give you a fifty-franc tip—" She pointed ahead through the windshield. "See that car there, the blue Citroën, three men have taken my friend, kidnapped him."

The taxi driver looked through the windshield. "It is a matter for the police—"

"There is no time. I must know where they are taking him. I will give you one hundred francs extra."

The driver capitulated. "For you, madame, I will follow."

"Thank you, thank you. But don't let them realize you are behind them."

He shifted, jolted forward until only a single automobile stood between him and the Citroën. Then he yanked his wheel, sending his taxi in between two cars in the creeping traffic.

Victoria sat back with relief as the dense traffic gradually loosened and the cars sped up toward the Place de la Concorde.

She sat forward again, tense and worried, wondering who the abductors were and what they wanted with Nick. Keeping her eyes on a portion of the sloping back of the Citroën, she prayed that the abductors would not get out of sight.

"They must not be aware we are following," she implored the driver.

"Never mind, madame. I am clever. I have an older brother in the Sûreté."

The police, she thought again. At what point should she seek help? She knew the answer. Not until she was certain where those thugs were taking Nick.

She held on to the overhead strap as her taxi careened through streets of Paris and sections of the city totally unfamiliar to her. Beyond the window, she sought the sight of famous landmarks but recognized none. They were passing shops and a department store, and she tried to memorize their names. She craned her neck to try to make out if Nick was visible in the rear seat of the Citroën ahead, but she was not able to get a full view of the car.

The Citroën breezed through a yellow light as it turned red, and so did the car ahead of them, and Victoria prayed her driver would do the same. The stoplight had turned red, and her driver valiantly sailed through it.

The pursuit had continued for fifteen or twenty minutes and they had entered a district that she had never visited when the car that separated the Citroën from their taxi pulled out of line and eased toward a parking place. Now they were exposed to the rearview mirror of the Citroën directly in front, and Victoria

could only hope that the abductors' driver would not become
suspicious of her taxi.

She was conscious of the fact that the Citroën was slowing,
and her own taxi was also slowing.

"Where are we?" she asked her driver.

"Tenth Arrondissement, approaching the Musée de l'Affiche."

"The poster museum?"

"*Oui.*" He was gradually braking. "I think they are looking to
turn off."

"Follow them."

"No, we must watch. We will see."

The vehicle in front had come almost to a halt, and Victoria
realized that only the two abductors were visible, that Nick had
disappeared from view. There could be only one logical explanation—Nick had been ordered down to the floor.

The car ahead had halted, and the taxi driver was forced to
apply his foot brake hard. He hammered at his horn angrily,
honking away.

"Don't do that," Victoria cried out. "You'll only attract
attention."

"I am acting naturally. Someone blocks a taxi, and we blow
the horn. They expect it. Just leave it to me, madame."

The Citroën had started moving once more, turning into a
cross street.

She heard her driver. "I think this is their destination."

She searched upward, saw the street signs. They were on the
Rue de Paradis. The cross street into which the Citroën had
entered was marked Rue Martel.

"Still the Tenth?" she asked.

"The Tenth," said her driver. "A workers' district."

He accelerated his taxi, drove it past the Rue Martel.

"Hey, aren't you going to follow them?"

"No. Too easy to be noticed. I think they will not run away.
See, they are slowing. I think they are getting ready to park." He
slid the taxi into a no-parking zone. "You go out to the corner,"

he said. "Walk in a normal way to cross the street. Look down the Rue Martel and see if they are parking. If not, I will back up fast and chase them."

He was idling the taxi alongside the curb. Victoria did not question his street wisdom. She unlatched the rear door and stepped out to the sidewalk.

Pulling herself together, she strolled to the corner. She glanced down the Rue Martel, trying to appear as casual and disinterested as possible. The Citroën represented the only activity in the street. It had gone less than halfway up the thoroughfare, and abruptly it swung left off the street into the driveway of some kind of building and in seconds it had disappeared.

She teetered on the street corner, feeling certain that she had not been seen or spotted as a threat.

She waited for someone to emerge from the building. No one appeared.

Resolutely she turned away from the Rue de Paradis and entered the Rue Martel. She strode briskly, as if the far end of the street were her destination—a French student on her way to her apartment from school.

On approaching the building where she had seen the Citroën turn in, she slowed her pace ever so slightly. She was next to the driveway for a building bearing a sign that read. No. 10. This wasn't it, she knew, but the one after.

She walked on. She was passing an old building with letters that indicated it was No. 12. There was another driveway—a *porte cochère*, really—at one side of this building, and out of the corner of her eye she could see that there was an inner courtyard beyond. Several cars were parked inside, but she could not see the blue Citroën. Yet she was positive that it had gone into that courtyard.

She stolled a few more steps, but no farther.

She had discovered what she needed to know.

Pivoting, she went past the driveway of No. 12 once more, then retraced her steps to the Rue de Paradis.

She wondered what was going on. Why would anyone want to kidnap Nick Ramsey? For what reason? For ransom? Had they mistaken him for someone else, a rich American? Above all, who were they?

Stepping back inside her taxi, she tried to make up her mind about her next move.

There was one obvious thing to do. Go to the police immediately. But something made her hesitate. It was the memory of Edward Armstead's earliest advice on that day he had admonished her that her first duty must always be to report to the New York *Record* first.

Christ, if she did that, the delay might put Nick in greater jeopardy.

She assured herself that it would postpone her report to the police by only a few minutes.

She decided to report to Edward Armstead first.

He would know exactly what must be done.

She saw the taxi driver studying her inquiringly. She nodded. "I know just where they are," she said. "Take me to the Plaza Athénée as fast as you can. A shortcut, if possible. I will report the whole matter from there. But hurry. Make it fast enough and I'll promise you a one-hundred-and-fifty-franc tip."

"*Très bien,*" he said, hunching over the wheel. "Hold on— here we go!"

It was strange being sightless so long, and sightless still.

From the instant of his abduction to this moment here, some-where in Paris, Nick Ramsey had not suffered fright. He had contended with the emotions of surprise, bewilderment, confusion, but not fear. So positive had he been that his kidnapping was an error, a mistake in identity, that he was certain that the blunder would be realized and he would be freed.

Once they had him in the back seat of their car, and had left the Champs-Élysées, they had ordered him to kneel down on the floor. Reluctantly, with the metal of a gun pressed hard against his temple, he had done so. At that point he had been blindfolded.

Several times during the ride to wherever he had tried to speak up, protest, point out their gross error, and each time one of them had harshly told him in English to shut up. Neither the two in the back seat nor the driver otherwise spoke to him or to each other.

Ramsey had attempted to calculate the time his ride had taken, but the darkness was too disorienting to enable him to think. There had been street sounds throughout the journey, even up to a minute before they had come to a final stop, so he guessed that they were still inside Paris and not in the suburbs.

He had wondered how long Vicky would continue to wait for him at the café, at what point she would become concerned, investigate his whereabouts, become alarmed, consider him missing. He had wondered what she would do, and had tried to conjure up what he might do in her place. He had doubts that kidnapping would ever enter her mind. There was an unreality to such a conclusion. He was, after all, a nonentity, not a promising captive for ransom.

After the vehicle had stopped and the engine was shut off, he had allowed himself to be pulled up and out of the car. He had been hurriedly prodded across what he assumed was a cobblestone paving and over some kind of threshold. Then, judging from the change in temperature, he had been led indoors.

With assistance, he went up three flights of stone steps, was brought to a halt, heard a door creak, felt soft carpeting beneath his shoes, guessed that he had been jostled through several rooms, felt himself being forcibly pushed down until his behind made contact with a wooden chair.

Now his blindfold was being unknotted and yanked off.

Ramsey expected to be blinded by light, but the transition from unseeing to seeing was easy because he had come out of darkness into little better than darkness.

A single low-wattage bulb off to one side of a small, drab, nearly barren room gave only minimal illumination. What Ramsey could make out in the eerie yellow light was a man seated directly in front of him, seated on a chair turned backward, straddling the chair, half smiling at him. On either side of this man, behind him, Ramsey could make out the shapeless forms of three, four, other persons.

Ramsey's gaze returned to the one facing him. This was a youngish man, as far as Ramsey could tell, perhaps middle or late thirties, with thick black hair carefully combed sideways, long sideburns, large brown eyes, straight wide nose, sunken cheeks, fat lips. The flesh on his face was loose, like the flesh of a pudgy person who had lost much weight.

When this one spoke, his voice was modulated, cultured, the accent barely British. "Welcome, Mr. Ramsey," he said. "I hope you have not been too inconvenienced."

"What is this, some kind of joke?" Ramsey demanded, surprised that his name was known.

"Hardly a joke."

"What in the hell is going on? Who are you? Where am I? What do you want with me?"

"I shall answer one question at a time. First, let me introduce myself. I am Ilich Ramirez Sanchez."

Confusion was immediately swept from Ramsey's mind. His senses flooded back, and full memory surfaced. "Carlos," Ramsey blurted.

"The terrorist, you might add. Carlos the terrorist, as you journalists always put it."

Ramsey stared at the long-hunted Venezuelan kidnapper and killer, filled with wonderment. "What on earth do you want with me?"

"To talk, simply to talk," said Carlos.

Ramsey was not listening. "If you want ransom, or anything like that, you've got the wrong person. I'm only a newspaperman, an American newspaperman, and not a very well-known one at that."

"We know who you are and what you are."

"Then this makes no sense. What can you want of me?"

"I have told you," said Carlos. "I decided it was time we have a brief talk."

"About what?"

"About your shoddy work on the infamous rag, the New York *Record*." The smile had evaporated. The soft face and soft tone had hardened.

"My work?" said Ramsey, puzzled.

"Your lies, Mr. Mark Bradshaw."

Ramsey's mouth fell open. "Bradshaw? You think I'm Mark Bradshaw? You're wrong, all wrong. You yourself greeted me as Ramsey. You know I'm Nick Ramsey." He hesitated, and added lamely, "I can prove it. I can show you my passport."

"Anyone can put any name on a passport. We have dozens of passports with dozens of names. As you have investigated us, we have investigated you. We have followed your inquiries, your travels, your stories. We have every reason to believe that you are really Mark Bradshaw, the journalist jackal who has been attributing all of the recent terrorist activities to me. I have had enough. I have decided the time has come to call you to account."

Ramsey sat nonplussed. "Believe me, I didn't write those stories."

"Oh, no?" said Carlos. "The stories appear. They are exclusive in your newspaper. They are spread worldwide. Carlos supplies weapons to the Basque kidnappers of the Spanish king. Carlos kidnaps the secretary-general of the United Nations. Carlos steals the Dead Sea scrolls. None of them have I done. None of these reflect my methods. Not once was a meaningful ransom asked."

Ramsey's journalistic scent was aroused. "The killing of the Israeli prime minister," he said. "You have taken cabinet ministers hostage before. You have killed."

"I had not a thing to do with the killing of the prime minister of Israel," said Carlos. "Only a fool would try to extract ransom from a country that will pay no ransom. Israel refused to comply with the ransom demands for the Dead Sea scrolls. This morning the thieves gave up and returned the scrolls, told the government they could be found in a garbage can near the port of Haifa. The whole thing has the mark of a PLO operation. Yet, frankly, none of these terrorist acts bears the imprint of political terrorists. Whoever is performing these acts is motivated by something other than politics. None of these are Carlos operations. Yet Mark Bradshaw reports each of these as being directed by Carlos. I believe *you* are Mark Bradshaw.''

"I've told you that you are grossly mistaken."

"You do not deny that you and the lady you use as an assistant both work for the New York *Record*. You do not deny that one of you was on the scene of each event when it happened."

"I only deny that I am Mark Bradshaw. He wrote those stories. I did not. He accused you of the operations. I did not."

Carlos was briefly silent. "If you are not Bradshaw, who is? Can you lead me to him?"

"I cannot. I don't know him."

"That sounds unlikely."

"It's true."

"I choose to think you lie," said Carlos. "I put you on warning, and if you are not Bradshaw, you put him on warning." He enunciated the next words coldly. "One more such fabrication about me in your newspaper, and you are dead. I will blow your head off. For good measure, I will blow your lady's head off. Do you hear me?"

"I hear you," said Ramsey. "And if I'm not Bradshaw?"

"Then find the one who is and relay to him my warning."

"I'll do my best." He paused. "What next?"

"Next?"

"What are you going to do with me?"

"I have no further use for you. I wanted to be sure you got my message. You will be blindfolded again, and released. I suggest strongly you do not write of this meeting."

The terrorist was about to rise when Ramsey spoke out once more. "Carlos—"

"What is it?"

"One question." Ramsey could not resist. He was fascinated by the man's ego. "For one who has had so many crimes attributed to him, why do you object to being connected with the crimes we've been discussing?"

"Professional pride," said Carlos, without humor. "What has been happening is not my style. I wish credit only where credit is due. When the history of our time is written, I want my role to be portrayed accurately. You understand?"

Ramsey nodded.

Carlos rose. "Final word of caution, Mr. Ramsey. Be sure you keep your head—without a hole in it. Adios." Carlos receded into the darkness.

Victoria was in the entry hall of the Plaza Athénée suite, at the mini refrigerator pouring her second Coca-Cola, when she heard the telephone ringing.

For more than an hour since her return from the Rue Martel, the location of the kidnappers' hideout, she had been trying to contact Edward Armstead in New York City. Armstead had been in and out of his office at the *Record*, and neither his secretary nor McAllister had any idea where he had gone.

"Maybe Harry Dietz might know," McAllister suggested. "I know Mr. Dietz walked out with Mr. Armstead, but Mr. Dietz was going back to his own apartment at the Sherry Netherland to pick up something. He should be back in the office in a few hours. He might know where Mr. Armstead can be found."

Victoria had not wanted to wait for Dietz's return to the *Record*. She had hoped to catch him at the Sherry Netherland, but he had not yet arrived at the hotel. Victoria had phoned Dietz again. Still not in. She had become frantic, torn by indecision, trying to decide if she dared waste so much time attempting to get Armstead. Fearful of what might be happening to Nick in the hands of abductors, she had almost made up her mind to notify the French Sûreté. But before doing so, she had determined to try Dietz one last time. A third call had been put through to the Sherry Netherland and through to Dietz's apartment, and to her vast relief Dietz had answered the phone.

Victoria had explained that she had an urgent matter to discuss with Mr. Armstead. Could Dietz help her locate him?

She had detected real reluctance on Dietz's part. He had been definitely hedging. "Well, I'm not sure. Maybe this is something I can help you with?"

Momentarily she had considered spilling it all out to Dietz, but some instinct had told her to hold out for Armstead, to speak to the publisher himself.

"I really think I should speak to Mr. Armstead."

"Umm. And you are sure it is urgent?"

"Most urgent, believe me."

"All right, Victoria. I might have an idea where he could be. Let me find out."

"Can I try him—wherever—directly, to save time?"

"Nooo. I think not. I'd better do it. If he is free to speak to you, I'll have him call you as soon as possible."

"At the Plaza Athénée, Paris."

"I know, Victoria. You stand by."

Interminable minutes had passed, while the telephone remained mute and Nick, she was sure, remained helpless in the hands of kidnappers.

At last the telephone was ringing, and she was hurrying, Coke in hand, into the living room of the suite. Putting down her glass, she grasped at the receiver and fell down on the sofa.

It was a female French operator. "Miss Victoria Weston?"

"Yes."

"A telephone call for you from New York. Mr. Armstead is calling."

"Please put him on."

Edward Armstead's voice came on, low and hushed, but distinct and tinged with annoyance. "What is it, Victoria? What's so important?"

"I'm sorry to disturb you, Mr. Armstead, believe me, but I have to. There's trouble here. Nick Ramsey's been kidnapped."

"He's what—been kidnapped, you say?" The annoyance had vanished from Armstead's tone, which took on a note more of curiosity than concern. "Am I hearing you right?"

"You heard me right. Nick was kidnapped, abducted in front of my very eyes just a little more than two hours ago. Let me tell you fast."

In a torrent of words, she related how she had met Nick at the airport, been dropped off, arranged to meet with him at the café on the Champs-Élysées, and had seen him abducted and forced into a car by two men. By some miracle she had managed to follow them, and had found out the address where Nick was being held.

For the first time Armstead broke in. "Any idea who did it?"

"Not the faintest."

"You haven't heard from his captors yet?"

"Not a peep. It's probably too soon. Should I have reported this directly to the Sûreté? I thought I should notify you first."

"You did the right thing, Victoria."

"Should I get in touch with the police now? I have the address. It is 12 Rue Martel. I can notify—"

Before Victoria could continue, or Armstead reply, another voice intruded. Victoria's head jerked up as Ramsey came into the room. "Is that Armstead?" he wanted to know. "Tell him they were letting me go when I heard one of them say that by morning they were moving to another safe house. Apparently they keep on the move all the time."

Mesmerized by Ramsey's unexpected appearance, Victoria listened to him, ignoring whatever Armstead was saying on the phone. Aware once more of the publisher on the other end of the line, she exclaimed into the mouthpiece, "Mr. Armstead, Nick just walked in! He's safe and sound!"

"He's there?" Armstead said.

"Right here. He wants to speak to you."

"I want to speak to him," said the publisher.

"One sec—"

Victoria handed Ramsey the telephone and gave him a quick kiss as she slid over on the sofa to make room for him. He closed his hand on top of the mouthpiece and addressed Victoria. "You actually knew where they took me?"

"I saw it happen on the Champs-Élysées. I managed to follow you."

He regarded her with real admiration. "You're quite a kid," he said. "Maybe I'll treat you to champagne tonight."

She beamed at him.

Ramsey removed his hand from the mouthpiece. "Hi, Mr. Armstead. I gather you heard all about my little episode from Vicky."

"I heard," said Armstead. "I want to hear from you what was going on. Who wanted you? Why? And how come you're free?"

"You'll find it hard to believe," said Ramsey. "I was picked up on the orders of Carlos, and taken to Carlos himself."

"Who?"

"Carlos, *the* Carlos."

"The terrorist?"

"Numero Uno in person. He had me grabbed. He wanted to talk to me."

"For God's sake, why?"

"Because he was sure I was the one and only Mark Bradshaw of the New York *Record*, and he wanted to tell me—warn me—that if I continued writing stories for the paper accusing him of more kidnappings, he'd blow my brains out. That was it."

Armstead's voice faltered. "You mean he denied kidnapping Bauer, stealing the Dead Sea scrolls—"

"—or murdering the Israeli prime minister. He insisted that he had no part in any of those operations. In fact, he resented being linked to them." Ramsey caught his breath. "I better tell you the whole thing play by play."

Ramsey saw Victoria hanging on every word, eyes wide again, and he winked at her and concentrated on his telephone conversation once more. He launched into a full recital of his enforced meeting with Carlos.

During Ramsey's recounting of his adventure, Armstead did not interrupt once.

Only when Ramsey finished did the publisher speak. "That's it?" he said.

"The whole thing."

"Helluva story," said Armstead. "You'd better write it up for us, get it in fast."

"Happy to," said Ramsey, "if you want a reporter with a hole in his head. That's what Carlos promised if I said a word."

"No, I don't want your life endangered."

"On the other hand, if we notify the police where they can find Carlos and his gang, and they're in custody, Vicky and I can cover the whole thing and file it."

There was a pause. "No, definitely no," decided Armstead. "As soon as the police know, everyone will know. We'll lose our exclusivity. Let me handle Carlos my way. I want to be sure we have the jump on the others. I have my own Sûreté contacts."

"Do it your way," agreed Ramsey. "But you'd better move before Carlos does. He's slippery."

"Don't worry. Leave him to me."

"Okay," said Ramsey with some reluctance. "But there is one thing I must do. In case Carlos gets away—"

"I told you I'd take care of him."

"But if he manages to get away, as he always has, I'd better locate Mark Bradshaw. I'd better let him know that Carlos has a contract out on him if he mentions Carlos in print once more. Can you tell me where to get in touch with Bradshaw?"

There was a silence. Ramsey waited, meeting Victoria's inquir-

ing gaze. Finally, Armstead spoke. "I prefer that you leave
Bradshaw to me. And Carlos, as well."

"As you wish, sir."

"Leave everything to me," Armstead repeated with finality.
"Look. You and Victoria go downstairs and have a drink on me.
You deserve it. Be back in your suite by—let me see, what time
is it?—by midnight your time. I'll be calling you with a full
report, and with your next assignment."

Victoria watched Ramsey hang up, and saw his disgust.

She came closer to Ramsey. "What is it, Nick? What was he
saying?"

"Armstead wants to do everything himself. He insists on it.
Apparently he has his own contacts in the Sûreté. He's afraid that
if we go to the police, we'll blow his exclusive. All he's worried
about is his goddam story."

"Well, all I'm worried about is you," said Victoria heatedly.
"It's too risky, playing around with Carlos. I think we should go
directly to the police."

"And get fired," said Ramsey, standing up. "No, I don't
think so, Vicky. I think we've got to let him play his game, and
see what happens."

"I don't like it," protested Victoria.

"We have to give him a chance. He's calling us back at
midnight." Ramsey reached down and pulled Victoria to her
feet. "Meanwhile, Armstead insisted we go downstairs and have
drinks on him."

"I don't want drinks," said Victoria. "I'm hungry."

"All right. You have dinner. I need drinks."

She allowed him to lead her to the entry and the door to the
suite. He opened the door. She held back. "Nick, you haven't
told me. What did Armstead say about Bradshaw?"

"Only that he'll take care of Bradshaw."

"Do you think he will?"

Ramsey hunched his shoulders. "Why not?"

She left the suite. Ramsey closed the door. She followed him
to the elevator. "Nick, I want to talk to you about Bradshaw."

He watched the elevator rise, come to a halt. When it opened,
he gestured her inside. "Later," he said. "Let's see what
Armstead comes up with. Right now, you have dinner and let me
have a few quiet drinks."

Armstead remained seated, immobilized, in the middle of Kim
Nesbit's apartment for a long time, staring at the olive-green
telephone he had recently used. He played and replayed his
conversations with Victoria Weston and Nick Ramsey over in his
mind, and tried to think.

He had left the office to come to Kim's apartment in the late
afternoon because he'd had a sudden urge to possess her, his first
in many days. He'd been high from all his successes, pleased
with himself, pleased with the tip from Bruce Harmston that
Time magazine was considering giving him a cover, had already
assigned a photograph session, and Armstead had wanted to
celebrate. After letting himself into Kim's quarters, he had been
mildly annoyed to find her napping—more likely, passed out—on
her bed. He had not liked her condition—her blond hair tangled,
her mascara smudged beneath her closed eyelids, her breath
reeking of whisky—and she was sprawled still in her nightclothes
at midday. But his annoyance had been overcome by the sight of
the flesh of an inner thigh through the parting of her white silk
robe. The realization that she was nude underneath had heated his
desire. It had been difficult to awaken her, but once she was fully
awake and sobering, she whimpered her pleasure at the sight of
him and clutched him, holding him tightly, promising to make
him happy, happier, the happiest.

He had allowed her to go to the bathroom to freshen herself
and get ready, and had removed his jacket and been about to
undress when the telephone rang in the living room and it was
Harry Dietz. Armstead had had no wish to call back that Weston
girl at this time, or from this place, but his concern at the urgency

of the call had got the better of him. He had phoned Victoria in Paris, and spoken to Ramsey as well.

Now he was trying to decide what to do.

Glancing down the hall to the bedroom, to be certain that Kim had not emerged from the bathroom as yet, satisfying himself that she would still be a while with her bath, makeup, lotions, perfumes, lingerie, he decided that there was time to make another call. From his wristwatch he guessed that Harry Dietz would still be at the Sherry Netherland. This was something to be handled through Harry.

He dialed the hotel and soon had Dietz on the other end.

"Harry, I called the Weston girl in Paris."

"Was it as important as she said, or a false alarm?"

Armstead dropped his voice. "It was important all right."

"Yes?"

"Ramsey, Nick Ramsey, is back in Paris. He was nabbed by the Carlos gang on the Champs-Élysées."

"You're kidding."

"The Weston girl saw it and followed them. She discovered where Carlos is hiding out."

"Hey, what a story. If we give it to the police—"

"We give it to every newspaper on earth," interrupted Armstead. "I had to restrain Ramsey from blowing the whistle on Carlos to the French police. That's no good."

"You're absolutely right, Chief. What can we do about Carlos?"

"I'm not sure yet," said Armstead thoughtfully. "But I want to keep an eye on him until we deide how to handle it. Is Gus Pagano there?"

"Just returned to Paris."

"Good. Give Pagano an immediate call. Tell him Carlos and his gang are holed up at 12 Rue Martel. They may be moving to another location before midnight. Tell Pagano to get his ass right over to that area and put a tail on Carlos. I want to know where he is when I've figured out how to bust the story."

"Will do," promised Dietz. "Sa-ay, you haven't told me—why did Carlos pick up Nick Ramsey?"

"Thought he was Mark Bradshaw. Doesn't like Bradshaw's stories blaming everything on him. Swore he'd kill Ramsey or Bradshaw if another Bradshaw by-line appears."

Dietz laughed. "He'd kill Bradshaw?"

"Or Ramsey," said Armstead. "Ramsey doesn't think it's very funny. He's determined to find Mark Bradshaw, not only to warn him, but to get Carlos off his own neck. He pressed me pretty hard on that."

"What did you say?"

"That I'd handle Bradshaw myself. Look, Harry, I'm a little worried about Ramsey. He didn't like me taking Bradshaw away from him. He may be in an inquisitive mood, start poking around on his own. That could cause some trouble. What do you think?"

"I think you should pull him out of Paris immediately—in fact, bring him back from Europe."

"Just what I was thinking," said Armstead. "Okay, here's what I want you to do. I'm supposed to give Ramsey a call at the Plaza Athénée by midnight his time. I want you to make that call for me."

"And tell him what?"

"First tell him that I got in touch with my Sûreté contacts in Paris. But it was too late. Carlos got away. We lost him. Now that he's loose again, we're worried about Ramsey's life. We want none of our staff in danger. Our first duty is to protect our reporters. Therefore, for his own sake, we are recalling him. As of tomorrow morning, Ramsey is to leave Paris, fly to Washington. Tell him we're transferring him to special duty in the Washington, D.C., bureau. Tell him to bone up on President Callaway's agenda during his meetings with the British prime minister in two weeks. Tell Ramsey we may send him along with the President. Will you take care of that?"

"What about Victoria Weston? Maybe you should take her out of Paris, now that Pagano's back in town?"

"Victoria Weston," Armstead reflected. "No, not yet. I want her in Paris digging up research on Lourdes, for a backgrounder on the Pope's upcoming visit to the shrine there. Just play it safe, have Pagano leave for Lourdes tomorrow. Have you got all that?"

"First, call Pagano."

"He's to tag after Carlos. Then have someone else do it after Gus heads for Lourdes."

"And you want me to get Nick Ramsey at midnight their time and instruct him to leave for Washington—?"

"Wait a minute," said Armstead, rising. "Maybe it would be better coming from me. Let me handle Ramsey and Weston from the office. You take care of Pagano. Look, we have to do this right. I'll be in the office in twenty minutes. Meet me there."

As he put down the telephone receiver, he had a glimpse of Kim Nesbit in the entrance to the hallway. She stood there in a pink filmy something or other, smiling sweetly at him. Then she turned away and disappeared.

Armstead had entirely forgotten about her and why he was here.

Slowly buttoning his shirt again, tightening the knot of his tie, he started for the hallway.

When he entered the bedroom, Kim had just slipped out of her negligee and thrown it on the chaise longue. She was wearing a white silk Chinese pajama top that barely covered her pubic hair, no more. She pirouetted toward Armstead, smiling seductively, arms outstretched.

"You're still dressed, darling," she said. "I thought you couldn't wait. I know I can't. I'm so happy you're here. It's been too long."

Her speech trailed off as she realized he had gone past her, avoiding her arms, and had reached for his coat jacket and was getting into it.

Her expression changed. "What are you doing?"

"I'm sorry, Kim. I've got to rush back to the office. Something just came up."

She hurried to him, throwing her arms around him. "Oh, darling, don't, please don't go. Give me a little time. Let's have a little time together. I've hardly seen you. I want you, I need you."

"Later," he said brusquely. "I've got more important things to do right now."

He pulled himself free by force, spun away and left the bedroom. She stumbled into the hallway after him. At the living room, she clung to him, entwining her arms around him again.

"Darling, please, please," she implored. "There's us. The world can live a little while without you."

"It can't!" he said fiercely, seizing her by the arms and freeing himself.

He stormed across the living room.

"Don't," she called weakly, "don't leave me alone again."

At the door, opening it, he hesitated, as if to say something more. He saw her, almost oblivious to him, starting to pour a drink.

He went wordlessly through the door, slamming it shut.

Having finished his conversation with Ramsey and Victoria in Paris, Armstead hung up the receiver of his office telephone and fell back in his swivel chair, utterly drained.

He began to think that what he wanted now was the tall, strong drink he had failed to get at Kim Nesbit's. As he was about to act on it, his buzzer sounded.

It was Estelle. "Mr. Armstead, I'm leaving now, but I wanted to tell you Bruce Harmston is here. He wonders if he can have a minute with you."

Armstead groaned audibly. "Is it something that can hold until tomorrow?"

He heard Estelle speaking to Harmston, and then she was back on the line again. "Mr. Harmston says it would be better if he could see you right now."

"Okay, okay, send him in."

Moments later, Harmston was seated edgily before him, the forehead below his receding hairline perspiring, his moon face troubled. "Mr. Armstead, I hate to bust in on you like this, but it's something I have to handle as soon as possible. It's *Time* magazine again."

Armstead showed his annoyance. "What in the hell do they want now? I've given them an interview, I'll sit for pictures—"

"Oh, you've been most cooperative, they know that. But they're still not satisfied with what you told them—or, in their words, did not tell them—about your star foreign correspondent, Mark Bradshaw."

"Bradshaw, Bradshaw, they're driving me nuts."

"I'm sure you are aware, sir, we've been getting many inquiries about Bradshaw. I've managed to concentrate all stories on you, on your intuitive genius, your brilliance. Everyone is accepting that—it's so obvious—but still they want to know more about the man you've been assigning to cover those exclusives. *Time* has been the most persistent. The editors feel you're being evasive. They're insisting on another interview with you, a brief one just about Bradshaw—who he is, how you found him, how you work with him. Do you think—?"

"Fuck *Time* magazine!" Armstead burst out. "I'm not wasting another second on them, even if it costs me the story."

"No, no, Mr. Armstead, don't misunderstand. They want to feature you. They want to play up the story. They just thought the lack of information on Bradshaw left a big hole in their profile. But they're going ahead with the piece, of course—"

"Sorry, Bruce, you tell them I'm simply too busy to see them again. Besides, my handling of Bradshaw, working with him, is a highly classified and private business matter. I'm not giving our private methods out to anyone. Our success depends on secrecy, and I intend to maintain it. No, I'm not going to discuss Bradshaw with them or with anyone else.''

Like all good press agents, Harmston was dogged. Not even a tornado would turn him away. He was clearing his throat now. ''Mr. Armstead, if you could just let me throw them a bone—something, anything, from you through me—to placate them.''

''Like what?''

''Like a few biographical tidbits. Anything. I don't have even a line about Bradshaw on file. I know your wish for secrecy, but—you understand, I have to do my job—''

Armstead did understand. Harmston was a veteran loyalist, and deserved better. But Armstead also knew that he must tread cautiously. Harmston had never been let in on what was going on. Only Dietz and Pagano, in Armstead's inner circle, were informed. No one else, no one, nor would they ever be. Still, Armstead realized that he would be giving away nothing if he threw the dogged one a bone.

''Okay,'' said Armstead, more agreeably. ''Maybe I can give you a few bio facts—very little, but something that will placate everyone.''

''Thank you, thank you very much,'' said Bruce Harmston, fumbling in his jacket for his miniature notebook and pencil. ''Any tidbit about Mark Bradshaw will be extremely useful. It will stop all the clamoring.''

Armstead closed his eyes, considering what to say. When it was formulàted in his mind, he spoke. ''Bradshaw, Mark,'' he said. ''Born in Liverpool, England. A Cambridge man. Was on the staff of two London dailies. Published three exposé books.'' Armstead paused. ''The ones badgering us need not try to trace him. He was born, educated, worked under another name. He took the name Bradshaw only after I saw merit in him and personally hired him. He's on my private payroll full time.''

Armstead stopped speaking.

Harmston lifted his head. ''Is that all?''

''That's all.''

"I mean—could you just give me something about where you keep him headquartered?"

"I keep him under a rock. I let him out at night."

"Mr. Armstead—"

"That's all, Bruce. Sorry. See you soon."

Unhappily, Harmston came to his feet, pocketing his notebook. "Well, thank you. It's something. I'll try to make it go a long way. Yes, hope to see you soon."

He backed off, turned, and left the office in haste.

Armstead sighed. It had been a long, hard day, especially the very end, this taking care of Nick Ramsey and then the Mark Bradshaw matter.

He pushed himself upright. He was ready for that tall, strong drink. He would find Dietz. They would have a drink together.

It was close to two o'clock in the moring in Paris.

In her bedroom, at the Plaza Athénée, Victoria Weston removed her robe, laid it neatly across a chair, tied the ribbon at the cleavage of her white silk nightgown, kicked off her slippers, turned off the bed lamp, and got into bed.

Lying on her back in the darkness, she unhappily reviewed the last of the evening with Nick.

For her, at least, their dinner had been unsatisfactory. She had eaten, as she wanted to, but had not enjoyed it. He had left his food mostly untouched, and had drunk too much. She had tried, several times, to bring up the subject of what had been troubling her about the Armstead operation, about the mystery of Mark Bradshaw, about the strangeness of their own assignments. She had not been able to communicate successfully with Nick. He simply had refused to listen to her, preferring to talk, when he did talk, about Israel and Egypt. She liked him too much to have pity for him, and had kept wondering why he drank so much and why he seemed to be constantly avoiding her.

Before midnight they had returned to the suite for their prearranged call. Shortly afterward, Armstead had telephoned from

New York. Armstead had spoken to Nick, and then to her. There had been disappointments. Armstead had revealed that he had tipped off his connections in the French Sûreté about Carlos, but Carlos had moved on before the police could trap him. A sensational story had been lost for all of them. Further, Nick had been informed that, for his own safety, he was being transferred from Paris to Washington, D.C., in the morning. As for herself, she was to stay on in Paris alone to gather material for a feature story on Lourdes that was to run in advance of the Pope's visit there next week. Before finishing with Armstead, she'd had the temerity to ask him if he had contacted Mark Bradshaw. The publisher had replied, "I've taken care of Bradshaw," that and no more.

After the phone call Victoria had made up her mind that this would be the time to discuss the whole puzzle with Nick. But again Nick had evaded discussion. Too busy for any serious talk, then and there. He had to get downstairs, he insisted, and arrange with the night concierge for an early flight to Washington, D.C. Don't wait up for me, he had said, speech slurred from alcohol, pecking her on the forehead with a kiss, don't wait up 'cause I got too much to do. Meaning, Victoria was sure, not only making his reservations but visiting the Plaza Athénée bar to have one or two more for the road.

Now, in bed, knowing Nick had not returned from his protracted excursion to the lobby, Victoria discovered that sleep would not come. Weariness was dominated by unanswered questions. She tried to understand Nick. She tried to understand Armstead and his elusive Bradshaw. She tried to understand why she and not the Paris bureau had been handed the routine assignment on Lourdes.

Trying to put everything out of her mind, she beckoned sleep as she might a lover.

Sleep would not join her.

Fixing on her illuminated travel clock, she could make out that she had been suffering insomnia for at least forty minutes. For the first time in months, she considered taking a sleeping pill, but just then she thought that she heard the noisy rattling of the door to the suite. She definitely heard a door being shut, listened harder, and knew that someone was bumping into furniture in the living room. When she heard the other bedroom door close, she knew that Nick had returned.

She lay still a long interval, wide awake, trying to decide whether she should corner Nick in the morning before he left or make an effort to confront him now. Tomorrow he might elude her. Right now, confined to his bedroom, he could not escape. Drunk or not, he would have to listen. This was the moment.

Throwing off her covers, she fumbled for the bed lamp, turned it on, and swung off the bed. She drew on her robe, glanced at the mirror, patted down her hair, and went into the living room. She crossed past the television set and the desk and stood before Nick's door.

For an instant, she hesitated. Maybe he was not in condition to hear her out.

Never mind, dammit, she told herself, it had to be now.

She rapped on the door.

No answer. Perhaps already asleep.

She rapped again, more sharply.

This time, Nick's muffled voice. "Come in."

She opened his door and went inside his room.

The bedroom was dimly lit by lamps on either side of the unmade bed. Nick had turned from the bureau to face her, and he was undressed, naked except for his white jock shorts.

Victoria gave a small gasp, ready to leave, saying. "Oh, I'm sorry. I didn't know—"

"Get off it, Vicky. You've seen plenty of men before." He grinned. "Not that I've been much of a man these days."

She remained rooted, staring at him, realizing his body contradicted his self-deprecation. He was plenty of man. Her surprise was that he was neither bloated nor flabby from drink. His hairy chest and stomach were flat and his thighs strong. But when he stepped away from the bureau toward her he almost lost

his balance, and when he spoke his words were thick. "Wanna
join me for a nightcap?" He held up his brandy glass.

"Thanks but no, Nick. I really wanted to talk to you briefly
about something before you left. When are you leaving?"

"The hotel? Eleven o'clock." He walked carefully around the
bed and sat on it, drinking, looking intently at her over the glass.

"I guess it can wait," she said awkwardly. "You'd better get
some sleep. Maybe we can talk in the morning. It *is* important."

"No, Vicky," he said, setting his glass down on the marble-
topped bedside table. "Less—let's talk. Been wanting to talk to
you for a long time."

"Well, if you really feel like it."

"Feel like it," he said. "Wanna talk about something important to me." He patted the bed. "Sit here."

"Okay," she said bravely, going to the bed, sitting. "But let
me start first, then it'll be your turn."

He stared at her blearily, shook his head. "No," he said. "My
turn first. My turn's more important. About us."

She raised her eyes to meet his, at once curious, wondering,
waiting.

"About us," he repeated. "Never made a pass at you. Wanted
to every time. Never did. Explain—lemme explain."

"You don't have to, Nick."

"Have to, because." His speech was cottony. He was making
an effort to pull himself together, be articulate. "Been a bachelor.
Fell hard for a young woman, six, seven years ago. Was afraid to
get involved, so close, but she loved me as much, I believed, I
thought. We got married. Right after, found out she was pregnant
by another guy, another guy she really loved, but he wouldn't
make it legal so she faked it with me to get married. I wanted to
kill myself or her. I wanted to."

She took his hands. "I'm sorry, Nick."

"Old story, old hat. But never did it, never killed anyone. Just
divorced her, left her. Vowed never to trust another woman,
never to let myself be hurt. Meant loneliness, frustration, started

drinking, never stopped drinking. Good company. Course had one-night stands all the time, fucking, no commitment, never trusted another one again. Never fell in love, till I met you.''

She felt her heart hammering.

''Was afraid to fall for you,'' he was saying. ''Afraid to trust any woman who meant so much—''

''I mean so much to you?''

''What the hell, I'm in love with you, Vicky, and not holding back.''

''Oh, Nick.'' She was on her feet over him, almost moved to tears. She sought his lips and kissed him and kissed him. ''I've been so in love with you from the start.''

His arms came heavily around her, pulling her down to his lap, kissing her back. ''Vicky, come to bed with me.''

She felt him hardening beneath her, and heat pervaded her from cheeks and breasts to the inside of her thighs. She caught her breath, tried to be flippant. ''I—I thought you'd never ask.''

He started to bring her down on the bed with him. ''Now, darling.''

She squirmed free. ''Yes, now,'' she said huskily. She came to her feet. ''Let me go into the bathroom first. I'll only be a minute.''

Barefoot, she hastened to his bathroom, closed herself in. Divesting herself of the bathrobe, hanging it up on his hook, she reached down and pulled up her silk nightgown, drawing it up over her breasts and her head. She was flushed, throbbing with excitement. He loved her. He wanted her. They would never be apart again.

She looked into his mirror over the sink. She wished that she had her makeup, her lotions, her perfume. But never mind. Her reflection told her what he would see, and what he would see was a flawless naked young woman in full blossom of love, from hardened nipples to moist vagina.

He would enjoy her. And she wanted him.

Not another second of their togetherness to lose.

She left the bathroom, turning down the light, went in measured step around the corner and, in her nudity, entered the bedroom as unselfconsciously as possible.

He was waiting for her on the bed, she could see.

She advanced to the side of the bed, arms limply at her sides, breasts rising and falling.

She could see him fully now. He was lying on his side, still in his jock shorts, his head deep in a pillow. His eyes were shut. He was snoring lightly. He was sound asleep.

He had passed out completely.

Glaring down at him, she remained transfixed, wanting to cry, and wanting to laugh.

Considering his inert figure, she tried to assess his earlier confession. Uninhibited, had he truly spilled out his love for her, or had he been merely plain stupid drunk and capable of saying anything?

The answer?

She'd once, as a youngster with her father, attended a movie festival of silent films, clips of silent day Saturday serials. They always left you hanging at the end of an episode. To be continued, they said.

She smiled ruefully to herself.

To be continued, she told herself.

She turned away, walked back into the bathroom, retrieved her nightgown and bathrobe, and dragged them behind her through his bedroom, across the living room, and into her bedroom.

If she was not fulfilled, she was at least sleepy at last.

As for the rest? To be continued.

11

At ten-thirty in the morning, Victoria Weston came down to the lobby of the Plaza Athénée, took her reserved copy of the day's *International Herald Tribune* from a concierge, and sank deep into an easy chair at the far side of the room. Partially hidden by the newspaper held open in front of her, she kept an eye on guests entering the main lobby from the elevators in the inner lobby beyond. She recalled that Nick had mentioned he would be leaving the hotel for Charles de Gaulle Airport at eleven o'clock in the morning, and she was determined to catch him before he departed.

When she had awakened earlier, she had thrown on a robe and crossed the living room to his bedroom door. She had knocked loudly several times, but there had been no reply. Tentatively she had opened the door and called out to him, but still there was no response. She had gone inside. He was neither in the bedroom nor beyond the open bathroom door. She spotted his packed bag, typewriter, trench coat on an armchair. So he was away somewhere, but he had not yet left for the airport. After that she had hastily dressed, taken the elevator downstairs, and tried both bars, but no Nick. In the court restaurant, picking a table near the entrance, keeping a watch on the inner lobby, she had gulped down a quick breakfast. Still no sign of Nick. This meant he was out on some private business, like seeing Sid Lukas or maybe saying good-bye to a girl friend in the area. She knew he could return to the hotel through some other entrance, possibly the Relais Plaza bar, but he could not leave the hotel without paying his bill. Realizing this, she had planted herself in the corner of the main lobby.

Absently scanning the paper as she waited, her thoughts were really on last night, on last night's fiasco, and Nick's unexpected profession of love for her. He had been terribly drunk, she knew, and babbling anything, maybe even insincerities. At the same time, he might have known what he was saying and meant every word of it. She could not be sure, but once she had a chance to speak with him and hear him out, she would know one way or the other.

Victoria had reached the editorial page of the *Herald Tribune*, observing also that her wristwatch was at nine minutes to eleven, when she saw him striding into the lobby, preceded by a bellboy gripping his heavy suitcase and his portable typewriter. The bellboy continued straight to the revolving door leading to the Mercedes sedan waiting on the narrow pavement between the sidewalk and the Avenue Montaigne. Nick had detoured to the concierge's counter. Victoria saw him handing out some francs, obviously a tip, and kept him in view as he moved along to the cashier's counter, where he was signing his bill.

Now, tugging on the trench coat he had been carrying, he headed for the revolving door. He looked well-groomed, casual but neat in his beige sports jacket and slacks, and the picture of sobriety. He was inside the revolving door and outside on the sidewalk, when Victoria leaped to her feet. Casting aside her newspaper, she hurried across the lobby in pursuit.

The chauffeur had already left a group of his colleagues to hold the rear door of the Mercedes open for Nick, and Nick had already tipped the bellboy and the doorman and entered the back of the car when Victoria reached it, nodded to the chauffeur, and ducked inside.

Wedging into the back seat between Nick and the window, Victoria settled in and offered up a winning smile. "Mind having company on the way to the airport?"

Surprised, Ramsey made more room for her. "I'm delighted," he said. "But how did you know when I was leaving?"

"I'm psychic," she said. She waited for the chauffeur to start the car and drive it away, turning right to head for the autoroute and the airport, before elaborating. "No," she said, "we talked last night and you mentioned when you were leaving." She paused. "Don't you remember?"

His expression was honestly bewildered. "We talked last night? After I knew when I was leaving? I remember seeing the night concierge and—" He faltered. "—and then I came up and went to sleep."

"We talked in between," she said adamantly.

Ramsey shrugged. "I guess maybe we did." He tried to smile. "I guess maybe I had a drink too many."

"I guess maybe you did," she said, also trying to smile, but her lips hurt and her heart sank.

He was a total blank. He had been blind drunk. His memory apparatus had been fogged in.

The shortest love affair, non-love affair, in history, she thought miserably. It would be hopeless to remind him. It would be embarrassing, too, because maybe the sober Nick Ramsey, the real person, entertained no such romantic feelings toward her.

To hell with it, she decided. There was nothing more she could do but absorb her loss.

"I really needed to talk to you, Nick, before you left. I tried several times, you know. Even last night at dinner."

"At dinner?" He showed a glimmer of remembrance. "Yes, after the Carlos episode, before Armstead called to transfer me. I guess I was still shaken up by Carlos."

"Whatever," she said. "But you have been putting me off."

"I'm sorry."

"I thought this was a good opportunity to discuss it."

"Go ahead."

She twisted toward him. "Nick, something strange has been going on, and it niggles at me. I want to get to the bottom of it. I very much need your good judgment."

"All right. Let's hear. What's so strange?"

"The wave of terrorism going on since we've been in Europe."

"Vicky, there's been terrorism over here for years."

"Not like this," she insisted. "Not so much, not so bunched together, one incident after another. Not so spectacular, either. These have involved only big names—king of Spain, secretary-general of the UN, prime minister of Israel. And important artifacts stolen—the Dead Sea scrolls. That's not how it used to happen."

"What are you leading up to?"

"Well, Carlos and his gang have been blamed for every one of these acts, even supplying weapons for the ETA operation in Spain. You were with Carlos yesterday. You heard him deny taking part in any of them."

"I'd hardly consider Carlos a reliable source on what he did or did not do."

"Do you think Carlos was telling you the truth?"

"I honestly don't know."

"I don't know either, but let me tell you what I think. I think Carlos told you the truth. I don't think he had anything to do with the terrorist acts that have been happening right under our noses."

"What makes you so sure of that?"

"Simply by reviewing what has been happening."

Victoria launched into a point-by-point recounting of the recent kidnappings, robbery, killing. "I agree with Carlos," she concluded. "Not one of them his style. Not the operations. Not the ransoms. All this is not Carlos. It's someone else, someone else who is doing it."

Ramsey stared thoughtfully out the car window at the passing suburban landscape. "If not Carlos, who?"

"I don't know," said Victoria helplessly. "I thought maybe you would have some ideas."

"There are a hundred splinter terrorist groups around," said Ramsey, "some large, some small. It could be any one of them, even a number of them."

"It's the same group all the time," said Victoria without equivocation.

"What makes you so positive?"

"Bradshaw, Mark Bradshaw," Victoria said simply. "He's the common denominator. Whenever something's happened, he's been there."

"So have you or I, almost every time."

"But he's been there first. He gets it to the *Record* first. It doesn't make sense. How does he know that secret terrorist acts are going on before anyone else?"

"Intuition, I guess," said Ramsey.

"It has to be more than intuition," said Victoria. "I'm suggesting that Mark Bradshaw has some connection with the gang of terrorists pulling off these acts. He may know someone in the gang. Again, he may actually be part of the gang."

"Aren't you being fanciful, Vicky? The guy's just a reporter working for Armstead, the way we are."

Victoria fixed her gaze on Ramsey. "Prove it," she said.

"What?"

"That Mark Bradshaw is a reporter on the New York *Record*."

Ramsey frowned. "What's to prove? I'm not naïve, but like one famous American, I believe what I read. And I read Mark Bradshaw's by-line in the paper. That's for real."

"That's a line of type, Nick. That's not a person."

"I've never known a by-line that did not represent a person or persons."

Victoria would not let go. "If Mark Bradshaw is a person, where is he? Who is he? Have you met anyone who has met him, seen him? Everyone on every paper is asking questions about Mark Bradshaw. So far, no answers. Well, I say he's the key to what's going on, to who is pulling off all these terrorist acts. I say find Mark Bradshaw, and you find out the truth about what's going on that's so suspicious."

"Vicky, maybe there's nothing going on that's so suspicious."

"I choose to think there is. I thought you might agree with me. Anyway, you're leaving, and I'm staying here. I'm to do the Lourdes background job, and I'll do it. But I'm also going after Mark Bradshaw. I'm determined to find out who he is. I hope you agree with me."

Ramsey fell silent. He stared reflectively once more out of the car window. At the turnoff to Charles de Gaulle Airport he lit a cigarette and let down the car window a few inches.

Not until the Mercedes drew up to the curb under the airport overhang, and the chauffeur left his seat to remove the bag and typewriter from the trunk, did Ramsey speak. He covered Victoria's hand briefly. "I agree," he said. "You do what you can to track down Bradshaw. If you find yourself getting nowhere, I suggest you try the personnel director at the *Record*—Katherine Crowe. You met Mrs. Crowe the day you came to work. Anyway, she's an old friend of mine. You can talk to her on a confidential basis. If you need further research on Bradshaw, use someone on the outside—it's always better to work with someone outside the office, especially on a matter like this—get hold of Howie Dittman on the New York *Telegraph*. He moonlights as a researcher. He'll do anything for me and he's a whiz."

"One second," said Victoria. She had her notepad on her knee. "Howie Dittman," she repeated, writing. "New York *Telegraph*." She looked up. "You're sure you won't regret getting involved, Nick?"

"Never mind. Do as I say." He reached for the handle of the car door. "You know, there was something I meant to tell you last night—but, well, it can wait. We'll be together again one day soon."

"Oh, I hope so, Nick." Impulsively she leaned over and kissed him.

"You go on," he said. Stepping out of the car, he turned back. "Just watch where you're going, and always look behind you. Remember that."

"I'll remember."

"If you need me, you know where I am."

"Yes, Nick."

He picked up his suitcase and his typewriter and headed into the airport terminal.

At the Plaza Athénée once more, Victoria occupied herself by checking out of the suite and transferring her effects to a single room on the same floor. Once settled, she ordered salad and quiche from room service. Having finished lunch, she was tempted to undertake the hunt for Mark Bradshaw, wherever it might lead her, but she knew that she dared not divert herself with that yet.

Armstead had given her a definite assignment, and her immediate job was to deliver it. The Pope was leaving the Vatican to visit the miracle site of Lourdes—His Holiness would be there in four days—and Victoria was expected to research and write a feature story on what the Pope would see. She had been ordered to file it with McAllister late the following afternoon.

She tried to figure out where to start her research, and finally decided to start in the obvious place. She would go to the Paris bureau of the *Record* and search through its reference files for clippings on Lourdes. This would give her sufficient background to know what she was doing, and perhaps provide a lead or two to sources that might offer some firsthand copy.

It was a short walk to the building on the Rue la Boëtie, a block from the Champs-Élysées. She took the rickety elevator up to the second floor, entered the *Record* bureau, greeted the two French girls at work in the main office, and put her head in on Sid Lukas, the myopic bureau chief, who was editing some dispatches at his desk in his tiny cubicle of an office.

"Hi, Sid," Victoria called out. "Mind if I rummage through your reference files? Doing a backgrounder on Lourdes."

"Make yourself at home. Doubt if you'll find much of use."

"We'll see."

She backtracked to the main office and the long row of green metal reference files, and when she found the manila folder bearing the word LOURDES she pulled the folder and took it to an empty table. It was, as Lukas had warned her, an unpromising file as to bulk. Seated, she removed the two-dozen clippings and carbons of filed stories, spread them out, sorted them into categories, and dipped into her purse for notepad and pen.

She began to read the clippings and carbons with care, occasionally making notes. First the historical basis for the fame of Lourdes. The fame of the small town had its birth on February 11, 1858. A simple fourteen-year-old native of the town, Bernadette Soubirous, a onetime shepherdess, a mediocre student at a parochial school, a girl who had long suffered from asthma, had gone to the outskirts of the town with her sister and a friend to gather firewood. Trailing behind the other two, about to cross the mill canal near a grotto, Bernadette heard a distant murmur that she thought was a gust of wind. Later, she would recall the moment. "I lost all power of speech and thought when, turning my head to the grotto, I saw at one of the openings of the rock a rosebush, one only, moving as if it were very windy. Almost at the same time there came out of the interior of the grotto a golden-colored cloud, and soon after a Lady, young and beautiful, exceedingly beautiful, the like of whom I had never seen, came and placed herself at the entrance of the opening above the rosebush."

The beautiful, barefoot young Lady, draped in a white robe and blue sash, white veil, yellow rose on each foot, was carrying a rosary with white beads on a gold chain. When Bernadette tried to make the sign of the cross, she found that her arm was paralyzed. Instead, the vaporous Lady made the sign of the cross and instantly Bernadette's stricken arm was well and mobile. Bernadette, who had been saying her rosary, was still on her knees when her sister and friend came back. Bernadette told them of her vision. They mocked her and called her an imbecile. Bernadette's sister reported the adventure to their mother, who forbade Bernadette to return to the Grotto of Massabielle.

But no restriction could keep the fourteen-year-old girl from the grotto. She was drawn there time and again in the next five months. Nor could any imposition of secrecy keep word of the vision from the townfolk. Soon they began to follow Bernadette to the grotto. In that period, the Lady in white appeared before Bernadette eighteen times, but did not speak to her until the third visit. In subsequent visits, the Lady ordered Bernadette to drink from a fountain and to bathe in it. Guided by the apparition, Bernadette dug a hole in the ground and finally water appeared. Then she later discovered a spring that gushed from the back of the grotto. On Bernadette's fifteenth visit to the grotto 20,000 persons gathered to watch, held in order by uniformed soldiers. Three weeks later the Lady revealed her identity: "I am the Immaculate Conception." Shortly afterward seven seriously ill persons, praying at the grotto, enjoyed miracle cures.

Bernadette isolated herself from public view, spending the last twelve years of her life as a nun and a recluse. In her final three years she was gravely ill, suffering from tuberculosis of the lungs, until her death in 1879. She gained immortality in 1933 when canonized as a saint by the Roman Catholic Church.

Her birthplace, Lourdes, scene of these religious wonders, became a worldwide legend, the foremost miracle site on earth. Because the Lady had requested a chapel, the Upper Basilica and the Rosary Basilica were built near the Grotto of Massabielle. In the years and decades that followed, sixty-four miracles were recognized by the Church out of the five thousand cures attributed to the holy water flowing from this grotto.

Peeling through the clippings, Victoria found more of the same, and yet more. Lovely, colorful stuff, Victoria thought, and it would be a useful underpinning to her story. But largely unanswered was the question Armstead had emphatically posed: What was there in Lourdes that the Pope himself would see when he arrived for his visit in a few days?

There were indeed some present-day descriptions of Lourdes, mostly the Michelin guidebook sort of thing, but they were spare and colorless.

Putting the clippings away in the manila file folder, Victoria knew that it was not enough for her purpose, and she needed more by late tomorrow afternoon.

She went back to call upon bureau chief Sid Lukas once more. He was still hunched over his battered desk, a burning cigarette between the stained fingers of one hand, a pencil stub between the fingers of the other. Despite the efficient black aerator on a corner of his desk, a pall of smoke hung over him like a cloud.

Victoria stepped inside his cubicle. "Thanks, Sid."

"You're welcome," he said, without looking up.

"You're right. There wasn't much."

"It's not much of a story anymore. In these days of computer body scans, who gives a damn about Lourdes?"

"The Pope does. He's going to be there in a few days."

"That's his business. Who else gives a damn?"

"I do, Sid. Can you give a girl a hand?" She advanced tentatively toward his desk. "I need your help."

For the first time he straightened up from his work, and flattened his back against his swivel chair. "All right," he said, grinding out his cigarette. He peered at her through his thick lenses. "Name it. What can I do?"

"In my story, Armstead wants me to paint a picture of Lourdes today, what the Pope will see."

"Have you looked at Michelin?"

"There was an extract in the file. I need more and more human interest, something an expert on Lourdes could tell me firsthand."

"There are plenty of theologians in Paris who must know Lourdes upside down."

"Somebody, maybe one of your reporters, scribbled a note on a piece of paper attached to one clipping. It said, 'Try Dr. René Leclerc.' "

"Leclerc, Leclerc, yup, that's your boy. I remember. Was about three or four years ago. We wanted to get material for a feature on Lourdes. A priest at Notre-Dame advised us to see Dr. Leclerc. He's the super authority on Lourdes. We located him, but he was out of Paris at the time and we couldn't wait. If he's still here, and he probably is, he has an apartment in the Sorbonne section. You won't have any trouble finding him. He'll give you what you want."

She blew a kiss at Lukas. "You're a dear, Sid."

"Never mind, get on with it," he said grouchily.

She was at his door, about to leave, when it occurred to her that this was a good time to ask him about the other priority matter on her mind. "Oh, Sid, one other matter—I hate to bother you, but there is one more thing."

He sat back again, resigned. "What is it?"

"Mark Bradshaw," she said.

"Who? What? Ah, you mean Armstead's hotshot new star."

"Remember, I dropped by here late yesterday afternoon for a little while. Actually, I was poking through your files to see some of the other by-lined stories Mark Bradshaw wrote. I couldn't find one written before the king of Spain's kidnapping. You were busy but I interrupted to ask you if you'd ever met Bradshaw."

"And I said no."

"Then I asked you to find out whether your staffers had ever met him or knew him. Did you?"

"I always do what I promise to do," said Lukas, lighting a cigarette. "If someone had known him, I'd have buzzed you. No one has ever laid eyes on him."

"Well, I'd like to talk to Bradshaw," said Victoria.

"Try the home office. They'll tell you where he is."

"I did, they wouldn't. I thought maybe you could do me a favor, query the other bureau chiefs from London to Baghdad. Learn where I can find Bradshaw."

"You want me to query all the bureau chiefs. Is it that important?"

"To me. Yes."

"Okay. Will do. Phone me back day after tomorrow." He paused. "Don't thank me. Just do me a favor."

"Anything."

"When you find Bradshaw, ask him for me how in the hell he does it. He's incredible."

She wanted to amend that to say, not incredible—he's simply not credible. But she held her tongue. "I'll ask him just that," she said, and left.

There had been little difficulty in locating Professor René Leclerc. He was one of the more eminent lecturers at the Sorbonne, indeed an expert on Lourdes, and he had readily taken Victoria's call. Although protesting that he had a busy teaching schedule, and that it would be difficult to see Victoria so soon, he had seemed eager for the publicity and granted the interview.

In the morning Victoria drove over the Seine to the Left Bank, and was able to park a mere two blocks from the designated building of the Sorbonne University. Inside, an usher preceded her up "C" staircase into a hall that led to a public waiting room. The room was stuffy, poorly lit, and Victoria was shut into it. For twenty minutes she waited, trying to occupy herself by reviewing her questions. Just as she had begun to worry that he would not keep his appointment, a frail, thin man, perhaps seventy years old, opened the door. "I am Monsieur Leclerc," he said in English. "You are Miss Weston? Please come along."

His small, spartan office, separated by a glass wall from the staircase, was furnished with no more than a bare wooden desk, one file, three chairs.

As Professor Leclerc eased into the chair at his desk, Victoria became aware that his face, deeply lined, looked as brittle as papyrus, and that he wore a hearing aid. His youngest feature was his eyes—clear brown, bright, alert. He apologized for his tardiness. He had been lecturing to a class of five hundred students on comparative religion, a two-hour class that had unaccountably run over to nearly two and a half hours. "We become more garrulous as we age," he explained shyly. "Do not let me go on that way with you. I do not have the time."

Victoria plunged immediately into her prepared questions, skipping the ones on the history of Lourdes to make sure that she got in the ones on the layout of the shrine that the Pope would be visiting. Professor Leclerc, who apparently considered Lourdes his private preserve and the Pope's visit a personal one, presented his answers with clarity and enthusiasm.

Victoria listened and jotted notes for more than an hour. Professor Leclerc had begun by explaining that Lourdes lay at the foot of a valley that led up into the French Pyrenees. He described the Boulevard de la Grotte that brought pilgrims and tourists, and would bring the Pope himself, to the "Domaine de la Grotte." He described the benches in front of the shrine, and the interior of the cave, with the white and pastel blue statue (somewhat blackened by years of candle smoke) of the Lady herself set in a niche, and the holy stream below it covered by a glass panel. He discussed the Upper Basilica and the Rosary Basilica and the thirty-acre park that surrounded both.

He spoke now of the Underground Basilica, the St. Pius X Basilica, the most mammoth man-made subterranean structure on earth. "This basilica," he said, "completed in 1958, measures 81 meters by 201 meters and is covered by a grassy esplanade. It can hold 20,000 pilgrims, more than the entire permanent population of Lourdes. It is used for ceremonies in poor weather, in winter, or to hold excessive crowds. The Pope will bless the thousands who will convene in this Underground Basilica. But do not forget, the Pope will be only one of four million persons visiting Lourdes this year.''

Victoria had recorded all of this, but her writing hand was becoming cramped.

Professor Leclerc seemed to be aware of her distress, for he stopped discoursing abruptly to inquire, ''Forgive me, madame, but do you have a watch with the time?''

Victoria consulted her wristwatch. ''Twelve thirty-two, Professor.''

He pushed himself erect, wheezing. ''I must take leave. I am late for a lunch appointment. I hope my descriptions were clear enough?''

Victoria scrambled to her feet. ''More than clear. I can't tell you how grateful I am.''

But Professor Leclerc was not wholly satisfied. ''Too bad I did not have the map to show, an excellent map, the best, issued several years ago by the Lourdes *Hôtel de Ville*. Unfortunately, I gave my only copy to another American who came by yesterday.''

Victoria's concern was immediate. ''Another American?''

''Yes, but have no fear, he was not a competing journalist. He informed me that he is a historian preparing a definitive work on world miracle sites, so-called.''

Victoria remained suspicious. ''Did he—did he give you his name? Was it Mark Bradshaw, by chance?''

''No, no, nothing like that. It was—'' He tried to remember. ''*Voilà*, Ferguson, Mr. James Ferguson, of a New York university. A rather lean young man with curly black hair, a prominent nose, a beard. An arresting appearance. I have no idea how erudite, since he spoke very little. Perhaps you knew this Mr. Ferguson, and he might share with you his map of Lourdes?''

''I wish I knew him, but I don't,'' said Victoria.

But five minutes later, walking back to her car, the name James Ferguson kept coming back to Victoria like the refrain of an old song. She did not know James Ferguson, but she thought she had heard or seen the name somewhere.

But where?

After lunch in the Plaza Athénée, Victoria went up to her room, took out her portable typewriter, and examined the pages of notes that she had made on Lourdes. At last, when she had absorbed them all and organized them, she began to write.

In an hour her feature story was finished, and it was good. After editing it, she was ready to telephone the *Record* in New York. It would be nine-thirty in the morning in New York, and the offices would be filling. It was unclear to her whether she was supposed to file the story with Armstead or Dietz. Nevertheless she put in a call direct to the publisher. Neither Armstead nor Dietz was in his office, so Victoria had herself connected with McAllister. He was present and ready to have her dictate the story on a recorder.

No sooner had she hung up on McAllister than the telephone rang. The caller was Sid Lukas.

"Zilch," he said.

For a moment, Victoria, her mind still on the Lourdes story she had delivered, was confused. "What do you mean?"

"Zero on Mark Bradshaw," Lukas said.

Her disappointment was immediate. "You mean nothing?"

"I queried every damn bureau this side of the Atlantic and in the Middle East," said Lukas. "Asked each chief if Mark Bradshaw worked out of his bureau, or had ever worked for him, and if he knew Bradshaw could he give me a current address and telephone. The response was one hundred percent negative. None had ever employed him. None had ever met him. Several added that they could certainly use him out their way. Everyone was curious about him. For such a hotshot, you would think he'd have been more visible." As an afterthought Lukas added, "But maybe that's the point when you're pulling off beats like that. Being invisible, I mean."

"Maybe that's the way it's done," admitted Victoria.

"Sorry I can't be of help to you, Vicky."

"Gee thanks, Sid. I'll buy you a cigar someday."

After putting the receiver back on the hook, she sat contemplating the instrument. Disheartened but not defeated, she resolved not to quit so easily. She even felt a challenge. With growing determination, she decided to chase the elusive by-line down to its primary source.

Before leaving, Nick had told her that if she ran into trouble, to contact a good friend of his in the personnel department of the New York *Record*. She remembered that this friend of his, Mrs. Crowe, was trustworthy. Feeling better, Victoria did a direct overseas dial to the New York *Record*. The switchboard connected her with a female voice that announced, "Mrs. Crowe speaking."

"This is Victoria Weston," said Victoria. "I'm with the paper."

"Yes, I know. I remember you."

"Of course," said Victoria. "I'm phoning from Paris."

"You sound like you're next door. Can I do anything for you?"

"It's a personnel matter," said Victoria. "I've been working with Nick Ramsey, and he suggested I call you. He told me to say that it was confidential."

"And so it will be."

"I'm calling about another member on our staff. Mark Bradshaw. I have to contact him. Could you check—"

"What a coincidence," Mrs. Crowe interrupted. "You know, for weeks we've been getting at least one call a day inquiring about him. Everybody from *Newsweek* to the *Columbia Journalism Review* wants coverage. Doubleday and Simon and Schuster want to talk to him about a book. CBS wants to consider him for an anchor spot. Now, today, yours is the second call in a row concerning Mr. Bradshaw. About an hour ago someone, a reporter from *Time* magazine, wanted information on Mr. Bradshaw."

"*Time* magazine," said Victoria. "Why?"

"Apparently the editors are considering doing a cover story on Mr. Armstead and his fantastic string of exclusive terrorist stories. Of course, Mr. Bradshaw has been playing a major role in getting those stories. So they wanted to know something about him. I'm afraid I couldn't help them, any more than I can help you. We simply have no card on Mark Bradshaw. As far as we're concerned, he does not exist as a member of our staff."

"But he *has* to be," insisted Victoria.

"I know," replied Mrs. Crowe, with resignation. Suddenly her voice came alive. "Wait. I have one more idea. Hold on, dear."

Victoria held on, entertaining a bit more hope and wondering what Mrs. Crowe was up to.

It was a full minute before Katherine Crowe's voice came on again. "Miss Weston?"

"I'm still here."

"I gave it the old college try, but it didn't work. It occurred to me that the one person who might know where you could find Mark Bradshaw would be Estelle Rivkin, Mr. Armstead's secretary. So I took a chance and buzzed her. I told her I had you on hold in Paris, and that you wanted to know where you could locate Bradshaw. All Estelle could say was, 'I don't have the faintest idea. I'd guess Mr. Armstead has him under personal contract and works with Mr. Bradshaw himself.' I'm sure Estelle was leveling with me. She doesn't seem to know a thing. I believe her."

Victoria sighed. "Well, I guess that's it. Many thanks for the old college try, Mrs. Crowe."

Once more Victoria dropped the phone receiver into the hook. Her frustration was accentuated, and now overlapped by a patina of worry. Nick, at their parting, had suggested that she speak confidentially to Katherine Crowe, but not to reveal her quest for Bradshaw to any other person at the *Record*. Any other person might include Edward Armstead's private secretary, and

Mrs. Crowe had gone ahead on her own and spoken to her. In a sense, Victoria's secret cat was out of the bag. But it was surely unlikely that Estelle Rivkin would find the incident important enough to repeat to her busy employer. Victoria relegated her worry to minor concern and, undaunted, tried to think whether there was anything more that she could do.

And then she realized that there was one last resort.

At his departure, Nick had suggested the names of two persons for her to consult, if she needed them, in her hunt for Mark Bradshaw. One had been Katherine Crowe at the *Record*, and that contact had been a failure. The other had been—she recalled Nick's exact words—*Howie Dittman on the New York* Telegraph. *He moonlights as a researcher. He'll do anything for me and he's a whiz.*

Howie Dittman would be her last shot.

The Plaza Athénée telephone had become like another limb, an extension of her body. She was on the telephone now, making one call, two calls, before she reached the *Telegraph* and was put through to Howie Dittman's desk. There had been seemingly countless rings, and Victoria had become discouraged and was about ready to hang up, when a male voice answered.

"Yeah?"

"Is this Mr. Dittman?"

"Naw. I'm at the next desk. He went home an hour ago. Any message?"

"I'd like to speak to him at home."

"I dunno. Not supposed to give out home numbers." The male voice was wary. "You want him on business or social?"

"Social," Victoria declared, and let her own voice go cute. "This is Kitty, his new girl friend. Maybe he spoke of us. He was expecting me to call, but I couldn't get to the phone till now. And I've misplaced his home number."

The voice on the other end had softened. "All right. One second and I'll get it for you." The voice quickly returned. "Got a pencil?"

"Sure."

"Endicott 2-9970. Got it?"

"Sure."

"If you can't find him, maybe call me back. I'm Ozzie. I'm not busy tonight."

"Sure."

She hung up. Ozzie. Howie. Je-sus. Okay, Howie.

The phone once more. The long direct dial. She got Howie Dittman on the first ring. After Ozzie, she had not known what to expect, but Howie Dittman was a serious type, with a low voice and what sounded like a controlled stutter.

After she had introduced herself, she started to explain that she was a friend and colleague of Nick Ramsey. But Dittman interrupted her before she could finish.

"I know about you," Dittman said. "Nick gave me a call from D.C. yesterday to tell me you might contact me and to cooperate."

Victoria felt a warm tingle for Nick, who had been thinking of her from so far away.

"You in Paris?" Dittman asked.

"Yes, I'm still in Paris, at the Plaza Athénée Hotel."

"Then we better get right on with it. Let's not run up your costs."

This reminded Victoria to make certain that she paid cash for these phone calls, to be sure that they were not charged to the *Record* and somehow came to the attention of Armstead or Dietz.

"I need some quiet and fast research help from you," said Victoria. "I want to find out what I can about a person, a media person who's received a lot of attention in the media itself. I want to learn whatever can be known about him. I want to trace him. I have to speak to him."

"His name?" inquired Dittman, businesslike.

"Mark Bradshaw, a foreign correspondent on the New York *Record*."

"What else can you tell me about him?"

"Not a darn thing. That's just it. He's pretty famous by now, I'd imagine. He's done those front-page scoops for the *Record* starting with the kidnapping of the king of Spain—"

"Yes, I know, right through to the killing of the Israeli prime minister. His name has become quite well known, Miss Weston. Yet you can find out nothing about him?"

"Not a thing. I need help. Don't bother with the New York *Record*. I've tried it, fairly thoroughly, and officially Bradshaw is not on the paper, except on the front page. I don't understand it."

"Obviously he's working for the paper in an unofficial capacity, or on a personal basis with someone high up there."

"That's what it sounds like. I want to get to him."

"You think someone wants to keep you from getting to him?"

"I don't think anything as dramatic as that. In fact, except for Nick, you, a friend of Nick's at the *Record*, the publisher's secretary, and the bureau chief in Paris, no one even knows I want to meet Bradshaw."

"Is that what you want to know? How to meet him?"

Victoria backtracked. "Well, maybe not exactly, although it might come to that in the end. No, what I want from you is *something* about Bradshaw, and most of all, where he can be reached. You think you can help?"

"I can try."

"Nick said you were a whiz."

"I'm hardly that. But I am good at what I do. I'm just smart about where to look and I work hard. I have access to all kinds of sources that wouldn't be available to you in Paris. In my experience, there is a mention of every person in existence somewhere, right down to the least-known nonentity. Mark Bradshaw is hardly a nonentity, so I hope to find something."

"That's wonderful."

"When do you need this material?"

"Yesterday."

"Oh, it's one of those. Will tomorrow do?"

"I'll be right here at the Plaza Athénée cuddled up to the phone."

"I'll give it this evening," said Dittman. "I'm off tomorrow, so I can give it tomorrow morning and afternoon, too. I should have something for you by six our time tomorrow—possibly before—what's that your time?"

"Midnight."

"Stand by tomorrow around midnight."

Through with the telephone for the day, she fell back on the sofa, hoarse and exhausted.

But hopeful. Dittman had kindled the last flicker of optimism. If Carlos had not been responsible for the terrorism that had been part of her life these recent weeks—and this she believed—she might soon know who was really responsible, and be onto the biggest story of her career. Tomorrow night she might have Bradshaw, and Bradshaw no doubt would provide the answer.

The following day, a cool, gray autumn Paris morning and afternoon, Victoria, with no word from the *Record* on a fresh assignment, with her hunt for Bradshaw at a temporary standstill, welcomed an opportunity to devote herself entirely to shopping. To have free time in Paris, and acceptable credit cards, was as promising as a Muslim's dream of heaven.

In the morning she hopped into her rented red Renault and made for the Galerie Maeght on the Rue de Téhéran. There she whiled away two hours inspecting posters and lithographs, and at last selected two signed lithographs, one by Joan Miró and one by Calder, to be mailed to her mother in Evanston. Preparing to leave the Right Bank, she detoured her car to Aux Trois Quartiers, the fashionable department store on the Boulevard de la Madeleine, and bought herself two silk scarves and a marvelous white cashmere sweater. Hungry, she walked to the Rue de Rivoli, and under the shopping arcade located W. H. Smith & Sons bookstore, and after surveying the English-language bestsellers, mostly British, on the front stand, she bought three paperbacks, one suspense,

one romance, and a reprinted classic by Samuel Butler to make
her feel less guilty about reading the other two. Then she climbed
up the wooden staircase to Smith's tearoom and ordered two
small sandwiches, one chicken, the other cheese, and a pot of hot
tea.

By midafternoon she had crossed over the Seine to the Left
Bank, and parked in a narrow street off St. Germain-des-Prés.
Her first destination was the Galerie Claude Bernard in the Rue
des Beaux-Arts. After studying and enjoying the numerous
Giacometti oils and sculptures on exhibit, which she could not
afford, she searched for something for her father that she could
afford. She rummaged among the racks of posters and lithographs,
and found a wildly amusing signed poster in color by Fernando
Botero. She bought it and arranged for it to be shipped off to
Georgetown.

The rest of the afternoon she spent wandering up and down
both sides of the Rue Bonaparte window-shopping, eventually
taking time out to warm herself with a cup of coffee at the
Brasserie Lipp.

After that she hurried back to her car and on to her hotel, to
change for dinner. She had been invited to have dinner with Sid
Lukas and his French wife, Odette, at their apartment in the Rue
de Téhéran. Odette, whom Victoria had not met before, proved
to be a sharp-tongued but bright middle-aged Frenchwoman of
inherited wealth, and the apartment was so richly furnished that
the only object that seemed out of place was Sid Lukas himself. Two
other couples had been invited, the first a handsome French
publisher who disdained everything American, and his intimidated
poet wife. The second included an impish, overweight Hungarian
film maker, who had made countless deals but no films in twenty
years and liked to quote the witticisms of Georg Lichtenberg—
"Perhaps in time the so-called Dark Ages will be thought of as
including our own"—or Stanislaus Lec—"The dispensing of
injustice is always in the right hands"—and his plain Czech wife
who always remembered to give attribution to the aphorisms. At

dinner the talk was cynical and sophisticated, and the meal served on silver platters carried by a Filipino houseboy wearing immaculate white gloves.

Victoria might have been thoroughly uncomfortable except for the presence of Sid Lukas, who was slouchy and homey and liked to use American slang whenever possible, probably to tease or annoy his chic French wife.

After dinner, assisting Victoria from the table, Lukas asked her, "Are you on a new assignment?"

"Bradshaw," she whispered. "The hunt for." She glanced at him. "Between us."

"Between us," he promised.

Actually, her mind was entirely filled with Bradshaw, aware that the time was nearing when Howie Dittman might soon introduce them, and Victoria was hardly attentive to the after-dinner conversation.

At five minutes to eleven, when the Hungarian film maker begged to be excused because of a toothache, and left with his Czech wife, Victoria was quick to leave with them.

Once ensconced in her room at the Plaza Athénée, she changed into her nightgown, eye on her travel clock, biding her time. When the minute hand reached fifteen to twelve and the telephone remained still, Victoria's stomach tightened, a sign of nerves.

Nine minutes to midnight and the telephone rang.

The caller was Howie Dittman from New York.

"Miss Weston? I've located Mark Bradshaw for you."

"Wonderful! Where is he?"

"In the 'Annual Media Almanac,' page fifty-four."

Uncomprehending, she blurted, "I don't—"

Howie Dittman did not let her finish. "Let me explain," he went on. "Three years ago a very reliable publisher of reference books in New York here, Ravenna Books, put out a new kind of Who's Who listing the living people in journalism, radio, television, slanted for that market. That was the first edition of the 'Annual

Media Almanac.' It was also the last and final edition. While a few copies sold, found their way into a handful of firms, the reference book did not catch on. So the publishing house dropped it as an annual. There was only this one relatively obscure edition. I stumbled on a copy late today.''

"And Mark Bradshaw is in it," Victoria said with a rush of excitement. "What does it say about him? Where do I find him?"

"Whoa, not so fast—let me finish," said Dittman. "As with every media personality listed, Bradshaw had an address where he could be reached. His address was a post-office box number at the Times Square Station. I could have written or wired him care of that post-office box, but I knew that I was calling you tonight, so I didn't waste time. I tried to find out whom the box number belonged to. Not easy. But I found out."

"Where Bradshaw can be reached?"

"I found out his box number was the box number of Ravenna Books, publisher of the defunct 'Annual Media Almanac.' ''

"He works for them and the *Record*?"

"Miss Weston, he works for no one," said Dittman. "Mark Bradshaw does not exist."

"What?"

"You heard me. There is no Mark Bradshaw. Once I knew whom Bradshaw's box belonged to, I guessed what was going on right away. I remembered once hearing that the highly respected 1888 Appleton's Cyclopedia of American Biography was exposed between 1919 and 1936 for listing among its real people eighty-four biographies of nonexistent, fictitious persons. Then I remembered reading somewhere that one of our major contemporary biographical guides—I've forgotten which one; again, a sort of *Who's Who*-type reference—used to mix in a half dozen or so phony names with make-believe biographies. They did it to tell whether unsavory and fraudulent characters were using their reference work to solicit victims by mail. Well, I suspected that was the explanation for the insertion of the name Mark Bradshaw

in the 'Annual Media Almanac.' I lost no time in getting over to
Ravenna Books, caught the executive editor just as he was
leaving work. He squirmed a little, didn't like to admit it, but
finally had to confess that Mark Bradshaw was one of ten phony
names invented and inserted in the 'Almanac' to draw letters
from borderline characters who might pester their very real entries.
I'm afraid there is no real Mark Bradshaw. I'm sorry.''

Victoria let it sink in. She had difficulty speaking out. She
started to say, "But why—?" She choked it off, knowing it was
pointless to discuss the matter with Dittman, and instead she
said, "I'm sorry, too. Thanks for your good work. Let me tell
you where to bill me." She gave him her New York apartment
address, and hung up.

Sleep would not come easily this night, Victoria knew. At least
not while there were so many unanswered questions rattling
around in her head. The thing to do was to try to get the answers
from someone who was sympathetic. It would be the best anti-
dote for insomnia. The riddle must be put to rest.

She was wide awake and on the telephone once more, after an
overseas dialing to the Washington, D.C., bureau of the *Record*
in the National Press Building. Nick Ramsey was in and the
operator was putting him on the line.

She heard, "Nick Ramsey here."

Her emotion was one of immediate relief. "Nick, it's Vicky."

He sounded genuinely pleased. "Great to hear from you.
Where are you?"

"Gay Paree."

"Why aren't you asleep?"

"Too much on my mind. I had to talk to you. I have something to tell you—"

"Let me tell you something first," he cut in. "That was an
excellent backgrounder you did on Lourdes, excellent. I suppose
you heard what happened at Lourdes last night?"

Her voice quickened. "No, what? I haven't had TV or the radio on yet."

"A near disaster," said Ramsey. "The Pope was being taken down to the underground St. Pius X Basilica in Lourdes—being escorted, with hundreds of people milling around, pressing and pushing—when the lights suddenly failed. There were some frightened or unruly people, a near panic—the Pope was saved from being trampled to death only by the prompt reaction of his heavy security guard. When the lights came on, there were at least forty pilgrims injured, some seriously—"

"But the Pope was all right?"

"I told you, he had a heavy security guard. Thanks to that—"

"Nick, I'll bet you they—whoever they are—they got the lights off and tried to kidnap the Pope, and they couldn't make it."

"Now you're being far out. There's absolutely no evidence of that. If it had been planned, you can be sure Mark Bradshaw's by-line would have been emblazoned on the front pages as usual. If there's no by-line, there's no story."

Victoria sucked in her breath, exhaled, and finally said, "Nick, that by-line, that's a lie."

"I didn't hear you."

"That Bradshaw by-line over each exclusive, it's a lie. He didn't get the Dead Sea scrolls scoop. He didn't get, or write, any one of them. Mark Bradshaw doesn't exist."

There was silence on the Washington end, and then Ramsey's voice again. "Vicky, what are you talking about?"

"I've been chasing Bradshaw the last couple of days. I got your friend Howie Dittman to help. You remember, you gave me Dittman's name."

"Go ahead."

"I hired him to research Bradshaw. He did. Let me tell you what he just found out." She relayed to Ramsey everything that Dittman had told her right up to the admission of the "Annual Media Almanac" editor that Mark Bradshaw did not exist, that

he was a concoction of their staff to bait fraudulent charity
solicitors and other unsavory letter writers. "That's why I'm
calling you, Nick. I'm going crazy trying to figure it out. What
do you make of it?"

There was no immediate reply from Ramsey. At last he said,
"I don't know, Vicky. I'm not sure."

"Why would Armstead by-line those big stories with the name
of someone who doesn't exist?"

"We-ll, that's not entirely unknown," said Ramsey slowly,
"using a false house name. It protects the publisher from building up a real correspondent or columnist who becomes such a
hotshot that he can make exorbitant salary demands or even quit
and go to a rival paper. If you've got a make-believe house
name, you own what you build up and you keep it."

"Okay. But how come the name Bradshaw for the house name?
How did Armstead come to pick a name of a non-person?"

"Even that can have a simple explanation," said Ramsey,
making an effort to be reasonable. "One day Armstead heard
someone who'd been on the 'Annual Media Almanac' tell an
anecdote about those false names in the book. Good story.
Someone told it. Armstead heard it, and when he wanted a house
name he remembered it and used it. He just put Mark Bradshaw
as a by-line on those exclusive stories."

"Knowing all the while that Bradshaw didn't exist, didn't
write them."

"I guess so."

"But Nick, somebody did get those scoops, somebody wrote
those stories. What I'm asking is—who?"

Again there was a marked silence from Ramsey.

Victoria persisted. "Somebody on the *Record* found out about
the king of Spain, the UN secretary-general, the Dead Sea scrolls,
the prime minister of Israel, before anyone else found out. Who
could know about these things just as they happened, know about
them and give them to the *Record* alone and instantly?"

"Vicky, I can't imagine."

"I can imagine. Armstead could have a contact with someone who has a connection with a terrorist gang, or even someone who is part of a terrorist gang. That someone could be selling material to Armstead on the spot. Can you buy that?"

"No. Too fanciful."

"Well, I have no other answer. I was hoping you might."

"Not at the moment. Let me think about it. Right now I've got to run over to the White House and hear Hugh Weston's statement on the President's decision to add a nuclear arms reduction plan to the London agenda."

"Okay," said Victoria unhappily. "Say hello to my father."

"Listen, Vicky, let me give the whole thing more thought." He was obviously attempting to cheer her up. "I'll try to see you shortly. You haven't forgotten, have you? Your father is taking a small group of the White House press corps with him on Air Force One to London. We'll be accompanying the President to cover his meetings with the British prime minister. That's very soon. I'll try to skip out for an afternoon and fly over to see you. We can talk the whole thing over. How's that?"

"I can't wait that long, Nick."

"What are you going to do?"

"I'm going right on—right on until I solve this, no matter what."

After eighteen holes of golf and a convivial lunch, Edward Armstead had returned to his office to be ready for the scheduled phone call. It had come on time, and he had been engrossed with it the past ten minutes, and now he was finishing up.

"Okay, that explains it, Gus," he was saying. "I wish it had worked, but it didn't. Like Cooper said, you can't win them all. Just tell him for me not to fret. Maybe the next one will be easier. Tell him to stand by."

Setting down the phone, Armstead saw Dietz hovering in the doorway.

"Hey, Harry, what are you doing here? You're supposed to be taking the day off."

"I've been hanging around waiting for you. I knew you had this call coming from Pagano, and I was waiting for you to be finished with it." He entered the office and went thoughtfully to one of the chairs before Armstead's desk and sat in it uneasily. "Did he tell you what went wrong in Lourdes?"

"It was just an impossible setup. They got the lights out and had their men in place, but there was a mass of people, too many people, who got out of hand. Also, too much security around the Pope. It became high-risk so Cooper aborted it. I hate to face our first complete miss, but I wouldn't want them to try anything they couldn't finish."

"Agreed," said Dietz.

Armstead studied his associate's face. "Something else seems to be troubling you, Harry. What's on your mind?"

"A couple of things I wanted to mention."

"I'm listening."

Dietz slid forward in his chair, assuming a confidential air. "I suppose you know *Time* magazine has been prying into your affairs."

"Bruce Harmston has that under control. He's even encouraged them. Up to a point. They won't find out much."

"I don't know. That's playing with fire."

"They won't," said Armstead with finality.

"All right. If Bruce is looking over their shoulder, I won't worry." Dietz hesitated. "But there's something else—"

"Yes?"

"Do you realize that the new girl on your staff, Victoria Weston, has been snooping around, trying to find out about Mark Bradshaw?"

Armstead grinned. "I'm afraid she won't get very far."

"She already made a call from Paris, got Mrs. Crowe in personnel to ask your secretary where Bradshaw might be found."

Armstead waved it off. "Aw, that's only natural. Jealous of someone who broke several big stories ahead of her. She wants to meet him, find out how it's done. You and I know she's not going to get anywhere."

"Still—" said Dietz. "Chief, I don't like it. I don't like all this curiosity. You've pulled off some great ones without a ripple. I say call it quits while you're ahead."

"Aren't you being a bit of a worrier, Harry? It's foolish to quit when you're on top of the world."

"I'd advise it," said Dietz gravely.

Armstead's euphoria dissolved before his associate's gravity. Armstead nodded. "Very well, Harry, let me sleep on it. Let's see what tomorrow brings."

Tomorrow brought *Time* magazine.

An ebullient Edward Armstead arrived in his office, a copy in his hand. He saw that Dietz was seated in front of the oak desk, waiting for him.

Beaming, Armstead held up the magazine, pointing to the portrait sketch of himself on the cover, the vaporous, indistinct face of a second man in the distant background (presumably the elusive Bradshaw) and the boldface cover line. The cover line read: JOURNALISM'S ALMIGHTY. "Have you seen it, Harry?" Armstead boomed out. "Not bad, eh?"

Dietz lifted a magazine off his lap. "I have it. I read the piece."

Going to his desk, Armstead continued to be enchanted with the cover. "I guess it looks like me. A little jowly, maybe."

"The portrait is good enough," Dietz assured him. "It represents you as vigorous, fresh, farseeing."

"I suppose I couldn't do better myself," said Armstead, settling into his swivel chair. He continued to contemplate the cover with pleasure. " 'Journalism's Almighty,' " he read. "Almighty. How do you like that?"

"It's true," said Dietz.

Armstead shook his head in wonder. "Not even my father ever had that."

"Have you read the story inside?" Dietz inquired.

"Of course. Pretty fair-minded, I thought. Even Hannah liked it."

For a moment Dietz looked puzzled, but then seemed to remember. "Your wife read it?"

"She wanted to find out about me." Armstead laughed coarsely. "Yes. Even the old bag liked it. What did you think, Harry?"

"Impressive, no question. Maybe a little snotty about Bradshaw, about our treating him like a prima donna, withholding information about him as if we're afraid we'll lose him to a competitor, but overall an impressive piece. It's brought in a swarm of telephone calls. Estelle has recorded most of them for you to handle when you have time." He reached to the desk top for several memos. "I brought in a few of the more important ones I thought you'd want to see right away."

Armstead took them.

"You'll see one call was from Hugh Weston, the President's press secretary, with President Callaway's congratulations and a presidential invitation to dinner at the White House the night before he leaves for London."

Armstead had found the phone message. "How do you like that?"

"I think Weston wants an answer right away. The President is having a number of media bigwigs, but you'd definitely be the star. I didn't know if—if you'd want to go."

Armstead looked surprised. "Wouldn't miss it for anything in the world." Armstead fingered the magazine lovingly. "So you found the story, the profile, impressive?"

"Very." Dietz paused. "Only thing that troubles me a little—it could lead to more prying around in your affairs. Did you give any more thought to what we discussed yesterday?"

The publisher's expression had sobered. "You mean the advice you gave me? Yes, I have." He sat back in his swivel chair and met Dietz's eyes squarely. "You're right," he said, "I've decided to take your advice. I'll quit—but only after one more big one, *the* big one."

"Chief, I'm not sure of that one."

"I am," said Armstead, without equivocation. "I'm on the upside. A man in my position doesn't go out with a miss, with a failure like Lourdes."

"But nobody knows about that."

"*I* know it, Harry. I won't let myself go out with a whimper. I'm going out with a huge topper. I want my last act to be a big bang." His expression creased into a smile. "I know what I'm doing, Harry. You can trust the Almighty."

Dietz was resigned. "Whatever you say."

"The last one," Armstead promised. "And I say let's get moving on it fast."

"Very well."

Armstead was all business now. "Pagano should be back in Paris. Get him for me. I want to tell him to arrange one more meeting for me with Cooper—in Paris, tomorrow night at the Lancaster."

Dietz frowned. "Chief, I want to caution you. Our nosy girl reporter Victoria Weston is in Paris right now, standing by for an assignment. I wouldn't want her to see you."

"No chance," said Armstead airily. "I'll be in the Lancaster only one night, and never leave the hotel. If it worries you, I'll ship the Weston girl off to London and have her stand by there."

"Better."

"Meanwhile, first things first. Get Pagano for me. And on your way out tell Estelle to book me on the Concorde's early flight tomorrow morning." He winked at Dietz. "The last one, Harry. I promise you."

*   *   *

At daybreak Victoria was snuggled in her bed, fast asleep, when she stirred, reacting to some distant sound. Gradually the sound penetrated, half awakened her. Opening her heavy-lidded eyes, she listened and realized it was the bedside telephone persistently ringing in her ear.

She struggled to a sitting position on the mattress, trying to clear her head, and her hand groped for the phone receiver. She had hold of it, dropped it, retrieved it, and brought it to her mouth and ear.

"Hello."

"Hi, Vicky. It's Nick. I know you're an early riser, but—did I wake you up?"

"No," she lied.

"I think I did." He paused. "My God, just looked at the time. It's almost midnight here, so it must be nearly dawn in Paris."

"Never mind, Nick. It's good to hear from you at any time. What is it? Something up?"

"Not exactly. Well, maybe yes, maybe no. I wasn't satisfied with the way our last conversation ended."

"How did it end?"

"You were wondering how Armstead was getting all those beats he's been crediting to the nonexistent Bradshaw. I said I wanted to think about it, and I'd be in London in a week or so with the President. I said I'd try to sneak an afternoon off to come over to Paris and talk to you. And you said—"

Victoria was fully awake now. "I said, 'I'm going on—right on until I solve this, no matter what.' "

"That's what I'm calling to find out about. What you've been doing—"

"I've been shopping, overeating, waiting for an assignment, and trying to think, in that order."

"But have you gone on with your investigation?" Ramsey pressed.

"I've done nothing more," she replied. "I've been stymied. I don't know which way to turn."

"Maybe I can help you," Ramsey said. "I don't know either, but let's see. I've been giving your theory some serious thought."

"Yes?" she said eagerly.

"Your theory is that Armstead has some inside contact with a terrorist gang. I don't think that's true, but I don't know any other possibility. So let's say I go along with you. If our boss has made contact with a gang, I still believe it has to be the Carlos crowd. It's the only one I know of capable of staging all those recent operations. I know you disagree."

"Nick, I'm open to anything at this point. Okay, let's say the Carlos crowd. Even though Armstead told us he followed through with the Sûreté and tried to have them arrested and missed them."

"Honey, along with your theory goes the theory that Armstead is a liar. He didn't try to have Carlos arrested because Carlos is the source for his stories."

"I'm going along."

"Then hear this. If the Carlos gang *is* involved with the Fourth Estate, perhaps I can help you. A long shot. But maybe I can unstymie you and get you going again."

"How possibly?"

"Let me tell you what happened to me an hour ago. I was up here in the press building alone, having a late drink—"

"Naturally."

"—when I decided to write down everything that happened when Carlos kidnapped and interrogated me. So I started writing—"

"Are you finally going to file a first-person piece on your encounter?"

"I still wouldn't dare. No, nothing like that. I—" He suddenly sounded embarrassed. "—I got an idea about doing a novel about a character like Carlos. In no way as trite as it sounds. A fresh approach."

"That's wonderful, Nick!"

"Forget I ever mentioned it. When it's done, and if it's good, I'll accept congratulations." He hurried on. "Anyway, in the interests of making the novel authentic, I made up my mind to set down all the facts about my meeting with the real Carlos. So I had just started to write when bingo, something happened."

"What?"

"Remember, after Carlos released me I told both you and Armstead that I heard someone say the gang was moving to a new hangout the next morning. Well, I'd forgotten, simply didn't recall until I was writing things down, that there was more to it, that I'd overheard a fragment more."

Victoria had her ear clamped to the phone, and was listening intently. "Go on, go on," she encouraged Ramsey.

"The Carlos terrorist who said they were moving the next morning also said, 'We're moving over to No. 10. We'll be holing up there.' Of course, none of them gave much of a damn what they were saying in front of me, because I'd been brought in blindfolded, and was being taken out blindfolded, and didn't have the slightest idea where I was in Paris." Ramsey paused. "But you did. You knew where they'd taken me."

"Off the Rue de Paradis, to an apartment at No. 12 Rue Martel."

"Was there a No. 10 Rue Martel?"

"There certainly was, next door!"

"A long shot, Vicky, a long shot—but wouldn't it be logical—?"

She felt feverishly high. "It would, it sure would."

"I don't like sending you there, but if you're going on—"

"I'm going on, Nick."

"Then go take a look. But not alone. I want you to take someone with you, Sid or one of his staff. Promise me that."

"I—I'll try to take someone," she said.

But she knew that she wouldn't. She was going to prove she could do something important on her own.

"Yes, do that," he was saying. "Take a good look. Who knows? But don't get too close. I don't want to lose you."

"You care?" she asked, happy as an idiot.

He avoided a reply. He said sternly, "Keep this in mind. You're not after Carlos."

"I'm after bigger game," she said quietly.

"Keep in touch," he said. *"Bonne chance."*

It was a gloomy, rain-swept night in Paris, and most of the life in the Champs-Élysées district was indoors.

Not far off the main artery, the Hotel Lancaster stood in illuminated splendor. It seemed that every guest's room or suite was brightly lighted except for the windows of one suite on the third floor.

In the shaded lamplight of the bedroom of that suite, Edward Armstead tried to stand still as he allowed Gus Pagano to adjust the new ski mask over his head and face. Through the mouth slit, Armstead asked, "How many did you say are here?"

"Only Cooper and Quiggs this time. They run the show."

"They have any idea of what I'm bringing up?"

"No," said Pagano. "With an operation of this magnitude, I thought you should be the one to present it."

"I'm ready," said Armstead.

Pagano opened the bedroom door, and they went into the small living room with its overstuffed period furniture and fireplace. The room was darker than the bedroom had been, and at first Armstead could not make out the occupants. Finally he spotted them on a two-cushioned sofa on the far side of the room.

He went toward them with Pagano, shaking hands with both Cooper and Quiggs before sitting down in a straight chair across from them.

"I want to thank you for everything you've done," said Armstead. "I never dreamed it could go that smoothly."

"Sorry about Lourdes," Cooper apologized. "I didn't like the odds. Better a miss than a mess."

"You made the right decision. But all the others were fine."

"Planning," Cooper said. "We're proud we pulled each one off without detection. We did have six fatalities, five on their side, one on ours, but that's a low rate of loss in this business. We hope you got full value for your money."

"No complaints," said Armstead. Then, with a lilt of amusement in his voice, "I'm sure you've already guessed why I commissioned the operations and what I've been after."

"We may have speculated," said Cooper evenly, "but we've never tried to find out. We wouldn't want to be in the position of being tempted to blackmail a client. We feel we've upheld our end, and we're pleased you're happy with your end of the bargain. You've paid us handsomely and we thank you."

"We all thank you," said Quiggs.

"Not yet," said Armstead. "It's not quite over with. I have one more job for you, one last one before we thank each other and our partnership is dissolved."

"One last one," said Cooper. "Fine. I assume it must be an operation of importance to bring you over here personally."

"It's important all right, the most important job of all," said Armstead, fishing into the pocket of his suit coat. He withdrew a folded sheet of bond paper, and slowly unfolded it. "I don't believe in committing my assignments to paper. Never have, until now. This one I typed out myself after checking in. I wanted every aspect of the operation to be perfectly clear. Once you've read it, I'll tear it up and flush it. Here it is."

Extending his hand for the sheet of paper, Cooper said, "Sounds like a blue-ribbon one."

"The most useful one of all, for my purpose," Armstead said.

Cooper and Quiggs read the typed page together. Armstead glanced at Pagano nervously, and then watched Cooper and Quiggs in silence.

After they had scanned the page together, Cooper reread it by himself. At last he neatly folded the sheet once, twice, and handed it back to Armstead.

Cooper's soft voice ended with stillness in the room.

"I'm afraid not," said Cooper. "Can't do it. Not in our line. Too tough."

Armstead was breathing quickly. "You have to do it. You did the others."

"This one is different."

"You can't be objecting to the idea."

"Christ, no. We don't give a damn about the operation or the victim. They're all more or less the same to us. That's not it. I'm simply saying this one is too difficult."

"Even for double the money? I'd guarantee you ten million dollars."

Cooper shook his head. "For no amount of dollars. It is basically a technical problem. We're not equipped to undertake this kind of operation. We couldn't get the plane. We couldn't get the pilot you'd need. In fact, no one could—" He hesitated. "—except, of course, Carlos. I've heard he has this kind of person in Japan. Carlos and his gang could probably pull it off. In fact, I'm sure he could. But not anybody else. Certainly not us."

Armstead had taken grasp of something. "But you think Carlos and his gang could do it?"

"I'm certain they could. But they wouldn't."

"Why not?"

Cooper spoke with evident sincerity. "Put it this way. Me and my boys, we're in business. We're sensible businessmen. For us, most operations are a living. Not so with Carlos and his loonies. They're not businessmen. They're fanatics. Your money would never impress them. They're political creatures who perform for causes, like it's a religion. They'd find no real cause involved in this, so they'd have no reason to want to do it."

Armstead was staring at Cooper through his eye slits. "I could give them a reason to do it."

Cooper was at once surprised and curious. "What possible reason?"

Armstead continued to stare at Cooper. "I could ask you to kidnap a man they'd do anything to get their hands on. I could ask you to kidnap this man, and the ransom would be to pull off my blue-ribbon operation. I know where the man to be kidnapped is this minute. I'd pay you the ten million to grab him."

Interest showed in Cooper's face. "Grab who?"

Armstead swallowed. "Carlos," Armstead said.

The other three were all staring at him now.

Armstead swallowed again. "Grab and hold Carlos," he repeated. "His gang will do anything I want to get him back. What do you say?"

12

Slipping into his lightweight plaid topcoat, which had been purchased three years earlier when he was corpulent and was now
too large for him, Carlos emerged from the driveway of No. 10
Rue Martel. Automatically he glanced to his left, to his right,
both sides empty of pedestrians except for some young woman
window-shopping at the corner of the Rue de Paradis.

Satisfied, Carlos took one sniff of the fresh early afternoon air,
cleaned by the previous night's rains, and proceeded to the
Citroën idling at the curb. Carlos noted that a meter had been
installed in the sedan, to camouflage it as a Paris taxi, and the job
was a realistic one. Yanking open the back door, Carlos climbed
into the rear.

His driver sat stonily awaiting instructions. The driver, wearing a heavy overcoat, a woolen scarf wrapped around his neck
and the lower part of his face, his usual cap pulled down to his
ears, had a fit of coughing.

"Sounds like you've got a cold," said Carlos.

The driver nodded, coughing once more into his handkerchief.

"Let's go, Jean," Carlos ordered. "De Gaulle. Turkish

Airlines— THY. No rush. No risks. I've left myself plenty of time to make one stop on the way, then check in, pick up some reading.''

Continuing to nod, trying to muffle his cough with the handkerchief in his free hand as he shifted gears with the other, the driver pulled the car away from the curb and started ahead.

Abruptly at the next driveway, which led into the courtyard of No. 12, the driver gripped the steering wheel with both hands, wrenched the car to the left into the darkened entrance, and once off the street jammed on the brakes.

Thrown forward, trying to regain his balance, Carlos bawled, ''You sonofabitch, what the hell's going on?''

As Carlos started to speak to Jean again, the driver whirled around, scarf thrown aside, and it wasn't Jean at all but a stranger. He stuck an arm over the back of the front seat and in his hand was an Astra .357 Magnum. He pressed the muzzle of the gun against Carlos's forehead. ''Shut up,'' the driver commanded. ''One move and you're dead.''

The trunk of the Citroën was already open, its lid pushed high. A man crawled out, slammed the lid shut as another man joined him, and then both dashed for the rear doors of the car and ducked in, one on either side of the stunned Carlos.

''What is—?'' Carlos had started to say, when the Astra was pulled away from his forehead and a swab of ether clamped over his mouth and nose. Carlos attempted to wrestle free, but the powerful men on both sides had him pinned back, while the hand of one exerted pressure on the soaked rag of ether covering his mouth and nostrils.

In short seconds Carlos's resistance subsided and he went limp and unconscious, sagging against one of his abductors. With practiced hands the man ran his fingers over Carlos's body, until he found and removed the Skorpion YZ61 gun.

Together, the pair pushed Carlos off the car seat and rolled him over and down to the floor.

''On our way,'' one of them called out.

The driver put the Citroën into reverse, and backed slowly out of the driveway into Rue Martel.

As the driver shifted into first, a voice in the rear shouted, "Hold it—here comes Pagano!"

Across the street a figure had materialized from the shadowed doorway of a closed shop and was running toward the car. The front door on the passenger side had been thrown open for him, and Pagano leaped in beside the driver and signaled ahead.

Stepping on the gas, the driver asked, "Anyone at No. 10 see this?"

"Nobody," Pagano assured him. Pagano turned to the pair in the back seat. "You got the carcass, Quiggs?"

"In dreamland," said Quiggs, poking his shoe into the uncon- scious lump on the floor. He looked up with a broad smile, exulting. "Boy, this was a piece of cake for ten million Ameri- can smackers."

Accelerating, the Citroën sped up the Rue Martel.

Seconds later, a red Renault turned into the Rue Martel, with Victoria at the wheel and following.

When Carlos completely opened his eyes and his head began to clear and he focused, he realized that two men were standing over him, observing him. He also realized that he was strapped tightly into a sturdy chair, his wrists tied behind the chair, his ankles, in front of the chair, also tied.

Carlos had difficulty speaking. His tongue was thick. With effort, he managed to articulate a question. "Who are you?" He turned his head in either direction. He was in a darkened room, a shabby living room, and he was aware that there were other persons somewhere in the room behind him. He managed another question. "Where am I?"

"Never mind where you are," said the taller of the pair, settling down in a chair directly in front of him. "Since we'll be together a little while, we don't mind introducing ourselves. I'm Cooper. This is Quiggs."

Carlos had found his voice. "You're going to pay for this, you dirty fuckers."

"I'm not exactly worried," said Cooper. "I think you're the one to start worrying—if you don't cooperate."

Carlos's eyes smoldered. "Carlos doesn't cooperate with anyone, if he doesn't want to. And I don't want to, not with a bunch of tinhorn scum and mercenaries. You let me go or—"

"Or what?"

"Or I'll see that each one of you is hunted down and cut to ribbons."

Cooper reached for Carlos's throat, placed his fingers around it, pressing his thumb against the terrorist's Adam's apple. When Carlos gagged, Cooper released his grip. "Listen to me, you fatheaded skunk, you're not going to see to anything, now or ever. You're going to have your head blown away. You're going to have your corpse, in chains, at the bottom of the Seine." Cooper straightened. "I don't want any more crap from you. Either you cooperate or you're wasted. You've got exactly one minute. Which is it?"

Carlos stared at him coldly, and at last gave a short shrug of surrender. "What do you want?"

"Your gang," said Cooper.

"You off your rocker, or what?"

"We need your men for an operation," said Cooper. "We want your gang, and your gang will be wanting you. We have a special operation in mind. We're not equipped to do it. Your men are. We want your men to pull if off. That's our ransom demand. Your men pull this off for us, and we'll set you free, return you to them."

Carlos fixed on Cooper with his lethal stare, lips compressed. Finally he spoke.

"What do you want done?" said Carlos. "Obviously I can't help. If you want something done, you'll have to put it up to my men, not to me."

Quiggs came closer, bending low. "Who do we contact?"

"I don't know. My partner, maybe. Without me there, he's the only one who can speak for the others. Robert Jacklin's the one."

"Where is he?" Cooper demanded. "At your hideout in the Rue Martel?"

"No," said Carlos. "Jacklin is in Istanbul laying the groundwork with the Turkish Popular Liberation Front for something of our own."

Quiggs displayed a Turkish Airlines ticket. "You were on your way to meet him?"

"Yes."

"How do we contact him in Istanbul with the ransom demand?" Cooper wanted to know.

"You can't. He has no address in Istanbul."

"But you were on your way to see him," said Cooper. "Where?"

Carlos grimaced and squirmed. "Will you loosen these goddam straps?"

"In due time," said Cooper. "Where were you meeting Jacklin?"

"Inside a mosque—the Blue Mosque—tomorrow—eleven in the morning."

"Where inside the mosque?"

Carlos was reluctant to answer. He glared at his tormentors, and finally gave in. "In front of the chanter's balcony."

"You'll have to explain that in a minute," said Cooper. "How do we identify Jacklin?"

"A scar—he has a scar on his right cheek." Carlos continued to glare at Cooper and Quiggs. "You know he won't talk to you."

"He will," said Cooper, "if he sees a ransom note from Carlos, a note in your own hand. You better play along with us, Carlos, if you want to see tomorrow."

Carlos had begun to calm down. His predicament seemed to

amuse him. A ghost of a smile played across his features. "I guess I have no choice," he said.

Cooper stood up, indicated the Turkish Airlines tickets that Quiggs was holding. "Give Gus these tickets. Tell him to get ready to take off soon as we get him the note. Tell him to inform our principal about the delay." He raised his hand to read his wristwatch. "Still time to make the three o'clock plane if he moves fast. I want him in Istanbul."

An hour ago, probably less, Victoria had seen most of the action in the Rue Martel. Standing at the corner, she had seen a man in a plaid topcoat emerge from No. 10 and enter a Citroën taxi, a car that resembled the auto that had whisked Nick away from the Champs-Élysées, only this one had been a taxi. She had been unable to identify the lone passenger exactly, although from Nick's earlier description and from her research notes she suspected that it might have been the world's most wanted terrorist, Carlos.

She had seen the vehicle dart away from the curb, brake, skid, and plunge into the next driveway out of view. Moments later she had seen it back out, but this time there had been three men in the rear seat instead of one, and suddenly the one in the middle had been pushed down out of sight.

Victoria had veered off, eased casually into the Rue de Paradis, then run to her Renault and got it started. When she careened into the Rue Martel, the taxi had nearly reached the far end of the block and was turning the corner. Grimly, Victoria had followed.

As luck had it, two stoplights had allowed her to keep within range of the fugitive taxi.

It had been a long, tense ride to the Left Bank.

She had observed them swing off the Rue de Seine into the Rue Jacob, and she had slowed to see the taxi vanish in a driveway beside a used bookstore on the street floor. She had been tempted to go after them in the Rue Jacob, but had been afraid that she might be spotted as suspicious. Instead, she had proceeded up the Rue de Seine, impatient to find a parking place, and at last found an illegal spot in the Rue Dauphine.

Victoria had hastened back to the Rue Jacob, wondered if it would be foolhardy to enter the empty street, and at last cautiously ventured into it. Crossing over to the other side, she strolled along past the bookstore and driveway on the opposite side. There had been no sign of the taxi. But upstairs, she could see there were apartments, windows shielded by gray metal shutters and fronted by black-painted balcony bars.

Worried about being noticed lingering, she had retraced her steps to the corner of Rue Jacob and the Rue de Seine, where she hoped to be made less conspicuous by occasional foot traffic.

She was still at her same post on the corner, after twenty minutes or a half hour, when she saw the Citroën taxi poke out of the driveway. There was no way she could clearly make out the two men in the front seat, but she knew that they were vital to her investigation.

She charged into motion, running as fast as she could to the Rue Dauphine to recover the Renault and give chase, but when she approached her car she saw that there was a blue uniformed policeman there, writing her a parking ticket.

It was hopeless now. She could never give chase. But she comforted herself with the fact that she knew where some unknown abductors had taken a member of the Carlos gang, probably Carlos himself.

She determined to return to her post and stand watch as long as possible, until she could more plainly see someone else emerge and obtain a description of him for Armstead. Then, she felt positive, she might have the story of the year.

Upon his arrival at the Yesilköy Airport outside Istanbul, Gus Pagano had been met by the car and driver he had reserved in advance. The car was a small Turkish-made Anadol, and the driver was a mustached Muslim student named Vasif.

After checking into a comfortable suite in the Istanbul International Hilton Hotel, Pagano had taken an evening tour of the city, crossing the Galata Bridge over the Golden Horn, into the old city of Stamboul, then scouting the Mosque of Sultan Ahmed, which he learned was the formal name of the Blue Mosque.

The following morning, on schedule, Pagano, again impressed by the Obelisk and six minarets of the early seventeenth-century Blue Mosque, traversed the vast courtyard to the gate that led to a terrace. He descended steps to a cobbled path, brushing off the swarm of hawkers with their postcards and cheap souvenirs until he reached the green awning that covered the entrance to the mosque. To the left of the entrance he saw a wooden rack resembling a bookcase, where visitors were leaving their shoes. Pagano followed suit, pushing off his Gucci loafers and placing them neatly on the rack.

He ducked under the green awning, and in his stocking feet went inside.

The sight that assaulted him was entirely new to his experience.

The interior was a mammoth, colorful, man-made cavern. At the top, a mighty central cupola was supported by four thick grooved marble pillars. All around, from top to bottom and on all sides, were windows, stained-glass windows, mostly blue—260 windows, Vasif had told him—and the entire rectangular stone floor was covered with handmade patterned rugs of every size, contributed by various Turkish villages as well as by world heads of state. The dusty interior air seemed permeated by some kind of mystical atmosphere, and scattered throughout there were ordinary people, Turks and some foreigners, on their knees in prayer.

Pagano heard someone breathing beside him and saw that it was his driver, Vasif, who had followed him.

"Extraordinary, no?" said Vasif.

Pagano was reminded that he was not here for sightseeing. "Where's the chanter's balcony?" Pagano asked.

Vasif pointed off to the right, to a square, windowless marble room within the mosque, atop which was a railed balcony.

"From the balcony the chanter calls the prayers," explained Vasif.

"Thanks," said Pagano. "I must be alone. Wait for me in the car."

Watching until his driver left the mosque, Pagano turned back and fixed his sight on the small structure that held the balcony. At its doorway, a lone male figure knelt in prayer. Pagano had what he wanted. He had a glimpse of his wristwatch. Three minutes after eleven. On the nose.

Pagano trod quietly over the array of carpets, advancing on the lone kneeling figure. When he came up alongside, he lowered himself to his kness and took in the other. This was an olive-complexioned ferret of a man with slick black hair and the livid welt of a scar on his visible right cheek.

Losing no time, Pagano said under his breath, "You are Robert Jacklin?"

Jacklin was surprised, and attentive. "Who are you?"

"I am here for Carlos," said Pagano.

"Why?"

"I am an emissary from a group in Paris that has kidnapped Carlos. We are holding him. You can have him back safe and sound if you comply with our ransom terms. I am to explain the terms to you."

Not a muscle moved on Jacklin's face. "How do I know you speak the truth?"

"I will show you a message from Carlos. You will recognize his handwriting."

"I must see it."

"Yeah, you'll see it, and then I will explain our demands to you. You will have time to consult with your compatriots in Paris. If you are willing to comply, you will meet with me—and my leader—at a table in the Bosphorus Terrace Restaurant of the Hilton at two o'clock tomorrow. Understand?"

Jacklin had raised himself off his knees. "Let me see the

evidence that you have Carlos in custody. After that, outline your
ransom demand. Please?''

"Very well," said Pagano.

At a few minutes before two o'clock in the afternoon, Edward
Armstead walked a step behind Pagano from the main lobby of
the Istanbul International Hilton Hotel into the stretch of side
lobby that led to the Bosphorus Terrace Restaurant at the far end.

Decidedly uncomfortable with the fluffy gray wig settled over
his real hair, with the puttied extension of his nose and his
flowing, pasted-down mustache, Armstead was nevertheless eager to go through any discomfort to attain the great achievement
he had in mind.

Now he would meet Carlos's right-hand man and he would
know whether the operation would be undertaken. All would
depend on the word from Robert Jacklin.

They strode past the alcove holding the cloakroom and WC's,
past the attractive walls tiled in green and blue, and stepped
inside the restaurant. The maître d' came forward. Pagano said,
"I believe you have a reservation for Mr. Walter Zimberg, a
party of three, on the terrace." The maître d' scanned his reservation sheet. "Yes, of course, on the terrace for three. One of your
guests has already arrived."

Their table was really two square tables set side by side along
a railing that looked down on a long, glistening pool. The neatly
dressed, lean, smallish young man with a prominent scar on one
tawny cheek did not bother to rise as Pagano pulled back a cane
chair for Armstead directly across from him.

"Mr. Robert Jacklin—Mr. Walter Zimberg."

Jacklin jerked his head in curt acknowledgment as Armstead
and Pagano sat down. Jacklin had a bottle of Kestana mineral
water standing on the green-and-white-checkered tablecloth before him, and he poured himself a second glass.

"I hope we haven't kept you waiting," said Armstead politely.

"No," said Jacklin. He eyed Armstead with a curl of his lips.

"Your disguise is a poor one, poorly done. I mention this for your future welfare. Not that it matters, of course. I don't really care who you are."

Taken aback, Armstead sought a response, but before he could speak, a captain appeared with three menus. "Perhaps you would like to start with a drink first?"

Jacklin placed his hand over his glass. "I'm all right."

Armstead opened the menu, then turned it over. "Do you have some white wine? Ah, yes, your beverage list. Want to share a bottle with me, Gus?"

"Why not?" said Pagano.

"May I recommend the Cankaya," suggested the captain.

"Whatever's the best," said Armstead. "While we have you, let's order a bite. What about the scrambled eggs here?"

"Menemen," said the captain. "Eggs with tomatoes, green peppers, parsley, and white cheese."

"I'll have the same," said Pagano.

"I'll have the vanilla custard cream," said Jacklin, handing back the menu.

"Krem Karamel Vanilyah," said the captain, as he wrote. "You are sure you do not wish something to start with?"

"Nothing," said Jacklin.

They waited for the captain to go. Once he was out of sight, Armstead addressed himself to Jacklin quietly. "I assume by now you know what this is all about?"

Jacklin dipped his head. "I have a good idea, from the note Carlos wrote and from your friend here."

"Can you do it?"

"We've done nearly everything, at some time or other. Not exactly one like this, but others, more dangerous. This one is a little unusual."

The muscles in Armstead's features went rigid. "I am not asking your judgment. I am asking if you can do it?"

Jacklin's expression was bland. "We want Carlos back."

"You'll do it," said Armstead.

"We have to," said Jacklin. "Yes, I have talked to the others in Paris. They have agreed. We can do everything you want. Not simple, but it can be done. Fortunately, the key person required is available to us in Japan, through the Japanese Red Army. He will join us, if the price is acceptable."

"The price is Carlos."

"For us, yes. But for the key person in Japan, no. He has no interest in Carlos. He needs a guaranteed sum of money separately for his own purposes. Perhaps one million American dollars. I cannot say precisely. But he will cooperate if the price he requests is met. We must have him to make the operation work."

Armstead did not give it a second thought. "I'll see that the price is right."

They all fell mute as a waiter rolled up the table containing their quickly prepared lunch orders. He passed out the dishes.

When the waiter had retreated and they were alone, Armstead poked his fork at his eggs, but he was too anxious to be hungry.

Jacklin resumed. "The one in Japan will require a few days of special training."

"No problem about that?" said Armstead.

"None. The day before the operation, he will be brought from Tokyo to join us. Actually, to join you. He will insist on meeting you first, seeing evidence that his payment is on deposit in his wife's name. You can meet him anywhere."

"At his point of departure from the United States," said Armstead hastily.

Jacklin spooned his custard. "Very well."

Armstead continued. "My friend here—" He indicated Pagano. "—he will arrange everything with you in Paris. He is going back to Paris today."

"I will be there tomorrow," said Jacklin. "Mr. Pagano has the means to reach us by phone." Jacklin's gaze fixed on Armstead. "No change in schedule?"

"Still one week from today," said Armstead. "The timing will have to be perfect."

"It will be perfect," Jacklin stated, eyes holding on Armstead. "With the operation concluded, the ransom will have been paid. Then, Carlos. When do we get back Carlos?"

Armstead nodded. "Within an hour after I have verified the result, your Paris contact shall receive a call from Mr. Pagano. He will tell you Carlos is free and where you can pick him up." Armstead spoke the next words with deliberation. "You do your part. We'll do our part."

A ghost of a smile crept across Jacklin's face. "Terrorism depends on trust," he said softly, "even when we terrorize each other."

In the main editorial office of the Paris bureau of the New York *Record*, Victoria carried four distended manila folders of still photographs from the picture file cabinets and set them down on the metal reading table in the center of the room.

She sat down to confront a picture of the man she sought, and there was an unbelievable relief in getting off her feet.

This was the middle of the afternoon of the fourth day since Victoria had witnessed the abduction of a member of the Carlos gang—possibly Carlos himself—by strangers, who had whisked the victim off to a hideout on the Left Bank. She had been fortunate in being able to follow the abductors to the Rue Jacob. She had been unfortunate in missing a chance to follow two of them, a driver and a passenger, who had left the hideout on the Rue Jacob that first day.

Since that time, Victoria had been relentless in her vigilance. For three days, except for the briefest periods to munch a croissant or a sandwich or visit a hotel bathroom, and to catch six hours of sleep after each midnight, she had maintained her station at the corner of the Rue de Seine and the Rue Jacob. This morning and early afternoon had been her fourth day at the fatiguing game. She had not been sure what she was on the lookout for—actually, she supposed, it was to see someone emerge from the hideout, someone she could follow and later

describe. But her purpose had changed. Her original intent at
the Rue Martel, based on Nick's clue, had been to hope for
some kind of link between the exclusive stories that had appeared
in the *Record* and the Carlos gang. Some sight of Carlos himself,
or of an informant who might be followed. Instead, she had been
treated to an actual kidnapping, the snatching of someone leaving
Carlos's hideout, by a set of strangers. After that, her intent had
shifted to learning the identity of the strangers and the man they
had abducted. This might lead her, she believed, to the most
sensational news story of the year, reported by herself, and never
mind who had reported the previous terrorist acts.

But in her four-day vigil at the Rue Jacob, not one other
person had emerged from that driveway beside the bookstore, not
one. Perhaps, she wondered, they had only come out at night,
when she was asleep on the Right Bank. Yet they had to sleep,
too, and probably slept when she slept. By early this afternoon,
the vigil had become too difficult. Passing police, on routine
rounds, and proprietors in neighborhood shops had undoubtedly
begun to eye her with suspicion. The same young woman, always hanging around. To them she must have looked like a
hooker, or an advance scout for thieves. The discomfort created
by familiarity and, worse, the sheer exhaustion of constantly
standing there, moving around on her feet there, had begun to
take a toll on her calves and thighs, her spine and neck, and early
this afternoon she had begun to feel faint.

She had just about given up, considered quitting, when she
realized there was something more useful she might be doing.

In all this time, from the Rue Martel to the Rue Jacob, she had
seen only one individual clearly. The person who had emerged
from the Carlos hideout and been kidnapped. This was a person
she believed she could recognize if she saw him again, recognize
and possibly identify. This might tell her whether the victim had
been Carlos himself or a lesser member of the gang.

Photographs of Carlos did exist. She had fleetingly seen some in Nick's possession. She might find out exactly whom she had seen abducted if she sought out pictures of Carlos.

With this thought as a fresh motive, she had reason to quit her unproductive vigil at the Rue Jacob at last, and she had got into her Renault and driven to the Right Bank and to the offices of her paper's Paris bureau.

Now, from the bureau's photographic archives, she had four files of still pictures taken of terrorists and their victims.

She brought the first folder down from the pile, and slowly started to turn over the eight-by-ten glossies, one by one.

There they were, the rogues' gallery of violence worldwide. Italian underground revolutionary Feltrinelli, scholarly glasses and weak chin. PFLP leader George Habash, more menacing and formidable. The corpse of Aldo Moro. The Olympic Village room riddled with bullet holes. West German terrorist Gabriele Kroecher-Tiedemann. Hassan Salameh of Black September. Professor Antonio Negri of the Red Brigades. Libya's infamous Colonel Qaddafi.

On and on. One folder, two folders, no familiar face.

The third folder. Pay dirt.

Ilich Ramirez Sanchez.

Otherwise known as, and captioned, Carlos.

There were four photographs of him. A pudgy round face. A nice friendly face. The hanger-on at cocktail parties. The busboy. The exchange student. But no killer. And not the face of the man she had seen abducted in the Rue Martel.

A fifth photograph, and this one she recognized.

Dark hair, bushy eyebrows, wide nose, thick lips—hollowed cheeks, no pudginess, thinner, harder—and this one, too, was captioned Carlos, the most recent photograph of Carlos.

This was the one in the oversized plaid topcoat who had emerged from No. 10 Rue Martel. This was the one who had been kidnapped by strangers. This was the one being held captive in Rue Jacob.

No question.

Victoria heard a footstep, half-turned in her chair to find Sid Lukas peering over her shoulder.

"What are you up to, Vicky?" he inquired. "Can I be of any help?"

"Just going through your photo files on terrorists."

"I see you found Carlos."

"Yes. Have you ever seen him?"

Lukas emitted a short laugh. "If I had, the whole world would have known about it."

Victoria avoided his eyes, considering how far she might go. "Sid, what—what if you ever got a lead on him—some information—?"

"On Carlos?"

"Like where he might be hiding. Something like that."

Lukas grunted. "That would be the day."

"What would you do?"

"It's just never going to happen."

"But if it did?" persisted Victoria.

"Why, I'd go straight to the French Sûreté, of course."

"You would?"

Sid Lukas hesitated, furrowing his brow, considering the idea. "Well—given Armstead's predilection for exclusives, I might notify him first. I suppose I would." He shrugged. "But why daydream? Anyway, what are you up to? Still messing with the old terrorist series? Because if I can be of any help—"

Victoria came to her feet, invigorated. She pecked a kiss at Lukas. "You already have been, Sid. Thanks." She hastily began to gather together the pictures and files, and shoved them at the bewildered bureau chief. "*Many* thanks."

She knew what to do next.

In the Plaza Athénée bedroom, Victoria, having kicked off her shoes, stood on the carpet in her stocking feet with the telephone receiver clutched between her ear and shoulder, waiting for the connection.

She heard Harry Dietz answer.

"Oh, Mr. Dietz, hello. Victoria Weston in Paris. Actually, I was trying to get through to Mr. Armstead."

"I know," said Dietz. "He's not available. He's been out of the city, just returned, and is probably still resting. I thought I could take your call and pass on anything."

"You can," Victoria said. "It's tremendous news, and for once I wanted to be the one to get the scoop." She caught her breath. "Carlos," she blurted, "I saw Carlos kidnapped!"

Dietz's voice was distant. "The terrorist leader?"

"I located his new hideout. I saw him come out of it. I saw him abducted. I saw where they took him, where they have him."

"Who took him—who has him—?"

"I don't know yet. Strangers. Another gang. They're holding him now. Nobody knows about it outside, except us. It's a tremendous story right now. Let's break it before the police find out."

"You're right—" Dietz's voice trailed off, then came on again waveringly. "But wait. Hold it, Vicky. You haven't told anyone about this, have you?"

"Of course not."

"Don't. I want to get this to Mr. Armstead first—before we go any further—he may have some ideas—"

"About what?" Victoria said impatiently.

"Well," Dietz hedged, "there just might be more—"

Victoria understood. "You mean about who has Carlos, who's holding him? I've tried to find out. I can keep trying."

"Something like that. Let me pass this on to Mr. Armstead and see what he advises. Yes, you're right, it is a hot story. But let's sit on it until I contact Mr. Armstead. You hang up, and stay where you are. I'll be in touch with you again in a few minutes."

*   *   *

Dietz knew that he had awakened Armstead from the moment he had heard his chief's voice. But Dietz also knew that what he had to tell Armstead was of vital importance, and that Armstead would not mind.

The call had been to Armstead's private line in his extremely private and locked-off study inside his Fifth Avenue penthouse. He had been sleeping and working there alone since inheriting the newspaper, not only to avoid the annoyance of Hannah, his wife, but to keep what he was doing away from her prying eyes. Normally Armstead would have been up at this hour, and readying himself for the office, but yesterday morning and this morning he had been sleeping later to recover from the Turkey trip and jet lag.

"What is it?" Armstead said fuzzily.

"You awake, Ed?" Dietz inquired, to give him more time. "I wouldn't have bothered you, Chief, but it's important."

"I'm awake. What's up?"

"I had a call from Paris just now, from our girl there, Victoria Weston. She was quite excited. Thinks she's onto a tremendous story." Dietz paused. "She claims to have seen Carlos kidnapped."

Dietz let the thunderbolt strike. He knew it would be a thunderbolt.

"What?" exclaimed Armstead. "How could she have?"

"I don't know," Dietz hastened to say. "I didn't want to push her yet. But she saw the kidnapping."

"Does she know who did it?" Armstead asked quickly.

"No. Strangers, she said."

"You're sure?"

"She didn't know, Chief. If she'd known anything about Cooper, or Cooper and us, she wouldn't have called."

"You're right," Armstead agreed. "She knows it happened— but doesn't know who did it."

"Exactly. She wants us to blast the story wide open. I stalled. I told her I thought I should consult you first—uh, that you might want her to find out more before we broke the story. She offered

to stay on and keep an eye on the hideout and find out who was
holding Carlos.''

"Nosy bitch," muttered Armstead. "She could cause real
trouble, throw a monkey wrench into our whole operation.''

"That's what has me worried. I persuaded her to stand by until
I contacted you. I promised to call her right back. What do you
want me to tell her, Chief?''

Armstead's answer was immediate. "Tell her to come home."

"What about Carlos?''

"Tell her we'll have someone in Paris keep an eye on the
hideout. Promise her she'll have the story as her own by-line
exclusive. But get her back here to New York. Tell her I want to
see her personally, hear firsthand what she's seen.'' He was
briefly silent. "After that, I'll decide what to do with her.''

"I wouldn't want her to become suspicious.''

"Don't worry, Harry. Leave her to me.''

13

The instant the bell over the entrance door to Dr. Scharf's reception room tinkled, indicating the arrival of the next patient, Edward Armstead gripped the arms of his worn armchair and hoisted himself to his feet. "Guess my time's up," he muttered, with a show of irritation.

Dr. Carl Scharf, partially slumped in the armchair opposite, fingers intertwined across his bulging belly, feet propped on the ottoman, remained unperturbed. He made no effort to rise. "Why don't you let me tell you when your time's up?" said Scharf for what must have been the hundredth time. "We were still talking—"

He watched Armstead stride to the couch to retrieve his overcoat, and he knew it was no use. Most patients usually reacted this way when the bell reminded them of the end of their fifty-minute hour, especially the more dependent patients, and Armstead was no exception. Dr. Scharf gave an inner sigh. There was no way to change this resentment. Patients became emotionally involved with their analysts. They gradually accepted their psychiatrist as friend and confidant, and were always resentful when reminded that they were being followed by other patients, that they were paying for this involvement, that these sessions were after all a business, and their analyst a businessman (or, at least, someone who treated them with concern for love—and money). However, Armstead had been more difficult than most patients, especially lately, with his reinforced ego that showed signs of insufferable arrogance. Armstead had originally come to him wanting love, and now seemed to demand it as his special prerogative, his right and his privilege.

Dr. Scharf wasted no more time in rising to his feet.

He joined his patient as Armstead finished buttoning his coat. Scharf wanted to soothe him. "Well, I'm certainly glad you'll be going to the White House to dine with the President," said Scharf. "Quite an honor. But you've earned it. I'll be seeing you right afterward. I want to hear about everything that happens."

"I'm not going," said Armstead brusquely. "I'm too busy for that nonsense." Noting the analyst's surprise, as they started for the exit door to the corridor Armstead added, "What the hell, Presidents come and go. Breaking bread with one of them really doesn't mean that much. My work is more important." He waited for Dr. Scharf to open the door for him. With an abrupt nod Armstead said, "Take it easy," and left.

Dr. Scharf had meant to say, "And you'd better take it easy, too," but had not said it.

He closed his office door and leaned against it, thinking.

He was worried about Edward Armstead. In this session, in the last, in the one before, more and more Armstead was beginning to show signs of megalomania. He was definitely in a hypomanic state right now, with a real psychotic-manic condition impending, an ultimate state that might seriously impair any balanced judgment he had in relation to others.

Dr. Scharf walked slowly back to his armchair, reviewing his patient's symptoms. There had been subtle indications for weeks, when Armstead revealed his behavior toward his wife, son, mistress, employees, of his hypomanic state. Armstead had been more frequently irritable, showing no consideration for others, only for his own satisfaction, showing the possibilities of cruelty and violence in his growing omniscience. This last remark, no time for the President of the United States, revealing a belief that he was more important than the Chief Executive, seemed to cap it all. Armstead had become, in his own eyes, omnipotent. Dr. Scharf tried to trace at what point, after the death of Armstead's father, he had seen it happening. Well before the *Time* magazine cover. Somewhere along the way, during Armstead's meteoric journalistic rise with all those exclusive stories, certainly by the time he had been the first to tell the world that the prime minister of Israel had been murdered.

It was an emotional problem, yet Dr. Scharf wondered. He considered the possibility that Armstead's state was organic, perhaps stemming from a frontal-lobe tumor. A thorough checkup by a physician might be called for—he might speak to the physician first about his own concern—and after that a visit to a top neurologist. But then Dr. Scharf remembered that not long ago Armstead, anxious about several dizzy spells, had visited both a physician and neurologist in turn, and been given a clean bill of health.

Dr. Scharf lowered himself into his armchair, absorbed with the problem of Armstead. It was not organic, the problem; it was a building psychosis. He might soon slide into episodes of a true manic attack.

Before he could put his mind to it further, the telephone interrupted. He guessed it might be his message service. When they rang in at all, it was usually during his break between patients. Dr. Scharf lifted the phone. There was, indeed, a message. "A Miss Kim Nesbit called. She asked that you return her call when you have time. She insisted you had her number."

Dr. Scharf replaced the receiver thoughtfully. He suspected that he knew why Kim had telephoned and wanted to speak to him. If he was right it was dangerous ground, but it could be useful. He wondered whether he should return her call before mentioning it to Armstead—that is, presuming Armstead would be the subject of her call.

The grandfather clock against the wall told him that he had five minutes of his own time before he would summon his next patient inside.

He opened his address book, found the telephone number, took the receiver from his phone once more, and dialed Kim Nesbit. A few rings, and she answered the phone.

"Kim? This is Carl Scharf. I received your message. It's been a long time."

"How you doing, Doc?"

"I'm fine, thank you. How have you been, Kim?"

"As well as can be expected." She gave a short laugh. "You should know."

His suspicion had been right. This was going to be about Armstead.

"Well, I haven't seen you for a while," he said. "I assume you're okay."

"Who's ever okay?" she said lightly.

He detected the slightest slur in her voice, but she sounded lucid. He judged that she was still sober.

"Well, if there's anything I can—" he began to say.

"I'll tell you why I gave you a call," she cut in. "I wanted some advice about a friend we both have in common."

"If I can help, I'd be glad to."

"It's about Edward Armstead. I presume you're still seeing him?"

"Well—" said Dr. Scharf guardedly.

She uttered another short laugh. "If you're seeing him—and I know you are—then you're doing better than I am. Of course, I do see him, you know he comes over. But not as much anymore. Only sometimes, when he wants to. He isn't exactly dependable."

Dr. Scharf refused to be drawn in. "You know, I'd be glad to give you guidance in anything I can," he said, "but I'm afraid it would be improper for me to discuss Edward Armstead. Yes, as he's told you, he is a patient of mine, Kim. It is a question of ethics, respecting confidentiality.''

"Oh, come off it, Carl,'' she said a little recklessly, "I don't want to know any of his secrets. I just wanted to sound off to someone I could trust, someone who knew him as well as I do. I wanted someone to tell me how to deal with him.'' Kim paused. "He's sick, you know,'' she said flatly.

To Dr. Scharf this astuteness was unexpected. It was the moment to withdraw from the conversation, find the means to terminate it. Yet Dr. Scharf was sorely tempted to let her go on, without committing himself. If Armstead was suffering a building psychosis, Dr. Scharf realized that confirmation would be helpful. Normally he would seek consultation with a fellow psychiatrist. But occasionally, cautious as he was, Dr. Scharf permitted himself to engage in the unorthodox. He considered doing so now, attempting to confirm his diagnosis with someone else who saw Armstead, under different circumstances, almost as frequently. Kim was not a doctor, but a former patient, generally trustworthy. And she *had* called him. This would not be exactly unethical, listening, advancing no opinions of his own.

Dr. Scharf decided to pick up on Kim's last remark. "You think he's sick? You mean actually?''

"Don't you? You should know. I mean he's sick in the head. He's got delusions. He really thinks he's running the world. Power is all he's interested in. He's so power-hungry, so obsessed with power, he can hardly get it up when we're in bed—and when he does manage, he goes slack on me, with his mind on a thousand other things. When he does make it with me, it's as if I'm not there, another human being. He treats me like one of those blown-up Japanese sex dolls.''

"I'm sorry, Kim.''

"He was all right in the beginning, after his father died, when he thought he wanted me. Now I'm not enough. He wants everyone in the world. To own them. Dominate them.''

"Are you going to continue seeing him?''

"I don't know," Kim said despairingly. "I don't give a damn." She reconsidered. "I suppose so. I suppose I'll see him when he comes around. It's the only game in town. If you hear of another one, let me know."

"Kim, whenever you feel like it, come in and see me."

"Maybe I will."

"I'd appreciate the chance to talk with you. Although I couldn't discuss Ed Armstead without his permission."

"Aw, forget it, and thanks for the free session."

"I wish I could help you with your concern, Kim. The fact is, I'm concerned about him, too, but I think you'll have to use your own judgment in handling Ed. Yes, he has seemed under—under a lot of pressure lately. But I'm hoping that will improve with time." He paused. "I think it would be wise for you not to mention that we spoke, until I can bring it up with him next week."

"I wish you wouldn't," she said plaintively.

"Well—"

"As for me, I won't say a thing. You have my word, Doc."

"Thanks, Kim," Dr. Scharf said uneasily. "Good-bye."

Dr. Scharf put down the receiver. Confirmed. He had walked an ethical tightrope, but it had been valuable, with no harm done. He would propose to Armstead that they resume seeing each other three times a week. Two times, at the least. He would suggest to Armstead's physician some tests—a workup—for possible use of lithium. He would do this very soon.

He stood up and started for the reception-room door. It was time for the next patient.

After leaving Dr. Scharf and settling into his limousine, Armstead had gone back to his office and spent a long and satisfactory afternoon getting his affairs in order. By five o'clock everything had seemed under control.

Dietz had reassured him that Victoria Weston would be no problem. She had been docile about her reassignment and agreed

to leave Paris for New York, pleased that Armstead wanted to
see her immediately and hear the details of the Carlos kidnapping.
After her arrival at Kennedy Airport tomorrow, she would be
coming directly to the *Record* building for the early afternoon
meeting with her publisher.

Confident that this potential leak on the Cooper gang had been
plugged, Armstead had devoted himself to seeing that preparations for his biggest story were progressing on schedule. Pagano
had returned to Paris, and Armstead had spoken to him at length.
Carlos was still a hidden hostage. Jacklin was doing everything
he had agreed to do to get his leader released. Members of the
Carlos gang were, from various points of entry, gathering in the
Bahamas and Cuba. Most important, the key figure in Tokyo—
Armstead had at last learned his name, Yosuke Matsuda—had
accepted the terms for his participation, was already in training,
and would shortly be on his way.

Relieved that the big one, the big story, was in the making,
moving inexorably to its climax, Armstead had been able to
attend to the loose ends awaiting his decisions at the newspaper.
He had conferred for over two hours with McAllister and the
department editors.

As the afternoon waned, when the day shift had departed and
there was no more for him to do, Armstead had begun to feel
very much alone. Except for Harry Dietz, and he had already had
a half-dozen conversations with Dietz that day, Armstead had no
one to talk to, he realized. He wanted a female companion, but
someone he could be comfortable with. Hannah was impossible.
He had no desire to endure her disapproval and suffering tonight.
He had instructed his secretary to phone and tell her that he was
too busy to come home for dinner.

That only left one other. He notified her that he was coming
by. At ten minutes after five, he admitted himself into Kim
Nesbit's apartment.

It immediately pleased him that, for a change, she was not in
her nightclothes and not in disarray. She was wearing a clinging

red silk dress that he had not seen before. She was groomed, her blond hair sleek and swept up in back, her makeup fresh and bright. She stood poised beside the nearest sofa, no drink in hand. It would be fun to undress her, fuck her, mess her up, enjoy her submission and entreaties, he decided.

To reward her, he went directly across the living room, embraced and kissed her.

He stepped away, frowning. She had not responded, and despite the faint aroma of mints, she smelled like a distillery.

"You all right?" he asked.

"Sure, why not?" said Kim, but the words had a drag and uncertainty to them.

"Aren't you going to offer me a drink?"

"Have a drink." She waved vaguely at the bar. "Have one."

"Want to make it for me?"

"Sure." She tried to leave the sofa, but staggered and held on to the side. "You better make it for yourself," she said.

Irritated, Armstead stepped over to the bar. Pouring himself a scotch and soda, he saw Kim feel her way around the sofa until she reached the far corner and then drop into it.

He intended to castigate her about her condition, but could see that her silk dress had been caught up above her knees. The milky thighs, and what lay between, diverted him. He could feel the beginnings of his first erection in a week. If he did it quickly, ignoring her, there could still be some pleasure.

She deserved one amenity. "What some black coffee?" he asked.

"Maid's gone," she said. "No. Make me a drink."

He did not want her senseless, and he did not want to waste any more time, so he moved to the sofa and sat down beside her, placing his drink on the coffee table.

Kim was seated, legs slightly parted, dress hiked higher to reveal a greater portion of the white flesh of her thighs.

Her glazed eyes followed his hand down to one thigh, as he

placed a palm inside it, caressing her, moving his hand under her dress.

"I've missed you, Kim," he said. "I want you."

"No," she said.

"Did you hear me? I want you."

"Do you hear me?" she mouthed thickly. "No."

His hand stopped. He could have easily subdued her, he knew, but he did not intend to take her by force. He had not been used to resistance, to being denied anything, for a long time, and he wanted her to be the one to give him what he desired.

"What's wrong?" he said. "Don't you want me?"

"I want you," she said. Her hand fell on his arm, until he withdrew his hand. "Not yet," she said. "I want to talk."

He decided to humor her. She wanted the buildup. "Okay," he said impatiently. "Let's talk. What did you do with yourself today?"

"Hairdresser. Watched television. Had—had a few drinks."

He tried to restrain himself. "You shouldn't drink so much."

"Where have you been?" she said. "You haven't been here in a week."

"I've been busy," he said. "I run a—" the words came to him from *Time* magazine. "—communications empire."

"You should have time for others—for me."

"Kim, be reasonable. I had to be in Paris. I was in Istanbul. I have thousands of people depending on me."

"I'm one of them. You could find time. I'm lonely."

He could detect a softening in her, and was conscious again of the hardening between his legs. "I am finding time. I'm here." He reached out once more, with both hands, one inside her bodice, cupping her breast, the other under her skirt, between her legs, groping for the strip of panty covering the down.

She gave a convulsive wrench, pulling away from him, finding the strength to tug at both his arms until she was free. "No," she said, "I don't want you any—anymore—unless—"

His anger was mounting. "Unless what?"

"—unless you promise to see me the way you did. You treat me like dirt now. I'm a person—a person—"

"You're what I want you to be," he said furiously. "You're nothing except what I want you to be. Who do you think you are, treating me this way? Everyone who's anyone in the world depends on me, even the President of the United States. What people know, what happens to them, depends on me. It's all on my shoulders." He had leaped to his feet, standing over her, eyeballs bulging. "I *am* the news. I *make* the news. I *make* life that goes on in the world."

She looked scared. "No, Ed. Don't talk like that. It's not true. You're influential, but you're not—"

He snatched at her wrists, gripping them fiercely. "Don't you tell me what I am and am not. I know what I am. It's in the magazines. I'm the Almighty."

"You're acting crazy," Kim whimpered. "Please—"

He tightened on her wrists, twisting, hurting her. "Don't you tell me I'm crazy—"

"Everyone says so," she cried out. "Everyone knows. Even Dr. Scharf said—"

She caught herself, trying to swallow the words.

He stood over her, stone-cold, staring down at her. "Dr. Scharf," he said. "You saw him—?"

"No—no, no—"

He lifted a hand and slapped her across the face. "You saw him—?"

"No," she gasped.

Armstead slapped her hard again.

"I called him," she gasped. "I was worried about you—we spoke."

"Scharf talked to you?"

"Of—of course."

"And said what?" Armstead roared.

She pressed her lips tight. His palm rose and fell, once, twice, slashing her against the cheek and jaw.

"Stop it—don't, Ed—" she cried. "It was for you—for your sake I called—we talked—"

Armstead started to hit her once more, but her arm warded him off in fright as her tears mingled with blood.

"Tell me!" he demanded. "What did he say?"

"He agreed you're sick—actually, I said it—but he said you were under pressure—and he was concerned—don't, Ed, don't hit me anymore."

Armstead came to his full height, a grim smile on his face. "So now we have it straight. Scharf says I'm sick and Nesbit says I'm crazy."

"No, Ed, listen—"

"The hack and the whore," said Armstead. "Now we have it from the final authorities."

"Listen, Ed—" she implored.

But he had left her.

She looked woozily over her shoulder.

Armstead had stormed out of the apartment.

An hour later they were seated on a banquette at a table in the barroom of the Four Seasons, Armstead and Dietz, with Armstead speaking intently and Dietz listening intently.

When Armstead was through Dietz asked, "Are you sure, Chief, she wasn't making it up? You believe Scharf really talked to her?"

"Positive. I suspected the little fat weasel all along."

"And you think he implied what she claims?"

"You bet he did. Kim's not bright enough to make up something like that. She was quoting him all right."

"What does this add up to?"

"Adds up to the fact that Scharf believes something is wrong—he's concerned—and he might be snooping around, the way the Weston girl did, and we can't have anyone get in our way just when we're on the verge of the big one."

"Maybe you're right, Chief."

"I know I'm right," said Armstead emphatically. "I can smell danger. Scharf is danger."

"What do you want to do about it?"

"Stop Scharf before there's trouble. The minute you leave me tonight, I want you to arrange for somebody to get into his office and go through it. Can you?"

"No problem whatsoever," said Dietz.

"Get someone to enter his office tonight. Should be easy. Obliterate my name—from his Rolodex, appointment pad, billings, even notes on file, if he has any. Can you arrange this?"

"Will do."

"Then I want you to get rid of Scharf."

"You mean all the way?"

"Naw. What the hell. He has a wife and family. Just see that he's put out of commission for a while. Maybe an accident in the street tomorrow, when he's walking to work."

"Sure," agreed Dietz. "I can set it up. An accident. But I can't guarantee the extent of—of what happens."

"Just put him out of commission for a while. Make a point of that. Pay your man whatever he wants to do it right. I'm sure you'll set it up okay. I know I can always count on you, Harry. I'm getting hungry. What about you? The sautéed calf's liver is always good. Let's order up."

Edward Armstead's single hope, letting himself into the huge, elegant tenth-floor penthouse apartment, was that his wife Hannah would not be awake. He did not want to be answerable to her for again avoiding dinner and her person. He did not want to listen to her complaints about her delicate and ailing body and his own inattentiveness. He wanted to be alone, in the unassailable safety of his soundproof study, at his Victorian library table-desk, to start writing the big story, the most sensational exclusive story in the history of journalism.

From the entry hall, Armstead peeked into the broad living room, into the drawing room, and there was no sign of life.

Good, he told himself, because if Hannah stayed up late she usually sat in her wheelchair in the living room, nodding off before the oversized television screen. After that she was in bed asleep at ten o'clock, and it was already ten thirty-five. Relieved, he entered the wide corridor that led past the two bedrooms on one side and to the ponderous oaken door to his private study opposite.

Treading gently across the corridor carpeting, he saw that the door to the first bedroom, Hannah's bedroom, was open and the lights were on. His heart fell. This meant that Hannah was awake and waiting for him. Praying that he was wrong, slowing, he glanced inside and came to a halt. She was there all right, in the wheelchair beside her bed. He met the hollow eyes, fixed in her sunken and wrinkled face, and holding on him with defiance.

"You still up?" he said. "You should be getting some rest."

"So should you," she said. "I've been waiting up for you. Where have you been so late?"

"Having dinner with Harry Dietz. We had some business to talk over."

"Before that?"

"In the office, of course."

"You left the office at five o'clock," Hannah said.

Armstead ground his teeth. She was going to be difficult, the old harridan. Somehow, she knew where he'd been in between. Best to admit it, thwart her by admitting it, put it in the right light, and then she would have no grievance at all. But before he could speak, she spoke again.

"After you left the office, Edward, you went to Kim Nesbit's apartment."

Armstead snapped his fingers. "That's right. Almost forgot. Just looked in on her to see if she was feeling better."

"You looked in on her for over an hour."

"For chrissakes, Hannah, what is this? Kim's practically a relative. She took my father's death pretty hard. Since then, I've looked in on her two or three times to give her my condolences."

"Two or three *dozen* times," said Hannah bitterly. "Some condolences."

"You goddam witch!" shouted Armstead. "You've been spying on me, having me followed—"

Hannah compressed her lips, hands tightening on the arms of the wheelchair until her knuckles were white. "I just know," she said, voice cracking. "I have my sources. I won't let you humiliate me."

"I'll do what I want to do," Armstead shot back. "There's nothing you can do about it."

"There's plenty I can do, if I want to. You're forgetting my father helped finance your father when he was in trouble. My father left his stock to me. I have ownership in at least half your public holdings. I could sell off, cause you a lot of trouble." She was wheezing now, trying to catch her breath. "Edward, I don't want to do anything like that. I only want you to be kind, behave decently."

"I'll be what I want to be," Armstead said angrily. "Don't you get in my way. And if you ever have anyone follow me again and I find out, you'll be sorry for it, goddam sorry. Just remember, Hannah, I warned you."

With that, he grabbed the knob of the bedroom door and slammed it shut between them.

Blind with fury, he continued up the corridor to the thick oaken door of his private study. Reaching into his pocket for the heavy key—the only key to this room in existence—he tried to calm down. Everything was going smoothly, perfectly, except for the women. All his troubles were coming from women. First that young snoop, the Weston girl in Paris. Then Kim, the whore, selling him out, collaborating with his own analyst. And now the death's-head in the bedroom. Having him followed, actually threatening him.

Inserting the silver key in the dead-bolt lock that secured his study door, he paused to examine the full implications of what Hannah had been saying. She knew about his visits to Kim, every visit, because she had hired a detective agency to follow him, shadow him, to observe his every move. He didn't give a damn how many times they had seen him call upon Kim. But they might have seen him consorting with someone else. Like Pagano, for instance, although there could be innocent explanations for that. Still, Hannah's jealous pursuit of him could unwittingly lead to dangerous fallout. Especially in the next few days. Something must be done quickly.

He turned the key, shouldered the heavy door open, and entered his private study. Before turning on the lights he stood in the darkness, thinking.

The thought came to him that it might be wise to show Hannah some contrition.

Like personally serving her breakfast in the morning. Yes, he would do that. He would take over from the housekeeper, prepare and serve Hannah her breakfast in the morning.

Ollie McAllister, who had rarely been summoned from his managing editor's desk to meet with the publisher in executive territory, came tentatively into Armstead's office carrying a single folder.

Swinging restlessly from side to side in his leather-upholstered swivel chair, puffing steadily on the first cigar of the day, Armstead observed his approach. Recently he had not dealt regularly with any editors on his staff, preferring to confine all meetings to Harry Dietz, but Armstead had come in early this morning, before Dietz had arrived at work. Armstead had toiled hard and long last night on the first draft of his masterpiece—the big story—and after that had slept lightly, subconsciously aware that he had to be up early enough to make Hannah's breakfast and serve it to her. Hannah had been grateful almost to tears for his consideration.

Dietz's not being in yet had been a minor disappointment for Armstead. There had been some unfinished business to be taken care of later last night and earlier this morning, and Armstead had been eager to know the outcome. He had waited over an hour for Dietz, and when Dietz had still not checked in, Armstead's impatience wore thin. At that point, before ten o'clock, he remembered another way he might learn the outcome of the unfinished business. He buzzed Ollie McAllister and requested the early summaries of local news from the metropolitan news desk.

Now the inquisitive McAllister was before him with the folder.

"Sit down, sit down, Ollie," the publisher directed.

McAllister folded himself uncomfortably into a rattan chair across from his publisher's desk. "You wanted only the early news summaries from the metropolitan desk," McAllister said, just to be certain.

"I've been neglecting cityside news," said Armstead, "but the last few days I've been having a look. Nothing to cheer about. Pretty dreary stuff."

McAllister was immediately apologetic. "There hasn't been much locally. All the best stuff has been coming from abroad. Our Bradshaw exclusives have been dominating the space."

"Of course," said the publisher. "Anyway, I thought I'd have a look, to see if we can beef it up. Let me see today's summaries."

McAllister half rose, to pass the folder over the desk to Armstead. "Thirty possible stories at this hour. I've allocated nine columns out of the 190 columns available for the news hole—nine columns for local news. We're basing it on a sixty-page first edition."

"Let's see what we have," said Armstead, opening the folder on his desk and rolling his chair up to it.

Armstead flipped through the summaries from the metropolitan desk, pretending to read several. He pulled one page loose. "What's this about the new bozo who's announcing himself as a mayoral candidate? Doesn't seem very substantial to me."

"True, he's a novelist, but we thought it might develop into something colorful."

"Christ, Ollie, he's got a new book coming out. This is a

publicity ploy. Don't give him more than a few inches.'' He
shoved the summary back into the stack and continued to leaf
through the others. He separated out another page. ''Man bites dog?
You've got to be kidding.''

''He actually did,'' said McAllister, hoping for a smile. ''They
put him away, of course.''

''And we're putting the story away,'' said Armstead, crum-
pling the page and dropping it into his wastebasket. ''We don't
have room for loonies in this newspaper.'' He resumed turning
the pages, stopped once more. ''Siamese twins in Bellevue.
Caucasian. They're okay?''

''Thriving.''

''Follow up. Freaks are another matter. Readers like freaks.''

''Yes, sir.''

Armstead continued leafing through the early summaries, scanning them, seeking the outcome of his unfinished business.
Abruptly he stopped, lifted out a page.

''What's this? Psychiatrist seriously injured by a hit-and-run
driver. In critical condition. Where did this come from?''

''Simms covering the police beat. Phoned it in this morning.
The shrink was crossing the street from a parking lot to his office
—a car came off the curb fast—maybe the driver didn't see
him—smacked the pedestrian on the left leg and side, real impact,
threw him thirty feet and pancaked him against a parked vehicle
—then took off.''

''Any lead on the hit-and-run?''

''No near eyewitnesses. Happened too fast. That part is
hopeless.''

Hiding his satisfaction, Armstead concentrated on the news
summary. ''Mmm. Dr. Carl Scharf. Never heard of him. Have
you?''

''No. But we intend to check him out. Can be a story if he has
anybody well known as a patient.''

Armstead snorted. ''No chance. You see where the psychiatrist's
office was? On Thirty-sixth Street off Broadway. What kind of

psychiatrist would have an office in that neighborhood? He must be nobody, and his patients are nobodies.''

"As I said, we can check it out.''

"Don't waste the time," said Armstead, wadding up the sheet of paper. "About as interesting as the mugging of a housekeeper." He threw the ball of paper away.

"I guess you're right, Mr. Armstead.''

Armstead hastily leafed through what remained in the folder, snapped the folder closed, and stood up with it. "I think you're right about the local stuff's being on the slow side." He handed the folder back. "Well, do your best, Ollie. Thanks.''

He watched his managing editor leave.

He found his onyx desk lighter, flicked on the flame, applied it to his cold cigar.

A brief image of his cherubic analyst came to him. The bastard had betrayed him. Served the sonofabitch right. He hoped Scharf wouldn't die. But if he did, he deserved it.

Anyway, one leak plugged.

That left a second one to take care of after lunch.

An hour after lunch, Dietz put his head in.

"Victoria Weston is here to see you, Chief.''

Armstead beckoned him. Dietz stepped inside, shutting the door behind him.

Armstead said, "I read in the local summaries about the psychiatrist who got in the way of a hit-and-run driver.''

"I was going to tell you myself but I overslept. Sorry, I was up most of the night on that matter.''

"Good job, Harry. The summary mentioned he was in critical condition. How critical?''

"Too early to say. I inquired at the metropolitan desk about several stories, and made this one of them. Scharf, at last word, was still unconscious. Concussion, multiple fractures, maybe a broken back. He was still in surgery.''

Armstead unpeeled a fresh cigar. "Hope he makes it. Keep me up. Again, my appreciation. Now let's have a go at Miss Weston."

Armstead was busily sorting through some memoranda on his desk when Victoria Weston was shown in.

"Hello, Mr. Armstead. Been a long time."

He pointed her to a chair across from him and sat back. As he put a light to his cigar, his eyes followed her. She had set down her purse and raincoat and seated herself. She was wearing what was obviously a new French outfit, velveteen jacket, lacy white blouse, paisley skirt. She was poised, pretty, but too intent, Armstead judged. She might be difficult.

"How was the flight from Paris?" he inquired.

"Smooth. I had to settle for a late plane or I'd have been in yesterday."

"Well, anyway, you got some sleep, I hope, shook the jet lag."

"Oh, I'm fine all around," said Victoria.

"I wanted to tell you how pleased we are with you. Your features, they were excellent. And you were on the spot whenever news was breaking."

"I'm afraid it didn't do you much good," said Victoria. "You had everything before I could get it to you."

"That's what comes of having a first-rate news organization, Victoria. Anyway, we were glad you were there as a backup, in case anything misfired."

"Mr. Armstead—" she said.

Here it comes, he thought. She is going to be difficult.

"—only one thing upsets me," she was saying. "Your bringing me back at this time. As I told Mr. Dietz, I had the lead on a tremendous scoop, something I was sure you'd want—"

"Of course, we'll pursue it. However, I felt I should discuss it with you first, in person."

"But it could evaporate, even while we talk," she protested.

"Don't worry, Victoria. The moment we heard about it, we assigned a staff member in Paris to keep an eye on the place.

Where was it? The Rue de Seine and the Rue Jacob. We have someone on watch. But I wanted to learn more, firsthand from you, before chasing it down further. I wouldn't want to make any mistakes, to hurt our credibility. We've built up a fine record in a short time, and every exclusive story of ours has proven to be one hundred percent true. We're the envy of the whole country, leading everyone in circulation. I wouldn't want to endanger this record by trumpeting a beat I could not substantiate. That would be our first sour note. So—''

"But Mr. Armstead," she interrupted, "I was there, I saw it happen. I saw them kidnap Carlos."

"Did you?" Armstead exhaled a cloud of smoke. "Victoria, forgive me, but I'm an old hand at this sort of thing, and you are new and relatively inexperienced. In my day, I've attended too many murder trials where five eyewitnesses give five different descriptions of the murderer. I mean, we're all only human—''

"Mr. Armstead, believe me."

"I do believe you. But my natural instinct to step into something like this warily, to be cautious before becoming involved, made me want to speak to you first. The fact is, I think this has possibilities for a front-page lead. That's why I brought you all the way here. To determine for myself whether we are onto something. So let's start from the beginning. You were on the Rue de Paradis, keeping an eye on the Rue Martel—''

"Keeping an eye on the hideout Carlos was using."

Armstead held up his cigar hand. "One moment, Victoria. The last information we had was from Nick Ramsey, after he was picked up and overheard someone in the Carlos gang saying they were moving. And, indeed, when I notified the Sûreté they staged a raid on No. 12 Rue Martel, and the apartment was already empty. Carlos had moved on."

"But I found out he had only moved next door."

"How did you discover that?"

"Why, from—" She looked at Armstead blankly. "I thought I'd told you. Maybe I forgot to. Anyway, after Nick got to

Washington he recalled something he had overlooked telling
you—it had slipped his mind—and we were talking and he told
me about it. The member of the Carlos gang who had mentioned
moving also mentioned that they were moving to No. 10. I
remembered that there was a No. 10 next to the old hideout at
No. 12.''

"Enterprising of you, Victoria, but a long shot. There must be
countless house numbers in Paris designated as No. 10. The
terrorist could have meant any one of them in any one of dozens
of other streets.''

"Yes, he could have,'' conceded Victoria, "but he didn't. He
meant No. 10 Rue Martel, next door. Which was what Nick and
I had reasoned. Why should the Carlos gang members expose
themselves to public view by moving around the city? Wouldn't
it be safer to move right next door? As it turned out, that's what
they did.''

"How can you be sure?''

"Because I saw Carlos himself, their leader, leave the building.''

Armstead sucked at his cigar. "Victoria, how do you know it
was Carlos? Have you ever met or seen him in person?''

"Of course not,'' replied Victoria, exasperated. "But earlier,
when we were on the terrorist series, Nick described him to me
and showed me photos of him in clippings. I was almost sure it
was Carlos. Finally, after a few days, I decided to make absolutely sure. I went to our Paris bureau, took out all the photographs on file, and there was a recent picture of the man I had
seen step into the Rue Martel and get kidnapped.''

"What made you think he was being kidnapped?''

"Because—'' Victoria faltered. "He—he got into a taxi, in
the back seat like a passenger, and sat in the middle. Then the
taxi started off, suddenly swerved into a second driveway and
disappeared. In seconds it backed out, and I could see that on
either side of the back seat there were two other men, and Carlos,
who had been in the middle, couldn't be seen. They'd obviously
pushed him down to the floorboard, were holding him by force.''

"You didn't see that happen?"

"No—no I didn't, but it was obvious."

Armstead remained skeptical. "Maybe it was Carlos still sitting up in the back seat, only he had moved over to one side when the taxi went into the driveway to pick up another passenger. Isn't that possible?"

"It's possible," Victoria had to admit, "but I don't think that's what happened."

"You don't *think* that's what happened," repeated Armstead. "And after that?"

"I ran for my car and was able to follow the taxi to the Left Bank, the Rue de Seine, and the Rue Jacob. The hideout of the other gang—the one that had abducted Carlos."

"You saw this so-called other gang carry Carlos into their hideout?"

"No—no I didn't. I was parking."

"Did you ever see any members of the so-called other gang?"

"Once. But not really. I saw two men leave in the taxi. I wanted to follow them, but a policeman was giving me a parking ticket. They got away."

"If we showed you some photographs of terrorists in various gangs, do you think you could identify those two men?"

"I—I'm afraid not. I didn't really get a clear look at either one. They moved out so fast."

"But you still think members of another terrorist gang are holding Carlos? I wonder why they'd risk it?"

"I can't imagine."

"Neither can I," said Armstead with an air of finality. "It is possible there may have been some extramural feuding between gangs. But I doubt it. I strongly doubt it. I can't see anyone monkeying around with Carlos. Still, someone might. For that reason, I'll follow through."

Victoria was not ready to be dismissed. "I was hoping you'd send me back, let me follow through."

Armstead put the stub of cigar in an ashtray. "I appreciate

your persistence, Victoria. But in this case I don't think it's justified. We'll look into the matter in Paris on our own, use someone who's on the scene. We have plenty to keep you busy right here."

"I'm sure you have." She rose, gathering up her raincoat and purse. "I'm sorry this didn't work out."

"If it does, you'll be the first to be informed and to be given a share of credit. Take the rest of the day off, and come back to work in the morning."

"Thank you, Mr. Armstead. I want to spend a little time at my desk, see what's piled up. Then go back to my apartment and unpack and get some sleep."

"You can use a company car until you get your own."

"Thanks again."

Before leaving editorial, Victoria had stopped at her desk to check and sort out the accumulation of mail that had been unattended since her departure for Europe. It had taken her fifteen minutes to clean off her desk and fill her wastebasket as she discarded junk mail, publicity handouts, outdated interoffice memos.

Finishing, dispirited by her interview with Armstead, she stepped into the aisle, about to depart, and bumped into Harry Dietz, who was hurrying back to his office. He caught her, steadied her, and apologized.

Releasing her, Dietz searched her face. "Hey, why so gloomy, Victoria? Isn't it good to be back home?"

"Well—"

Dietz nodded understandingly. "I know. Mr. Armstead filled me in briefly on your talk. Listen, we all make assumptions, mistakes. But in case there is anything to it, he'll follow through. You can depend on him. If it works out, he'll give you due credit. I promise, you'll share the by-line with Bradshaw. How's that?"

Without waiting for her reply, Dietz hastened off.

Going to the elevator, Victoria tried to mimic his question in her head: *How's that?*

Getting into the elevator, she angrily replied to his question with her answer: *Fuck off, Mr. Harry Dietz.*

Stepping out of the elevator into the lobby, she halted, reviewing what Dietz had told her.

He'll follow through. You can depend on him. If it works out, he'll give you due credit. I promise, you'll share the by-line with Bradshaw.

With Bradshaw.

There was no Bradshaw. They knew it. She knew it. But—they did not know she knew it.

Plainly, it was all a sham. Whatever Armstead had promised her, he had not meant. He had not believed her story at all. He had merely dusted her off.

Her anger mounted at the injustice of it. Armstead and Dietz, they were treating her like a child, an inexperienced cub reporter.

Yet, she had seen the happening in Paris, seen it with her own eyes, and trusted what she had seen. She was not wrong. They, the big shots, the know-it-alls who knew nothing, they were wrong. Suddenly she wanted to show them up, prove herself.

There was a public pay phone near the exit. It was vacant. Victoria made her way to the booth, closed herself inside, and located her personal credit card. When she had it, she put through a long-distance call to Paris.

Fifteen minutes later, in his own office on the sixth floor of the Armstead Building, Harry Dietz received an unexpected telephone call that disturbed him. After listening, Dietz said, "No, I don't know anything about this. Maybe the chief does. Let me see if Mr. Armstead is in. If he is, I think you should speak to him. Let me put you on hold."

Dietz pressed the hold button, came to his feet, strode to the private door leading to the publisher's office, knocked sharply and looked in. Armstead was at his desk and alone.

Dietz let himself into the office and hurried to the publisher's side. "Chief, there's a call—"

Armstead cocked his head questioningly.

"—I have a call from our Paris bureau, from Sid Lukas, that perhaps you'll want to take."

"Sid Lukas?" Armstead noted the time on his desk clock, and calculated the hour in Paris. "At this time? What's going on?"

"Let him explain," urged Dietz.

Dietz went to the front of the desk and perched on the end of a chair while the puzzled Armstead depressed the button on his telephone console and lifted the receiver.

"Sid?" said Armstead.

"Mr. Armstead, I didn't want to bother you, but Mr. Dietz thought you might be able to help."

"About what?"

"Victoria Weston's call ten minutes ago. I gather she's in New York again. I just missed her call, but she left a message. I gather it was vital or I wouldn't have bothered."

Armstead was at once alert, staring at Dietz. "Go on, Sid."

"I was in Lyon on a story," said Lukas, "and just got back to Paris. Thought I'd drop by the office to see if there was anything essential on my desk before going to the apartment. I checked out our message service, and there was one message that sounded critical. A long-distance from Vicky Weston. I figured she was still at her desk, so I called her there. When there was no answer, I asked to be transferred to Mr. Dietz, who felt I should speak to you."

"Here I am," said Armstead. "What do you want to know?"

"I was hoping you could fill me in on Vicky's message. It's a bit cryptic. I guess she didn't want to leave the full message with the service."

"What's the message?" asked Armstead, although his expression indicated that he knew.

"The message says, 'Tell Mr. Lukas I had to leave Paris in the middle of an important story. No one believes I have it, but it's true. Remember when I was going through the terrorist photos in your office two days ago, and we discussed the leader? I know where he is right now. I think you should follow through. I'll be back in my apartment in an hour. Phone me at any time after that for full details. Victoria Weston.' And she left her phone number." Sid Lukas paused. "Of course, she was referring to Carlos. She knows where he is. That could be pretty important, all right. I could use the details this minute. I was hoping you could help me. If not, I can get the details from her a little later. Do you know anything about this, Mr. Armstead?''

Armstead forced a chuckle. "Sid, sorry to burst your bubble, but it's a phony. Yes, I saw Miss Weston today. She spilled the whole thing to me. I pointed out she'd been misled, and was trying to mislead everyone else. I proved it to her, and told her to forget it.''

"Then why in the hell is she bothering me?" Lukas complained.

"Because she's like all kid reporters," said Armstead. "She wants to prove herself, make it overnight. She's obsessed with the idea that she saw someone who looked like Carlos, when in fact we happen to know Carlos is in Tripoli right now. There you have it. Ignore Vicky's fantasy. Forget the whole thing.''

"All right, Mr. Armstead. Thanks. Sorry to trouble you. But geez, I don't know what to say to her when I call her tonight.''

"Don't bother calling her. You don't have to. Go to sleep."

"Okay. Maybe I'll give her a call anyway, just to be courteous. I'll be polite, but double-talk her.''

Armstead contained himself. "Whatever you like, Sid. If you want to call her tonight to be polite, go ahead. Anyway, sorry the story didn't shape up.''

The second Armstead hung up, Dietz was leaning against the far side of the desk, his face anxiety-ridden. "You're not letting him call her, Chief? My God, she might persuade him to look into it—he might get the Sûreté to the hideout on the Rue Jacob, and they'd not only find Carlos, they'd find Cooper and our whole crowd—and they'd find us. We'd—''

"Calm down, Harry," said Armstead. "Victoria Weston is not going to get any call from Sid Lukas tonight or any night."

"Why not?"

"Harry," Armstead said with a smile, "she's going to be dead. And you're going to see to it right now."

After the telephone call to Paris from the lobby, Victoria had gone down to the Armstead Building garage to borrow a company car. The last available car was on a grease rack, and Victoria had been delayed a half hour while a mechanic finished servicing it. Once in possession of the Ford, she drove it out into the thick of the Park Avenue traffic.

She was eager to return to her apartment and not miss the call from Sid Lukas. She knew that he would call once he got into Paris from out of town and checked his message service. The chance for a scoop on Carlos was an opportunity Sid would not be able to resist. He would call, all right, and she wanted to be there when the phone rang. It would be worth anything to show up those arrogant nitwits, Armstead and Dietz, and prove that she was no simpleton, but someone as smart as, if not smarter than, the two of them.

Stalled by the traffic, starting and stopping constantly, Victoria had time to relive her interview with Armstead and short meeting with Dietz, and she was again smarting at their treatment.

Imagine their daring to try to con her into believing they would follow through on the Carlos story, and Dietz saying that Bradshaw would be doing it.

Bradshaw. That Dietz would pretend he existed, and got them all those sensational scoops when she knew—

That instant, she *knew*.

She felt the goose pimples grow on her arms, and her fingers clenched the steering wheel more tightly as her body went rigid. It was coming to her in a rush, the incredible answers to the questions that she had been asking herself in these last weeks. Like a streak of lightning throwing a bright, stark light on a dark area, illuminating all that had been hidden so long.

In those stunning moments of revelation, Victoria could see the whole truth. It was too shocking, even horrifying, to believe, but it was the truth, there could be no other. It was coming to her—who Mark Bradshaw was; why she and Nick had always been sent to scenes where terrorism was about to happen, to file advance background stories where terrorism would occur; how the *Record* had obtained exclusive stories on the kidnapping of the Spanish king and abduction of the UN secretary-general and theft of the Dead Sea scrolls and murder of the Israeli prime minister and near kidnapping of the Pope in Lourdes; why Carlos was not being picked up and jailed; why she had abruptly been ordered to leave Paris and return to New York.

All this made sense if—she tugged at the steering wheel, breaking out of the traffic, and pulled up against the curb to hear her heart thumping and her senses telling her the ultimate truth —if Edward Armstead was behind everything, was himself the mastermind and promoter of his own terrorist gang, was himself the real Bradshaw secretly spewing out all those circulation-building and power-making scoops and exclusives.

It had to be Armstead, none other. It couldn't be, but it had to be.

The logic was there, and the certainty. But not the proof.

How to prove it?

If only she were an experienced investigative reporter, she

would know which way to turn. But then it occurred to her that if she wasn't one, she knew one, and it was to him she must turn.

She must call Nick Ramsey as speedily as possible.

Pulling away from the curb, she slipped her Ford into the train of traffic once more, and trembling with excitement, she sought a public telephone.

Because it was so difficult to find both parking and a public telephone, Victoria considered going on to her own studio apartment on West Seventy-third Street. But she realized that it might take too long and she could miss Nick Ramsey, and that wouldn't do, not right now. She remembered telephone booths nearby, and easy parking, and she turned off Park Avenue, crossed Fifth, maneuvered her way to Rockefeller Plaza. There she braked before the NBC Building, left her Ford and a generous tip with the doorman, and ran inside to find a telephone booth.

In minutes she was putting through her call to the New York *Record* bureau in Washington, D.C.

Nick Ramsey was still at work.

"Are you free to talk?" Victoria wanted to know.

"For you, anytime," he said. "Just sitting here trying to wind up a backgrounder on the President's conference in London."

"Listen to me, Nick—"

"Hey, what's up? You sound pretty excited."

"I am excited, ready to burst. I'm in New York—"

"How come? I thought you were calling from Paris. What's going on?"

She tried to be as quick as possible. "Nick, your tip led me to Carlos. I saw him kidnapped by another gang."

"You actually saw that? Why would anyone want to—or dare to?"

"I don't know. I reported it to Dietz, and the next thing I knew I was ordered to return to New York and tell it all to Armstead. I did. He didn't believe me, but promised to look into it. If my story is confirmed, I'll share a by-line with Mark Bradshaw.''

"With Bradshaw? But he doesn't—''

"You know, I know, but Armstead isn't aware that we know. That put me onto it. How could I have been so blind? It was right under my nose. The real truth. Who's behind the latest terrorist wave—who's writing those exclusives for the *Record*—''

"I'm listening,'' she heard Ramsey say. There was no chiding in his tone. She tried to picture him at the other end, telephone pressed to his ear, countenance serious and sober, grimly prepared to hear her out. "Go ahead, Vicky,'' he added.

Encouraged, she went on. She poured out everything that was on her mind. She omitted nothing. Even as she spoke, her certainty grew. Not once did Ramsey interrupt or challenge her. He was fully attentive as she built her case. At last she was through, and she wanted his response.

"There you have it, Nick,'' she concluded. "There you have it all.''

A short silence followed. "Edward Armstead,'' he murmured finally. "So you think it's Armstead.''

"I *know* it's Armstead.''

"But if he did it, why—why would he do it? He has all the money in the world.''

"He doesn't have identity, or didn't have when he took over. You yourself told me that once. He has to be somebody. He wants power. And he seems—I don't know—a little mad.''

"Could be,'' said Ramsey, but a doubt had surfaced. "Yet, it can't be. You've made a case. But somehow the thought of it seems farfetched. Armstead hiring mercenaries, employing terrorists, committing criminal acts, murdering—it just doesn't seem possible.''

"Anything is possible, Nick, anything. The logic is there. You can't dispute the logic. There is no other explanation.''

"I can't think of a better one,'' Ramsey admitted. "Suppose

everything you've said is true. What can you do about it? What can you do without proof?''

"I can go to the police, try to have them investigate."

"They'd throw you out on your ear. You know it."

"I know it," Victoria confessed miserably. "I do need proof. I guess that's why I'm calling you. I need help. Maybe you can suggest something. What would you do if you were in my shoes?"

Ramsey was intent now. "The first thing I'd do is look out for myself, proceed with caution, watch every step I make. Because if you are anywhere near the truth, Vicky, you're in danger of treading on a land mine. If Armstead is involved, he already has you marked as a threat. Perhaps that's why he brought you home. If you persisted, got too close to him, Armstead might be forced to—to eliminate you."

"Fair warning," said Victoria. "But the next step. If you were me, what would you do next?"

"Well . . ." The utterance trailed off. "Proof, you want proof. Almost impossible to imagine where you could find it. However, there are two sources, both close to Armstead, and—this is my guess—with not too much love for him. One is his wife Hannah. She's had a bad time with him for years, especially in the last year or two. Have you met her?"

"I've heard of her."

"The other is Kim Nesbit. Does that ring a bell?"

"A faint one. She was a Broadway actress, a singer, something, and Ezra J. Armstead's mistress."

"That's all you know?"

"That's all."

"Now she's Edward Armstead's mistress. He inherited her from his father."

"You're kidding."

"You better believe me. Kim's in bad shape, I hear. Armstead has treated her abominably. The word gets around. I don't know how she feels about him right now. She might feel loyal. She might feel angry, vengeful. If you get lucky, you might hit pay dirt.''

"And if I'm unlucky?"

"She might pass on to Armstead what you're doing."

"I'll take my chances. Now I've got to find them."

"I have Hannah and Edward Armstead's penthouse address right here. And Kim Nesbit's condo address."

"How do you know all this?" she said.

"I'm an investigative reporter, remember? On any job, I always make it a policy to investigate my boss first."

"Okay, the addresses."

He read them to her and she wrote them down.

"I suggest you start with Kim," he said.

"Exactly what I intend to do. Thanks, Nick—I miss you."

"I miss you, too. I wish I could be there to give you a hand, but you know I'm off for London the day after tomorrow. If you need me, I'll be at the Athenaeum Hotel—"

"Okay."

"Better yet, if you need some fast advice or help, call the White House and ask for Sy Rosenbloom. He's on the President's staff, an aide in the West Wing, and he'll be staying behind. Your father knows him and likes him. Sy is one of my closest friends. We were roommates in college."

"Sy Rosenbloom. I'll remember. Are you going to tell him what's going on?"

"No, not that. Certainly not at this point. But he already knows about you, and he knows we've worked together. Of course, if things get rough and you're in real trouble—if you need advice, help, someone to bail you out—you can tell him everything, the whole thing. But always try to get me first."

"I will. Have a good trip, Nick."

"Never mind about me. It's you I'm concerned about. You will be careful?"

"Very."

"When are you starting after the proof?"

"Tonight, Nick. In exactly one minute."

There were two surprises awaiting Victoria after she rang the condo doorbell.

The first was that Kim Nesbit, apparently having used the peephole, opened the door herself. The other was that Kim Nesbit appeared to be so young. Victoria had expected someone much older. After all, she had been the mistress of Armstead's father. Yet, in the unlighted entry hall, attired in Oriental kimono and pajamas, her features smooth, her flaxen hair as long and light blond as Victoria's own, she seemed astonishingly girlish.

"The guard downstairs told me you were with the paper," Kim said.

"I am," said Victoria.

"What do you want with me?"

"I'd like to speak to you briefly, if I may."

Kim Nesbit remained suspicious. "What about?"

Victoria felt uneasy, but knew she would have to be forthright. "I understand you're a friend of Mr. Armstead."

"Friend, ha. Maybe I am a friend. What about it?"

For the first time Victoria sensed that Kim might be drunk. "I hoped that I could discuss him with you."

"This isn't an interview, is it?"

"No, it's something personal," Victoria said hastily. "It's really something I'd like to discuss with you in private."

Kim looked her over. "Ed didn't knock you up, did he?"

"Oh, God, no. Nothing like that."

"All right," said Kim grudgingly, "come on in."

Victoria walked past Kim through the dark entry, to be blinded by the white brightness of the large living room. Kim, behind her, said, "Sit down anywhere. Would you like a drink?"

Victoria shook her head. "No, thanks."

There were three pillow-strewn green sofas, and Victoria chose the one to her left. She watched Kim go to the bar, retrieve a half-finished drink, come toward her. Victoria could see that the woman's gait was unsteady, and the harsh lighting in the living room had aged her considerably. She was disheveled, and there were lines of discontent in her face.

Kim sat down on the middle sofa, took a slow swallow from her glass, and set it on the coffee table.

"What about Ed Armstead?" said Kim. "What do you want to know, and why?"

Victoria's fingers worried her purse. "I'm not sure how to begin," Victoria said.

"Just begin," said Kim.

"I work for Edward Armstead, as you know. I'm one of the new reporters at the *Record*. I went to Europe for him, with another reporter, to research a series on modern-day terrorism, and some other stories. During that period, and recently, a lot of things happened that made me worry a little."

"Worry about what?"

"About Mr. Armstead himself. I—I don't know how to say it. I want to be honest with you, but I'm a little afraid. I'm afraid you might repeat to Mr. Armstead what I have to tell you."

"And he'll fire you?"

"Something like that."

"I don't know what you have on your mind, or if I can help you with it. But one thing for sure. You can be as honest as you like. You don't have to worry about me repeating anything. Repeat anything? I'm not speaking to the bastard anymore. I hate his guts." She picked up her glass, took another swallow. "What's the bastard done to you? Go ahead, tell me."

"Nothing. He's done nothing to me personally. But I am concerned about what he may be doing to other people."

Kim seemed to have misunderstood. "He's done plenty to me, to his wife and to me. Neglecting us, abusing us. He's a bastard. Most people don't know it, but he's a real bastard."

"I don't know anything about that," said Victoria. "I meant, the way he's been treating people worldwide. The harm he may be doing them. I'm referring to his interest in terrorism. He seems to be close to terrorists, possibly condoning, possibly even inspiring, some of their activities. Certainly, he knows more about each recent terrorist act than anyone else. He seems to be writing about it as it happens. He's the first in print with each event. It leads me to believe he has some terrorist connection.''

Victoria had been more direct than she had intended, but she felt that she could trust this woman, and was now relieved that she had put it on the line. She waited for Kim's reply.

Kim was finishing her drink. ''Terrorists,'' mumbled Kim vaguely. ''You think he has something to do with them?''

''I want to know what you think, Miss Nesbit.''

Kim contemplated her empty glass. ''Power,'' she said. ''He likes it. He'd trample on anyone for power.''

''Do you mean that?''

''He'd do anything for power.''

''Like what?''

''He'd kill for power.''

Victoria was not sure that Kim was sober enough to know what she was saying. ''Can you prove it?'' Victoria asked.

Kim relapsed into silence for a spell. ''I can tell you plenty—'' she muttered. She raised her head. ''—but I won't.''

''You won't?''

''I can't.'' With effort, she managed to rise. ''You better go.'' She headed to the bar, weaving, to pour another drink.

Victoria came up swiftly and followed her. ''If you don't feel well, maybe we can talk another time.''

Kim set her glass on the bar. ''Another time, yes. I'm going to lie down.''

Victoria was scribbling on her pad. She tore the page out and pushed it into Kim's hand. ''Let me give you my address and phone number,'' Victoria said. ''I'll be there almost every evening.'' She sought Kim's attention. ''I hope you consider what we've been discussing, and get in touch with me.''

''Maybe,'' said Kim. ''Good-bye.''

*   *   *

Entering the luxurious lobby of the On Fifth Towers, Victoria
went straight to the uniformed guard at the table.

She had to make sure that Armstead was not in the apartment.
"Has Mr. Armstead come home yet?" she inquired. Flipping
open her red wallet, she showed her press pass. "I'm with
Armstead Communications."

"Not yet. Mr. Armstead's not back yet."

"Actually, it's Mrs. Armstead I want to see. Is she in?"

"She's always in." The guard reached for the phone. "Who
should I say is calling?"

"Miss Weston. I work for Mr. Armstead's newspaper, the
Record. Say—say I have something to deliver to Mrs. Armstead."

The guard rang up, repeated the message, listened, nodded at
the phone and hung up. "Okay, Miss Weston. Go on up to the
penthouse."

Ascending in the noiseless elevator, Victoria knew that all her
hopes for a lead were pinned on Hannah Armstead. The session
with Kim Nesbit had been futile. She had probably been too
intoxicated to understand anything Victoria had said to her. Kim
had definitely been hostile to her lover, yet too frightened to
reveal any information. Too frightened or too drunk. Hannah would
be another matter. Nick had advised her that the Armsteads got
on badly. At the same time, Hannah was Armstead's wife, and
no matter how she felt about him, she might be more protective.
Victoria knew she would have to proceed with care.

There was only one apartment on the penthouse floor, and the
grand entrance door off the elevator bore a single word lettered in
brass: ARMSTEAD.

Getting up her courage, Victoria pressed the doorbell. She
could hear the faint chimes inside.

She hoped that Hannah herself would answer the doorbell. At
first, no one answered. Victoria was about to ring the bell again
when the door opened.

A flat-faced, brawny woman—she appeared to be of Nordic or

Germanic origin—wearing a starched white nurse's outfit, filled
the entry space.

"Yes?" she said.

"I'm with Armstead Communications," said Victoria, "and
I'm supposed to see Hannah Armstead."

"Sorry, miss. You picked the wrong day. Doctor's orders are,
she's to have no visitors today."

"This is a personal matter. Mrs. Armstead would consider it
vital."

"Not today, miss. I've got to obey the doctor."

"Is Mrs. Armstead ill?"

"After breakfast, she suffered a severe attack of ptomaine
poisoning. They had to use a stomach pump on her."

"Will she be all right?"

"She can thank the Good Lord. They got it all out in time.
She's recovering, but she's weak, and not allowed to see anybody for a day or two."

With a sigh of relief that Hannah had survived, Victoria said,
"I'd like to leave her a personal note. Do you mind giving her
one?"

"No harm in that," said the nurse.

"Just give me a second—" Victoria found her pad and pen,
realizing she would have to take a chance with what she wrote.
She saw no choice. So she wrote, "I work for your husband.
Must see you privately about him. Utmost importance. Please
don't let him see note or my name. Thanks. Victoria Weston."
Beneath her name, she printed her apartment telephone number.

Tearing off the slip, she folded it and gave it to the nurse.
"This is for Hannah Armstead. For her eyes only. No one else is
to see it."

"Whatever you say, miss."

"You don't know how much I appreciate this."

Starting for the elevator, Victoria changed her mind about
riding it down. There was always the chance that she might run

into Edward Armstead riding it up. The one person she wanted to avoid right now was Armstead. She detoured toward the staircase.

Going down the steps, she realized that she should hurry if she wanted to get back to her apartment in time for the call from Sid Lukas in Paris. But then she slowed.

Somehow, Carlos didn't matter anymore.

Victoria was after bigger game.

In his Sherry Netherland bedroom, Harry Dietz, fully dressed, had propped the pillows of his bed against the headboard and reclined against them as he began to scan the first edition of tomorrow's New York *Times*. He liked to pay attention to what the opposition was doing daily, yet this evening he was barely attentive to the print.

The telephone at his bedside should have rung an hour or more ago. Gus Pagano, called back to New York, had been given his orders, but his report was long overdue. Dietz was an efficient man who expected efficiency in others. Pagano's tardiness was inexplicable, unless something had gone wrong. Dietz began to worry.

That instant, he heard the welcome jingle of the telephone. He took up the receiver.

"Hello," he said anxiously.

"It's Gus."

"About time," said Dietz with mingled irritation and relief. "The job finished?"

"Finished, hell," said Pagano, revealing his own irritation, "it's not even started."

Dietz sat up on the bed. "What do you mean?"

"I thought you told me the blond was heading straight back to her apartment at West Seventy-third."

"She was. I even checked the garage. She signed out a company car over an hour and a half ago. She was going to her apartment."

"Well, she never made it," said Pagano. "I've got our hit man on the other line, holding. He says she's not there."

"Has he been inside?"

"Twice already. No problem getting in. She doesn't have a special lock. No Medico cylinder lock, nothing like that. Probably promised to her for later. For now, just a rinky-dink one. A hairpin job. He got in okay. But no one was there. He waited awhile and tried again. Still nobody there. You sure she was going to the apartment?"

"Where else would she go?" Dietz said with exasperation. "I don't know what's delayed her but she'll be there."

"What do you want our man to do?"

"Can't he just stay someplace outside the apartment and watch for her arrival? And then follow her in."

"Won't work. He wanted to do that but there's no safe observation point on that floor."

"Then let him go inside her apartment and wait for her."

"Too dangerous," said Pagano. "What if she came in with three or four people? They might trap him."

"Goddammit," said Dietz, "then let him go on doing what he has been doing. Let him wait a half hour and go back. I want him to go back every half hour until he finds her and does the job."

"I'll tell him." Pagano hesitated. "You know, each time he does it, he's exposing himself more. The risk is higher. It's going to cost more."

"Fuck the cost," said Dietz shrilly, out of temper. "We just want him to do the job. I have to go to the office now. The next time you call, I want to know we've got rid of her. You hear me?"

"Hear you loud and clear."

"Call me there."

Dietz hung up angrily. Only thing Pagano had to say was, It's going to cost more. Highway robbers. All they ever thought of was money. Didn't anyone ever take pride in his profession anymore?

He swung off the bed, preparing for a late conference at the office with Armstead, with a man who took real pride in everything he did.

Kim Nesbit had tried to nap, and maybe she had. An hour had passed since she'd gone to lie down, and now she was wide awake once more. Her hangover wasn't bad, all things considered—the smallest throb of headache, puffiness around the eyes, dry mouth and tongue. Overall, she felt somewhat sobered.

Sitting up, she wondered whether she should go to the bathroom for aspirin or go to the bar for a drink.

She went to the bar for a drink.

After pouring scotch on the rocks, she shambled about the living room. It was like being at the bottom of the Grand Canyon alone. She turned on the entry hall light, saw that tomorrow morning's two newspapers—the *Record* and the *Times*—had been slipped through the mail slot in the front door. She stooped, reached for them, brought them to the middle sofa, dropping them there to read later.

Coming around the middle sofa, sipping her soctch, she saw that a cushion was indented and she bent over to puff it up. She saw that a cushion on another sofa had been used and, patting that one to straighten it out, she dimly remembered that she'd had a visitor earlier in the evening.

The girl from the paper who'd wanted to know some personal things about Ed Armstead.

She sat down with her scotch, drank it and tried to recall more. Her memory, usually foggy, had more visibility than a few hours ago. She recalled the girl with clarity, and tried to hear her again. The girl had wondered about Ed's front-page exclusive stories on terrorist acts, and had speculated on the possibility that Ed might have a personal connection with terrorists. For some reason Kim had characterized Ed as a perfect bastard, which was true, and as a power-hungry monster, which was also true. After that, Kim could not recall their conversation.

Swallowing the last of her scotch, Kim trudged back to the bar for a refill, dropped two ice cubes into the empty glass and dribbled three ounces of scotch out over the ice. She held up the amber-colored glass, examined it, decided that she had been niggardly with herself, deserved more, deserved a longer drink, and she lowered the glass and added two more ounces of scotch. Better. Sipping her drink steadily, she began thinking of Ed Armstead once more.

He *was* a bastard, a lousy bastard. Neglectful of her needs and cruel to her person. She was glad to be rid of him.

She surveyed her barn of a living room. Inanimate objects as far as the eye could see. No living, pulsating, warm human being around, except her own lonely little self here in the corner of the sofa.

Christ, loneliness was the worst curse on earth, and she was lonely, isolated from all humanity and by herself, alone with herself, a person she could not cope with.

She needed someone, sometime, a flesh-and-blood man.

The only man she knew was Edward Armstead. A bastard, sure enough, but at least her bastard.

Yesterday they'd had a fight. She'd called him everything on earth, terrible things. He had done the same to her. He had roared out of the apartment in a fury. At the time, she had not wondered if he would ever come back. Now she wondered if he would. Had she alienated him forever? She wanted him in her unpopulated life once more. Even if he didn't come by enough, he did come by sometimes. Even if he wasn't loving and kind, he did want her body, did join her, did enjoy her.

A crumb, a morsel, not to be ignored when you are starving.

She sorted out strategies, means of winning him back.

One floated upward through the fog and appealed to her. The girl earlier this evening, the girl from his newspaper snooping around into his private life. That was a valid excuse for calling him, calling him with a favor, to alert him, to warn him that one of his staff was prying into his affairs behind his back.

He would be grateful, touched by Kim's concern for him and her caring, and appreciative of her intelligence and warning.

He would see who counted in his life. All would be forgiven. He would be back, and the room no longer a desert.

She fumbled for the piece of paper with the girl's name, address, number that she'd left on the bar, found it under her glass being used as a coaster, and with the soggy piece of paper in hand she reeled to the sofa, fell into it next to the olive-green telephone, and dialed Ed Armstead's private number with its private line in the study of his apartment. She held on as it rang and rang. No answer, nobody there. That meant if he wasn't there, he was probably not out somewhere but still in his office.

Kim's forefinger sought the dial again. She misdialed twice, but the third time had the satisfaction of dialing it right. The phone rang once, and was picked up.

"Hello, Ed," she said. "This is Kim."

"This isn't Edward," a voice replied. "This is Harry Dietz."

"I was calling Ed on his private line. I want Ed."

"I was at his desk, working. Let me see if he's around."

"You go and see," she said.

Abruptly, as though someone's hand had clamped over the other mouthpiece, all sound was choked off.

But not completely.

The hand over the mouthpiece had apparently slipped a little. She could hear a distant voice in the background, and she heard it state with annoyance, "I told you what to say, dammit. Tell her I'm not here." It was Ed's voice in the background. Then Dietz's voice full volume into the phone. "I've been looking, Kim. He's not here."

Kim was livid with rage. "You prick, he's right there, I heard him! You tell him to come to the phone right now, I have something important for him. Tell him if he won't come, he'll be sorry."

There was a pause, and Dietz intoning again, "Kim, he's not here."

"You tell that motherfucker to drop dead!" she screamed, and she slammed down the phone.

For five minutes she lay back in the sofa stewing, trying to give her heart time to stop pounding.

I'll get him, the bastard, she told herself. I'll get him if it's the last thing I do.

She resumed her drinking to help the fog descend.

While there was a shaft of clarity remaining, Kim tried to map her revenge.

That girl who had come calling, the one from his staff. She searched for the soggy piece of paper, and blurred as the name was, she was able to make it out. Victoria Weston. The one who had been looking into Ed Armstead, who had suspicions about him.

Yeah, that girl, maybe that was the way to get even, to find something to tell that girl. But what? She beseeched her faded memory to provide some remembrance of yesterday's quarrel, for something Ed had revealed to her. She revived one crazy outburst, fragments she could recall of it: *what happens to people depends on me*—or something like that—and: *I make the news, I make life that goes on in the world.*

Words to that effect. Had they implied that he was directing terrorists? Maybe yes, maybe no. Would they be useful for Victoria Weston, have some special meaning to her? They might, but probably not.

Kim wanted to hurt the arrogant bastard the way he had hurt her. But her evidence against him was weak. Too weak to carry to Victoria Weston.

Oh, what the hell, to hell with it, Kim decided, drinking, feeling better.

She picked up the nearest next morning's newspaper, a habit, to go through it until she was so weary she would sleep without difficulty. She saw that she was holding the New York *Record*, and she defied him by tearing at it and throwing it to the floor. She reached for the New York *Times*, and laughed at how angry this would have made him had he known. Blinking, she attempted to read the front page. Ezra—E. J.—used to advise her that a newspaper a day was better than an apple a day. It helped round out a woman, made her interested and interesting, so that when she appeared in public she was conversant with what was going on. There were some nice things to be said about Ezra. He had got too busy, of course, and too old, but he had always been kinder than his son. In the years after receiving his advice, she had never failed to read a newspaper a day. Blinking at the front page, she realized the true fact, that she hardly read anymore. At this hour, the newsprint was always out of focus. What she really did was go through the front section, fixing on the various headlines and concentrating on women's styles in the department-store advertisements.

She turned the page, then another and another, lingering over ads, peering at headlines. On page six, she had gone over a Bloomingdale's ad featuring new Italian purses and handbags when the headline of a small story directly above it caught her eye. It was a word in the headline that held her attention. The word was PSYCHIATRIST. Then she made out the words SERIOUSLY INJURED.

Mildly piqued, she squeezed her eyes to make the newsprint stop jiggling and stand still.

She had started to read the small story when the name Dr. Carl Scharf leaped out at her. With supreme effort she made out the words that followed, and she could feel her heartbeat accelerate.

The fog in her head could not obliterate the sense of what she was reading. Dr. Carl Scharf, crossing the street to his office, had been the victim of a hit-and-run driver. Seriously injured, multiple injuries. At last report in critical condition in Roosevelt Hospital's intensive care ward. Surgery, surgery, surgery. A list of Dr. Scharf's degrees, honors. Police said the driver had sped away after the accident, and there were no clues pointing to the person responsible.

Kim let the story go out of focus again, and dwelt on what part of it had adhered to her mind.

Accident . . . no clues to the person responsible.

She shuddered.

Wavering across her mind were the images and words that had taken place before the accident. Dr. Scharf's talk with her about Edward Armstead. Scharf: *I'm concerned about him.* Scharf: *Seems under a lot of pressure.* Herself: *Sick, you know . . . delusions . . . thinks he is running the world.* Scharf: *Wise for you not to mention that we spoke.*

Yet she had mentioned that Scharf had spoken to her—drunkenly, stupidly, unforgivably blurted it out to Edward Armstead. Herself: *Even Dr. Scharf said . . . you were under pressure . . . he was concerned.* And Ed had almost killed her.

Kim shook the newspaper helplessly.

And now Ed had tried to kill Dr. Scharf, too.

There.

There it was. No accident. A deliberate attempt. She knew the person responsible.

Oh, there was no doubt in her mind, no doubt whatsoever, that Edward Armstead had been responsible for trying to eliminate Dr. Scharf. Why? Because Scharf, his psychiatrist, had betrayed him? No, not that, because such a reaction would have depended on human sensitivity and emotion. Ed Armstead no longer possessed either. Then what other motive? To prevent someone who suspected he was maniacal from exposing his behavior—and maybe his crimes.

His crimes.

That young woman, the one on the newspaper, she had hinted at it, or tried to speak of it, and had wanted corroboration.

By God, she would get it now, any help that Kim could give her.

Kim wobbled off the sofa, stood erect, her feet planted on the rug, her body swaying. She was terribly drunk, she knew, but she was also sober, some sensibility of conscience in her was sober.

Could one be drunk and sober? No, of course not, but she was both.

There was one thing more she wanted to do before acting. A good pedestrian thing. A friendship thing. A caring thing.

She called Roosevelt Hospital.

Yes, nurse, I'm a relative and I must know.

Well, I shouldn't be talking until the attending doctor—well, I can tell you, the patient is out of the woods, still in intensive care, successful surgery, on the road to recovery, but it'll be a long haul, a long one.

He'll live?

Yes, he'll live.

Thank God. The phone call over, Kim knew there was more to appreciate from God. There was his directive. Vengeance is mine; I will repay, saith the Lord.

She would be acting for the Lord.

Putting one foot before the other, Kim started for the bedroom, to change from her kimono and pajamas into an outdoors sweater and slacks and her fur coat.

To go to see Victoria Weston as quickly as possible.

At Victoria Weston's apartment door in the brownstone on West Seventy-third, Kim rocked dizzily, meant to knock, instead hammered her fists against it.

A breathless voice from inside. "Who is it?"

"It's me, Kim Nesbit. For chrissake let me in."

The door was unlocked, then flung wide, and Victoria, who had begun undressing, now in her bra and petticoat, reached out to catch Kim before she could fall.

"Miss Nesbit, I hadn't expected—" Victoria gasped, busying herself trying to support Kim and keep her on her feet.

"I must talk to you—got lot to tell you—got to talk," Kim mumbled. "Got a lot to say about Ed—Ed Armstead—the way he told me—told me he was running people's lives—making news—maybe with a gang, I don't know—and trying to have

someone killed, his psychiatrist, who was becoming suspicious—
Geez, kiddo, I'm drunk. Got to admit it. Drunk as hell. Lemme
sit down.''

Victoria helped her off with her fur coat and led her to the
sofa, which had just been converted into a sofa bed for the night.
Victoria lowered her to a sitting position on the side of the bed.
"Let me get you some coffee," said Victoria. "Will you drink
black coffee?"

"Anything," sighed Kim.

"Just sit right here. Let me go in the kitchen and prepare some
instant coffee. Just wait. I won't be more than a few minutes. I'll
be right back."

Victoria studied her visitor. Then, reassured, she pulled on her
robe and disappeared into the kitchen.

Kim sat swaying on the edge of the bed, her hands pushing
back her flaxen hair, pressing her temples, covering her eyes.

She wanted to close her eyes, rest, rest forever. She fell on the
bed, raised her legs onto the bed, squirmed backward until the
back of her head found the softness of the pillow and her body
was stretched out supine. Lying there on her back, she tried to
resist sleep; but immediately surrendered.

Eyes closed, she drifted into darkness.

Not even the silent opening of the apartment door dispelled the
darkness.

The front door continued opening wider, and the figure of a
man appeared quietly, sidling sideways into the room with practiced agility.

In a split second he had surveyed the room. His catlike gaze
came to rest on the figure lying stretched out on the sofa bed.
There she was, at last. The blonde on the bed.

A looker, yet. He was tempted to rape her first. But that would
be unprofessional, a self-indulgence. He had pride in his profession,
a job to be done quickly and perfectly.

It was too easy, really.

On his noiseless tennis shoes, he moved gracefully to the foot of the bed. His right hand touched the metal in his pocket. He brought out the Walther P-38 and the bulky silencer, put them together, released the safety catch, circled his forefinger around the trigger, and lifted the gun above the foot of the bed. His right arm went straight out, the gun an extension of his right hand.

He pointed the gun at the center of the blonde's white forehead.

He tugged at the trigger.

Swoosh.

She gave a convulsive jerk—the impact, he knew—and lay still, very limp and very still.

He arced the P-38 down by ten inches, the aim lower, and shot her in the heart.

For good measure. It was fun anyway. The second shot had drawn blood, which was seeping through her sweater.

He turned, glided away, slipping through the crack in the door, vanishing behind the neatly shut door.

From the kitchen, Victoria appeared, cup of coffee and saucer in hand, brow knit at what she thought had been some kind of unusual sound.

The room was as before. The door closed. Relieved, she turned to Kim Nesbit, stretched out on the sofa bed.

At first she did not understand.

And then she did, reeling backward against the wall, letting the coffee cup and saucer drop from her shaking hand.

She tried to find her voice. Only a gurgle and nausea rose in her throat.

She retreated from the deathbed and began screaming. She stumbled to the door, screaming, and into the hallway, screaming at the top of her voice.

Outside the windows and beyond the balcony of Edward Armstead's office on the sixth floor of the Armstead Building, the gray of earliest morning was giving form to the skyscrapers across Park Avenue.

At the publisher's desk, Armstead behind it, Dietz in front of

it, the pair were having their first hot coffee of the new day.
Armstead, lounging in his swivel chair, the latest morning edition
of the New York *Record* laid up against his crossed knee, was
reading the story on page three.

"You had to run it, I guess," he said.

It was not a question, but Dietz chose to answer it. "We had
to run it," said Dietz. "It would have been awkward and suspicious if we hadn't."

Armstead dipped his head in assent. "You're right." He finished the story and cast the newspaper aside. "A discreet job."

"We tried to bury it."

Armstead shook his head. "Poor Kim. How could Pagano's
guy have botched it so badly?"

"It's understandable," Dietz reasoned. "He'd been given an
assignment. He'd never seen the intended victim before. He'd
been told, 'Get the blonde who lives in that apartment.' So he
went in, got the blonde—the wrong blonde—while the real one
was in the kitchen."

"Which still leaves some work undone."

"I'm afraid so."

"Where is our Victoria Weston?"

"She disappeared from the apartment. No idea where she
went."

"We'll have to find out, Harry."

"We will, Chief."

Armstead emptied his cup of coffee. "What in the hell was
Kim doing in her apartment anyway?"

"I don't know. Again, I'm sorry about the mistake."

"I am—and I'm not," said Armstead, standing up. "She must
have gone there to talk. She probably never got the chance." He
smiled and started to unwrap a cigar. "Looks like luck's on our
side all the way."

Hannah Armstead had already been awake, sitting up in bed
removing her hairnet, and reading the story in both newspapers,

when the nurse came in to tell her that her physician was on the phone.

"I gave him a full report," the nurse said. "He was very pleased. He prefers that you eat as little as possible today, but if you are really hungry and want breakfast—"

"I want breakfast," Hannah said.

"The doctor would like to speak to you."

"Very well. Help me out of bed first, and help me with my dressing gown. Roll up the wheelchair."

Once she was settled in her wheelchair and the nurse had gone to prepare breakfast, Hannah picked up the phone.

"Congratulations," the doctor said. "You're on your way to a full recovery. You'll be fine."

"Was it ptomaine?"

"Possibly. There was a posionous substance in the porridge. Whether the fault of the manufacturer or some boric acid—you had some in the kitchen for cockroaches—got into the mix by mistake, I can't say. If you would like us to pursue it further—"

"Never mind."

"I can come by and have a look at you later."

"Don't bother. I feel fine. I'll spend the day resting and sleeping."

"Well, that would be best. You just take it easy. If there's the slightest problem, any distress, call me. Otherwise, I'll see you tomorrow definitely."

"Tomorrow, yes."

"Incidentally, Mrs. Armstead, I rang up your husband before calling you. He'd been so upset yesterday. But just now I was able to reassure him that the prognosis was for a perfect recovery. He was rushing out of town, but told me he'd be seeing you before he leaves. Anyway, I was glad to give him the good news. He was quite relieved."

I'll bet he was, thought Hannah.

"Thank you, doctor," she said.

After hanging up, Hannah reread the story in the *Record*.

Onetime Broadway musical comedy star, Kim Nesbit, slain by an unknown intruder. Next, Hannah reread the story in the *Times*, front page and more explicit. Blond feature player in many Broadway musicals of two decades ago, Kim Nesbit, was mysteriously shot to death in a friend's brownstone apartment last night. Police theorized that she had been awakened from a nap by the entry of a burglar, and he had killed her. The principal backer of Miss Nesbit's lavish musicals had been the late Ezra J. Armstead, founding giant of Armstead Communications.

Neither newspaper acknowledged the presence in Miss Nesbit's life of Edward Armstead—in one instance, Hannah thought, the omission had been deliberate, in the other, through ignorance of the truth.

But Hannah knew the truth.

She put aside her newspapers as the nurse set the sparse breakfast tray before her.

With one eye on the time, she munched her soft-boiled egg and drank her tea. A few minutes after finishing breakfast, Hannah took up the remote control and turned on the morning television news.

Stoically she withstood coverage of a West Virginia mining disaster, and suffered through preparations being made for President Thomas Callaway's flight to the meeting with the British prime minister in London tomorrow morning. After the commercials there was the top of the local city news, and Hannah came forward in her wheelchair. The old brownstone apartment building on West Seventy-third Street, scene of a tragedy last night. Shots of the small studio apartment inside rented by a Manhattan newspaperwoman, Victoria Weston. A grisly closeup of the blood-stained bed. A montage of still photographs of the late Kim Nesbit in some of her Broadway roles. The questioning of a New York City poice detective on the killing . . . no clues, no nothing, dead end on a death. A fleeting attempt at interviewing the occupant of the apartment, Miss Victoria Weston, a pretty young thing but absolutely ashen as she left the scene of the murder with two policemen. Dissolve to the opening of a new day-care center in Harlem.

Hannah pressed the button of her remote control unit and blanked out the television screen.

Victoria Weston.

Hannah swung her wheelchair around and rolled it to the head of her bed. Her fingers felt underneath her pillow until they touched a folded piece of paper. She withdrew it, unfolded it, and once more read the cryptic message that had been left for her last night:

"I work for your husband. Must see you privately about him. Utmost importance. Please don't let him see note or my name. Thanks. Victoria Weston."

The pretty young woman who was employed on Edward's newspaper. The young woman in whose apartment Edward's mistress had been murdered last night. The young woman who had tried to see Armstead's wife last night.

Please don't let him see note or my name.

A young woman who was afraid of Edward Armstead.

A young woman who wanted to hear something or tell something about him.

Utmost importance.

Hannah rang the kitchen and summoned the nurse.

When the sturdy nurse stood at attention before her, Hannah said, "Helga, I don't need you anymore today. You can go home now."

"Mrs. Armstead," the nurse protested, "I've only just begun the day. Doctor's orders were—"

"Never mind what the doctor's orders were. I spoke to him. He said if I did not need you, I could send you home. I won't need you anymore today. I have a friend on the way over, and she'll look after me until bedtime. You'll be paid for the rest of the day. Thanks, Helga, thanks for everything."

"If you say so."

"I say so."

Hannah sat listening, and ten minutes later when she heard the nurse departing and was certain that Helga was gone, she rolled her wheelchair to the telephone.

She dialed the number that Victoria Weston had left for her.

Not unexpectedly, the voice answering the telephone in the apartment was that of a policeman. "Officer Flaherty."

"I'm a friend of Victoria Weston's. I'd like to speak to her."

"She's not here, madam. She's temporarily moved out."

"Can you tell me where I can reach her?"

"I'm sorry, not permitted, madam. My instructions are to take any messages for Miss Weston. She'll be calling in today."

"Are you sure?"

"I'm positive. If you leave me your name and number, I'll give it to her."

"All right, officer," said Hannah. "Can you take this down?"

"I'm ready, madam."

"Tell her Mrs. Hannah Armstead phoned and would like to see her as soon as possible. Tell this only to Miss Weston and no one else."

"You can depend on me, madam. Do you want to tell me where she can reach you?"

"She knows where to reach me," said Hannah. "Be sure to have her phone me first." With that, she hung up.

Throughout her short life Victoria Weston had been a young person, and death had been far away. It had been an intellectual reality one did not have to deal with emotionally or in the foreseeable future. Last night Victoria had encountered death for the second time. One minute she had listened and spoken to a drunken but vibrant living human being, and minutes later she had looked down upon that human being and found a corpse, lifeless forever.

This experience had been even more shocking than the one with the Carlos informant in Paris.

Another consideration, almost as frightening, had come to her shortly afterward. The possibility that the gunman had been ordered to murder the occupant of the apartment—herself—and had mistakenly killed Kim Nesbit instead.

Of course, the police had theorized that the killing had been haphazard, an accident committed by a trigger-happy, perhaps drugged intruder and thief. If Victoria could have believed that, she would have been less fearful. But she had not believed it. A robber robbed. Kim's unseen killer had not lingered to steal a thing. He had entered with one purpose, to kill, and he had killed and vanished. This Victoria had believed from the first, and believed still.

Someone had been ordered to liquidate Victoria Weston.

By sheer luck she had escaped death, but she knew that death would not be disappointed.

Her survival instinct had told her to flee, and late last night she had fled. Her instinct had told her to disappear from sight. flee from the place that was known, hide out somewhere in the city until she could decide what to do. She had remembered a second-rate but homelike hotel that would give her temporary anonymity and safety, the Royalton on Forty-fourth Street, where she had once stayed several days with her father on one of his business visits to New York. She had thrown together some things for overnight, abandoned the company car, appreciated the escort of two police officers and their patrol car, and checked into the Royalton Hotel as Barbara Parry.

All of last night and into the early morning hours, even with sedatives, she had not been alone. The specter of death had been at her shoulder. The specter had resembled Edward Armstead, accompanied by his invisible hoodlums. She had wanted to resign from all scoops, investigative do-gooding. She had wanted to tell him she'd quit if he would quit. But she knew that he could never quit.

And so death was near, and she was afraid. She wanted to cry into her pillow last night, and she did cry. It was so unfair, so unfair to have to die. How could you die so soon, when you had never possessed a man you loved, or carried a growing child in your belly, or tasted grapes in the lovely Napa Valley, or cozied up before your own farmhouse fireplace on a Vermont Christmas morning, or seen the Taj Mahal in a summer's moonlight, or watched the dawning of a new day from a balcony in Venice, or read the poems of Shelley you'd always meant to read, or sat in the dark enrapt by Greta Garbo as Camille one more time?

What had put her onto these images of things that would never be? She remembered. An elocution class in high school. A short story by Aldous Huxley, a story called "The Gioconda Smile." Detached from its reality, she had memorized the passage to recite it, and word for word it passed through her head once more. "Death was waiting for him. His eyes filled with tears; he wanted so passionately to live. . . . There were still so many places in this astonishing world unvisited, so many queer delightful people still unknown, so many lovely women never so much as seen. The huge white oxen would still be dragging their wains along the Tuscan roads, the cypresses would still go up, straight as pillars, to the blue heaven; but he would not be there to see them. And the sweet southern wines—Tear of Christ and Blood of Judas—others would drink them, not he. Others would walk down the obscure and narrow lanes between the bookshelves in the London Library, sniffing the dusty perfume of good literature, peering at strange titles, discovering unknown names, exploring the fringes of vast domains of knowledge. He would be lying in a hole in the ground."

She would be lying in a hole in the ground.

No, no, no. It must not be. Not yet. Not so unfairly.

She was too young. She deserved her white oxen, her straight cypresses, her southern wines, her dusty perfume of strange titles.

She dozed and dreamed.

After a frightful night, she had slept and awakened, and finally slept again until ten-twenty in the morning. She had awakened with hysteria somehow exorcised.

After breakfast in her room, eating hungrily while she read the morning papers, Victoria's confidence had grown. She was alive and young, and death was far away. Yet she had been unable to decide what to do next, stay or run. She would think it out during the day. Meanwhile she decided to call her parents, in case they read about what had happened in her apartment, to let them know that she was well. She had telephoned her father in Washington, D.C., and her mother in Evanston and told them about what they had not read, and reassured them she had been a peripheral figure in a not uncommon New York story. Then she had called Nick Ramsey, not only to tell him that she was well, but to seek his advice. She had been told that Nick was out of the office and would not be back, since he was flying to London at nine o'clock the next morning. She had not left her name.

She had realized that this time she was on her own, all on her own.

Now, wondering why the telephone did not ring, it occurred to her that it wasn't supposed to ring. Except for the two policemen who had escorted her here, no one knew where she was. This by design. Then Victoria remembered the arrangement she had made last night when leaving her apartment. The policeman who would be on duty in her apartment today, an officer named Flaherty, would answer her phone and take any messages for her. He would pass them on to her when she called in.

Victoria had forgotten to call in, and now she did so.

Officer Flaherty answered her phone. Victoria identified herself, and learned that there were four messages for her. The first three were from the media—two from television stations, one from a radio station—and Victoria told him to tear them up.

The fourth message was from Mrs. Hannah Armstead.

Hannah Armstead was ready to see her!

Victoria's last vestige of fear dissolved into thin air. Her sluggish adrenaline was flowing. Her decision was made for her in those moments. No more running. She was staying. Kill or be killed, she was staying.

She dialed Hannah Armstead's number.

She expected the voice that answered the phone to be old and wavering. Instead, it was strong and resolute.

"Yes, who is this?"

"Mrs. Armstead? This Victoria Weston. I have your message."

"Good. I want to see you. To what end I do not know, but we shall find out."

"I can come right over."

"No. Not yet, Miss Weston. I take it you do not want to see or be seen by my husband. Well, I've had word he will be coming by briefly to pack before going out of the city overnight. We will have to wait until he comes and goes. That should be sometime this afternoon."

"I'll stand by, Mrs. Armstead."

"You wait until I call you. Where should I call?"

"I'm registered in the Royalton Hotel under another name— Barbara Parry."

"I see." There was a long pause. "Are you afraid, Miss Weston, that my husband wants to kill you?"

"Well—"

"You probably should be," said Hannah Armstead dryly. "You wait for my call."

It was not until after seven o'clock in the evening that Victoria received the all-clear summons from Hannah Armstead.

"You can come over now," said Hannah.

"I'm on my way," said Victoria.

On the way, in the taxi, Victoria's entire being tingled with anticipation. Not until she arrived at the entrance to the Armstead penthouse was her enthusiasm for the quest dampened by any feeling of wariness. Her hand hesitated before touching the doorbell. Could Hannah be in league with her husband to bring Victoria here and end her investigation? Or could Hannah, acting under duress, have been forced to lure Victoria into a trap? Possible, but unlikely, she reassured herself. Her finger pressed the doorbell.

Seconds later the entrance door opened inward. An elderly lady in a rose-patterned bathrobe, seated in a wheelchair, had opened the door.

"I am Hannah Armstead," she said.

Victoria observed a woman whose features were withered, here entire aspect frail, yet the eyes were alert and bright and the small mouth shrewd.

"You are Victoria Weston?" she said.

Victoria Weston nodded.

"Don't worry," said Hannah, "he's not here. No one else is here. We'll be quite alone. Do come in."

Victoria's guard fell, her apprehension totally disarmed. Sheepishly, she followed the moving wheelchair into the living room. "He came and went an hour ago," Hannah said over her shoulder. "I don't expect him back until tomorrow. Tonight we can talk together in privacy."

"Thank you, Mrs. Armstead."

"You can make that Hannah. I'll call you Victoria. I expect this meeting will be personal, and first names should make it easier for both of us. Sit there, Victoria." She pointed to a highbacked wing chair turned toward the fireplace with its carved eighteenth-century mantel and Carrara marble surround. As Victoria seated herself in the armchair, Hannah guided her wheelchair to one side of the fireplace and pivoted it to face Victoria directly.

"Very well," said Hannah, "let's lose no time. Why did you want to see me? What is this matter of utmost importance that you wrote me about? Obviously it concerns my husband."

"Yes, it concerns Mr. Armstead."

"In case you find this difficult, I can allay any hesitation on your part," said Hannah. "I don't like my husband anymore. This was not always so. But it has become so in recent years, and increasingly so in recent weeks. He has discarded all civility, until his behavior sometimes is that of a beast. Or, more correctly, that of a madman. I've reached the point where I am afraid to see

him come home. With that background in mind, perhaps it will
be easier for you to proceed.''

Victoria's heart went out to this intelligent, kind lady. ''Much
easier, Mrs.—so much easier, Hannah.''

''Tell me—why are you here?''

''Because I think your husband might be the brains behind an
international terrorist group.''

Hannah offered no reaction, only a rhetorical question. ''The
man portrayed on *Time* magazine as journalism's Almighty, the
most discussed publisher of modern times, the leader of terrorists?''

''I know how improbable it sounds—''

''No, no. Go ahead. I want to hear exactly how you arrived at
this conclusion. You have evidence?''

''Circumstantial,'' said Victoria hastily, ''but most persuasive.''

''I'm eager to hear,'' said Hannah.

''I'm eager to tell someone who might be sympathetic. If
you're ready, I'll go on.''

Victoria hurried through her observations, deductions, a recital
of her growing suspicions of the man who was her employer.

She spoke of the series of tremendous scoops that had sent
Armstead's newspaper circulation soaring and driven the ratings
of his television stations upward. All of these scoops had been
credited to Mark Bradshaw, a person who did not exist. Each of
these scoops had been preceded by Victoria or her colleague Nick
Ramsey's being sent to the scene of a forthcoming terrorist event.
In every instance, she or Nick had been assigned to investigate
the scene of violence in advance and file background material on
it. In one case she thought that she had seen a person, a Gus
Pagano, a criminal type who had been on Mr. Armstead's payroll
as an informer, in the area of a terrorist attack. An American
named James Ferguson had acquired a detailed map of Lourdes
in Paris before what may have been an aborted kidnapping of the
Pope, and she had recalled seeing the name James Ferguson in
the register of a hotel in Nyon, Switzerland. Victoria went on and
on, to the experience of witnessing the kidnapping of Carlos by

strangers, reporting it to Mr. Armstead and not being allowed to follow through.

When she had talked herself out, she awaited Hannah's reaction.

Throughout, Hannah had listened closely without a single comment or interruption. Her eyes held on Victoria, her lips working almost imperceptibly as if she were masticating, her veined hands folded motionless in her lap. Having heard Victoria's every word, she looked off absently as if pondering.

She spoke finally, her voice barely above a whisper. "Yes," she said, "the possibility of all this had occurred to me once or twice recently. There could be no other explanation for Edward's run of good fortune—"

"Except to conclude that he might be inventing the news?"

"Inventing the news," Hannah repeated. "But I put it out of my mind as something inconceivable. Until yesterday, when my husband tried to poison me."

Victoria was astounded. "Mr. Armstead tried to poison you—kill you?"

"Yesterday morning he insisted upon personally making breakfast for me. A rare treat and a gesture of consideration, I assumed. He left for his office, and I ate my breakfast contentedly, and shortly afterward I was in agony. I was able to get to the telephone and call my doctor, and to unlock the penthouse door before I fell unconscious. I was saved in the nick of time." She paused. "No, Victoria, it was not ptomaine. Poison had been put in my food, accidentally or deliberately. I choose to think it was done deliberately—by my husband."

"But why would he do such a thing? Of course, I don't know your relationship—"

"We'd had an ugly quarrel the night before. I had let him know what I had suspected of his long absences, that he was involved in a love affair with Kim Nesbit."

Victoria was surprised to hear Kim's name from Hannah's lips. "How did you find that out?" she inquired.

"By the most obvious means," said Hannah. "I hired a

private detective agency and had Edward followed for several weeks."

"You told your husband you had him followed?"

"Not exactly, but I implied it."

Victoria considered this, and measured what she had to say next. "Hannah, he didn't try to kill you because you had found out about his other woman. He tried to kill you because you were secretly having him followed."

"I don't understand."

"By having him followed, you could become a threat to the hidden activity in his life. You could have learned about a lot of people he might be seeing—criminals or terrorists—and found out what he was really up to. He had to stop you before you learned the truth."

"I hadn't thought of that," said Hannah slowly. She addressed Victoria straightforwardly. "At any rate, he tried to poison me. Of that I was sure. But I didn't know what could be done about it, since I had no proof. I didn't know where to turn. Then, this morning, reading and seeing the news of the killing in your apartment, the killing of Kim Nesbit, I was firmly convinced that Edward might be behind it. He was the common denominator for the one and one who made two in your apartment. Kim had been his mistress. You were his employee, suspicious enough of him to risk sending me a note. I don't know if he meant to kill you or Kim—or why—"

"I don't know for certain either," said Victoria, "but I think I know why. Somehow, your husband learned I was suspicious of him and trying to get evidence on him from Kim. He ordered someone to get me out of the way, and they got Kim instead. Perhaps I would have been killed, too, if it had been known I was in another room."

"Anyway," said Hannah, "the note from you, after my being poisoned, coincided with the tragedy in your apartment. I guessed you were onto something of utmost importance, as you had written me. In my interest in my own survival, I had to find out what you had in mind.''

"Now you know," said Victoria.

"I know." Hannah shook. her head with conviction. "We can't let him go on. You heard me characterize his behavior in recent weeks as that of a madman, possibly that of a homicidal maniac."

"And the leader of the most active of terrorist gangs."

"That you believe?"

"Absolutely."

Hannah stared at her visitor. "But you can't prove it."

"No, I haven't been able to prove it. My last hope was that you could help."

Hannah did not speak immediately. She stared into space, as if trying to make up her mind about something. Finally she spoke. "I can help," she announced. "I can help prove—or disprove—Edward's involvement."

"You can?" Victoria was on her feet, electrified, to learn what Hannah Armstead had in mind.

Hannah raised a hand and crooked a finger toward the corridor leading off the living room. "Follow me," Hannah said. She began rolling her wheelchair rapidly toward the corridor and into it, with Victoria right behind her.

At the doorway of the first bedroom, Hannah gestured for Victoria to wait. Victoria watched her roll herself up to the bedstead, fumble for a cane leaning against the headboard. Using the cane for leverage, Hannah pushed herself up and out of the wheelchair and onto her feet. Unsteadily, she crossed over to her dressing table. To the left of her mirror, she pulled out a lower drawer. She sought something difficult to find, apparently well hidden, and triumphantly found whatever she had been seeking. Victoria could not make out what she had found, but it appeared to be more than one object, possibly two, which she placed in a pocket of her dressing gown.

Hannah hobbled back to where Victoria was standing. "Come

with me," she said. "If proof exists, I'm going to show you the only place we could find it."

Leaning on her cane, Hannah led the way up the corridor, with a curious Victoria at her heels. They passed the second bedroom and came to a halt before a formidable oaken door with an impressive burnished brass doorknob and dead-bolt lock. "Mr. Armstead's private study," said Hannah. "No one else is allowed inside without him there. I've never been in it with his permission. I've been in it once without his permission. This will be my second time." She fumbled in her pocket for one of the objects she'd had hidden in her dressing table. In her hand she displayed a key. "Edward thinks he has the only key to his study. He would not allow a spare one to be made. But I had one made without his knowledge, and this is it." She inserted the key into the dead-bolt lock. It fit. "I had it made without telling him. Not because I was suspicious at the time or wanted to spy, but because I still worried about him. He was spending so much time in his sealed room, working such long hours, that I was concerned for his health. I worried that one night he might have a heart attack, and it would be impossible to get inside and reach him when he might need help. So, secretly, I called in a locksmith and had this second key fashioned for his study. It was meant for an emergency. This, I believe, constitutes an emergency."

With a strong twist of her wrist she turned the key. There was a metallic sound. Hannah gripped the doorknob, put her shoulder against the massive door. Noiselessly the door swung inward.

"Has this room always been his private study?" asked Victoria.

"Yes, but never before locked," said Hannah, "until a few weeks before the king of Spain was kidnapped in San Sebastián, when he installed the special lock and issued the no-trespassing order."

Hannah and Victoria exchanged looks and went inside.

Victoria took in her surroundings. A handsome room with exquisite light brown paneling with neoclassical detailing, a wall of leather-bound volumes on one side, an immense television

screen on a stand in a corner, an oil portrait of Napoleon Bonaparte above the huge fireplace ahead, two pastel-covered armchairs behind an oak table, a wide couch draped with a velvet
coverlet, a door to a private bathroom, finally a Victorian library-
table desk with an electric typewriter on a stand beside it.

Hannah pointed to the straight chair resting between the typewriter and the desk. "He's been coming in here almost every
night, and he sits on that chair typing," she said. "I haven't seen
him, but I know he does it and has been doing it since several
weeks after he inherited his father's newspaper."

A kind of awe rooted Victoria to the spot. Her eyes were on
the typewriter. "Do you suppose he's writing those terrorist
stories?" she wondered.

"You want to know if I suppose my husband is Mark
Bradshaw?" Hannah said. "Let's find out."

She turned around and lifted a forefinger to the wall cross the
study and behind the pastel armchairs. "See that?"

Victoria had missed it the first time around. It was a medium-
sized painting, lightly framed, of a young boy, perhaps ten or
eleven, attired in a military uniform and posing as a juvenile
version of the Napoleon portrait hanging over the fireplace.

"A memento of Edward's childhood," Hannah explained. "The
safe is in the wall behind it."

Victoria glanced sharply at Hannah. "The safe?" she mouthed.

"The proof," said Hannah. "If it exists, it will be in that
concealed safe." She pulled a shred of paper from her dressing-
gown pocket. "Here's the combination. I found it, and copied it,
the only time I was inside this room before, the time with the
locksmith. Take this chair. Climb up and remove the painting.
You'll find the safe. I'll call the combination out to you. If
there's proof, it'll be inside. It is all the help I can offer you. I
wish you—not luck—I wish you truth."

Momentarily Victoria wavered. She remembered reading in
high school of a New England schoolteacher who had been the
first to theorize seriously that Shakespeare had not written his

own plays and that final proof might be found in Shakespeare's grave in the chancel of the Holy Trinity Church in Stratford-upon-Avon. When, after years of applying to open Shakespeare's grave, the schoolteacher had been given the opportunity to do so, she was afraid to follow through. "A doubt stole into her mind," her friend Hawthorne had written, "whether she might not have mistaken the depository . . . she was afraid to hazard the shock of uplifting the stone and finding nothing." She had retreated and quit.

In these frozen seconds, Victoria was afraid to hazard the shock of finding nothing. Then the madness would be her own, not Armstead's.

"I—I don't know," whispered Victoria.

"It'll be the last chance you'll ever have," urged Hannah. "We both deserve to know the truth."

Victoria bobbed her head. She dragged the straight chair across the study to a position behind the armchairs and under the youthful painting of the publisher. She climbed up on the chair, and with ease was able to lift the framed painting off its hook and hand it down.

A miniature silver combination-lock dial, set into a blue one-foot-square metal safe door, was revealed.

"I'm ready," said Victoria to Hannah, who stood beneath her.

Hannah peered at the directions on the shred of paper. "Spin the dial three times around to the left, and the fourth time around stop at 56."

Victoria spun the dial left past zero three times, and on the fourth time stopped at 56. "Okay."

"Spin it right two times, and the third time around stop at 26."

Victoria did as she was told. "Okay."

"Now turn it left once, and the second time around stop at 74."

Once more Victoria followed the instructions. "Done. Any more?"

"Turn the dial right to zero. That should do it."

Carefully, filled with doubt, Victoria moved the dial to zero.

Click. The bolt had retracted.

She pulled at the lever, and the wall safe was open.

She reached inside it, probing with her fingers, and felt a large manila envelope. She withdrew it. There was nothing else in the safe. She looked down at the brown envelope. It bore no identification, only a neat penciled date across it. Tomorrow's date.

"Only this," said Victoria, stepping down off the chair.

"What's in it?" said Hannah. "What's inside?"

Victoria pulled up the back clasp and lifted the flap of the envelope. There were three sheets inside. They were double-spaced and neatly typed.

There was a by-line.

By Mark Bradshaw.

There was a story.

Side by side, Victoria and Hannah scanned it together. After the first page, the two women stared at each other aghast.

"My God," whispered Victoria. "Hannah—"

Hannah was trembling. "I can't believe it—"

"You'd better!" a voice rasped at them from across the room.

Both women looked up, horrified, petrified at the sight of Edward Armstead inside the open door. He wore a set smile upon his face as he started into the room.

"It is not always, ladies, that you can read tomorrow's news today."

He stopped beside his desk, leaned over, and ripped the telephone cord out of the wall.

He resumed his slow advance across the room toward the two women huddled together.

Reaching them, his smile was almost benign. He raised one hand, and almost delicately removed the pages from Victoria's hold.

"I came back for this," he said. "Foolish to have overlooked it in my haste to leave.'' He folded the pages of the story with care and slipped them into his overcoat pocket. "Now, if you'll excuse me—oh, yes, Hannah, the duplicate key, please—"

Dumbly, his wife handed the key to him. As he turned to go, she suddenly came to life, clutching at him with both hands. "Edward, you can't!"

With a shrug, Armstead shook free of her. "My dear," he said, "everyone has to die sometime, doesn't he? As for yourself and your friend, you won't have to wait past morning."

He walked back through the room into the corridor. He turned, and gave a courteous nod.

The door closed. The dead bolt sounded. The study was sealed.

Hannah awakened gradually, and when she was able to open her eyes, she was disoriented. It took seconds for her to realize that she was lying on the couch in her husband's study. The events of the evening, the night, the long hours of imprisonment, surfaced. She was too exhausted to be horrified. She moved her head sideways and made out Victoria standing beside her, staring down at her.

"I—I must have fallen asleep," said Hannah. "Did you sleep at all?"

"Briefly," said Victoria, "in an armchair."

Hannah stared at the ceiling. "I think you had better tell me again what it was," she said. "The story he wrote. The story he is running today. I barely had a glimpse of it. I missed most of the details. The—the President's plane—"

"Air Force One will be hit in midair over the Atlantic by another plane," said Victoria, her voice hollow. "The collision will make Air Force One explode. There will be no survivors. President Callaway will die. His press secretary, Hugh Weston, will die. The newspaper correspondent Nick Ramsey will die.

More than one hundred occupants of the President's plane will die.''

''Edward wrote that.''

''As if it had already happened. It will happen in little more than an hour.''

''At what time?'' asked Hannah.

''The story announced that it had happened at 9:32 this morning.''

''What time is it now, Victoria?''

Victoria glanced at the clock on the desk. ''It's 8:08 in the morning right now.''

Hannah shuddered. ''How? How will he do it?''

''His story didn't dare tell too much. His lead, of course, was that President Callaway had been deliberately killed in a midair crash. Details were not known, but there was word from Havana TV that a Cuban Air Force MiG-27F, an imported Soviet plane, had been stolen by one of Castro's more violent anti-American factions from a military base near Cienfuegos. The pilot may have been a deranged ex-kamikaze officer who had written a threatening letter a week before, a crank letter not taken seriously. He had been assigned to kill President Roosevelt in 1945, had failed, and to restore his honor had determined to kill another United States President. With the help of Cuban reactionaries, this Japanese had made off with the MiG Foxbat fighter, obtained and charted Air Force One's flight course from Andrews Air Force Base in Maryland to London, and plunged the stolen craft into the President's plane 120 miles off the Atlantic coast, some forty minutes after it took off. Then there followed a fuller recounting of those who were believed to have perished—the President and everyone else aboard. That was all I had time to read.''

Hannah was sitting up. ''It's unimaginable. Edward must have hired the best professional terrorists in the world to attempt this.'' Her head bowed in grief. ''We were right, Victoria. My husband's gone insane.''

"But logical enough to have arranged this," said Victoria.

"He's utterly insane," Hannah said again.

Victoria began to pace wearily. "What do you think will happen to us? What will he do?"

"He made that clear, Victoria. By morning—any time now—he will send someone—probably two of them—to unlock the door and take us away somewhere and kill us the way poor Kim was killed."

"But he could have killed us himself last night," Victoria said.

Hannah was shaking her head. "No, Edward's too smart for that. Kill us, and be left with the bodies? Easier to have someone more professional do it, march us out of here and do it."

"There's a guard downstairs in the lobby. He'd know."

"It's my guess the guard won't be there. They'll take him by surprise and put him away somewhere. Then they'll come up for us."

Victoria's eyes roved the paneled study. "Hannah, there must be some way out."

"You know it's impossible," said Hannah helplessly. "We spent hours last night, after he left, checking every inch of the walls, the room. There's no way out until someone takes us out."

Victoria ceased her pacing. "I—I don't care about myself, Hannah, I honestly don't. I'm sorry for you."

"Never mind about me—"

"But what sickens me most is thinking of all of them in that plane—my father, and a man I love, truly love, and the President himself and all the rest of those innocent people. Nothing like this, nothing, has ever happened in history. Hannah, it mustn't happen."

"Maybe it won't," said Hannah as kindly as she could.

"But you think it will?"

"I'm afraid it will. What's to prevent it? There's not a thing we can do." She closed her eyes. "We've lost."

*   *   *

Four hours earlier, an eerie scene had taken place.

The eeriest in his experience, Armstead decided as he allowed Gus Pagano to guide him into the vaulted living room of the dilapidated wooden mansion on the outskirts of Newport, Rhode Island.

Armstead, adorned with wig and false mustache and glasses, had arrived in a leased Learjet, been met by Pagano in a nondescript Dodge sedan, and had been driven through the town to this crumbling, isolated twenty-two-room mansion. The Carlos vanguard had rented it from an absentee landlord, and had used it as the base of operations and as a safe house.

Leaving Armstead in the living room, Pagano explained, "It's perfect. No outsiders ever come here, and we'll fly Matsuda to the Bahamas from the private airport runway, which, as you know, is only a short ride away. Everything is in readiness, and time is running out, so the meeting will have to be short. But he insisted on the meeting before going ahead."

"Okay by me," said Armstead.

"You've got what he wants?" asked Pagano.

"No problem."

"Wait here. I'll get him."

Pagano left the room, and Armstead was alone, marveling at his surroundings. This room had probably hosted the likes of Diamond Jim Brady, James Gordon Bennett, Jay Gould . . . a pantheon of giants. He studied the once elegant run-down nineteenth-century furniture, and was amused that the original china cuspidors with their hand-painted flowers still rested in their places.

Ancient history.

Armstead strutted to the center of the room. He was living history, and after today no media Hall of Fame would fail to award him its most prominent pedestal.

He heard someone enter, and he wheeled to greet his star.

Instead of one, there were two of them advancing toward him.

The first he recognized as Robert Jacklin, whom he had not seen since Istanbul and who had been directing the entire operation for Carlos. The second was the star, a diminutive, bowlegged, elderly Japanese, perhaps five feet two, perhaps sixty-five years of age, attired in a leather helmet bearing the emblem of the Rising Sun and an ill-fitting dark business suit, the jacket carrying another representation of the Rising Sun, a felt badge of the Nipponese Imperial Air Force of 1945.

"Mr. Walter Zimberg," said Jacklin curtly, "Flight Lieutenant Yosuke Matsuda, once of the Japanese Special Attack Corps and the leader of your mission."

Armstead offered his hand and an uncertain smile. Lieutenant Matsuda took his hand and shook it heartily, offering a wide grin that revealed an upper row of gold teeth.

"He speaks limited English," Jacklin said. "Understands almost none. However, I am fluent in Japanese and will help out, since it's necessary."

"Good," said Armstead. He was fascinated by the lieutenant's gold teeth. "How could he afford those teeth?"

"Prewar gift paid for by his parents."

"Okay," said Armstead.

"I will explain what has brought him here. Flight Lieutenant Yosuke Matsuda was stationed at Konoya Air Base, a member of the 721st Air Group and of a suicide squadron sent out against a United States aircraft carrier on April 17, 1945. Matsuda's assignment was to make a kamikaze assault on the aircraft carrier in his Suisei 4YI dive bomber, driving his plane with its 520-pound bomb attached to the fuselage into the carrier's bridge tower where President Franklin D. Roosevelt was supposed to be stationed as an observer."

"Hold on," said Armstead. "When did that happen?"

"On April 17, 1945."

"But President Roosevelt was dead by then. President Truman—"

Jacklin wagged a finger. "You and I know that, but Lieutenant Matsuda did not know it at the time. The main fact is that Matsuda failed to carry out his mission. At the last minute, going into his final dive, he lost his nerve. He did not want to die. He had a bride waiting for him in Tokyo. He wanted to return alive to her. So he aborted his kamikaze attack, avoided the carrier's bridge and crash-landed it in the water. He was picked up alive and made a prisoner of war. After the war he was released to go back home and join his bride. But he had disgraced himself, was without honor, and in the years after was never able to obtain gainful employment. He and his wife and their three children have lived in poverty in all the years since. His wife is a cripple. Lieutenant Matsuda has lived for one thing. To find a means of providing security for his wife and children. He let it be known that if he had a kamikaze assignment to perform over again, he would do it if it would bring him what he needed, an annuity for his family. When Carlos heard of this from the Japanese Red Army he contacted the old aviator, and kept him under wraps for a day when he might be useful. The day has come."

Armstead continued to eye the bantam, grinning Japanese uncertainly. "What if he aborts this mission, like he did the first one?"

"No chance of that," said Jacklin. "His only desire is to provide for his family. Also, there is the matter of honor, as he will tell you. He is even carrying an *omamori* in his pocket."

"A what?"

"The wooden Buddhist good luck charm, to guarantee success of the mission."

Observing that Armstead seemed satisfied, Jacklin addressed Lieutenant Matsuda in Japanese. Matsuda jabbered back in Japanese. Jacklin faced Armstead. "Yes, he says that he is ready to go right now, carry out the mission, if you will prove to him that you have made the deposit in the DKB—the Dai-Ichi Kanayo Bank—in Tokyo for one million American dollars."

"It is taken care of," said Armstead, withdrawing the DKB

receipt from inside his jacket pocket. "Here is a duplicate of the receipt. The money is in his wife's name. Your representative in Tokyo is presenting the original to his wife today."

Jacklin took the receipt and showed it to the Japanese pilot. Matsuda read it, and finishing, offered his shining mouthful of gold teeth. Matsuda spoke in Japanese.

"I will interpret," said Jacklin. "He is satisfied. He thanks you. But he wishes you to know, as I told you he would, that there is also a point of honor involved."

"What point of honor?"

"Long ago he failed to fulfill a mission as he had been ordered. He welcomes this second opportunity, to kill a different President, namely Mr. Callaway. This time he will succeed. Have no concern. He will carry it out."

Armstead's attention lingered on the Japanese uneasily. "He looks so ridiculous. Is he capable?"

"Perfectly. Sufficiently trained to bring the new jet fighter to the target."

"How was he trained?" Armstead wondered. "And the plane, how are you getting the plane?"

"Not too difficult," said Jacklin. "We bought off one of Castro's pilots for a large sum. Right about now he's starting on a routine training mission, but instead of returning to base in Cuba he'll defect and land on a deserted airstrip in the Bahamas. Never mind where—the drug syndicate also uses it, and they don't want the location publicized. There the defector will be met by our people and replaced by Lieutenant Matsuda here, who'll take over." Jacklin tapped his wristwatch. "We must hurry to the airport if we're to be on schedule."

He took the little Japanese by the arm. The Japanese showed his gleaming teeth a last time. *"Tenno banzai,"* he said with restraint, inoffensively, and he swaggered out of the room with Jacklin.

Five minutes later Armstead walked away from the mansion

with Pagano. When they reached the car Armstead said, "You'll be flying back to New York with me. You haven't forgotten?"

"I haven't forgotten," said Pagano.

"Here are the two keys," said Armstead. "One to let your men into the penthouse. The other to let them into the study. The second we're back in New York, you'll turn the keys over to them."

"It's set, boss, don't worry."

Armstead climbed into the front seat. "There can't be any slipup."

"There won't be. The bodies will never be found." He trotted around to the other side of the car and crawled in behind the wheel.

Armstead touched him. "Gus—?"

"Yeah?"

"They won't feel it, will they?"

"Won't feel a thing, I promise. Just like Nesbit. No pain. No nothing. Relax, boss. The Jap will take care of the big story. I'll take care of the rest. Have yourself a smoke. Sit back and enjoy."

He started the car, and they drove off.

In the sealed study of the Armstead penthouse, the two women had resigned themselves to the inevitable.

Hannah sat hunched on the couch. Victoria slumped in an armchair. Both were paralyzed by lassitude and helplessness.

Victoria was hypnotized by the clock on Armstead's desk. She followed the darts of the minute hand. One more dart. Victoria squirmed.

"They are taking off," she intoned.

In a state of daze, Hannah raised her head. "Who?"

"Air Force One from Andrews Air Force Base in Maryland. It's exactly nine o'clock. Air Force One is taking off with all of them. I guess that means the ex-kamikaze is taking off, too." She rearranged herself in the armchair to speak directly to her companion. ''I guess that means your husband will be sending someone for us.''

''I suppose so.''

Victoria gave her first show of spirit in hours. ''When they come—Hannah, I'm not going to let them take me out anywhere for execution. When they get us downstairs, I—I'm going to make a run for it.''

''They'll shoot you dead in the street.''

''Let them,'' said Victoria. ''I'll wind up the same way whatever happens, but maybe they'll be caught. Maybe you'll be able to get away.''

''Not on these legs, Victoria,'' Hannah said, rubbing one of the spindly calves protruding from beneath her robe. ''I'm not going very far on these legs.''

Victoria roused herself fully, fists knotted. ''We can't just sit and let them take us like helpless Jews being herded to Auschwitz. We've got to resist. I can't believe there's no way out of here.''

''We've been through this, Victoria. There's no way that I know.''

Victoria struggled to her feet, casting about. ''Windows. I've never known a room to be without windows. There might be one superficially covered up.''

''I was here during the early remodeling. It was planned to be constructed without windows. There are none.''

''If there were some heavy object—like a sledgehammer—a mallet—we could use it to break through a wall.''

''Victoria, what would Edward be doing with anything like a sledgehammer or mallet in this room? If there had been an object like that, he would have removed it when he left. He's too smart to leave behind a potential weapon.''

Victoria strode to the heavy electric typewriter. ''If I could lift this and slam it against the wall—''

''You'd get nowhere. Those walls are reinforced like a vault with steel and concrete.''

Victoria stepped closer to Hannah. "You said you had no live-in help?"

"I have no live-in help."

"Surely you can't manage an establishment like this by yourself? There has to be someone who comes in to clean, make the beds, do the cooking. You must have some kind of maid?"

"I used to have a wonderful black lady here every day, but weeks ago Edward made me get rid of her. He insisted that he wanted privacy, no one puttering around. He personally hired a part-time cleaning woman. She comes in two days a week for three or four hours. A young woman from Guatemala who can't speak much English, let alone read it."

"When is she coming in?"

"Not today. Sorry, Victoria. And the building's resident house-keeper sends someone to do the beds and clean up only when we ask her to. This is an impossible household. Edward made it into a monastery. For obvious reasons."

"Wasn't he afraid of break-ins? There must be some kind of internal security system."

"None, none whatsoever. Edward felt the guard downstairs was enough. Besides, he wouldn't permit any mechanism to be installed that might give outsiders access to this apartment or his room." She rambled on. "The only thing he let the contractor install was the smoke detector, because he has a terrible phobia about fires."

Victoria was instantly alert. "Smoke detector? Where?"

"Right here, of course."

Victoria's eyes swept the high, open-beam ceiling. "I don't see it."

"You can't like that," said Hannah. "Edward had it installed beyond that farthest wooden beam because it was so unsightly. You can't see it, but it's there."

Victoria went swiftly to the other side of the study, stood under the wooden beam and peered upward. She could make out a round metal disk, painted light brown, six inches in diameter, with a tiny red light in it, hardly visible. "There's a metal thing up there, round—"

"The smoke detector."

"What does it do?" asked Victoria tightly.

"Why, it goes off, of course, if there should be a fire and smoke."

"Goes off?" pressed Victoria. "How?"

"It rings out loud, like they all do, to warn the occupant of this room. But this kind of smoke detector is more sophisticated than some. When it goes off, it also sends a silent alarm to the company that put it in. They immediately notify the nearest fire department, and a fire truck comes—"

"Hannah!" Victoria cried. "That's a way out!"

Hannah was bewildered. "I don't understand—"

"It's a way to let somebody know we're in trouble. We start a fire here. It makes the detector go off. It summons help—"

Hannah had risen. "A fire? Why, yes. But that's really dangerous. We could be trapped by the flames—"

"We'll control the flames. What have we got to lose? Look what's going to happen to us anyway."

Hannah had shed her inertia. "What a clever idea, Victoria. It could be a way to call for help."

Victoria had already spun into action, dragging the straight chair to a spot beneath the smoke detector. "Do you have any matches?"

"Edward would." Hannah was opening her husband's humidor and feeling around the desk top, without luck. She drew out the single drawer under the desk top, rummaged inside, and then held up a green packet of book matches. She hobbled to Victoria, handing the packet to her. Victoria climbed up on the chair, stood on her toes, stretching one hand as high as she could. She lowered her outstretched hand. "I can't reach far enough to get anywhere near the detector. It's too high. Only a real fire might— Hannah, that newspaper, get me the newspaper off his desk."

Hannah obeyed as quickly as she could.

"Perfect," said Victoria. Loosing a section of the newspaper, she rolled it diagonally until it resembled a long cone. "I'm going to light one end and stick it up there. That could do it."

Securing the paper cone under an arm, Victoria struck a match.

"Careful, Victoria," Hannah called out.

Victoria applied the burning match to the large end of the rolled newspaper. At once the newspaper burst into flame. As the flame grew bigger, wider, redder, more intense, Victoria stretched upward on her toes, stabbing the burning cone of newspaper as high as she could under the smoke detector. From the makeshift torch, a curl of smoke began rising toward the detector as the fire itself crept downward toward Victoria's fingers.

"Look out!" Hannah shouted.

Victoria ignored her as she frantically implored the metal detector, "Go off, go off!"

Suddenly, with a high shriek, it went off. It was ringing loudly and steadily, the fire alarm fully operative. Victoria's hot face was aglow in the blaze of the torch. Abruptly, she screamed out in pain as the lowest fringe of fire licked at her hand. Flinging the torch aside, clutching her scorched fingers, she jumped down from the chair.

Hannah gripped her by the shoulder, pointing off. "Victoria—!"

The blazing cone of newspaper that Victoria had flung aside had landed under the folds of a decorative maroon drape. The drape was being transformed into a deep red and yellow bonfire as the flames licked up it, enlarging, spreading.

"Put it out—we've got to put it out!" Victoria yelled.

Fascinated, Hannah watched as the speeding flames began to form a red halo around the upper part of the room. "No, Victoria, it's too late—we can't put it out—in minutes we'll be trapped, suffocated—" She tugged desperately at Victoria. "This way— the bathroom—the fire people advised us—get into the bathroom, into the shower—turn on the shower—"

The smoke was blinding now. Bent low, Victoria stumbled after Hannah through a small doorway. Hannah fell back against the door, shutting it tightly. She came away from the door, pushing Victoria across the tile flooring to a glass shower door. "Inside," she ordered, "let's get inside."

They were both huddled in the confines of the shower. "I can smell smoke," coughed Victoria. "It's seeping through. If the smoke doesn't get us first, the fire will. Should I turn on the shower?"

"Not yet," said Hannah. "That'll be our last resort. Listen, Victoria."

They both strained to listen and could hear the shrill, insistent sounding of the fire alarm.

"If the system's working all around," said Hannah, breathing hard, "the men must have been alerted at the fire station. If they have, they'll know there's trouble. They'll be here."

"I hope so," sputtered Victoria, racked by coughing. "I don't think they can make it in time." She sought the time on her wristwatch. "It's been eight or ten minutes."

Peering through the glass shower door, she could see the bathroom door begin to blister and roast, and hear the crackle of the blaze closing in. The smoke in the bathroom was thickening, covering the glass surrounding the shower, coming in through the cracks in the shower door.

Victoria saw a dry towel on a handle. She picked up the towel, clawed in her pocket for a handkerchief, twisted the handle on the tile wall until a stream of cold water spurted forth. Victoria held towel and handkerchief under the spout, shut off the water, and shoved the soaked towel at Hannah. She clamped the wet handkerchief against her own mouth and nose.

Her eyes smarted and stung in the rising smoke, and her persistent coughing was choking her.

She heard a tremendous noise over the crackling of the fire, and put her ear against the shower glass.

It was distinct, loud and powerful, the hacking and hammering, and then there was a crushing blow against the bathroom door, a smashing that shattered the door, a blast of water rushing in, and the hissing sounds of fire being doused and drowned. Victoria fumbled for Hannah, but realized that Hannah had sunk to her knees in near collapse.

Through the smoked-up glass Victoria thought that she could see two figures, in masks and fire-resistant coats, enter the bathroom. She freed the shower door, screaming, "Here! We're here!" As she stepped out, a fireman prevented her from falling. Panting, Victoria pointed behind her. "'She's in there—help her!''

The second fireman squeezed past, followed by a third, and as Victoria was led stumbling out of the charred bathroom and smoldering shell of Armstead's study, she could see Hannah being lifted out of the shower and carried away.

She found herself in the corridor, waiting while Hannah was being brought into the second bedroom, Armstead's bedroom, and lowered onto the double bed. Victoria left the firemen, who were running, one after another, into the study with their chemical fire extinguishers, and she entered the bedroom. Hannah's limp form had been surrounded by paramedics, three young men and a woman in white, clean and promisng as angels, all bending over Hannah, working on her.

One of them, a young man with a neat beard, ambled over to Victoria.

"You all right, miss?"

Victoria's coughing had ceased, and she nodded vigorously.

The paramedic's thumb jerked over his shoulder toward the bed. "Don't worry, your mother's going to make it. Smoke inhalation, but she's coming back. They got her out in time."

Victoria continued to nod, and looked toward the bed. Hannah's eyes were wide and Victoria thought they were beckoning her. Automatically she went to the bed, and could see that Hannah was feebly trying to bring her closer. Victoria knelt and quickly put her head next to Hannah's.

"You're going to be as good as new," Victoria promised her.

Hannah was trying to whisper, and Victoria placed her head

nearer to Hannah's moving lips. "Vic—" Hannah murmured. "Don't let them kill him—he—he's just sick, very sick."

Victoria nodded, pushed away, and rose, mumbling her thanks to the paramedics, who were busy with Hannah again.

Victoria glanced around her. Everyone was busy everywhere, the paramedics here in the bedroom, the bulkily dressed firemen coming and going in the corridor. Grabbing her purse, Victoria retreated toward the corridor, sidled into it, and hastened toward the living room. She stepped over the fire hose and carefully avoided the occupied firemen and policemen. No one saw her leave.

Outside the penthouse, in the hallway, a cluster of fire officials were engrossed in conversation. Victoria considered revealing to them the plot against Air Force One. But instinctively she knew that it would take too long to explain, prove, convince them. Casually Victoria followed the snaking fire hose, edging toward the stairway. This was no time to be detained for questioning. Once on the stairs, she began to descend as swiftly as possible without tripping and falling.

She did not have to look at her wristwatch. She knew that time had almost run out.

Victoria came to a halt before the first open store on Madison Avenue, bracing herself against an edge of the front display window to catch her breath.

She had come on the run, from the apartment building's Fifth Avenue exit, past the crowd of courious onlookers and the lineup of fire engines, plunging into one of the seventies blocks, wasting no time to gain entry to any of the brownstone residences, drawing the stares of wondering pedestrians, until she reached Madison Avenue.

She rushed into the open store, an elongated narrow liquor store, the bell above the entrance jangling her arrival.

The proprietor, half hidden by the cash register, showed himself, a partially bald, dumpy, middle-aged tradesman who resembled someone who might have a shop in the Piazza San Marco.

"What can I do for you, lady? Hey, there—you look like you been out all night."

"I've been in a fire," Victoria blurted, feeling she must explain her bedraggled hair, smudged face, dirtied and torn dress. "I need a telephone—"

"Right in front of you, lady."

There was a single public booth, and she stepped into it. Closing herself inside, she pawed through her purse for a credit card, could find none, but felt her bulging change purse. She pulled it out, grateful for the first elementary lesson she had learned as a cub reporter. Always carry change, lots of it, for telephone calls. The telephone was a reporter's main artery, and what pumped it alive was change. She dumped the coins on the shelf and took the receiver off the hook.

She tried to remember the number, and it came to her. She dialed the area code for Washington, D.C., 202, and the number for the White House, 456-1414.

She had the switchboard, a female with a mechanical voice. Victoria hesitated, uncertain whom to ask for. Maybe the plane, Air Force One, had been delayed, had not left yet. Maybe her father was still in the White House.

"I want to speak to Hugh Weston, the press secretary."

"I'll connect you."

A young woman's cheery voice answered. "Press secretary's office."

"I must speak to Mr. Weston. Is he still there?"

"Sorry. He'll be out of the city for a week. If you'd like to leave your name—"

"This is an emergency. It concerns the President's life. Is there anyone—"

The young woman remained unperturbed, still cheery. "Let me turn you over to the chief of White House operations. Hold on."

Seconds later, a smooth male voice was on the line. "This is Frank Oliphant. Can I be of help?"

"You can," said Victoria. "I'm Press Secretary Weston's daughter—"

"Perhaps you'd better speak to his office. Let me—"

"I just did," said Victoria with exasperation. "They told me to speak to you. This is a real emergency. The President's life is in danger. Any minute he could—"

The chief of White House operations interrupted, trying to soothe her. "I wouldn't worry about him right now, Miss Weston. He's safely on his way to London in Air Force One. But if this is regarding some future threat, I'd be happy to make out a report on it. If you'll give me your full name and address, and the circumstances, I'll write them all down for investigation."

Frustration was strangling Victoria. The idiot was coddling her, treating her like any routine crackpot. An unbelievable disaster was impending, on the verge of happening, and there was no one to pay attention, give it credence. Officialdom treated every stranger as a crackpot. Disbelief, abetted by routine, hampered most emergencies. Pearl Harbor, she had read, had been like this.

As she was about to hang up in a fury, a name sprang to mind. Sy Rosenbloom.

Nick had said to her, the last time they had talked: *If you need some fast advice or help, call the White House and ask for Sy Rosenbloom. He's on the President's staff, an aide . . . if things get rough and you're in real trouble . . . you can tell him everything.*

"Let me speak to Mr. Sy Rosenbloom," she shouted into the phone.

"Who?"

"Mr. Rosenbloom. He's a presidential aide. He's in the West Wing of the White House."

"One moment, madam, let me check the directory . . . Yes, I have it, I have his extension. I'll try to put you through."

A lapse of seconds. Put me through, put me through, she beseeched the mute telephone.

An older woman's voice, a more human voice, came on. "Mr. Rosenbloom's office."

"Hello, listen. This is urgent, really urgent. I must speak to Mr. Rosenbloom. This is Victoria Weston, and he—"

"You've just missed him, Miss Weston. He left with another staffer for a cup of coffee. I'm sure he'll be back in less than a half hour."

Victoria was desperate. "Please, do me a favor. I told you this was urgent, honestly it is—it's a matter of life or death. Could he still be in the building? Can you catch up with him?"

The secretary responded seriously. "He might be. If I find him, who should I say is calling? Did you say Weston—?"

"Victoria Weston. Tell him Hugh Weston's daughter, Nick Ramsey's friend. He knows about me—please hurry!"

"Let me put you on hold."

Victoria, head throbbing, held on in limbo. The minute hand on her wristwatch had moved again. The operator broke in, and Victoria fed more coins into the monster machine and waited.

A cool and boyish cultivated voice was on the other end. "Miss Weston?"

"Oh, yes!"

"Sy Rosenbloom. Sorry for all the trouble. Delighted to speak to you. Of course, I know all about you from Nick and from your wonderful father. Nick told me there was a chance you might call. Is there anything—?"

"Sy, listen to me, listen!" Victoria pleaded. "The President, my father, Nick Ramsey, everyone on Air Force One is going to die any minute. We've uncovered a plot, an assassination plot now underway—don't tell me I'm crazy, I'm not crazy, it's all true—a plot for a stolen Cuban Air Force plane being piloted by a terrorist who's going to crash it into Air Force One."

Victoria could hear the sharp intake of breath on the other end. "You're serious? Positive about this?"

"Oh, Sy, I am, I am, believe me."

"I do believe you. When is this supposed to happen?"

"Now. Any minute—in mere minutes."

"I'd better get you through to Air Force One. It'll be faster. You can alert them. Where are you?"

"In New York, in a pay booth on Madison Avenue."

"I'm putting you on hold," snapped Rosenbloom. "Stay right there."

She became aware of two other persons standing outside the telephone booth, waiting to use it. When Victoria did not leave the cubicle one of them rapped on the glass angrily. Victoria refused to budge. Now they were calling back to the proprietor, and he was coming around the counter.

The proprietor hit his knuckles against the door of the booth.

Victoria folded it open a few inches.

"Lady, you can't hog the telephone forever," the proprietor admonished. "Come on out of there and give these people a chance."

"I can't," pleaded Victoria. "I'm waiting to talk to the President of the United States. And don't call the booby hatch." She shut the booth door.

A voice came over the telephone.

Victoria pressed the receiver to her ear. "Yes, it's me."

"It's Sy Rosenbloom. Hold on, Victoria. You're being put right through to Air Force One."

Twenty-two minutes out of Andrews Air Force Base, riding serenely above the clouds and the blue Atlantic, the 747 jumbo jet designated Air Force One was in the early stage of its flight to London.

Inside the aircraft, Hugh Weston, the presidential press secretary, had been summoned from the copying machine to take a telephone call in the plane's communications center. As he entered, the master sergeant indicated the free telephone on the table. "For you, Hugh."

"Who is it?"

"No idea. Only know it's an emergency call patched through the White House situation room from somewhere else."

Puzzled, Hugh Weston picked up the receiver and was astonished to learn that it was his daughter.

"Vicky, what's going on?"

She started to tell him, words tumbling out, and a minute later he stopped her.

"Vicky, I don't want to waste a second. I'd better alert the President—and put Nick on to hear the rest of it. You say he has the background and you can shorthand it for him—and then Nick will be able to answer any questions President Callaway may have? Sit tight, Vicky. Nick'll be right on."

Hugh Weston set the receiver down beside the phone, and tapped the master sergeant on the shoulder. The sergeant slipped off one earphone.

"Max, see that my telephone is left open."

Weston rushed into the aisle, spotted a young man in a blue blazer, a flight steward, and flagged him.

"Listen, you get back to the press pool and get hold of Nick Ramsey and send him back here, on the double."

The flight steward went scurrying off to the rear compartment, where a dozen reporters and columnists were playing cards, reading, napping. Within a half minute, a rumpled and breathless Ramsey stood before the press secretary.

"Hugh?"

"Nick, my girl's on the line from New York—"

"Vicky?"

"She just escaped being killed by Armstead. She's uncovered unimpeachable evidence that Armstead has sent up a stolen MiG fighter, manned by a terrorist, a kamikaze type, to blow us all up, the President, all of us. Could Armstead do a thing like this?"

Without hesitation, Ramsey said, "Yes, he could."

"Then you think it's true?"

"If Vicky says so, and has seen the evidence—Hugh, it's true."

"She says it's going to happen in nine minutes. I'd better notify the President. Vicky's on the phone to give you details. Get them, fast as you can, and come to the President's suite. I'll be in there with him."

Little more than sixty seconds later, Ramsey had jammed down the telephone receiver and rushed into the aisle and to the presidential suite forward. The gold-and-blue presidential seal was painted on the door panel, and Ramsey hit it with his fist.

"Come in!" called out the President. "Door's open."

Ramsey hustled inside to find President Callaway on the very edge of his leather swivel chair, palms flattened on the polished desk, the beribboned Army General Judson, highest-ranking military presence on the plane, standing stiffly beside him, and Hugh Weston, positioned expectantly in the leather chair on the opposite side of the desk.

Without any greeting, the President said, "Are you convinced Miss Weston has her facts right?"

"No question, Mr. President," said Ramsey. "She held the evidence in her own hands, the story Armstead had written for tonight's edition, headlining the news that Air Force One was blown up in a midair collision."

"How?"

"Using a stolen Cuban Air Force fighter plane, with some kind of suicidal ex-kamikaze as pilot. Armstead has a professional terrorist group on his payroll, to make news exclusively for him. Miss Weston has been onto Armstead for some time. Now he's got his terrorists to steal one of Castro's fighter planes, install in it an ex-kamikaze pilot, and send him to blast us out of the sky."

"When is this supposed to happen?"

Ramsey's eyes shifted to the wall clock. "In eight minutes, Mr. President."

The Chief Executive swung his chair sideways and looked up at General Judson. "What's our protection on this flight, General?"

"Nil, sir, as you probably know, following our policy of recent years to downplay any military security. We're supposed to resemble a civilian flight. There may be some Duck Butts—Air Rescue Service cargo planes in the area—"

"They won't do a damn bit of good," snapped the President. "I'm asking about protection."

"We'd better make sure the MiG is stolen and in terrorist hands."

"Make sure fast," said the President, shoving his white telephone at him. "If it is, find out if there are any of our fighter aircraft within range, in the air or aboard carriers. You should be getting an answer in microseconds. Because if there is no help—"

General Judson was already on the white telephone, contacting the National Military Command System center at the Pentagon.

Buckled tightly to his seat in the cockpit of the sleek MiG-27F interceptor as it hurtled through the sky, the helmeted Lieutenant Yosuke Matsuda kept his eyes fastened to the on-board computer readouts. He had punched in the time data and the longitude/latitude coordinates at takeoff, along with the coordinates for the intercept point he had calculated. The computer, working with the inertial navigation system, would digest the inputs and display continuously corrected readings for both the distance remaining and the time left before he would make his glorious dive from 70,000 feet, the MiG's optimum ceiling. In the final minutes, his forward-looking radar would pick up the President's blip on its screen as the American 747 flew at 35,000 feet on its path over the Atlantic Ocean. Then he would take over from the autopilot for the moment of destiny that had eluded him for so long.

His obliteration was drawing closer and closer, and yet Matsuda was smiling, gratified by the million dollars in the Tokyo bank that would support his family, and pleased that after so many decades he would absolve himself of the dishonor that had haunted him all his life.

In his death, he could be good father and great hero, at last.

The final ride was a dream. He had no worries, no confusion. There was no necessity to employ further radar, computers, display scopes to fire off a missile at the target.

In this instance he and the plane were the missile, the projectile itself, that would destroy the enemy American President, and his party, and his plane.

Matsuda noted that the machmeter had settled down to a steady 2.3, well below the 2.8 redline speed at which the designers could no longer guarantee the ship's integrity when it carried missiles. He ignored the fuel gauge. With full a load the MiG's range was over 1,600 miles, more than ample for his one-way flght. The powerful Turmansky twin turbojets would get him there just after the presidential plane reached a point 120 miles off the Delaware coast.

For some minutes Matsuda's thoughts drifted back to his family—to their immediate grief, their ultimate security—as his jet flew along the prescribed heading. Then, as a warning beep broke in on his reflections, he saw a blip suddenly appear on the radar, indicating an object 150 miles ahead. Eyes on the radar, he absently reached into his inside pocket for the color snapshot of his wife, Kieko, and their three children, that he had carried with him. He glanced at the picture, a last loving farewell. He could imagine them venerating his memory at the sacred Yasukuni Shrine. Then, the final moment at hand, Matsuda dropped the photo into his lap, disengaged the automatic pilot and took over the control stick manually. He dipped his left wing slightly for a better view and peered downward through the canopy.

Far off, but enlarging rapidly, he had his first visual sighting of the aircraft known as Air Force One. With a golden grin Matsuda prepared to push the control stick forward, which would send him into a screaming dive toward his target.

*   *   *

In the conference room, adjacent to the presidential suite of Air Force One, the three of them were bending, pressing their faces against three windows, waiting for the moment of extinction. At one window, President Callaway, at the next window Hugh Weston, and at the third window Nick Ramsey. Beyond the open door beside them that led to the communications center, their fourth member, General Judson, was frozen before the radar equipment, reporting to the President on the intercom amplifier the movement of the blip now plainly visible on the radar screen.

From their windows in the conference room, President Callaway, Weston, and Ramsey could see nothing in the blue beyond, not even a speck in the sky.

The pilots and crew had not been consulted. There was hardly time, and evasive action would have been impossible. Their plane was a sitting duck. Nor had any passengers been warned. They were helpless, and if informed would only die in fright and panic.

The plane's communications center had already delivered word, and a warning, from the National Security Agency that, via spy satellite, an unidentified airplane with characteristics of a fighter had been detected and was closing on Air Force One at great speed. Appropriate action was being attempted.

Jusdon's super-emergency call had also alerted the high command to contact the nearest defense capability, summon American cover fighters in the general area, but there was no way of knowing exactly when the collision would occur and whether help could reach them in time.

Results indecisive. All hope up in the air, as they floated through the air, the target of a madman loosed by another madman.

For Ramsey, at the window, immediate death remained unacceptable and an unreality. His intellectual mind ticked off losses: never to love and make love to Vicky, never to write the book he had under way, never to enjoy another apéritif at Fouquet's, never to be a father and perpetuate his name. To know only nothingness. Inconceivable.

The amplifier crackled. Ramsey heard the general's strangled voice attempting the countdown of doom from the radar. "Bastard's a hundred miles away . . . eighty miles . . . sixty . . ."

No sooner had the reverberation of General Judson's voice ceased than he ran into the conference room, uncontrollably furious, stumbling toward the windows. He pushed himself next to Hugh Weston at the middle window. With the others, he scanned the empty, forbidding sky.

At his own window, Ramsey strained his eyes, seeking their executioner. There was nothing, only innocent clouds. Instantly he was chilled by the general's outcry. "Hey, up there, look up there! The sonofabitch is coming down at us like a bat out of hell!"

Heart hammering, Ramsey squinted off to the left, lifting his sight, and could make out the sliver, the ominous sliver, in the blue sky, distant but pointed at them, coming from above at incredible speed, diving, growing in his vision until he could see it was the feared configuration of a MiG fighter.

"Je-sus, like a fucking bat out of hell," the general was gasping. "Coming two thousand miles an hour straight for us!"

"We're goners," the President groaned.

Ramsey had caught another sliver, two slivers, out of the corner of his eye, and staring down through the window, he shouted, "Look—look below!"

They had burst out of a cloud formation, the two of them, zooming and screaming upward.

"F-15 long-range fighters!" the general bellowed. "Our own!"

"By God, lookit!" the President yelled.

They all saw the Advanced Medium Range Air-to-Air Missiles leave the defending planes—the AMRAAM's come bursting out—sizzling through the sky like twin avengers, going with the speed of lightning, homing in on the oncoming attacker.

Awed, mouth agape, Ramsey could see the kamikaze destructor almost upon them and the twin missiles almost upon the kamikaze destructor.

Which would hit and obliterate first? He steeled himself for the impact of carnage and death.

But before his eyes the blue sky grew into a huge orange ball—the kamikaze MiG exploding in a mass of flame and debris, debris sailing off, debris falling toward the ocean, no full part of the attacker in the sky, only smoke, and bits and pieces floating away.

Air Force One had shuddered violently under the pressure of the nearby explosion.

It was shaking still, but now leveling out, and continuing uninterrupted to London.

And four men were hugging each other and dancing in the big warm room.

Finishing her call to Air Force One, Victoria had only one more thing to say. "I'm praying for you and Dad," she said, and then she blurted out, "Nick, I love you." But she had realized that the phone was dead, that Nick had already hung up and was doing what could be done.

Replacing the receiver on the hook, Victoria had remained rooted in the stifling telephone booth.

Unfinished business, one piece of unfinished business, one more call to be made.

Captain Timothy Crawford, detective division of the New York City Police Department. In haste, Nick had asked her what she was going to do next, and in haste she had told him. "Don't confront Armstead alone," Nick had warned her. "Contact the New York City police, detective division, speak to my friend Timothy Crawford, tell him everything. He'll know what to do."

She had contacted Captain Crawford, identified herself, mentioning Nick Ramsey, and she had spilled out her story. "The last is enough to act on," Crawford had assured her. "About the rest, we'll have to be sure, and see what happens to Air Force One. But the last will do. A charge of attempted murder, with

you and his wife making the charge. Can you get over to the
Armstead Building right away? Meet you there.''

Emerging from the booth, trying to suppress any further thoughts
of Air Force One and her loved ones, she had run a gauntlet of
five angry persons awaiting their turn to use the telephone, but
she had been deaf to their curses. She had run out of the liquor
store into Madison Avenue and waved down a cruising taxi.
''Armstead Building on Park Avenue,'' she had instructed the
driver.

Now, approaching the showdown, the fear that had been gripping her in a viselike hold began to tighten. She could see the
fourth of four police squad cars drawing up before the entrance to
the Armstead Building. She tried to concentrate on what was
immediately ahead.

''I'll get out here,'' she told the driver. As he braked to a halt,
she pushed three dollar bills into the slot under the partition, and
unlatched the rear door.

''Hey, what's going on?'' the driver called out.

''Plenty,'' she called back. ''You'll read about it in the papers.''

There was a gathering of a dozen uniformed policemen and
plainclothesmen on the sidewalk, and she tried to guess which
one would be Detective Timothy Crawford, and guessed it might
be the behemoth of a man with the ruddy face, the one in the
middle.

She guessed right. The burly man was approaching her. ''You
Vicky Weston? I'm Crawford. You can see, we're all in place.
You think he's in?''

''He'll be in all right,'' Vicky promised. ''He's standing by
for news of the big blowup, so he can break his story. He's
probably in his office at the back of editorial on the sixth floor.
I'll show you the way.''

''Better stay out of this part, Miss Weston. Could be dangerous.
I'm taking up a detail of men.''

''Will you know which one is Edward Armstead?''

Captain Crawford showed his crooked teeth in a half smile.

"His face has been plenty visible for weeks. The Almighty, right? Couldn't miss him." He wheeled toward the arrest team. "All right, boys. Four of you up the stairs. Three of you with me up the elevator. The rest of you stake out down here and all around the building in case he tries to get away."

They were barging into the lobby, and Victoria was right behind them.

She squeezed into the elevator, apologizing to Crawford. "I've got to be there."

Breaking into the sixth-floor foyer, Crawford held his men until the other half of the arrest detail came up the staircase. Crawford ordered these arrivals to stand guard. He raised his hand, and signaled the rest into the city room.

Victoria dashed ahead, followed by Crawford and his squad. The room was full, buzzing with activity when they entered and moved purposefully between the endless desks toward the executive offices in the rear. Gradually all work ceased as editors, reporters, rewrite men remained motionless and curious, watching the steady march of the five of them through the vast room to the publisher's office.

Passing her own desk, Victoria heard her telephone ringing. She tried to ignore it, then saw someone else pick it up.

"For you, Vicky," the reporter called to her.

"Not now," said Victoria.

"He says you'll want to hear. He says his name is Sy Rosenbloom."

Victoria stopped, looked at Crawford. Victoria said, "A second. It must be about—Air Force One." She hurried to the phone, listened briefly, felt her strained facial muscles beginning to relax.

She returned to Crawford's side, face wreathed in a smile. "Air Force One made it," she said. "Interceptors shot down Armstead's terrorist."

Crawford's crooked teeth revealed his pleasure. "Okay, then we only have to wrap it up."

The march resumed. Victoria preceded them into Estelle Rivkin's reception room. Estelle brought her head up from the typewriter and tried to understand the interruption. "What do you want?"

"Is Mr. Armstead in?" demanded Victoria.

"He was. He's in, but he may be with Mr. Dietz. Let me ring him."

Crawford stepped forward. "Don't lift a finger, lady. We'd like to surprise your boss." His head made a gesture toward Armstead's door.

Victoria threw the door open, heart beating faster as she watched the police hurry into the publisher's office. Then she went inside, in time to hear Captain Crawford announce, "No one here."

At that instant the door across the room opened, the door into the corridor that led to Dietz's office, and there was Edward Armstead holding aloft some sheets of paper, his head turned as he laughed jubilantly at Dietz behind him. Victoria thought there was someone else, too, partially visible, possibly Pagano. Armstead was still laughing, speaking to Dietz over his shoulder. "Greatest electronic contraption I ever heard of. Jacklin said he heard the midair explosion clear as day. Now we've got the big one. I'm—"

"Chief," Dietz croaked. "Turn around—"

Puzzled, Armstead swung around and saw the police. "What in the hell is this?"

Crawford took a step toward him. "Edward Armstead, you are under arrest for criminal conspiracy and attempted murder."

Victoria emerged from behind the other police, and stood beside Crawford. Armstead had not been aware of her before and his eyes widened.

"We got out, Hannah and I. We told it all." Victoria was having difficulty with her voice, but she went on. "You've got no story. The explosion you heard about was the explosion of your kamikaze, shot down by interceptors. Air Force One is safe."

Armstead was shaking his head in disbelief, looking wildly at everyone in the room with the glazed eyes of a lunatic, backing away slowly, until he had backed against the sliding doors to his balcony.

"Read him his rights, boys, and then book him!" Crawford called out.

"No!" Armstead shrieked, yanking the sliding doors wide open and whirling around toward the balcony.

Crawford instinctively whipped out his service revolver and was taking aim when Victoria grabbed at his wrist. "Don't—don't kill him. His wife, she—he has no place to go out there. He's sick, crazy."

The detective was staring at Armstead. "Look at him. Nuttier than a fruitcake."

Armstead was climbing to the top of the cement parapet. He was teetering on the narrow railing.

"I can't let him," growled Crawford, moving toward the balcony. Victoria was running alongside the detective, calling out to Armstead, "Let them help you! They want to help you!"

Swaying there on the railing, Armstead knotted his right hand into a fist and shook it at Victoria. "You—you bitch—you'll never make a reporter—ruining the story of the century! All of you—leave me alone—I want to see my old man! I need him!"

With that, he stepped off the balcony rail into space and plummeted out of sight.

Victoria screamed, but he was gone. She stumbled onto the balcony. Crawford was already there, bent over the railing, peering down at the street six stories below. As Victoria came up to him, Crawford firmly turned her away. "It's a long way down. You wouldn't want to see what happened."

"He's dead."

"Very."

They had left the balcony for the office when they were startled by a gunshot reverberating in the corridor beyond the door that Armstead had left open.

Two policemen dashed into the corridor in the direction of the sound, and Crawford and Victoria followed them into the corridor. The police had hurried into the next office, and one of them quickly emerged. "The guy in here—suicide—shot himself in the head."

Crawford looked at Victoria. "Who is he?"

"Armstead's assistant. Harry Dietz."

Crawford grunted. "They've sure saved the state a lot of trouble."

Later, after Dietz's body had been removed and Crawford was leaving, Victoria caught up with the detective as they entered the city room.

"Tim," Victoria said. "About Mr. Armstead's fall—"

"Yes?"

"It was an accident, you know."

Crawford stared at her a long time. At last he gave a short shrug. "Could have been. Whatever you say. It's your story now."

He walked off.

After the immediate sensation, and the tumult, and the questions, and her lies, Victoria was left alone to write her story.

But not right away. There was one more thing to be done. She picked up the telephone and placed a call to Sid Lukas's Paris apartment.

Lukas answered the phone himself.

She started right in about Carlos, but Lukas stopped her. "Vicky, I've got to tell you, Edward Armstead doesn't believe you saw Carlos and made it clear he doesn't want me to pursue the story."

She hesitated, considering telling Sid Lukas the full truth, that there was no Edward Armstead anymore. She decided against it. This would only divert him from what she wanted him to do, require explanations when there was no time to lose. Lukas would learn what had happened to Armstead soon enough. Right now, the subject was Carlos.

"Sid," she replied, "Armstead doesn't want you to pursue the story because it's Armstead's own terrorist gang that has Carlos."

"What? What are you saying?"

"You heard me. Don't make me explain. Don't waste a minute. You'll know about everything in the morning. Just believe me that Edward Armstead turned terrorism into a big business. Have the Sûreté pursue Armstead's gang, and Carlos. Tell the Sûreté to get to No. 3 Rue Jacob as fast as possible. I'll fill you in on the rest tomorrow, I promise. But do something, Sid, soon as you can."

"If this is a false alarm, Vicky, it'll ruin me with Armstead and the Sûreté."

"They'll decorate you, Sid, I guarantee it. Go to it, this minute. Will you?"

"Okay, Vicky. No. 3 Rue Jacob."

Done.

Hanging up, she pulled her chair closer to the desk. Now, the story.

It was to be tomorrow's lead front-page story, unless Air Force One chose to announce its own close call. Victoria, at the keys of her word processor, went to work, working hard on it, writing and rewriting.

Several hours passed. The editorial room thinned out, quieted down, and it was late afternoon when Victoria was through with the story. She punched the printer beside the word processor, and the final draft was automatically typed out.

Tearing it free, Victoria leaned back in her chair and reread it one final time.

The story of the Almighty's accidental fall to his death, at the peak of a distinguished career. His life. His achievements. His instinct for news. His memorable exclusive stories:

All of that. Nothing else. Hannah had implored someone to be kind.

Victoria rolled up the story.

Hannah's legacy.

Drained, Victoria managed to get to her feet. With weariness, she trudged to Ollie McAllister's coop. He was hunched over his desk, studying copy for the first edition to go.

He glanced up. "Got it?"

"All done," said Victoria. She tossed the pages on his desk. "Long day. Good night."

She walked slowly through the editorial room. Outside the end alcove, she could hear the Teletypes clattering away. She paused to go inside the wire room, making her way to the machine that was spewing out the latest news from Europe via London. She watched the automatic keys hitting the roll of paper, which cascaded to the floor. She picked up the stream of paper that had already been printed out, seeking a Paris dateline.

There it was, second story from the top.

BULLETIN MATTER . . . FIRST LEAD PARIS . . . TONIGHT THE FRENCH SURETE RAIDED A LEFT BANK HIDEOUT OF THE LEGENDARY TER-RORIST CARLOS, WHO SUCCESSFULLY ESCAPED MINUTES BEFORE POLICE BROKE INTO HIS APARTMENT. HE HAD BEEN HIDING WITH ANOTHER TERRORIST GROUP LED BY SOMEONE KNOWN ONLY AS COOPER. MEMBERS OF THIS GROUP, ALONG WITH COOPER, ALSO SUC-CEEDED IN EVADING POLICE. ONE MEMBER WHO HAD LINGERED BE-HIND TO DESTORY EVIDENCE, AND HAD BEEN MORTALLY WOUNDED, GAVE HIS NAME AS PETER QUIGGS, OF LEEDS, ENGLAND. HE CON-FESSED BEFORE DYING THAT THE COOPER GANG HAD BEEN RESPONSI-BLE FOR MANY RECENT TERRORIST ACTS. SURETE INVESTI-GATING FUTHER . . . XXX . . . MORE.

Victoria dropped the Teletype printout.

Someone had alerted Cooper just before the raid, allowing Cooper to release Carlos and escape himself with most of his men.

Someone had got to him first.

Of course, that someone was Gus Pagano. She was sure that she had seen him with Armstead and Dietz. Afterward, she had not seen him at all. He had got away. She knew that she would never see him again. He was not the Almighty. He was the Survivor.

She heard her name, and saw that it was Ollie McAllister outside the Teletype alcove, holding her story. She went to him.

McAllister was shaking the story and studying her owlishly. "Vicky, it says here—it was an accident. Is that true?"

She met his eyes. "Ollie. I was there. I say it's true. I think the new owners of the paper—Hannah Armstead and Roger—would agree with me."

"Then, it is true," said McAllister.

Victoria made to leave, when the managing editor's hand caught her. "One more thing."

Victoria waited.

McAllister was tapping the story again. "The by-line here. You want it to stand? It reads 'by Mark Bradshaw.' "

"Yes, Ollie." She smiled. "I want it to stand."

And she left for the elevator.

One week and one day later.

The evening of his homecoming. He would be here any minute, and Victoria had begun the celebration by herself.

She had spruced up the old studio apartment, turned away as workers removed the sofa bed in which Kim Nesbit had died, watched as they replaced it with a fresh new one. She had bathed herself and perfumed herself, and changed into the sheer shift of a nightgown she had saved for a night like this since Paris. The chilled champagne bottle was uncorked on the table beside her, and she reclined against the pillow placed against the back of her new sofa bed, enjoying her fourth glass of champagne while waiting.

The fourth glass went down quickly, and she was sipping from her fifth glass when she heard the buzzer.

She set down the goblet, jumped off the bed, running to the

door, undoing the elaborate new safety locks, flinging the door wide, knowing it would be he.

Nick Ramsey, carrying a suitcase and typewriter, grinning, walked in, dropped the suitcase and typewriter, and lifted her up and off the floor.

They were hugging each other and kissing.

"You're here, Nick, you're here."

"You bet I am," he said. "That's quite a getup you're wearing or not wearing."

"I'll take it off," she said gaily.

"Not yet," he said, removing his jacket. "Did you save a glass of bubbly for me?"

"Right here," she said, padding on bare feet to the table and filling the other glass. He had undone his tie, and was unbuttoning his shirt. "You know, Vicky—"

"You're staying tonight," she said.

He grinned again. "I thought you'd never ask." He stripped off his shirt. "Where's the bathroom? I see it. Don't move. I'll be right back."

He disappeared into the bathroom.

Victoria bounced herself down on the bed, lay on her back admiring her legs, and hummed foolishly.

She'd never felt more light-headed.

She reached over to get the rest of her fifth drink, then poured her sixth, and feeling drowsy after it, poured her seventh and finished it.

Five minutes later, Nick Ramsey came out of the bathroom, naked. "Vicky?"

There was no response. He did a half circle around the bed and looked down at her. She was curled on her side under the blanket, eyes shut, breathing nasally. She was sound asleep. Ramsey glanced at the champagne bottle. Empty. Asleep or passed out.

Smiling, he let her rest, walked to the other side of the bed, and slid under the blanket beside her. She did not stir. Still smiling, he lay back, closed his eyes, and soon, he, too, was asleep.

In the early morning, they were both awake and sober—but high—higher and happier, in each other's arms, than they had ever been in their entire lives.